Ellen Creathorne Clayton

Queen of Song

Vol. 2

SALZWASSER
VERLAG

Ellen Creathorne Clayton

Queen of Song

Vol. 2

Reprint of the original, first published in 1863.

1st Edition 2022 | ISBN: 978-3-37500-489-7

Verlag (Publisher): Salzwasser Verlag GmbH, Zeilweg 44, 60439 Frankfurt, Deutschland
Vertretungsberechtigt (Authorized to represent): E. Roepke, Zeilweg 44, 60439 Frankfurt, Deutschland
Druck (Print): Books on Demand GmbH, In de Tarpen 42, 22848 Norderstedt, Deutschland

QUEENS OF SONG:

BEING MEMOIRS OF SOME OF THE MOST

CELEBRATED FEMALE VOCALISTS

TO WHICH IS ADDED

A CHRONOLOGICAL LIST OF ALL THE OPERAS

By ELLEN CREATHORNE CLAYTON.

IN TWO VOLUMES.

VOL. II.

WITH SIX PORTRAITS.

LONDON

M.DCCC.LXIII.

CONTENTS OF VOL. II.

QUEENS OF SONG.

CHAPTER I.

GIUDITTA PASTA.

WHEN Mr. Ayrton undertook the management of the King's Theatre in 1816, he commenced his task with an enthusiastic desire to render the Opera attractive, not merely by an array of brilliant talent, but by that perfection in the representation of the works of the great masters which was due alike to the composer and the audience. He had engaged several vocalists of talent, nearly all of whom were to be heard in England for the first time. When at the house of M. Paer, in Paris, he met with Signor and Madame Pasta, a tenor and a mezzo-soprano, and engaged both for the ensuing season, at the modest salary of four hundred pounds for the two.

Giuditta Pasta was then eighteen. She was born at Sarrano, near Milan, in 1798, of a Jewish family named Negri. She received her first lessons in music from Bartolomeo Lotte, chapel-master of the Cathedral of Como, and was admitted at the age of fifteen to the Conservatorio of Milan, then under the direction of Asiola. In 1815, she left the Conservatorio, and, making her early essays at the theatre of an amateur, obtained engagements at the second-rate theatres of Leghorn, Parma, and Brescia; appearing only in subordinate parts, her voice and style at that time unfitting her for any other. In 1816 she sang, together with Mdlle. Cinti, Miss Corri, and some other young débutantes, in the train of the haughty Madame Catalani, at the Favart; being precisely the kind of subordinate vocalist suited to one of Madame Catalani's exacting disposition, for she attracted no attention whatever. Pasta, when first seen in London, only appeared as a glimmering little star just risen above the horizon, in the sunblaze of the fame of Fodor and Camporese. As for her husband, finding there would be no chance whatever for him in competition with a singer like Crivelli, he wisely relinquished all idea of making a début. The King's Theatre opened Jan. 11, 1817, with Cimarosa's opera of *Penelope*, Madame Camporese taking the leading part, and as one of the papers said, "two subordinate singers, named Pasta and Mori, came forward also, in the characters of Telemaco and Arsinoe, but their musical talent does not require minute delineation."

Giuditta Pasta's voice was hard and unequal, and

she had the greatest difficulty in managing it, while its natural tone was far from being perfect. She had expression, and could descend from the sharp notes of the soprano to the grave tones of the contralto; but she always wanted flexibility, and did not appear to advantage in bravura music: some persons, however, perceived in her the germs of future excellence. In appearance, she was below the medium height, but admirably proportioned, with a queenly Roman head and beautiful features, a high forehead, dark expressive eyes, exquisitely formed lips, and a finely shaped nose. The serious cast of her countenance, and the simple majesty of her air, denoted that her genius lay in the loftiest walk of tragedy, especially as she had much dramatic energy, while her gestures and her attitudes were noble and graceful.

She next appeared as Cherubino in the *Nozze di Figaro*, in which she performed very creditably. She also appeared in Paer's *Agnese* with Madame Camporese and Signor Ambrogetti; and when *La Clemenza di Tito* was brought forward, Pasta was given the part of Servilia, which she went through very well, but with some of the awkwardness of inexperience. She also performed the rôle of the pretended shrew in *Il Sbaglio Fortunato*, by Ferrari.

It could not be disguised at the close of the season that poor Madame Pasta, though sometimes spoken kindly of by the critics, had proved a "failure." She meditated deeply on the causes of her non-success, and felt the impetus of genius which urges those gifted with the spark of divine fire to persevere; so she returned to Italy and studied assiduously for more than a year, under the guidance of M. Scappa. An English nobleman who saw her in Italy at this time, said that her exertions were unremitting. "Other singers," said he, "find themselves endowed with a voice, and leave everything else to chance. This woman leaves nothing to chance, and her success is therefore certain."

That success was awaiting her reappearance in Italy. She created a marked sensation when she made her début afresh in Venice in 1819. At Rome, in April of that year, she performed men's parts at the Argentina, with Tacchinardi, in such operas as Rossini's *Aureliano in Palmira*, Mayer's *Danaë*, Nicolini's *Cesare nelle Gallie*, and in 1820 she appeared at Milan and Trieste. In the autumn of 1821 she was engaged at the Théâtre Italien of Paris, where she fixed the attention of the fastidious French public; but it was at Verona, during the Congress of 1822, that she obtained her great success. She then returned to Paris, reappearing at the Italiens, March 30, in the opera of *Romeo e Giulietta*, and was received with the homage paid only to the highest talent.

Madame Pasta was then laying the foundation of one of the most dazzling reputations ever gained by prima donna. By sheer industry she had extended the range of her voice to two octaves and a half; from A above the bass clef note to C flat, and even to D in alt. Her tones had become rich and sweet, except when she attempted to force them beyond their limits; her intonation was, however, never quite perfect, being occasionally a little flat. Her singing was pure, and totally divested of all spurious finery; she added little to what was set down by the composer, and that little was not only in good taste, but had a great deal of originality to recommend it. She possessed deep feeling and correct judgment. Her shake was most beautiful: Signor Pacini's well-known cavatina, *Il soave e bel contento*—the peculiar feature of which consisted in the solidity and power of a sudden shake, contrasted with the detached staccato of the first bar—was written for Madame Pasta. Her voice, though it had improved wonderfully, never appeared easy and clear in the emission of certain notes, and retained a veiled quality, from which it was only freed after the first scenes. Some of her notes were sharp almost to harshness, but this defect with the greatness of genius she overcame, and even converted into a beauty; for in passages of profound passion her guttural tones were thrilling. The irregularity of her lower notes, governed thus by a perfect taste and musical tact, aided to a great extent in giving that depth of expression which was one of the principal charms of her singing: indeed, these lower tones were peculiarly suited for the utterance of vehement passion, producing an extraordinary effect by the splendid and unexpected contrast which they enabled her to give to the sweetness of the upper tones; causing a kind of musical discordance, which, animated by her pathetic expression, created in the heart of the listener an indefinable feeling of melancholy. Her accents were so plaintive, so penetrating, and so profoundly tragical, that it was impossible to resist their influence.

She had a transcendent gift for acting; indeed, her genius as a tragedian surpassed her talents as a singer. Her imaginative power and fine sensibility enabled her to throw herself completely into the characters she assumed: when on the stage she ceased to be Pasta, she was Tancredi, Romeo, Desdemona, Medea, or Semiramide. "Nothing could have been more free from trick or affectation than Pasta's performance," observed Ebers. "There is no perceptible effort to resemble a character she plays; on the contrary, she enters the stage the character itself; transposed into the situation, excited by the hopes and the fears, breathing the life and the spirit of the being she represents." Prompted by the inspiration of her genius, every gesture, every movement, became a study for a painter or a sculptor; and the passions of the soul animating her noble countenance, vivified the ideal personation. Some of her attitudes were matchless for grace and originality, their effect being heightened by "a resemblance in the grand contours of her figure to the antique, and more particularly to the Niobe." Her personal qualifications, combined with her innate genius and high cultivation, made her soon the first living actress in Italian tragic opera. Talma himself, hearing her declaim, said, "Here is a woman of whom I can still learn." On the stage she habitually assumed the majesty of power in repose, and while ardent in passionate scenes, with the intuition of genius she restrained her energy within due limits. "One turn of her beautiful head, one glance of her eye, one light motion of her hand, are with her sufficient to express a passion. She could raise the soul of the spectator to the highest pitch of astonishment and delight by one tone of her voice. 'O Dio!' as it came from her breast, swelling over her lips, was of indescribable effect."

Outwardly calm and sustained, though poetical and enthusiastic in temperament, the crowning excellence of her art was its grand simplicity. Sublime and terrible as she was in the expression of vehement passion, there was yet a measured force in the display of her power, which was always under the control of her taste and judgment. She never wasted energy; nor in the expression of the deepest pathos, or the most exalted passion, did she ever exceed the bounds of art. She was always vigorous, but never violent; always supremely graceful, but never artificial or affected; and she was always greatest when she had the greatest difficulties to encounter.

Madame Pasta's personation of Romeo, a part originally written for Grassini, by Zingarelli, was beautiful and pathetic in the extreme. The passionate grief of the young Montecchi, in the third act, was subdued by a tearful pathos. The recitative, "O mia Giulietta! O sposa!" when Romeo drinks the poison, was an effusion of despairing melancholy; and in the air which follows it, "Ombra adorata," (written by Crescentini, the singer,) in which the unfortunate lover dwells on the idea of his spirit joining that of his beloved in Elysium, she seemed to be sustained by hope, resignation, and sublime faith. In a word, it would be difficult to conceive anything more profoundly affecting than Madame Pasta's Romeo.

Her next important character at the Théâtre Italien was Tancredi, which she made her own; and it was one of her most finished, enchanting, and deeply interesting impersonations. She looked resplendent in the casque and cuirass of the Red Cross Knight. No one could ever sing the part of Tancredi like Madame Pasta; her pure taste enabled her to add grace to the original composition by elegant and irreproachable ornaments. "Di tanti palpiti" had been first presented to the Parisians by Madame Fodor, who covered it with rich and brilliant embroidery, and gave it what an English critic, Lord Mount Edgecumbe, afterwards termed its country-dance-like character. Madame Pasta, on the contrary, infused into this air its true colour and expression, and the effect was ravishing.

But her great triumph was in *Otello*. In Desdemona she produced an indescribable effect upon the audience. Of the impassioned energy, the spirit, the delicacy and tenderness which Madame Pasta infused into the character, pages might be written. In the celebrated scene which closes the second act, commencing thus—

> "Se il padre m'abbandoni
> Da chi sperar' pietà."

fear, anguish, and despair were successively expressed in her countenance, and her pathetic singing of the lovely melody, "Assisa a pisè d'un salice," touched every heart. In this part those melting tones, which are designated "the tears of the voice," were heard with touching effect. It was in the last scene, however, when, awakened by the raging Otello, Desdemona starts up, and the indignation and horror of conscious innocence are kindled within her, that the powers of Madame Pasta's performance were concentrated. Her transitions from hope to terror, from supplication to scorn, culminating in her vehement exclamation "Sono innocente!" electrified the audience: no language could convey an idea of the beauty, the intensity, the sublimity of her acting. Indeed, throughout the final scene, her acting was the perfection of tragic beauty: her last frenzied looks, when, blinded by her dishevelled hair and bewildered with conflicting emotions, she seems to seek fruitlessly the means of flight, were awful. In no other character were the varied resources of the art of the great tragedian drawn forth so consummately as in Desdemona; and it displayed the versatility of her powers to advantage when succeeding that of Tancredi. The contrast presented by her chivalric bearing as the young hero of Syracuse, to the gentleness and graceful simplicity of the artless Venetian lady, was very striking, and enhanced the appreciation of her genius. On the lyric stage she thus exercised a double sway; for such was her force of genius that she was able to excel in the new school of Rossini, and in the grand style of the ancient school. She shone in the operas of the Swan of Pesaro; and she could equally give effect to the sublime airs composed by Zingarelli for Marchesi, Crescentini, Grassini, and other models of what was then called "the fine school of singing."

Elisabetta was revived for Pasta, who, as the English Queen, was no less admirable than in the characters of Desdemona, Romeo, or Tancredi. The opera offered then a twofold interest, for Mdlle. Cinti, after a long absence, reappeared in the part of Mathilde. In October *Mosè in Egitto* was produced, Pasta filling the leading character with *éclat*.

In January of the following year, Madame Pasta

for the first time appeared before the public in her great masterpiece—the character of Medea, in Mayer's opera. Even her warmest admirers were taken by surprise by the grandeur of her impersonation. Nothing could surpass her performance of this character; it was a triumph of histrionic art, and afforded every opportunity for the display of all the resources of her genius—the varied powers which had been called forth and combined in Medea, the passionate tenderness of Romeo, the spirit and animation of Tancredi, the majesty of Semiramide, the mournful beauty of Nina, the dignity and sweetness of Desdemona. It is difficult to conceive a character more highly dramatic, or more intensely impassioned, than that of Medea; and in the successive scenes, Pasta appeared as if torn by the conflict of contending passions, until at last her anguish rose to sublimity. The conflict of human affection and supernatural power, the tenderness of the wife, the agonies of the mother, and the rage of the woman scorned, were portrayed with a truth, a power, a grandeur of effect, unequalled before or since by any actress or singer. Every attitude, each movement and look, became a study for a painter; for in the storm of furious passion the grace and beauty of her gestures were never marred by extravagance. Indeed, her impersonation of Medea was one of the finest illustrations of classic grandeur the stage has ever presented.

In the scene where Medea murders her children, the acting of Pasta rose to the sublime. Her self-abandonment, her horror at the contemplation of the deed she is about to perpetrate, the irrepressible affection which comes welling up in her breast, were pictured with a magnificent power, yet with such natural pathos, that the agony of the distracted mother was never lost sight of in the fury of the priestess. Folding her arms across her bosom, she contracted her form, as, cowering, she shrunk from the approach of her children; then grief, love, despair, rage, madness, alternately wrung her heart, until at last her soul seemed appalled at the crime she contemplated. Starting forward, she pursued the innocent creatures, while the audience involuntarily closed their eyes and recoiled before the harrowing spectacle, which almost elicited a stifled cry of horror. But her fine genius invested the character with that classic dignity and beauty which, as in the Niobe group, veils the excess of human agony in the drapery of ideal art.

The season of 1824 at the King's Theatre was remarkable for an unusually—an unnecessarily—large company of singers. No less than *six* prima donnas appeared: Mesdames Colbran Rossini, Catalani, Ronzi di Begnis, Vestris, Caradori, and Pasta. In the month of March, Madame Pasta was announced, and made her first appearance April 24. The opera selected for her appearance was *Otello*. It might almost be termed a début, public curiosity was so strongly excited; for Europe was now ringing with her fame. Every portion of the house was filled at a very early hour, the boxes and pit being so crowded that many elegantly dressed ladies were obliged to be content with seats in the gallery. To Madame Pasta was due the idea of reviving *Otello*. The music was worthy of a better fate than being allied to such wretched trash as the libretto in which Shakspeare's beautiful tragedy had been travestied by a certain Marchese Berio, and tortured to suit what he considered the exigencies of the lyric stage. The utmost skill both of composer and performer was requisite to make the libretto even tolerable to an English audience.

Madame Pasta's chaste and expressive style of singing excited the utmost admiration; it was never disfigured by meretricious ornament. "Moderate in the use of embellishments," says Stendhal, "Madame Pasta never employs them but to heighten the force of the expression: and, what is more, her embellishments last only just so long as they are found to be useful." In this respect, her manner formed a very strong contrast with that of the generality of Italian singers at the time, who were more desirous of creating astonishment than of giving pleasure. It was not from any lack of technical knowledge and vocal skill that Madame Pasta avoided extravagant ornamentation, for in many of the concerted pieces—in which she chiefly shone—her execution united clearness and rapidity. "Madame Pasta is certainly less exuberant in point of ornament, and more expressive in point of majesty and simplicity," observed one critic, "than any of the first-class singers who have visited England for a long period." "She is also a mistress of art," continues the same writer, "and being limited by nature, she makes no extravagant use of her powers, but employs them with the tact and judgment that can proceed only from an extraordinary mind. This constitutes her highest praise; for never did intellect and industry become such perfect substitutes for organic superiority. Notwithstanding her fine vein of imagination and the beauty of her execution, she cultivates high and deep passions, and is never so great as in the adaptation of art to the purest purposes of expression."

Madame Pasta appeared as Tancredi, May 18. Of this performance it was said by one enthusiastic writer, "She lends her soul to the character, and seems to feel deeply the sentiments which she utters with the heart-touching eloquence of harmony." "Di tanti palpiti," and some passages in the duet of the second act with Amenaïde, were remarked as the best examples of her peculiar manner; for though "Di tanti palpiti" had been set to a quadrille, and had been whistled through every street of the town, yet it excited a tempest of applause when poured from the lips of Madame Pasta. Madame Ronzi di Begnis, a young and lovely woman, a lively actress and a finished singer, imparted to the character of Amenaïde that passionate feeling and powerful expression in which she was superior to almost all the vocalists of the day. Her voice was not powerful, but she had the advantage of knowing its exact capability, and in her management of it evinced much taste and science.

The next character in which the great tragedian appeared was that of Romeo; Zingarelli's opera being produced first for her benefit, June 21. Giulietta was afterwards represented by Ronzi di Begnis, but for a few nights her place was supplied by Madame Biagioli, who undertook the character at three days' notice, on account of the illness of the fair young prima donna. The libretto of this opera is a poor one, but the music contains several beautiful pieces.

Semiramide was the last opera brought out for Pasta in 1824. She was superb and majestic as the Assyrian queen, and realized by her regal dignity and air of command the highest conception of the character of Semiramide. The scene in the first act, where the spectre of her murdered consort appears, she made fearfully grand and impressive; and those where she learns that Arsace is her son, and where she falls by his hand before the tomb of Ninus, were of almost indescribable effect.

Madame Pasta was now at the summit of her art, and "a reigning favourite on the stage, which she had once left without exciting regret." She was universally allowed to be the greatest performer in lyric tragedy who had appeared for years. And this recognition was due to her fine genius; she owed nothing to artifice or meretricious attraction. The exercise of her histrionic and musical gifts was controlled by a refined taste; and the imperfections of her voice were remedied by incessant cultivation, and veiled by a style noble, delicate, and pure. Nothing was left to chance. Her brilliant talents, united to amiable manners, made her the idol of the fashionable world; large sums were showered on her for appearing at private concerts, and she made a handsome profit by her subscription concerts at Almack's Rooms. Her salary at the theatre was 14,000*l*. Madame Colbran Rossini received 15,000*l*.

Despite the galaxy of talent at the King's Theatre, the Opera season of 1824 was a disastrous failure, partly owing to the enormous expense of an unnecessarily numerous company. Soon after the termination of the season, the contents of the King's Theatre were advertised for sale, and it seemed probable that it had closed to open no more. "Interminable disputes and litigations, mismanagements, and repeated losses," says Ebers, "seemed to threaten ruin to whoever should be bold enough to undertake it; but by some arrangement the sale never took place, and the same manager ventured to run the hazard of renewing his lease."

The management of the King's Theatre in 1825 made great exertions to secure Madame Pasta, who, then in the height of her popularity, was performing in Paris. She obtained a congé to the 8th June only, being bound under heavy penalties to return to Paris by the stipulated time. Great difficulties presented themselves in the way of completing the engagement, and these at first appeared insurmountable. One was, that Benelli, the manager and sub-lessee, quitted England, leaving unpaid the greater part of her large salary for the past season; Madame Pasta, therefore, was naturally unwilling to enter into a fresh engagement with the management. "She required, then, in addition to the remuneration which might be agreed on for the employment of her services during the period of her congé," says Ebers, "that she should be paid the whole portion of her last year's salary, left owing by the late manager." Mr. Allen was sent to Paris to try what could be done to induce her to come, short of such a demand, and at last all was arranged, and on the 10th May Madame Pasta made her appearance at the King's Theatre, in *Otello*, the opera, in all its principal parts, being cast as in the preceding season. It was generally decided that her singing during this season was improved, by being more finished.

Madame Pasta's arrival made a wonderful alteration in the prospects of the King's Theatre. Ronzi di Begnis, having totally lost her voice, had been compelled to throw up her engagement, and retired to Italy; Madame Vestris had seceded from the Opera; and Madame Caradori was unable to perform for some time. The manager, in despair, thought of engaging the young daughter of the tenor Garcia, who, he hoped, might help to prop the fortunes of the house; and she appeared, but through extreme nervousness proved a comparative failure.

The first novelty, and which was produced for Pasta's benefit, May 26th, was a revival of Paisiello's *Nina, Pazza per Amore,* woefully abridged, or rather mangled and curtailed into one act, and even then thought too long and tiresome; "so entirely has taste changed, and music," sighed Lord Mount Edgecumbe. Some declared that Nina, in which Madame Pasta had previously appeared in Paris, in 1823, was her finest performance as an actress, though not as a singer. The story is simple and affecting, being that of an unhappy young girl driven to madness by an unrequited passion, and then restored to reason by hearing an air which she had been accustomed to sing with her lover. Madame Pasta depicted the wandering of intellect finely and delicately, and with touching effect; and the gradual return of intelligence, brightening the spirit with joy and thankfulness, was exquisitely beautiful.

Her singing was characterized by simplicity and pathos, and the whole performance drew tears from her fashionable audience.

At this time some persons of fashion, seeking for a new sensation, arranged to have operas performed at their houses on *Sunday night:* more than one performance had been given, when they were suddenly checked. The Duke of York had been invited to one of them, and the performance was delayed for some time, as his Royal Highness did not make his appearance; at length a note arrived, couched in polite terms, but plainly intimating that the Sunday operas did not receive the countenance of the Court. Had these operas been continued, it is certain that, in addition to the shock that would have been given to religious ideas, they would have tended to ruin the Italian theatre; as it was, their effect was detrimental, as some of the singers actually left the rehearsals at the King's Theatre unfinished, to attend those at aristocratic houses. Many of the singers being engaged to perform nightly at three or four public and private concerts, the Opera was often paralysed by the indisposition of the vocalists in consequence.

Madame Pasta performed, during the season of 1825, on ten nights and in four characters, and she actually sang at twenty-four or twenty-five concerts, receiving twenty-five guineas for each. Her operatic engagement was 1,200*l.*, she sold her benefit to Ebers for 800*l.*, and within the brief space of four weeks she realized no less a sum than 2,400*l.* In 1826 she demanded 2,300*l.* for three months and a half, which was acceded to; and the security she demanded was managed by making the money payable in three instalments, the last to be paid previous to her appearance on the stage: in addition to her salary, she was allowed, during the term of her engagement, a private box, twelve pit and twelve gallery tickets.

She made her appearance the 23rd April, and her popularity absorbed universal attention. "At no period of Pasta's career had she been more fashionable," says Ebers, "than during this engagement. She had, literally, worked her way up to eminence, and, having attained the height, she stood on it firm and secure; no performer has owed less to caprice or fashion: her reputation has been earned, and, what is more, deserved."

Pasta had sung alternately in Paris and in London till 1826; but owing to some disagreement with Rossini, then charged with the direction of the Opéra Italien, she would not renew her engagement with him. On quitting England, in that year, she went to Naples. In 1827, she reappeared in London, being engaged at a salary of between two and three thousand guineas for twenty-three nights, besides a free benefit, which produced her 1,500 guineas. She repeated her usual characters, and her performance of Desdemona afforded an opportunity of comparison with Madame Malibran, with whom it was also a favourite character, and who performed it the same season. It was admitted that Malibran had the advantage in vocalisation and execution, and pure musical feeling, but in high and original conception, Pasta was incontestably superior; her reading of the part was totally different from that of her young rival, being characterized by greater nobleness and grandeur.

The novelty of the season was a serious opera, entitled *Maria Stuarda*, the music by Signor Coccia. The character of the unhappy Mary was sustained by Madame Pasta with an "impassioned dignity, with an eloquence of voice, of look, and of action which defies description, and challenges the severest criticism. It was a piece of acting which great natural genius, extensive powers of observation, peculiar sensibility of feeling, and those acquirements of art which are the result of sedulous study, combined to render perfect." The interview with Queen Elizabeth was deeply affecting. Mary first supplicates, but, roused by the taunts of her persecutor, reassumes for a moment the dignity of her character and station, and then sinks again under her sorrow. The abject humiliation of the Scottish Queen was touching in the extreme, and her burst of passion was a magnificent contrast to the misery previously expressed. The last scene, when Mary takes an eternal farewell of her weeping attendants, was unequalled for pathos, and crowned the triumph of the performance. Madame Pasta felt the situation so intensely, that when summoned before the audience she was always still labouring under great agitation.

In August, Madame Pasta went to Dublin, accompanied by Spagnoletti, Seguin, and Madame Castelli, and then left for Italy, appearing first at Trieste. While there, when walking with some friends, a ragged child, about three years of age, approached, and asked charity for her blind mother, in such artless and touching accents, that the prima donna burst into tears, and put into the child's hands all the money she had. Her friends began extolling her charity and the goodness of her heart. "I will not accept your compliments," said she, wiping the tears from her eyes. "This child demanded charity in a sublime manner. I have seen, at one glance, all the miseries of the mother, the wretchedness of their home, the want of clothing, the cold which they suffer. I should indeed be a great actress if, at any time, I could find a gesture expressing profound misery with such truth."

At Naples, Madame Pasta found less favour than at Trieste. *Medea* did not create the furore it had inspired in the colder inhabitants of the capitals of France and England, and Mayer's opera was supplanted by Pacini's *Niobe*, which succeeded better. The Neapolitans, caring more for the pure art of vocalisation than for the dramatic quality of a singer, appeared unable to appreciate at its full value the genius of Pasta, who, discouraged by their coldness, soon left Naples. She received more justice at Bologna, Milan, Vienna, and Verona.

In 1828, she appeared again before her English admirers in *Tancredi*, and afterwards performed in *Zelmira*, in which she sang with the most exquisite feeling. Her Zelmira was by many preferred to her Tancredi, as affording greater opportunity for the exertion of her dramatic as well as vocal powers; for she was always more at ease, more confident, in proportion to the magnitude of her task. After *Otello*, Mayer's grand serious opera of *La Rosa Bianca e la Rosa Rossa*, was produced, with new scenery, dresses, and decorations. The libretto was absurd, and utterly destitute of historical accuracy, while the music was not what might have been expected from the composer of *Medea;* being pleasing, but nothing more. Madame Pasta distinguished herself pre-eminently by her dramatic and vocal excellence, and, as the Earl of Derby, a young knight of the Red Rose, in a plumed helmet, looked the gallant cavalier to admiration.

The part of Armando, in *Il Crociato in Egitto*, was her next remarkable personation. The opera had been composed almost expressly for Signor Velluti, but Pasta's success in the character in Paris had raised the curiosity of the English public, and a violent contest ensued between the partisans of the signor and the great prima donna, which rose to such a height that there were sometimes outbreaks during the performances. Madame Pasta's version of the part was different in many respects from that of Velluti: she paid the most scrupulous attention to the tempo, which Velluti altogether disregarded in order to introduce his favourite roulades. Her conception of the part was completely original, so that many thought they now witnessed it really for the first time. A ludicrous incident occurred at the first representation, March 13th. On the conclusion of the trio, "Ma balzar' quel cor' senti," which she sang with Madame Caradori and Mdlle. Brambilla, Madame Pasta flew to her dressing-room to change her costume, but the audience not allowing the performance to proceed till the trio was repeated, the prima donna hurried on to the stage again, half Crusader, half Mameluke.

On her benefit night, May 15th, Madame Pasta attempted a daring experiment. Selecting *Otello* as the piece of the evening, she actually appeared as the jealous Moor, Mdlle. Sontag being the Desdemona; but the innovation was not liked: indeed the transposition of the music of *Otello* from a tenor to a mezzo-soprano voice naturally injured the effect of the concerted pieces; nor did the songs gain by the change. But her acting was passionately grand. She did not blacken her face, but assumed a brown complexion, in order that the expressive play of her countenance, which always was one of her most powerful aids in acting, might not be lost. The last scene, where Otello seizes Desdemona, who endeavours to escape, grasping her by the hair and dragging her to the bed, where he stabs her, was horrifying. "Some of the spectators, and those not a few, considered her whole deportment to have exceeded the effects which can be readily borne, and to touch the very verge of disgust." It was, however, a magnificent display of tragic power.

Never had Pasta's performance been so powerful as during this season. The presence of Malibran and of Sontag, two young and glorious rivals, excited her to superhuman efforts to retain her supremacy; and her energy, always marvellous, was now exerted to the utmost. But while increased effect was visible in her acting, her singing was deteriorated: she never acted so well, or sang so ill. Her intonation was materially affected by the exertions she made, and in her anxiety not to be outstripped, she lowered her standard of taste, and loaded her singing with the same redundancy of ornament in which her younger rivals indulged. She was considered by some to have fallen into the same class with Catalani; but her style had less force than that of Catalani only because it had less violence, while it was much more finished. She united the most elegant and cultivated vocal taste with dramatic talent of almost unequalled splendour. "Madame Pasta," said a clever writer, "is in fact the founder of a new school, and after her, the possession of vocal talent alone is insufficient to secure high favour, or to excite the same degree of interest for any length of time. Even in Italy, where the mixture of dramatic with musical science was long neglected, and not appreciated for want of persons equally gifted with both attainments, Madame Pasta has exhibited to her countrymen the beauty of a school too long neglected, in such a manner that they will no longer admit the notion of lyric tragedy being properly spoken without dramatic as well as vocal qualifications in its representative."

In 1829 Madame Pasta was in Vienna, where she was named by the Emperor of Austria first Court singer, and was presented by him with a superb diadem of the value of 400 ducats (about 180*l.*) She purchased a charming villa this year near the Lake of Como, whither she retired for some months in the summer, for repose from her exertions. During this year she performed in twelve operas by Rossini at Bologna, the great maestro himself directing the orchestra; and a medal was struck in her honour by the Società del Casino.

In 1830 she performed at Vienna, in *Otello* and other grand operas, and thence went to Milan, where she was singing with Rubini, Galli, Madame Pisaroni, Lablache, and David. Donizetti was then in that city, and wrote for Pasta, Rubini, and Galli his *Anna*

Bolena, which was very successful; the subject being chosen with the view of developing the predominant qualities of the three lyric performers.

Rubini, the "King of Tenors," was then about six-and-thirty. His talents were powerfully dramatic, his voice was a pure and high tenor, rising from *mi* to *ut* from the chest, and prolonged to *la* in the falsetto. With a great volume of tone and a delicious *timbre*, he had wonderful facility of execution; his style being distinguished by an extraordinary fluency in ornament, and a peculiar tremulo on the sustained notes, which gave exquisite effect to pathetic expression. He had been originally a choir-boy, but though his father thought highly of his talents and voice, some good people pretended that he would never be able to succeed as a singer. He worked hard, nevertheless, and after surmounting great difficulties and vicissitudes, went to Paris in 1825, where his success was triumphant. His manner was full of energy, and his execution facile and finished, even when indulging in the most daring and luxuriant ornamentation. These qualities he still possessed, when, at a subsequent period on the boards of our Italian Opera, he was one of the marvellous quartett composed of Grisi, Rubini, Tamburini, and Lablache.

In 1831 Pasta was engaged at Milan for twenty representations, at a salary of 40,000 francs: Milan thus possessing at once the two greatest singers of the time, herself and Malibran. It was at Milan that Vincenzo Bellini wrote for her his lovely opera, *La Sonnambula*, which was thus cast: Amina, Madame Pasta; Elvino, Rubini; Rodolfo, Mariano; Lisa, Madame Taccani. This delightful work was produced at the Teatro della Canobiana, and excited the most lively interest. Pasta and Rubini surpassed themselves. "Emulating each other in wishing to display the merits of the opera, they were both equally successful," said a critic of the day, "and those who participated in the delight of hearing them will never forget the magic effect of their execution. But, exquisite as were, undoubtedly, Madame Pasta's vocal exertions, her histrionic powers, if possible, surpassed them. It would be difficult for those who have seen her represent, in Donizetti's excellent opera, the unfortunate Amina, with a grandeur and a dignity above all praise, to conceive that she could so change (if the expression may be allowed) her nature as to enact the part of a simple country girl. But she has proved her powers to be unrivalled; she personates a simple rustic as easily as she identifies herself with Medea, Semiramide, Tancredi, and Anna Bolena."

In 1831, after an absence of three years, Madame Pasta returned to England, presenting herself in the character of Medea, with Rubini, Fanny Ayton, and Lablache. Her performance had lost none of its wonted vigour: on the contrary, her tragic acting was remarked as being, if possible, improved. In the scene with her children she rivalled Mrs. Siddons. Rubini performed the character of Egeus, and the duets between the great tenor and Pasta were exquisite. This was a happy year for Rubini, it being the first that he was allowed to have his enormous earnings in full, he having previously received only a small portion from Barbaja: those earnings had averaged 8,000*l.* per annum for many years. Rubini was very economical, and when he died, in 1854, left behind him a fortune of 90,000*l.*

In Gnecco's *Prova d'un Opera Seria*, Pasta appeared to unusual advantage, and showed much versatility in this amusing caricature of the rehearsals of a serious opera at the house of the prima donna and at the theatre. Alternately arch, whimsical, playful, and capricious, she provoked roars of laughter by her burlesque singing, without advancing a step towards vulgarity. Lablache, in the character of the composer, was irresistibly droll, especially in the quarrel scene between himself and Pasta.

Anna Bolena was produced for Madame Pasta's benefit, when Lablache performed Henry VIII. The mighty basso always thoroughly studied every part he undertook; and on this occasion he startled the house by his extraordinary resemblance to Holbein's portrait of the arbitrary monarch.

In December, Madame Pasta, after singing at Paris,

took leave of her French admirers with an extra performance, consisting of *La Prova d'un Opera Seria* and a concert, at which all the principal singers of the establishment assisted. Her last triumph was obtained at La Scala, in 1832. There was an admirable company assembled that season: Pasta, the young Giulia Grisi, Donzelli, and others. Bellini wrote for these artistes his opera of *Norma*. Pasta performed the Druidic priestess, Donzelli her lover, Pollione, and Giulia Grisi the fair Adalgisa. Madame Pasta appeared in this opera the following year in London. It was produced Thursday, June 2nd, for her benefit, being the chief novelty of the season, and was directed by the composer himself. Adalgisa was performed by Madame De Meric, Pollione by Donzelli, Oroveso by Signor V. Galli. It was not at first liked, though after a little while the public discovered its beauty. Pasta's acting alone saved the opera from being almost a fiasco.

For several years after this, Pasta continued to perform in Paris and the principal theatres in Italy with undiminished éclat. In 1837 she revisited England, and appeared at the King's Theatre in Medea, Norma, Anna Bolena, and other characters; but it now began to be remarked that though, as an actress, she was as great as ever, her vocal powers were beginning to fail, especially in regard to intonation. This was her last season in England, for it is not necessary to take into account a short visit in 1850, when she appeared only twice in public.

She continued, nevertheless, to receive continental honours. In 1839 she was elected an honorary member of the celebrated Accademia di Santa Cecilia at Rome; and in 1840, after a splendid season at St. Petersburg and Moscow, she was presented by the Czar with a valuable ring.

In 1841 she went to Berlin. The Berlinese regarded her with deep sympathy and commiseration, for she had lost almost her entire fortune—the well-earned reward of her splendid talents—by the failure of the great bank of Guymuller, at Vienna. She appeared at the Royal Opera House in a dramatic concert, with Herr Zschiesche and Dem. Lehmann, in costume, the music selected being from *Semiramide*, and (with Signor Gamberini) a part of *Otello*. Subsequently she appeared at the Königstädtischen Theater in *Anna Bolena*, with Signora Ferlotti and Signor Paltrinieri, a singer with a fine baritone. She also performed in *Norma* and *Tancredi*; then, in compliance with the wish of the King, twice in *Semiramide*, performing altogether eleven times. In October she was at Leipzig.

But neither her voice nor her physical strength were now what they had been; and she wisely retired from the scene of her triumphs. For many years she had resided during the winter at Milan or

Genoa, and during the summer at her villa at Como, occupying her leisure in giving to artistes very valuable lessons. Mademoiselle Parodi was her most distinguished pupil.

Madame Pasta had one child, a daughter, born about 1825.

CHAPTER II.

CATHERINE STEPHENS.

THE transition from the triumph of the commanding genius of a Pasta to the sweet and artless Catherine Stephens, is like the sensation one would feel on emerging from a classic temple or a gorgeous saloon into a scene of simple nature, clothed with the fresh beauty of the spring.

The year before Angelica Catalani made her début at the Fenice, there was born in London, on the 18th September, 1794, a child who was afterwards to earn for herself the fame of a prima donna; this was Catherine Stephens, the daughter of a carver and gilder, in Park Street, Grosvenor Square. At her earliest age she afforded evidences that she would be a fine singer some day: she lisped in song. Her elder sister (afterwards Mrs. J. Smith) had also a love of music, and the two girls trilled like larks. At length their father felt it his duty to have them properly taught.

While Catherine was trying to master the elements of musical science, her sister made her début at Liverpool; from whence she came to Drury Lane, appearing there in the character of Miss Hoyden in the *Trip to Scarborough*, and Lucy in the *Virgin Unmasked*. Catherine was then, in 1807, placed under the tuition of Gesualdo Lanza, a well-known musical professor. From him she learned quickly to sing at sight with perfect correctness, and went steadily not only through all the gradations of solfeggi, but through a severe course of vocal exercises, with the view of acquiring facility of execution; she also studied a multitude of pieces of music selected by Signor Lanza from the best English and Italian Operas and from Oratorios.

While with Signor Lanza, she sang at Bath, Bristol, and many places along the south coast, and on the 3rd October, 1812, she sang at Ramsgate, at a concert given by Mr. Samuel Wesley and Mr. Webb, jun.; "where," said Samuel Wesley," she received the greatest and most deserved applause." When there, being called upon to try, at sight, some manuscript glees, she acquitted herself in a manner which surprised the most excellent judges. Her friends becoming impatient at her apparently tardy progress under Lanza, transferred her to the charge of Mr. Thomas Welsh; and to poor Lanza's great mortification she appeared on the 17th or 18th of that same October, at Manchester, as "Mr. Welsh's pupil."

During her studies, Catherine Stephens had been heard by Signor Galiloni, who recommended her to the managers of the Opera-house, to supply the place of Madame Catalani; but not being perfect in Italian, she was then ineligible for the King's Theatre.

On the 23rd September, 1813, Catherine made her first acknowledged appearance, at Covent Garden, as Mandane in *Artaxerxes*, under the name of Miss *Stevens*, with complete success. Her execution of "Check'd by duty, rack'd by love," and "The Soldier tir'd," was particularly admired. But for great ladies she was not well suited, either in person, voice, or style. She was now nineteen; her figure, of medium height, was pretty, but inclined to embonpoint; her hair and eyes were dark, and though not, strictly speaking, handsome, her countenance had an indescribable fascination, owing to the ingenuous simplicity and unaffected sweetness of her nature. Her manner in private life was easy, mild, and artless, and she was blithe and joyous as a child: in truth, her animal spirits would sometimes completely run away with her; and even on the stage, while playing parts which needed a serious demeanour, if anything provoked her mirth, she would be in agonies, struggling between a desire to laugh and the fear of offending the audience.

The tones of her voice were rich and dulcet, and captivated the ear; its quality was full and liquid beyond that of any other singer then in England; its volume was such that it could be distinctly heard above the band and chorus, and its compass reached to the high D. Her ornaments were correct and neat, and her execution was good, but not remarkable either for rapidity or variety. She did not aim at "stage effect," and her singing consequently had the peculiar charm of sincerity and artlessness. She seemed to sing from the impulse of her happy joyous nature, and the delight she felt was conveyed to her audience. There was no fire, no deep sentiment, no dramatic power; she had high cultivation, science, polish, but she warbled so calmly and easily, that the audience, if not deeply moved, were charmed. Simple airs of innocent pathos were her speciality; loftier efforts seemed neither adapted to her taste nor suited to her talent.

She appeared as Polly in the *Beggar's Opera*, on the 22nd October; and after that she sang under her own name. Her personation of Polly was exquisite. "Two hours spent at this performance," said an enthusiastic admirer, "is a little glossy portion of the stream of life—a season of calm joy, which it is tranquillizing even to remember." The unobtrusiveness of her style, the very "bewitching awkwardness" of her manner, completed the pleasure which her performance afforded. On the 12th November she performed Clara in the *Duenna*. Then she appeared as Rosetta, which she acted charmingly. In the song, "Young I am, and sore afraid," the ill-repressed laugh, and the irony gleaming through her feigned tears, were most admirable. Her freshness, her simplicity, atoned for any coldness of conception. When she advanced to sing, with a lovely pleading look in her eyes, deprecating criticism, the heart was at once enlisted in her favour, and it was impossible to find fault with the singer while the woman thus disarmed the critic. The softness and delicacy of her voice, and the purity of her taste, were universally acknowledged, and she was admitted to be exempt from the prevailing sin of a mixture of styles.

Her own style was best adapted for ballad-singing: such songs as "Auld Robin Gray," and "Savourneen Deelish," she sang with so much ease, pouring forth her sweet, rich tones with bird-like volubility, that it was impossible to imagine her suffering from the distress which the song was written to portray. "Even the effects of her full and fine crescendo and dying fall are lost," observed a writer in the *Quarterly Musical Review;* "and it is by them that the workings of passion or the sinkings of the soul are pictured." But there is a peculiar charm in the simple utterance of a ballad by a sweet, round, ringing voice, which is deeply felt, and the heart is the more surely touched because of the absence of effort or intention on the part of the singer. If Miss Stephens was incapable of force, passion, or brilliancy, it was owing to an innate reserve that veiled her powers; for in private society she threw off every tinge of coldness. "I have heard her sing

'Auld Robin Gray' without the music, in a style that certainly came *from* the heart, and went at once *to* the heart," said another writer.

The public were charmed with a singer so thoroughly *English*, and the manager gave her what was then considered a large salary—twelve pounds a week for the first year for singing thrice a week, and twenty pounds the second year. Of this salary Mr. Welsh received half, though it was rather due to poor Lanza.

In March, 1814, Miss Stephens made her first appearance at the Ancient Concerts, in *Acis and Galatea*, and during this season her talents were severely tested in the most popular arias: such as "Ye sacred priests," "Angels ever bright and fair," "Holy, holy," "Mad Bess," "Pious Orgies," "I know that my REDEEMER liveth," "From rosy bowers," "Berenice, ove sei?" with many others. Immediately after her début at the Ancient Concerts, she sang at the fourth of the Philharmonic Society's Concerts, with Braham, and in July she sang at two concerts at York. Her singing of sacred music seemed to want that depth of pathos and exalted fervour which awaken the soul. She excelled in the simple, pure, chaste English style; and she was fitted for homely characters in low comedy, not for fine ladies or fashionable heroines. As a singer only, however, she pleased in everything; her dulcet notes were sufficiently charming in themselves, and a certain native quiet humour and sense of enjoyment supplied the place of higher attributes. Her execution of the "Pretty Mocking-Bird" was often cited as one of the most perfect specimens of vocal power ever heard. One result of her serene and smooth vocalisation was that the ear never became satiated with her effects; she had no favourite passages, no pet cadence introduced alike into all her songs: no musical mannerism disfigured her style.

In February, 1815, a piece called *Brother and Sister*, by Bishop and Reeve, was produced. In this Miss Stephens sang a song by Bishop, wherein, in imitation of Braham's song in *Narensky*, she gave an echo to her own voice. Its success was extraordinary: the echo of her own voice seemed as if it was produced, not by the singer, but by a viewless power, so aërial and delicate were its tones. She achieved a triumph in this song, which always remained a favourite.

Miss Stephens' character in private life was most amiable; polite and easy in her manner, she was also benevolent and charitable without ostentation. On the occasion of a benefit for Dulwich Hospital, she not only returned the price of her services, thirty guineas, but added ten from her own purse; and again in Dublin she gave to the poor 330*l.*, the proceeds of a benefit concert. And these are only a few instances of her generosity. She was wholly unaffected, and never arrogated to herself undue consideration because she was a popular singer. "I shall never forget seeing her at a private party," says an author in *Knight's Quarterly Magazine*, "where, with the most unaffected good-nature, she offered to sing second to a child with a very beautiful voice. 'If I am wanted,' she said; but she did not make the offer until a real difficulty had arisen about a singer, so it was evident that her only motive was to be of use." Towards her professional comrades she was exceedingly kind, and was ever ready to take their place even at a moment's notice if they needed it. She was industrious in study, feeling that it was necessary she should work to retain the reputation she had earned, and for eight or sometimes nine hours a day she practised all the year round, only relaxing when her throat needed rest from exertion, and then she would take a walk until it had recovered from the fatigue.

One gentleman who lost his heart to her in 1815, regularly attended all her performances; waiting till the doors were opened, he seated himself in the third or fourth row of the pit, and the instant the opera was concluded, flew round and placed himself at the stage-door, to catch a glimpse of the enchantress as she passed to her carriage. He was so desperately smitten that he followed her to Ipswich, and once even, it was believed, to Dublin, in hopes of meeting her if she by chance should go out for a walk; but he never had the courage to gain an introduction. The ill-fated gentleman, sad to relate, ended his days in a lunatic asylum; but whether he went mad through love for the charming Kitty, or whether he fell in love because he was a madman, is a problem not now to be solved.

The extraordinary popularity of Mozart's *Don Giovanni* at the King's Theatre induced the proprietor of Covent Garden to bring out an English version of the opera, arranged by Mr. Bishop. It was produced the 20th May, 1817, and the principal parts were well sustained by Sinclair, Duruset, and Miss Stephens. As Donna Anna she was not equal to Madame Fodor, but she was encored in the beautiful air in the second act. The success of this production originated the practice of adapting to the English stage the most eminent works of foreign composers.

The operas in which Miss Stephens performed were, however, generally very indifferent, and little worthy even of a passing notice—being nothing more than "operatic dramas." In February, 1821, she appeared in the *Beggar's Opera*, but very soon after she broke with Covent Garden in consequence of disputes with the manager. She received a salary of twenty pounds for playing thrice in each week, but she demanded an advance of five pounds a week. The manager objected; there being a rule requiring that if one performer's salary was raised, all must be advanced. The proprietors offered to make up the amount by presents, but the popular singer refused this reasonable arrangement; and then she demanded ten pounds a night. This was peremptorily refused, and she went off to Drury Lane, then under the management of Elliston.

She did not agree much better with him; indeed, he did not act well towards her. One of the conditions in the articles of agreement entered into by the leading performers was that they should not be required to appear in pantomimes; yet, on the production of *Harlequin and the Flying Chest*, Elliston summoned all his singers to take part in the music. Relying on the terms of her articles, Miss Stephens paid no attention to this call, so Elliston inflicted a heavy fine. She was indignant, and remonstrated: "I never agreed to go on in a pantomime," said she, a little passionately. "My dear soul," answered the wily manager, "I don't wish it. I only want you to join in the chorus off the wings;" and he retained the fine.

At Drury Lane Miss Stephens received but little attention, owing probably to the exceedingly indifferent music she was condemned to sing. The pieces were at first pretty good, though garbled and maltreated. Dramatised adaptations of Scott's novels, and different ephemeral operettas, formed the répertoire from which Miss Stephens had to choose her parts. In August, 1822, she appeared in *Der Freischütz*, with Braham and T. Cook. This opera gave great satisfaction to the frequenters of Drury Lane; but what with "introductions" and "omissions," it must have been a droll affair. In 1830, Bishop went over to Paris, when *Guillaume Tell* was at its height of popularity. He attended the performance two or three times, took notes, literally as well as figuratively, and returning to England, he produced, in conjunction with Mr. Planché, *Hofer, the Tell of the Tyrol.* This piece was very splendidly mounted, and brought forward at Covent Garden, May 1, 1830, with Miss Stephens, Madame Vestris, H. Phillips, and Sinclair, in the leading characters.

Miss Stephens' earnings were now on an average about 5,000*l.* per annum. The theatre yielded her 1,500*l.*; the Ancient Concerts produced 330*l.*; the oratorios 200*l.*; occasional appearances at the Philharmonic, City Amateur, and the City Concerts, about 200*l.* more. Her earnings by singing at private parties could not be computed: by a visit to Ireland alone she gained 5,000*l.* Young, charming, clever, and rich too—for she was prudent as fortunate—of a generous nature, an affectionate daughter, a kind sister, and an amiable friend—some surprise was felt that she should not have married. Lord Milton was at one time supposed to be madly enamoured of the fair English songstress; and the Duke of Devonshire, too, at whose splendid parties she frequently appeared, was thought to be in love with her. At last the Earl of Essex, a widower, who had long been her ardent admirer, offered her a coronet, was accepted, and the marriage took place, Thursday, March 14, 1838, at his lordship's house in Belgrave Square. The bridegroom was eighty-two, the bride forty-five. The earl settled on his bride a splendid jointure, and allowed her to leave her relations the whole of her own property, which had so long been at their disposal. He survived but a short time to enjoy her society, and by his death she became Dowager Countess of Essex.

CHAPTER III.

MARY ANNE PATON.

TOWARDS the end of the last century, a respectable and well-educated tutor, named Paton, was at the head of a mathematical seminary in Edinburgh, and his classes were so numerously attended, that, for a considerable time, he was in the receipt of 2,000*l.* per annum. His family consisted of Mary Anne, Isabella, and Eliza. Mary Anne, the eldest, was born in 1802.

Mary Anne had a gift and a passion for music from her earliest childhood. When only two years old she could name any tone, or semitone, on hearing it sounded. She sang like a skylark, and was perpetually warbling her "wood-notes wild," flying about the house, and scattering in sportive profusion trills and shakes on every note in her voice. She joyfully agreed, while yet a child, to undergo the drudgery of learning the harp and pianoforte, and when little more than four years of age, in 1806, she performed on these instruments. Not content with executing the compositions of others, she next insisted on producing some of her own, and in 1807 some fantasias, etc. were published under her name. Her infantile talent attracted the notice of the Duchess of Buccleugh, with whom, one of her biographers gravely asserts, Mary Anne, at the age of *five*, held a correspondence regarding some of her baby musical productions.

In 1810, Miss Paton appeared at several concerts in Edinburgh, where she sang, played on the harp and pianoforte, and recited Collins' "Ode to the Passions" (a favourite piece with young ladies at the period), "Alexander's Feast," and some similar morceaux. Some of these concerts were patronized by the Duchess of Buccleugh, the Duchess of Gordon, and other distinguished ladies. The young girl had no other instructors, it may be observed, up to this time, than her father and mother. This circumstance afterwards proved disadvantageous to her in many respects, when she came into competition with the leading singers of the day.

Miss Paton inherited her musical abilities by rightful descent. Her grandmother, though not a professional vocalist, was so good a performer on the violin, that her fame became widely spread in the neighbourhood of Strathbogie (now Huntley), in Aberdeenshire, where she lived. The Duke of Cumberland, on his way to Culloden, stopped to pay her a visit; and was so pleased with the style in which she executed some Scotch melodies, that he presented her with a superb scarf of silk tartan, which was long preserved in the family as an honourable testimony to her musical skill.

Mr. Paton quitted Edinburgh about 1811. He entertained peculiar ideas regarding the Christian dispensation, and orthodoxy taking the alarm, he gradually lost that professional connection which his talents and agreeable manners had drawn together; he therefore came to London, and opened an academy. Meantime, Mary Anne continued her studies, with little or no assistance from masters. She desired to place herself under the tuition of Mr. Bishop, but for some reason he declined receiving her as a pupil; and she met with a similar rebuff from many eminent professors, who felt certain that she had no chance of success.

Miss Paton appeared from time to time during 1812, 1813, and the early part of 1814 at fashionable concerts; but public concerts were then, unfortunately, monopolized by a few principal vocalists of acknowledged reputation, who introduced the pupils of such masters as could easily secure their success. Miss Paton offered her services, gratuitously, to almost every manager in the metropolis, without meeting with any encouraging response. Her health suffered very much about this period, and her general education not having advanced in proportion to her musical knowledge, her friends counselled her temporary withdrawal from public; she therefore refrained from singing, except occasionally at private parties. In 1820 she appeared at the Bath concerts, where she made a favourable impression, and she next sang at Huntingdon, at two concerts given by the organist of that town.

At last Mr. Morris, of the Haymarket, agreed to give her a chance of making an essay on the stage, and on the 3rd August, 1822, Miss Paton made her first curtsey as Susanna, in the *Marriage of Figaro;* foreign music with English words being now all the vogue. She was a very agreeable-looking girl; her figure was about the middle height, slender and delicate; her hair and eyes were dark, her complexion clear. Her face was not very beautiful when in repose, but when animated in acting or singing, its expression reflected every change of sentiment, and her countenance beamed with vivacity. Never was success more decided or more deserved. She subsequently performed Rosina in the *Barber of Seville*, and Lydia in *Morning, Noon, and Night;* an opera now forgotten: in it she introduced the Scotch ballad of "Mary of Castle Carey," a ballad in which she had been frequently applauded. She also performed Polly in the *Beggar's Opera.*

Two months after, Miss Paton was engaged at Covent Garden, replacing Miss Stephens in the first characters. Morris, in his farewell address at the Haymarket, alluded most kindly to her, and eulogized her talents. On the 19th October, she made her appearance at Covent Garden as Polly, and repeated that character two or three times; but her name was suddenly omitted from the bills until the 7th December, when she appeared as Mandane. Curiosity was naturally excited as to the reason of this singular conduct of the management: the singer's indisposition had been assigned as the cause, but the truth soon became known. Miss A. M. Tree, it appeared, had peremptorily refused to perform with Miss Paton, except on the condition of her rival playing second to her, which the quality of their respective voices rendered absurd; besides, Miss Paton had been engaged to perform first characters only. The part of Susanna in the *Marriage of Figaro* was given to her, and she was announced in the bills to appear in that character; but the manager informed her that Miss Tree had refused to play the Countess, and begged that she would take the part alternately with that of the Countess, that the piece might be brought forward, and her sister singer saved from incurring a heavy penalty. Miss Paton assented, in this instance only; but was afterwards informed by the manager that the same difficulties remained, unless she conceded the part of Susanna to Miss Tree on the first night. To this concession, also, she kindly agreed. On her benefit night this season her sister Isabella (afterwards of Drury Lane Theatre) made her appearance as Letitia Hardy.

The revival of Shakspeare's plays with music proved a more fertile source of jealousy between the rival sirens. In February, 1823, they performed together in the *Comedy of Errors.* Miss Paton, as Adriana, sang the "Willow" song from *Othello*, and "Come live with me and be my love," very sweetly; but she surpassed herself in "Lo! here the gentle lark," from *Venus and Adonis.* The duet with Miss Tree, "Tell me, where is fancy bred," was finely executed, and Miss Tree performed Luciana charmingly. Jones and Duruset were the two Antipholises, and Farren and Blanchard were very comic representatives of the two Dromios.

When Miss Stephens' engagement at the English Opera-house was concluded, Miss Paton took her place, to execute the music of *Der Freischütz*, which was produced July 22, 1823. Braham, who had an arduous part, exerted himself to the utmost in this opera, and Miss Paton, in the grand scena, "Before my eyes beheld him," displayed her vocal powers to the greatest advantage. She was essentially a British songstress. Her voice was sweet, brilliant, and powerful, its compass extending from A to D or E, or above eighteen or nineteen notes, and her intonation was correct. "Miss Paton," said an able critic in the *Quarterly Musical Review*, "is certainly gifted with extraordinary vocal powers, and with enthusiasm and intellectual vigour of no common kind. She has not yet reached her twenty-first year, yet her technical attainments, we are disposed to think, are nearly as great as those of any vocalist in this country." But there were certain slight reservations: "her shake," it was added, "was too close, too rapid, and too hard; the trifling accent which this grace will bear is wrongly placed," thus depriving it of its value in expression, to which every species of ornament ought essentially to contribute. "No difficulties appal or embarrass her," continues the same critic. "Nor is it to the execution of passages as they are written that she confines herself. Even in Rossini's most rapid airs she changes, and at the same time multiplies the notes, in a way that few, even of the most matured vocalists, venture to attain." Of the *judgment* of such alterations the critic declines to speak, merely stating a fact which demonstrated Miss Paton's facility. Her style was naturally florid, and she cultivated elaborate execution; it being the fashion of the time to admire exuberant ornament. In October, 1823, at a concert given for the benefit of the then nascent Royal Academy of Music, almost the only encore of the night was accorded to the duet "Sull' Aria," sung by

Miss Paton and Miss A. M. Tree. This sweet and beautiful melody was made "a mere ground for the ladies to embroider upon; and they manifested as much ingenuity and as much execution as possible, though at the expense of sound taste." In addition to the allurement of conscious power, Miss Paton began to imitate Catalani, and she did so with success, however much it was regretted by true lovers of song.

Miss Paton had warm sensibility, and this was "displayed in the vigour with which she embodies the conceptions of a composer, not less than in her fancy when she varies them. She gives impressive, passionate recitative with dignity or pathos, as these emotions vary. She can do this from herself." Unfortunately her finer qualities were sometimes obscured by her imitation of Catalani, which was so obvious that no one who had ever heard the marvellous Italian could avoid remarking it, especially when she sang one of Catalani's airs. "Miss Paton and Miss Stephens," says another critic, "are the two greatest English singers that we now have, or perhaps that ever coexisted (and we say this with a perfect remembrance of the claims of Mrs. Salmon, Mrs. Dickons, Miss Tree, and Miss Gradden); and our heroine has the best ear and the most extensive voice: in bravuras she is decidedly superior to her rival, and in many ballads equal to her; witness her 'On the Banks of Allan Water,' etc. etc. Miss Paton's voice is more brilliant, but less soothing than Miss Stephens'; and this quality, which Miss Stephens possesses so abundantly, seems a part of her nature. Miss Paton has compass, power, smoothness, enunciation; in fact, everything that would constitute a great singer, as far as singing is an art; but there is something beyond all this to be found. Her personal nature is exquisitely blended with the effect of art. Miss Stephens has a honied sweetness in her tone, a richness that seems to spring from her heart to her lips, and which we have found in no one else."

At this time Miss Paton became acquainted with a young gentleman named Blood, a surgeon of St. Thomas's Hospital, who was of good family, and (though he did not boast of the circumstance,) was a lineal descendant of the notorious Colonel Blood. He was a tall, elegant-looking young fellow, was accomplished, and passionately fond of music. He moved in good society, and was likely to advance in his profession, in which he was very skilful. His devotion to music, however, led him astray, and he went so far as to make his début at the Lyceum, as Don Carlos, in the *Duenna*, which was performed for the benefit of a friend, when he was warmly applauded. He also performed in Dublin and other places with much success, and afterwards obtained an engagement at the Haymarket Theatre, where he made his début under the name of Davis, as Captain Macheath; but his success was very moderate. Miss Paton being engaged at the Haymarket at the same time, performed with him in the *Beggar's Opera,* and was struck with his agreeable manner and handsome figure. A mutual attachment was the result of their acquaintance, and Mr. Blood made her an offer of marriage, which she accepted; his betrothed then exerted her influence with the manager, and obtained for him an engagement at Covent Garden Theatre. But an unforeseen obstacle arose to mar the happiness of the lovers. Mr. Paton, angered beyond measure, vehemently refused his consent to the match, and threatened the manager that if young Blood were permitted to come behind the scenes of the theatre to see Miss Paton, he should break her engagement. "If you marry him you will work for an adventurer," said her father: "if you must have a husband, wait, and you will, no doubt, get a lord." Rather than injure his betrothed in her profession, or with her family, Mr. Blood voluntarily threw up his own engagement. He had offered to make a settlement of 200*l.* per annum upon her parents.

Mary Anne, notwithstanding her father's opposition, at first determined to decide for herself. She said to a friend of her lover's, "Tell Blood that I would marry him, even if he were a shepherd's boy, and had no more than a penny a day." Indeed, she exceeded him in protestations of affection, and a day was ultimately fixed for their marriage. But on the very morning that was to see the lovers united, the bride for the first time hesitated and drew back; stating that prudential motives induced her for the present to recede. She then abruptly returned her lover's presents, with a message to the effect that he might shortly have occasion to put them to another use; and the rejected lover attempted in vain to gain an explanation of her strange conduct.

Piqued by this treatment, Mr. Blood returned to his own profession, and offered his hand to Miss Dance, another actress, of whom probably Miss Paton had been made jealous; he was accepted, and they were married, and went to reside at Bath, where he practised successfully as a surgeon.

Miss Paton was now observed to droop and become melancholy: her health appeared to be failing; she grew thin and wasted, and her aspect excited the compassion of every one who saw her. Whether on the stage or in the concert-room, every effort at gaiety was succeeded by a marked dejection, and she seemed utterly careless of herself, as if sunk in despair. Among the young men of fashion who had the privilege of going behind the scenes at the theatre, was Lord William Lennox, who soon fixed his regards on the young prima donna. His attentions were most assiduous, and eventually he made her an offer of his hand, on condition that the marriage should be kept secret. Timid, undecided, and easily swayed by others,

Miss Paton consented. Post-horses were ordered for a precipitate flight, and in 1824 the marriage took place, under circumstances of some mystery. Her father's prediction was fulfilled: she had "got a lord."

In 1824, Weber received a proposition from Covent Garden to write an opera, and after having long hesitated on the choice of his subject, he at length chose *Oberon*. As a clever critic observed, "He could not have selected one better adapted to the display of his peculiar genius. It contains descriptions of air, of earth, and heaven—the enchantments of fairy-land, the ardour of chivalry, the tenderness of passion, the dangers of the sea, and, above all, the magic powers of the ivory horn; and this variety, which would have paralysed an ordinary man, has only roused him to commensurate exertion, and affords him a field for the more ample display of the glory of his art." A correspondence was then opened between the director of the theatre and the composer, with reference to the epoch in which the scene should be laid; this being arranged, the management wished to have the piece ready in three months. "Three months!" echoed the composer, writing back. "Why, they would not be sufficient to read the libretto and sketch the plan in my brain!" Indeed, Weber employed nearly eighteen months in finishing his task.

When Weber arrived in London, his first visit, of

course, was to Covent Garden Theatre, where he saw his own *Freischütz* performed. His presence was discovered by the audience, and a storm of enthusiasm ensued. In one of his charming letters to his wife, he gave an account of his reception, and made some remarks on the performance of his opera. The passage ought never to be forgotten; showing, as it does, how different was the judgment on the merits of our English performers, given by a great German artist, from the supercilious tone adopted by many of our so-called critics, who think they display their acumen by depreciating the talent of their own country.

"Could a man," said Weber, "wish for more enthusiasm or more love? I must confess that I was completely overpowered by it, though I am of a calm disposition, and somewhat accustomed to such scenes. I know not what I would have given to have had you by my side, that you might have seen me in my foreign garb of honour. And now, dear love, I can assure you that you may be quite at ease, both as to the singers and the orchestra. Miss Paton is a singer of the first rank, and will play Reiza divinely. Braham not less so, though in a totally different style. There are also several good tenors, and I really cannot see why the English singing should be so much abused. The singers have a perfectly good Italian education, fine voices and expression. The orchestra is not remarkable, but still very good, and the choruses particularly so. In short, I feel quite at ease as to the fate of *Oberon*."

The production of *Oberon* was not effected without more difficulties than Weber had contemplated. Innumerable prejudices had to be overcome, particular singers conciliated, alterations made, and repeated rehearsals superintended, before the composer could inspire the performers with the right spirit of his composition. "Braham," said he, in one of his letters to his wife (March 29, 1826), "begs for a grand scena instead of his first air, which, in fact, was not written for him, and which is rather high. The thought of it was at first quite horrible; I would not hear of it. At last I promised, when the opera was completed, if I had time enough, it should be done; and now this grand scena, a confounded battle-piece and what not, is lying before me, and I am about to set to work, yet with the greatest reluctance. What can I do? Braham knows his public, and is idolized by them. But for Germany I shall keep the opera as it is. I hate the air I am going to compose (to-day I hope) by anticipation. Adieu, and now for the battle."

At rehearsal one of the performers was singing in the fashionable style, when Weber, looking attentively at him, said, "I am very sorry you take so much trouble." "Oh! not at all!" was the careless reply. "Yes," he added, "but I say yes; for why do you take the trouble to sing so many notes that are not in the book?" He disliked the superabundance of florid ornamentation which Catalani, Braham, and other eminent singers had brought into fashion; and he discountenanced as far as possible the habit many singers had of slurring over the verses. In one of the pieces in *Oberon*, Miss Paton, with all her taste and execution, was unable to produce the effect intended by the composer. "I know not how it is," she at last exclaimed, "but I can never do this as it should be." "The reason is," quietly replied Weber, "because you have not studied the words."

Oberon was finally produced the 12th April. When Weber entered the orchestra the house was filled to overflowing, for the expectations of the public had been raised to an extraordinary pitch. The audience simultaneously rose and saluted him by huzzas, by waving of hats and handkerchiefs. They insisted on encoring the overture, and every air was interrupted twice or thrice by bursts of applause.

To Reiza is allotted the most exquisitely impassioned music, and Miss Paton surpassed herself in brilliancy and spirit; her grand scena, "Ocean, thou mighty monster," was given with surprising energy, and in her most finished manner, and received with rapturous delight. The chivalrous character of Sir Huon was assigned to Braham, who sang with powerful effect. The beautiful, talented Madame Vestris was charmingly arch and vivacious as Fatima; her laughter at hearing the enchanted horn in the last scene was so hearty and natural that the whole house was infected with her merriment, and echoed it with peals of laughter. The scenery, dresses, and decorations were unusually splendid, and the scene in the second act, representing the reflection of the setting sun in the sea, surpassed everything of the kind seen before.

On the conclusion of the opera Weber was loudly called for, but it was with the greatest difficulty that he could be induced to make his appearance at the side-scenes. He was too modest to become the "lion" of musical parties, and consequently at his benefit concert the room was not half filled; "while on the same evening the concert of a favourite Italian singer, at the house of one of the nobility, was attended by four hundred fashionables, who paid a guinea apiece for their tickets." Just two months after the production of *Oberon*, Weber was found dead in his bed, in his room at the house of Sir George Smart. His head was resting on his hand as calmly as if in sleep. Ever since his arrival in England he had been in a declining and precarious state of health, and suffering from many anxieties.

At the Philharmonic Concerts, in August, Miss Paton executed a most difficult song from Spohr's *Faust*, which was sent to her, it was said, only the day before the rehearsal. She sang it to perfection. No other vocalist in London probably would have undertaken so hazardous a task, and her success displayed her science as a musician, and her extreme aptitude. "Miss Paton," it was agreed, "has indeed made a vast improvement this season, and taking into account her various abilities, she is perhaps unrivalled." It was to be regretted that she devoted her attention to such miserable trash as she sang on the stage, and scattered her energies upon trifles of the moment, in lieu of giving her study to works of an elevated character; but her facility enabled her to shine in a great variety of styles. "Taken in all styles, taken as a musician, Miss Paton is beyond all question the cleverest female singer we have; but there is not one song, properly so called, in which some one or other does not excel her. In a ballad, the finish, equality, and beauty of Miss Stephens' voicing, her delicacy and truth, place her infinitely above Miss Paton. In execution, Mrs. Salmon distances her not less. From mere distraction of pursuits she has never attained the gusto of the Italian manner; and in the church Miss Travis or any of the others exceed her. Yet if the trial were to depend upon diversity of talent, Miss Paton would outshine them all, without equalling, in their own province, any of them."

This year (1826) she was acknowledged and received as the lady of Lord William Lennox; but the union had proved a most unfortunate one. After her marriage the unhappy wife's health became so impaired that even when the curtain rose to crowded audiences, the public were never certain that they might not be met by a medical certificate of Miss Paton's "total incapacity to play that evening."

At the festivals of Salisbury and York, in 1828, the principal singers were Mesdames Catalani, Caradori, Miss Stephens, Mrs. W. Knyvett, and Miss Paton, with Braham, Phillips, De Begnis, and others. Catalani failed, Miss Paton as evidently rose in the general estimation, while Miss Stephens and Madame Caradori simply preserved the place they had already gained. "It, perhaps, may with truth be said," says an authority of the period, "that since the days of Mara no one has appeared equal to sustain the majesty of such a song as 'I know that my REDEEMER liveth.' Miss Paton certainly threw both energy and pathos into her singing, but still it partakes far more of the beautiful than the sublime of expression. The truth is, that the mind must possess a vigour and solidity which rarely consists with the diversity of pursuits incidental to a modern professional life; and perhaps it requires those severe studies and trains of thought which lead to the production of a composer in the great ecclesiastical style."

An estrangement from her husband, followed by a divorce, terminated her unlucky marriage. For her second husband Miss Paton selected Mr. Wood, a kind-hearted young vocalist, who had lately appeared on the Covent Garden boards. He was a fine and rather good-looking man, with a very sweet and agreeable voice, and, in some characters, was a pretty good actor. Mrs. Wood gradually recovered her health, which as Lady William Lennox she had lost; and the cheerfulness and gaiety of early days returned.

Her first appearance in public after her marriage with Mr. Wood, was on February 24, 1829, at Covent Garden, as Reiza, in Weber's *Oberon*. Ill health had been assigned as the cause of her long absence from the stage, and when she first became visible to the audience through the mist which envelopes the figure of Reiza on her appearance to Sir Huon, she was greeted by enthusiastic applause, which lasted several minutes, and on coming forward the ovation was renewed with equal vigour, and protracted to undue length. Her powers were found to be unimpaired, and were never more brilliantly displayed. Mr. Wood appeared as Sir Huon for the first time, and his vocal and dramatic efforts were spirited and energetic.

Mrs. Wood was engaged at the King's Theatre in 1831, being the first Englishwoman after Cecilia Davies who "achieved that distinction without a certificate of character from Italy." Her début took place the 5th April, in the opera of *La Cenerentola*. In so fine a house for sound as the King's Theatre, her full rich voice was heard to great advantage. Her enunciation of Italian was admirable, and her correct intonation and knowledge of music were fully appreciated by the critical audience. On the 17th, Pacini's absurd opera, *L'Ultimo Giorno di Pompeii,* was produced for the benefit of Signor Davide. Many persons did not much relish Davide's style. It was well said that "he sang too much in *italics;*" and he was characterized as a singer who "united the extravagancies with the beauties of genius."

From the King's Theatre Mrs. Wood went to Drury Lane, where she appeared in the *Barber of Seville.* Her singing was exquisite: the lesson song at the pianoforte in particular was given with extraordinary power and effect. Mr. Wood was only passable as Almaviva, and Henry Phillips, though he sang the music of Figaro with great beauty and science, was deficient in mercurial vivacity. An English version of *Robert le Diable* was produced at Drury Lane, 20th February, 1832. The cast was a pretty good one: Robert, Mr. Wood; Bertram, H. Phillips; Raimbaut, Templeton; Isabel, Miss Ayton; Alice, Mrs. Wood. The following night, a rival adaptation was brought out at Covent Garden, under the title of the *Fiend Father.*

Tempting offers induced Mr. and Mrs. Wood to cross the Atlantic in 1840. They appeared first at the Park Theatre, New York, and were greatly liked in America. A ludicrous incident marked their stay at Philadelphia. There was a shabby couple who desired to have the *éclat* of engaging the celebrated English prima donna to sing at one of their parties, and sent her an invitation. Being indisposed, Mrs. Wood declined, but they so urgently pressed her that she consented to join the party. When the entertainments of the evening had fairly commenced, and several ladies among the visitors had sung, the hostess invited Mrs. Wood to seat herself at the piano, as the company would be delighted to hear her beautiful voice; but Mrs. Wood, with a very serious countenance, begged to be excused. At first the astonishment created by this refusal was evinced by a dead silence and a fixed stare; but at length the disappointed hostess burst out, saying, "What! not sing, Mrs. Wood! why, it was for this that I invited you to my party, and I told all my guests that you were coming." "That quite alters the case," said Mrs. Wood; "I was not at all aware of this, or I should not have refused; but since you have invited me professionally, I shall of course sing immediately!" "What a good creature," rejoined the hostess; "I thought you could not persist in refusing me." So Mrs. Wood sang the entire evening, giving every song she was asked for, and being encored several times. In the morning, to the utter consternation of the rich, parsimonious couple, a bill for 200 dollars was presented to them from Mr. Wood for his wife's professional services, which of course they had to pay.

On their return, Mr. and Mrs. Wood judiciously invested their earnings in the purchase of an estate in Yorkshire, intending to retire and enjoy the ease and quiet which they had fairly won. But either a life of excitement had destroyed Mrs. Wood's taste for retirement, or the offers which she received from managers were too seducing; for when, in 1836, Rossini's *Cenerentola* was brought out at Covent Garden, April 13, under the title of *Cinderella, the Fairy Queen and the Little Glass Slipper*, Mrs. Wood performed Cinderella, playing the part with extreme simplicity, and singing with irreproachable taste. The music had been adapted by Mr. Lacy, who made liberal additions from the other works of Rossini.

Mrs. Wood afterwards appeared with Malibran, in the *Marriage of Figaro*, for the benefit of Charles Kemble; and in 1837 she sang at Drury Lane in the *Sonnambula*, etc.

Mr. and Mrs. Wood again retired to their Yorkshire home, where a new whim suddenly seized the lady, who had always been rather eccentric. She resolved to change her creed, turn Catholic, and become a nun; and in February, 1843, she withdrew to the convent at Micklegate Bar, Yorkshire. Her husband, uniformly kind and indulgent, was convinced that her ascetic fancy would soon die away, and as she took no irrevocable vow to lead a monastic life, but was only a probationer, he was content to await her return. Some malicious persons having spread a rumour that he had by his ill-treatment driven her to adopt this course, she published a letter exculpating her husband.

Finding she had no vocation for conventual life, Mrs. Wood quitted the convent, July, 1843, and returned to her home. Shortly afterwards she, with her husband, accepted a professional engagement, and appeared first at Leeds, where Mrs. Wood sang and played on the organ. In 1844 she was singing in opera at the Princess's Theatre.

Mrs. Wood continues to live in the neighbourhood of Leeds, in great peace and comfort; varying her occupations by taking a few pupils, some of whom have gained distinction.

CHAPTER IV.

WILHELMINA SCHRÖDER DEVRIENT.

Sophia Schröder was the Siddons of Germany. Her profound sensibility and fine perception of character, and her splendid elocution combined with a majestic form, rendered her one of the finest tragic actresses of her time. She was for years the ornament of the dramatic stage of Germany, where she made herself celebrated in the parts of Phèdre, Medea, Lady Macbeth, Mérope, Sapho, Jeanne de Montfaucon, and Isabella in the *Braut von Messina.*

Wilhelmina, the daughter of Madame Schröder, was born at Hamburg, October 6th, 1805. Her mother destined her for the stage, for which she was educated, and in her fifth year the child appeared on the Hamburg stage as a little Cupid; and in her tenth danced in the ballet at the Imperial Theatre of Vienna. However, she did not long remain in the ballet; for with the development of her powers came ambition, and, what is more important, skill and experience. Her mother, who wished her to perform in tragedy, obtained for her an appearance at the Burgtheater of Vienna, where she appeared, in her fifteenth year, in the part of Aricie in the *Phèdre* of Racine. She then perfofmed the character of Luise in *Cabale und Liebe*, and soon rose to be the representative of high tragedy; appearing as Ophelia in *Hamlet*, Beatrice in the *Braut von Messina*, and other leading parts.

The full scope of her genius, however, was not yet apparent. She then knew nothing of music; but at last she was able to study under the direction of an Italian master, named Mazzatti, who resided in Vienna.

She made her début in opera, January 20, 1821, as Pamina in Mozart's *Zauberflöte* at the Vienna Theatre. The beauty of her voice, her imposing figure and deportment, and her power of expressing emotion, produced a favourable impression. In stature she was above the middle height, and her figure was fully developed; though not handsome, but rather the reverse, her countenance had a sweet, noble, frank expression; and when excited by the ardour of feeling, her physiognomy was full of fire and passion. Her voice was a mellow soprano, which had the true metallic ring, and united softness with power and compass, though it was deficient in flexibility. Her intonation was remarkably perfect, her articulation singularly distinct, and her accentuation impressive.

She speedily became a favourite, but her triumph was achieved by her performance of Leonora in the *Fidelio* of Beethoven, in which she eclipsed all who had preceded her. This opera was represented for the festival of the Emperor's birthday, and the young débutante drew down thunders of applause. The character itself excites the deepest sympathy, and there are some most pathetic situations in the scenes where Leonora appears. Schröder's performance throughout was thrilling, but in the scene where Leonora enters the dungeon, her delineation of the agonizing emotions which rend the heart of the wife, was perfectly electrifying. She had studied this character profoundly. Her account of her first performance is very interesting.

"When I was studying the character of Fidelio at Vienna," she herself says, "I could not attain that which appeared to me to be the desired and natural expression at the moment when Leonora, throwing herself before her husband, holds out a pistol to the Governor, with the words 'Kill first his wife!' I studied and studied in vain, though I did all I could to place myself mentally in the situation of Leonora. I had pictured to myself the situation, but I felt that it was incomplete, without knowing why or wherefore. Well, the evening arrived; the audience knows not with what feelings an artiste, who enters seriously into a part, dresses for the representation. The nearer the moment approached, the greater was my alarm.

When it did arrive, and as I ought to have sung the ominous words, and pointed the pistol at the Governor, I fell into such utter tremor at the thought of not being perfect in my character, that my whole frame trembled, and I thought I should have fallen. Now, only fancy how I felt when the whole house broke forth into enthusiastic shouts of applause, and what I thought when, after the curtain fell, I was told that this moment was the most effective and powerful of my whole representation. So that which I could not attain with every effort of mind and imagination, was produced at this decisive moment by my unaffected terror and anxiety. This result, and the effect it had upon the public, taught me how to seize and comprehend the incident, so that which at the first representation I had hit upon unconsciously, I adopted in full consciousness ever afterwards in this part."

Not even Malibran could equal her in the impersonation of this character. Never was dramatic performance more completely, more intensely affecting, more deeply pathetic, truthful, tender, and powerful.

Some persons regarded her as more of a tragedian than a singer. "Her voice, since I have known it," observes Mr. Chorley (*Modern German Music*), "was capable of conveying poignant or tender expression, but it was harsh and torn—not so inflexible as incorrect. Madame Schröder Devrient resolved to be par excellence 'the German dramatic singer.' Earnest and intense as was her assumption of the parts she attempted, her desire of presenting herself first was little less vehement—there is no possibility of an opera being performed by a company, each of whom should be as resolute as she was never to rest, never for an instant to allow the spectator to forget his presence. She cared not whether she broke the flow of the composition by some cry heard on any note, or in any scale—by even speaking some word, for which she would not trouble herself to study a right musical emphasis or inflexion—provided, only, she succeeded in continuing to arrest the attention. Hence, in part, arose her extraordinary success in *Fidelio*. That opera contains, virtually, only one acting character,—and with her it rests to intimate the thrilling secret of the whole story, to develop this link by link, in presence of the public, and to give the drama the importance of terror, suspense, and rapture. When the spell is broken, by exhibiting the agony and the struggle of which she is the innocent victim; if the devotion, the disguise, and the hope of Leonora, the wife, were not for ever before us, the interest of the prison-opera would flag and wane into a cheerless and incurable melancholy. This Madame Schröder Devrient took care that it should never do. From her first entry upon the stage, it might be seen that there was a purpose at her heart, which could make the weak strong, and the timid brave; quickening every sense, nerving every fibre, arming its possessor with disguise against curiosity, with persuasion more powerful than any obstacle, with expedients equal to every emergency. . . What Pasta would be, in spite of her uneven, rebellious, uncertain voice—a most magnificent singer—Madame Schröder Devrient did not care to be; though nature, I have been assured by those who heard her sing when a girl, had blessed her with a fresh, delicious soprano voice."

Her fame increasing, the Fräulein Schröder resolved to undertake an art-tour in Germany. Early in 1823 she appeared at Cassel, producing a great sensation in Emmeline, Pamina, and Agathe. Seldom had any performer achieved such a popularity. From thence she went to Dresden, where she met with Carl Devrient, a clever vocalist from Berlin, with an agreeable voice, youthful and fresh. He was a favourite with the public, and as a tragedian he disputed the histrionic crown with Herr Seydelmann of Stuttgart. The Dem. Schröder was very much charmed with this young singer, who reciprocated the sentiment, and they were married; but the union did not prove a happy one.

For some time Madame Schröder Devrient remained at Dresden. Her most noticeable performance in 1824 was Euryanthe, with Madame Funk, Herr Bergmann, and Herr Meyer. For a short time she was at Munich, but returned again to Dresden. In 1825 the chief operas there were Cherubini's *Faniska,* Spohr's *Jessonda* (in which she sang with Mdlle. Voltheim, Bergmann, and Meyer), and the *Barber of Seville,* in which Bergmann performed Almaviva, and Keller, Bartolo. She was still performing there in 1826 and 1827. In 1828 she went to Prague, and thence to Berlin, where her marriage was dissolved judicially. She had one boy, born in 1824. At Berlin she appeared at both theatres in the chefs-d'œuvre of Weber, with the utmost success. Spontini at first conceived against her a violent antipathy; but this did not prevent her from obtaining the most astonishing success, especially in the part of Euryanthe. She then went to Vienna, where she performed with Cramolini and Madame Grünbaum.

A troupe of German singers, headed by Madame Fischer, a pretty, tall blonde, with a fresh voice, went to Paris in 1830. Madame Schröder Devrient formed one of this company, and made her début in May at the Théâtre Louvois (then under the direction of Röckel), in *Der Freischütz.* She was terribly agitated, but the encouragement which she received reassured her. The critics were delighted with the beauty and finish of her style. Madame Roland, Woltereck, and Wieser sang with her in *Der Freischütz.* She repeated the principal parts of her répertoire in *Fidelio, Don Giovanni,* etc., and also appeared, with Haitzinger, Wieser, and Madame Schmidt, in

Weber's *Oberon*, and in the *Serail* of Mozart. Her success was particularly marked in *Fidelio*.

Returning to Germany, Madame Schröder Devrient appeared next in Berlin with triumph, together with Scheckner and Sontag. In 1832 she was again in Paris, fulfilling an engagement of a year, when she imprudently accepted a proposition made to her by the manager of the Théâtre Italien to sing in a language and in the style of a school for which she had not the necessary qualifications. The theatre opened September 1, with a splendid company: Pasta, Malibran, Schröder Devrient, Rubini, Bordogni, and Lablache. The illness of Madame Pasta rendered it necessary for Schröder to appear in *Anna Bolena*, in which she failed completely. Bellini's *Pirata* was afterwards brought out with a decided success, to which the singing and acting of Madame Devrient and Rubini powerfully contributed. Madame Devrient performed the part of the heroine with great taste and expression, improving as she became more familiar with the usages of the Italian stage. On the 22nd November, she performed Desdemona for Malibran's benefit, Rubini being the Moor. Madame Devrient had certainly moments of inspiration in this performance, but she was not Desdemona.

In 1832, Mr. Monck Mason became lessee of the King's Theatre, at a rent of 16,000*l*. He had already dabbled a little in theatrical affairs, having written and composed a small opera, and was quite a musical enthusiast. His plans and projected improvements were of the most novel character, and on the most extensive scale, for he engaged an excellent company, not only of Italian, but of French and German singers. Among the latter he brought forward Schröder Devrient, who appeared in her favourite operas with Mdlle. Schneider and Herr Haitzinger; the latter a tenor, who sang with great feeling, but sometimes too vehemently. Madame Devrient also performed in Italian opera, appearing as Desdemona in *Otello*, July 17. On this occasion Roderigo's serenade was sung by Donzelli, who was the Otello. The English public did not care much about the German cantatrice, but the critics were delighted with her genius. "We know not," said one, "how to say enough of Madame Schröder Devrient, without appearing extravagant, and yet the most extravagant eulogy we could pen would not come up to our idea of her excellence. She is a woman of first-rate genius; her acting skilful, various, impassioned: her singing pure, scientific, and enthusiastic. Her whole soul is wrapt in her subject; yet she never for a moment oversteps the modesty of nature." This season was a most disastrous one to the unfortunate Mr. Monck Mason, who not only sacrificed his money and his energies, but was most unjustly attacked and lampooned.

The following year Mr. Bunn engaged Madame

Schröder Devrient to perform on alternate nights with Malibran, the company being abruptly transferred from Drury Lane to Covent Garden. The first piece in which the Germans performed was Mozart's *Zauberflöte*, produced for the first time on the English stage. Haitzinger, Dobler—a fine deep musical bass—and Madame Uétz—a very excellent actress, and a singer of great merit—supported the chief parts with Madame Schröder Devrient; but it was not a success. Weber's *Euryanthe* was also brought forward, for the first time in England; and of course Madame Schröder Devrient performed in *Fidelio*.

In January, 1834, she was engaged at Berlin, where she was to sing in twelve operas by native composers: *Fidelio, Don Giovanni, Euryanthe, Oberon*, and others. From thence she went to Vienna and to Russia. In March, 1835, she was at Dresden; by May, in Leipzig; then returning to Dresden, she obtained a congé of eighteen months to go to Italy, where she was welcomed with great enthusiasm. She paused at Breslau, giving in that town some representations which threw the public into a frenzy of rapture, according to the journals of the time. They conducted her in triumph to her dwelling, where the orchestra of the theatre had prepared a serenade for her. She was in Vienna in 1836 with Madame Tadolini, Genaro, and Galli, singing in *L'Elisir d'Amore*, etc.

The managers of Drury Lane applied to her in 1837 to supply the place of Madame de Beriot, and the people of Dresden—where she was performing when she entered into the engagement—gave her a flattering ovation before her departure. She personated the character of Euryanthe, and when the enthusiasm was at its height, Mdlle. Wust approached in her character of Eglantine, and presented a beautiful chaplet of flowers to the heroine of German song, reciting at the same time a complimentary address.

Madame Schröder Devrient played in *Fidelio*, for the first time in English, May 14th. The whole performance was lamentably inferior to that at the Opera-house in 1832. *Norma* was produced June 25th, Schröder Devrient being seconded by Wilson, Giubilei, and Miss Betts. She was either very ill-advised or over-confident, for her "massy" style of singing was totally at variance with the light beauty of Bellini's music. Her conception of the character, however, was in the grandest style of histrionic art. "The sibyls of Michael Angelo are not more grand," exclaimed one critic; "but the vocalisation of Pasta and Grisi is wholly foreign to her." During this engagement, Madame Schröder Devrient was often unable to perform from serious illness. She took her benefit July 7th, when *La Sonnambula* was performed; and Tuesday the 16th, the theatre closed with *Fidelio*.

From England she went to the Lower Rhine.

In 1839, she was at Dresden, with Herr Tichatschek, one of the first tenors of Germany, a handsome man, with a powerful, sweet, and extensive voice. In June, 1841, she gave a performance at Berlin, to assist the Parisian subscription for a monument to Cherubini. The opera was *Les Deux Journées*, in which she took her favourite part of Constance. The same year she sang at Dresden, with the utmost success, in a new rôle in Goethe's *Tasso*, in which she was said to surpass her *Fidelio*. She then went to Leipzig, and early the next year returned to Dresden.

For some years Madame Schröder Devrient resided in perfect seclusion in the little town of Rochlitz, in Saxony. She was almost forgotten, when suddenly she reappeared on the stage at Dresden, as Romeo, in Bellini's *I Montecchi ed i Capuletti*. Although not so great a singer as in the days when she had been accustomed to carry away her audiences by the irresistible power of her performance, yet her success was immense. Shortly after, Glück's *Iphigénie en Aulis* was revived. Madame Schröder Devrient performed Clytemnestra; Johanna Wagner, Iphigénie; Mitterwurzer, Agamemnon; Tichatschek, Achilles.

She was again at Dresden in 1849, when she married a rich Livonian propriétaire named Bock, with whom she retired to Livonia. In October, her mother died at Raudnitz, in Saxony, at the advanced age of eighty-four. The Emperor Francis I. paid Madame Schröder an honour which no other German artiste ever received. He ordered her portrait to be drawn in all her principal characters, and placed in the collection in the Imperial Museum.

About 1854, Scudo saw Madame Schröder Devrient at Paris, in many exclusive houses, and in a public concert, "where she sang with a very weak voice the melodies of Schubert." She was a woman of intelligence and acute observation; as an artiste, full of impetuosity and ardour; a lyric tragedian perhaps, rather than a singer in the ordinary sense of the word. She might be said to belong to the group of singers who were the interpreters of that school of dramatic music which arose in Germany after the death of Mozart.

Her son, Carl Devrient, appeared in 1857 with his father at Hanover, in *Don Carlos*, on the anniversary of the birthday of Schiller.

Madame Schröder Devrient died February 9th, 1860, at Cologne. The following year her bust was placed in the Opera-house at Berlin.

The great German artiste, whose life was much agitated by a variety of adventures, left a kind of journal wherein she recorded her different impressions, and which testified how much she had suffered during a career replete with triumphs. One of the Leipzig papers published numerous extracts from this journal.

CHAPTER V.

HENRIETTA SONTAG.

Henrietta Sontag, or Sonntag, born May 13, 1805, at Coblentz, was a graceful and vivacious child, with a lovely silver-toned voice, and the darling of her father, who was an actor of genteel comedy. From her cradle she was destined by her parents for their own profession, and when six years old, appeared for the first time on the stage, at the Court theatre of Hesse Darmstadt, in an opera entitled *Donau Weibchen* (the Daughter of the Danube). Her infantine prettiness, her naïveté, her joyousness, her silver-toned voice, and the accuracy of her intonation made her a pet at once. In her eighth year, her voice had already acquired much steadiness, and to gratify neighbours and friends, Henrietta's mother would place her on the table and bid her sing. A distinguished traveller relates having seen her sing in this manner the grand aria of the "Queen of Night," in the *Zauberflöte*, "her arms hanging beside her, and her eye following the flight of a butterfly, while her voice, pure, penetrating, and of angelic tone, flowed as unconsciously as a limpid rill from the mountain side."

In her ninth year, Henrietta lost her father, when the widowed Madame Sontag took her daughters to Prague, where Henrietta played the parts of children under the direction of Weber, then chef-d'orchestre of the theatre. These early successes obtained for her, as a very special favour, permission to attend the courses of the Conservatoire of Prague, although she had not yet attained the prescribed age—twelve—she being only eleven. During four years she here studied vocal music, the pianoforte, and the elements of harmony. Pixis, for whom she always retained a lively affection, taught her the piano; Bayer, the celebrated flutist, and Madame Czezka instructed her in vocalization; and the maître de chapelle, Tribensée, taught her the rudiments of music; and she successively won the prize in every class of this great school of music.

A sudden indisposition of the prima donna gave Henrietta an unexpected opportunity of appearing in the rather important part of the Princesse de Navarre, in Boiëldieu's opera of *Jean de Paris*. She was then only fifteen, and being very small, the little vocalist was supplied with heels four inches high, so when the little prodigy appeared on her cork pedestals, the house was filled with cheers and acclamations; but the emotion which agitated her did not injure her success. Her next part was the far more difficult one of the heroine in Paer's fine opera, *Sargino*. The brilliant success she had achieved decided her career, and, leaving the Conservatoire, she went to Vienna, where she had an opportunity of hearing Madame Fodor, who was engaged at the theatre there. Admiring the talents of the French cantatrice, Henrietta endeavoured to impress on her mind the practical lessons which she thus received, and which were as profitable as all the studies she had pursued in the Conservatoire. The admiration was reciprocated by Madame Fodor, who, on hearing the young girl sing for the first time, exclaimed,—

"Had I her voice, I should hold the entire world at my feet!"

Singing alternately in German and Italian opera, with the most experienced colleagues, Rubini amongst others, Henrietta Sontag was perfected in the two languages, and was enabled at the same time to choose between the brilliancy of Italian music and the sober profundity of the German school. The English Ambassador, Earl Clanwilliam, became one of her most ardent admirers; he followed her to the theatre, to concerts, and even in her walks to church. Sontag, in German, means Sunday, and the Viennese wits nicknamed the ambassador Earl Montag, as Monday follows Sunday.

In November, 1823, Weber produced his *Euryanthe*, at the Kärnthnerthor Theater, Mdlle. Sontag taking the leading part; but the public were so little pleased that they called the opera *L'Ennuyante*. With the exception of the chorus of huntsmen, the music was not liked.

Mdlle. Sontag, in 1824, was engaged to sing in German opera at the theatre of Leipzig. She gained great applause by the manner in which she interpreted the *Freischütz* and the *Euryanthe* of Weber, then almost in their flush of novelty. Her young sister Nina performed at the same time in children's characters. Here commenced the serious part of her art life.

Henrietta's voice was a pure soprano, reaching, perhaps, from A, or B, to D in alt, and though uniform in its quality, it was a little reedy in the lower notes, but its flexibility was marvellous: in the high octave, from F to C in alt, her notes rang out like the tones of a silver bell. The clearness of her notes, the precision of her intonation, the fertility of her invention, and the facility of her execution, were displayed in brilliant flights and lavish fioriture; her rare flexibility being a natural gift, cultivated by taste and incessant study. It was to the example of Madame Fodor that Mdlle. Sontag was indebted for the blooming of those dormant qualities which had till then remained undeveloped. The ease with which she sang was perfectly captivating; and the neatness and elegance of her enunciation combined with the sweetness and brilliancy of her voice, and her perfect intonation, to render her execution faultless, and its effect ravishing. She appeared to sing with the volubility of a bird, and to experience the pleasure she imparted. To use the language of a critic of that day, "All passages are alike to her, but she has appropriated some that were hitherto believed to belong to instruments—to the pianoforte and the violin, for instance. Arpeggios and chromatic scales, passages ascending and descending, she executed in the same manner that the ablest performers on these instruments execute them. There was the firmness and the neatness that appertain to the pianoforte, while she would go through a scale *staccato* with the precision of the bow. Her great art, however, lay in rendering whatever she did pleasing. The ear was never disturbed by a harsh note. The velocity of her passages was sometimes uncontrollable, for it has been observed that in a division, say of four groups of quadruplets, she would execute the first in exact time, the second and third would increase in rapidity, so much that in the fourth she was compelled to decrease the speed perceptibly, in order to give the band the means of recovering the time she had gained."

Mdlle. Sontag was of middle stature, neither full nor slender, with a face expressive of delicacy, sensibility, and modesty united; she had light hair (between blonde and auburn), fair complexion, large blue eyes, softly pencilled lips, and regular white teeth, and an aspect of sweetness and good-humour; but her features were by no means striking, or capable of vivacious or tragic expression. Her elegant form, the delicacy of her features, the exquisite proportion of her hands and feet, and her beautiful and soft expressive eyes, completed the enchantment exercised by this fair cantatrice. She could not command, but she won admiration by her easy, quiet, and reserved, yet artless and unaffected, lady-like demeanour. As an actress, though not great, she justly claimed applause. Neither in her action nor in her singing did she display any grandeur or depth of feeling; but while she could not aspire to be a tender and impassionate Leonora, a thrilling Medea, she was a captivating Rosina, a bewitching Susanna. In light and elegant comedy, whether as actress or singer, she has rarely been excelled. She possessed all the originality of her own nation, while emulating the flexibility of the Italians. With equal skill she could render the works of Rossini, Mozart, Weber, and Spohr, joining to the verve and power of the German the volubility and facility of French and Italian singers.

Such was her success in Leipzig that she was called to Berlin, to sing in the Koenigstadt Theater. Her studies at Vienna had prepared her to sing in the operas of Rossini; but the music of this illustrious maestro, which was enthusiastically admired in the capital of Austria, was not duly estimated at Berlin.

Mdlle. Sontag was therefore chiefly heard in some German operas, in which she gained great renown throughout Germany, and she made the fortune of the theatre which possessed her. It was not merely admiration and delight which she inspired, but an enthusiasm which manifested itself in the most extravagant demonstrations of rapture whenever she appeared. The old King of Prussia received her at his Court with paternal kindness.

About this time Mdlle. Sontag became acquainted with Count Rossi, a Piedmontese nobleman, then secretary to the Legation of Sardinia at Berlin, and their marriage was arranged to take place.

After a sojourn of two years at Berlin, Mdlle. Sontag determined to visit Paris. When she announced her intention, the Berlin public were very angry; they told her she might either go or stay, for they didn't care in the least, while they vented their spleen in very unequivocal marks of resentment, and, to spite her, petted a rival singer. Such conduct was not calculated to induce her to forego her intentions, and at the end of May, 1826, she profited by a congé, which was granted her, to go to the French capital.

In the Parisian salons, in the daily papers, in the cafés and restaurants, people laughed at the idea of *la petite Allemande*, who was daring enough to appear in the part of Rosina in *Il Barbiere di Seviglia*. What audacious self-confidence this Sontag — this

German Frau must be endowed with, to dare to step on a scene where Pasta, Cinti, and Fodor had shone! It was ridiculous! What *could* M. le Vicomte Sosthène de la Rochefoucauld be dreaming of?

On the 15th June, Mdlle. Sontag appeared, and curiosity to hear how the German vocalist would maltreat the music of Rossini caused the theatre to be filled to overflowing. The audience expected to see a bold, robust songstress with a harsh voice. What was their amazement when there flitted on to the stage, in all her shy, blushing beauty, a young girl of scarce twenty summers, whose aspect at once disarmed criticism. The first silvery tones of her voice in recitative produced a reaction in her favour; thunders of applause broke forth, and the singer's courage, which had wavered for a moment, was now assured. Her execution of the air with Rode's variations, in the second act, distanced even Madame Catalani, who had till then been invincible. The enthusiasm of the Parisian public rose to its full height, and was undiminished by twenty-three subsequent representations; and she immediately received the appropriate sobriquet of the Nightingale of the North.

The principal operas in which she appeared were, *Il Barbiere*, *La Donna del Lago*, and *L'Italiana in Algieri*. In this last, the leading airs were transposed for a soprano voice. On the occasion of her benefit she was crowned on the stage, and elegant devices of a complimentary kind were thrown at her feet. The charming young German was petted and caressed by the Parisian aristocracy, and, through the Prussian Ambassador, she was honoured with a state dinner. She was presented to Alexander von Humboldt and to the Princess Dalbergischen, and required no letters of introduction to render her welcome in the highest circles. At the house of Talleyrand, the young cantatrice being introduced, by the Duchess of Dino, to Madame de Baudemont the strong-minded Duchess von Lothringen, was thus complimented: "I would not desire that my daughter were other than you." The society of a German singer—a thing before unheard of—was now sedulously courted by ladies of the highest fashion in Paris; and Benjamin Constant and his wife (the Countess Hardenberg) made her acquainted with the élite of the Republican party.

Madame Catalani, it is reported, declared of her, "Elle est la première de son genre, mais son genre n'est pas le premier;" and a professor of great reputation and experience introduced a celebrated flute-player to her in these words—"Ecco il tuo rivale!"

Mdlle. Sontag was always supposed to be on the point of marriage, and princes, musicians, romantic young heroes, were imagined by turns to aspire to the honour of her hand, and to be dying of love for her. No singer was ever rumoured to have so many honourably disposed lovers at her feet. A musician of celebrity,* and a gentleman of high rank, asked her in marriage about this time: but she rejected both offers, without reserve, yet with kindness and delicacy; her troth had been already pledged. Her health failed for a time, but the sea-bathing of Boulogne restored her, and she was in blooming health when she started, at the end of September, 1826, on her return to Berlin.

She was offered fabulous terms in Paris if she would give up Berlin, but her heart and her duty steeled her against every temptation.

On her route she made large sums by singing, and received numerous handsome testimonies to the esteem in which she was held. Just before she left Paris, Ebers wrote offering her 2,000*l.* and a benefit for the season. This offer it was impossible for her to accept, as she was under a contract for Berlin; he wrote again, volunteering to pay the forfeit which she might incur by the breach of her contract; but, not wishing to break her faith with the Berlin public, she refused.

She received a hearty welcome in Weimar and Frankfort. In Hainz, the home of her parents, she went to see her grandmother, and she also visited her father's grave, and gave her needy relatives proofs of her generosity; she sang in the theatre for the poor, sought out the grey-headed Mathison, that she might

* Charles de Bériot.

receive the last blessing of the aged poet, and left the home of her father laden with love and kind wishes.

The Berlin people did not prove ungrateful for the preference their favourite had shown for them; though on her first reappearance in *L'Italiana in Algieri*, they affected to be still very cross, in order that they might be coaxed a little. There was a brilliant company of singers assembled that season in Berlin, and Madame Catalani and Mdlle. Scheckner shared the glory of the day with Sontag. The King of Prussia engaged her for his chapel at a yearly salary of 20,000 francs: about 840*l*.

Early in 1828 she was again in Paris, at the same time with Malibran, who had reigned the preceding season. Mdlle. Sontag appeared, as a novelty, in *La Cenerentola*; but the music of this opera suffered very much from being transposed for a soprano voice. The Parisian public, which always had a penchant for fomenting musical rivalries and jealousies, put in direct opposition the cool, placid German, and the ardent, passionate Spaniard; yet, excepting that they both could sing, there was very little in common between the two: however, the war waged long and hotly, occasioning ill-feeling and discord.

Mdlle. Sontag appeared in London at the King's Theatre, April 16, as Rosina in Rossini's *Il Barbiere*, a character which affords every opportunity for the display of lightness and gaiety; and of all modern operas, it is the best adapted to her style. Since Mrs. Billington, never had such high promise been made, or so much expectation excited: her talents had been exaggerated by report, and her beauty and charms extolled as matchless; she was declared to possess all the qualities of every singer in perfection, and as an actress to be the very personification of grace and power. Stories of the romantic attachments of foreign princes and English lords were afloat in all directions: she was going to be married to a personage of the loftiest rank—to a German prince—to an ambassador; she was pursued by the ardent love of men of fashion. Amongst other stories in circulation was one of a duel between two imaginary rival candidates for a ticket of admission to her performance; but the most affecting and trustworthy story was that of an early attachment between the beautiful Henrietta and a young student of good family, which was broken off in consequence of his passion for gambling.

Mdlle. Sontag, before she appeared at the Opera, sang at the houses of Prince Esterhazy and the Duke of Devonshire. An immense crowd assembled in front of the theatre on the evening of her début at the Opera. The crush was dreadful, and when at length the half-stifled crowd managed to find seats, "shoes were held up in all directions to be owned." The audience waited in breathless suspense for the rising of the curtain, and when the fair cantatrice appeared the excited throng could scarcely realize that the simple English-looking girl before them was the celebrated Sontag. On recovering from their astonishment, they applauded her warmly, and her lightness, brilliancy, volubility, and graceful manner, made her at once popular. Her style was more florid than that of any other singer in Europe, not even excepting Catalani, whom she excelled in fluency, though not in volume; and it was decided that she resembled Fodor more than any other singer: which was natural, as she had in early life imitated that cantatrice. Her taste was so cultivated that the redundancy of ornament, especially the obbligato passages which the part of Rosina presents, never, in her hands, appeared overcharged; and she sang the cavatina, "Una voce poco fà," in a style as new as it was exquisitely tasteful. "Two passages, introduced by her in this air, executed in a *staccato* manner, could not have been surpassed in perfection by the spirited bow of the finest violin-player." In the lesson scene, she gave Rode's variations, and her execution of the second variation in arpeggios was pronounced infinitely superior to Catalani's.

Mdlle. Sontag appeared successively in the *Cenerentola, La Gazza Ladra,* as Zerlina in *Don Giovanni*, and as Elena in *La Donna del Lago*, in which she achieved a new success. The part of Elena abounds in opportunities for the display of vocalization, and the tranquil situations do not demand energy or dramatic power.

She also performed Palmide in *Il Crociato* for Velluti's benefit.

At first the cognoscenti were haunted by a fear that Sontag would permit herself to degenerate, like Catalani, into a mere imitator of instrumental performers, and endeavour to astonish instead of pleasing the public, by executing such things as Rode's variations. But it was soon observed that, while indulging in almost unlimited luxuriance of embellishment in singing Rossini's music, she showed herself a good musician, and never fell into the fault common with florid singers, of introducing ornaments at variance with the spirit of the air or the harmony of the accompaniments. In singing the music of Mozart or Weber, she paid the utmost deference to the text, restraining the exuberance of her fancy, and confining herself within the limits set by the composer. Her success was tested by a most substantial proof of her popularity: her benefit produced the enormous sum of 3,000*l*.

Mdlle. Sontag was engaged by Laurent at the Théâtre Italien at a salary of 50,000 fr. per annum and a congé of three months in the year. She re-appeared as Desdemona, but the part was not suited to her. She, however, turned her attention seriously towards the study of sentiment and passion, and the manner in which she afterwards performed the part of Donna Anna in *Don Giovanni*, of Semiramide, and many other tragic characters, showed that she had to a certain extent inspiration as well as taste and grace.

The rivalry between Malibran and Sontag now broke out afresh with redoubled vehemence, and reached such a height that they would not even meet in the same salon; the partisans of each, as it always happens, contributed to give to this rivalry an aspect of vindictiveness, and on the stage, when they sang in the same opera, their jealousy was scarcely disguised. An Italian gentleman, the firmest item of whose musical creed was that none but Italians could sing, refused to admit that Sontag (whom he had never heard) could by any possibility be equal to the singers of Italy. With great difficulty he was induced to hear her; when listening for five minutes, he suddenly quitted his seat. "Do stay," urged his friend. "You will be convinced presently." "I know it," replied the Italian, "and therefore I go."

One evening, at the termination of the opera, the rival singers were called for, and a number of wreaths and bouquets were flung on the stage. One of the coronals fell at the feet of Malibran, who, considering it was meant for her, stooped and picked it up; when a stern voice from the pit cried out—"Rendez-la: ce n'est pas pour vous!" "I would not deprive Mdlle. Sontag of the coronal," answered Malibran, somewhat scornfully: "I would sooner bestow one on her."

There also commenced between Sontag and Madame

Pisaroni one of those vindictive contests of which musical history has so many instances; though no two vocalists could possibly be more different in voice and style as well as in person.

Having performed during 1827 almost exclusively in Berlin, Mdlle. Sontag appeared again in London in May, 1828, as Angelina, in Rossini's *Cenerentola*. She was charming, as she always was, her execution was brilliant as ever, and she looked unusually lovely in her splendid costume in the last scene. She also appeared in *Il Barbiere*, and as Semiramide for Madame Pisaroni's benefit; but there was a want of majesty and royal dignity in her deportment as the Assyrian Queen, which detracted greatly from her performance.

Malibran was performing at the same time, on alternate nights, and a reconciliation had taken place between the two rival artistes; this had been brought about, but not without much trouble, by M. Fétis, who was then in London. His benevolent purpose was aided by an unexpected circumstance. They had both promised to sing at a concert to be given at the house of Lord Saltoun, for the benefit of Mr. Ella.* Fétis, who was engaged to accompany the two singers, proposed to them to sing together the duo of Semiramide and Arsace. They agreed, and for the first time their voices were heard in combination; each strove to surpass the other, and the effect of the fusion of the

* Now the director of the "Musical Union."

two voices, so different in tone, character, and expression, was so fine, that a complete triumph sealed their reconciliation. In consequence of this, Laporte brought forward operas in which they could play together. They first appeared in *Semiramide*, and then in *Don Giovanni*, when Malibran took the part of Zerlina. Malibran's Zerlina was original and sprightly; and Sontag, who had already performed the arduous part of Donna Anna, in London, executed it in a most brilliant manner, delightful to the ear, if not so satisfactory to the judgment. They also appeared together in the *Nozze di Figaro*, on the occasion of Malibran's benefit. Mdlle. Sontag, as the Countess, performed with appropriate dignity, and the celebrated letter duet between the Countess and Susanna was sung by them in a style which was not to be surpassed. Sontag also appeared with her rival in the second act of *Romeo e Giulietta*, but the part of Giulietta was not suited to her.

Her sister, Nina, appeared at Mdlle. Sontag's benefit, in the *Zauberflöte*. The sisters bore a strong resemblance, both in person and in voice, but as a performer Nina was very inferior to Henrietta.

On the 29th January, 1829, she made her reappearance at the Théâtre Italien, as Rosina; she also performed during the summer in London, with Malibran. Her most remarkable performance was Carolina in *Il Matrimonio Segreto*, which she gave with great feeling and occasional comic humour; she also performed Desdemona several times. She reappeared in Paris, September 16, in *Semiramide*, Madame Pisaroni being the Arsace; and in October in *Matilda di Shabran*.

Mdlle. Sontag had now been for more than a year married to the Count Rossi, but the union was preserved a secret for a long time; his family not choosing to recognize a singer, and one who could not boast of descent from nobility. Count Rossi was a native of Corsica, a relative of Buonaparte by the Romalino family, and his sister was married to the Prince de Salm. The secrecy of Henrietta's marriage was unfortunate, and calumny for the first time assailed her; until at last the fact of her marriage transpired, when she determined to undertake an art tour through Europe and then retire. She had been ennobled by the King of Prussia under the title of Mdlle. de Lauenstein.

She made her adieux to the Parisian public in January, 1830, and, returning to Berlin, she there closed the first portion of her dramatic career, May the 19th, by the performance of the *Semiramide* of Rossini. The enthusiasm of the public was not to be described. From the Prussian capital she went to Russia, singing at St. Petersburg, Moscow, and Warsaw, with incredible success.

On arriving at Hamburg, on her return from Russia, she was received with every mark of distinction by the principal inhabitants of that city, and by the hereditary Prince of Mecklenburg, who happened to be on a visit there with his princess. She received an invitation from the citizens of Bremen, who offered carte blanche as to terms; but, gratefully declining the offer, she stated decisively her resolve to retire altogether from public life. At a supper given in compliment to her by a distinguished English merchant at Hamburg, she announced herself for the first time as the Countess Rossi. At Hamburg she sang for the last time in public, but only at concerts; in which she showed that her powers, far from having declined, had gained in compass, in execution, and above all in expression.

The Countess Rossi lived first at the Hague, then for a short time at Frankfort-on-the-Maine. In 1835, she was at the latter place, where, as a matter of etiquette, she took precedence of all the ladies of the corps diplomatique, her husband being Minister Plenipotentiary to the Germanic Diet.

In 1838, Madame Rossi paid a visit to Berlin, where she had the honour of dining with the Royal family; and after the repast she joined in several duets and concerted pieces with the princes and princesses.

She devoted herself on her retirement from the stage to the study of composition. At Vienna, and at the houses of Prince Esterhazy and Prince Metternich, in 1841, she executed a cantata entitled *Il Naufragio Fortunato*, for a soprano voice and chorus, of which she wrote a portion during a sojourn in Hungary. This work was received with the greatest enthusiasm by a brilliant and numerous company, and Madame Rossi received from the Empress an autograph letter, begging of her to sing her cantata in the concert which her Imperial Majesty was about to give in her apartments, to which were invited the Imperial family and all the court.

The political storm which swept over Europe in 1848 reduced the family of Count Rossi to ruin, and when the revolution broke out at Berlin Madame Rossi's fortune was lost. With a real nobility of soul the Countess firmly breasted the storm: she announced her intention of reappearing once more on the stage, and accepted an offer of 17,000*l.* from Mr. Lumley, of Her Majesty's Theatre. On the 7th July, 1849, she made her reappearance in *Linda di Chamouni*, as "Madame Sontag." Her reception was cordial and enthusiastic, and the most eager interest was evinced in this fresh début. Her voice had suffered little during a repose of seventeen or eighteen years; and still possessed its "exquisite purity and *spirituelle* quality," which rendered it a luxury to hear her. If her lower notes had lost a little of their fulness and freedom, the upper tones still retained their roundness and beauty; and her execution had lost nothing of that marvellous flexibility which was its characteristic. She still possessed "the finish, the charm, the placid and serene expression," which had formerly pre-eminently distinguished her; and always a thorough and conscientious artist, she still remained so, although she found herself in presence of a new public, who had become accustomed to a different style of singing.

All her former companions had long vanished from the scene. The brilliant Malibran had been dead for thirteen years; Madame Pisaroni had disappeared for the same length of time; and the "stars" who now shone on the musical world had not appeared when Henrietta Sontag left the stage in 1830. Giulia Grisi, Clara Novello, Pauline Viardot, Fanny Persiani, Jenny Lind, Marietta Alboni, Nantier Didier, Sophie Cruvelli, Catherine Hayes, Louisa Pyne, Duprez, Mario, Ronconi, Tagliafico, Gardoni—this brilliant galaxy of musical genius had arisen since the day she announced herself as the Countess Rossi; and Bellini, Donizetti, and Meyerbeer, had written their best operas since that day.

Lablache—the good-hearted, kind, joyous, dear old comrade of earlier days—was perhaps the only familiar friend she recognized on returning to Her Majesty's Theatre. Even the King's Theatre had been metamorphosed.

Madame Sontag appeared in her favourite character of Rosina, with Lablache and Gardoni: she also performed Amina and Desdemona. Had it not been that the attention of the public was absorbed by "the

Swedish Nightingale" and the "glorious Alboni," Madame Sontag would have renewed the triumphs of 1828. The next season she sang again at Her Majesty's as Norina, Elvira (*I Puritani*), Zerlina, and Maria (in *La Figlia del Reggimento*), characters which she performed for the first time. The chief novelty was *La Tempestà*, written by Scribe and composed by Halévy expressly for Her Majesty's Theatre, the drama having been translated into Italian from the French original. It was got up with extraordinary splendour, and had a considerable run. Madame Sontag sang charmingly in the character of Miranda; but the greatest effect was created by Lablache's magnificent impersonation of Caliban: no small share of the success of the piece was due to the famous danseuse Carlotta Grisi, who seemed to take the most appropriate part ever designed for ballerina when she undertook to represent Ariel. With the exception of Carlotta, all have passed away like a dream—Halévy, Scribe, Lablache, Henrietta Sontag.

When, at the close of 1850, the Théâtre Italien of Paris opened under the management of Mr. Lumley, Madame Sontag, as the prima donna, was welcomed with a new ovation. Respect, admiration, and deferential sympathy, animated the audience. "Even amid the loud applause with which the crowd greeted her reappearance on the stage," says a French writer, "it was easy to distinguish the respect which was entertained for the virtuous lady, the devoted wife and mother."

In 1851, Madame Sontag was again at Her Majesty's Theatre. She was next heard in Vienna and Berlin. In 1852 she accepted an offer to go to America. She appeared at Her Majesty's Theatre for a limited number of nights previous to her departure.

On her arrival at New York, September 19, she commenced a series of concerts at the Metropolitan Hall, with Salvi and Signora Blangini. From New York she went to Boston and Philadelphia. Her course was a triumphant one, and she became one of the greatest favourites that had ever visited the New World. A portion of the capital realized by her entertainments was devoted by her to the purchase of a château and domain in Germany. In New Orleans, in 1854, she entered into an engagement with M. Masson, director of the principal theatre in the city of Mexico, to sing in opera for a fixed period of two months, with the privilege on his part of continuing the arrangement for three months longer, at a salary of 7,000 dollars. Madame Sontag despatched her agent, Mr. Ullman, to Europe, to secure a company, and he had nearly concluded his mission when news arrived from America that she had died in Mexico, on the 17th June, of an attack of cholera.

Her funeral took place on the 19th June, in presence of an immense concourse of people, including the corps diplomatique. The funeral service was celebrated with great grandeur: the instrumental performers included the orchestras of the two Italian theatres; the nuns of San Francisco sang the canticles; the German Philharmonic Society intoned a prayer to the Virgin, and sang a chorus of Lindpaintner's "Ne m'oubliez pas;" and M. Pantaléon Tovar declaimed a composition in beautiful Spanish verse to the memory of the departed. It was nine o'clock in the evening before the ceremony was concluded.

The remains of the deceased lady were transported to Germany, to be buried in the Abbey of Marienstern, in Lausitz. Her husband had quitted Mexico immediately after her death, leaving the body of his wife to be sent to the port by a carrier, with other parcels.

CHAPTER VI.

JULIE DORUS GRAS.

THE chef-d'orchestre of the Valenciennes Theatre, at the beginning of the present century, was a Monsieur Dorus, who had been a soldier, and served his country on the field of battle, but had wisely turned his musical talents to account. He had two children, a boy and a girl, whom he resolved to bring up in his favourite profession.

The girl, Julie (born about 1808), had a clear, brilliant, though somewhat hard voice, and being smart and clever, she so quickly profited by the lessons imparted by her father, that ere she had entered her teens, she sang at a concert. The municipality of Valenciennes, perceiving the undoubted gifts of this little vocalist, adopted her, and sent her to the Conservatoire de Paris, with an allowance of 1,500 francs per annum for three years. She entered as a pupil in December, 1821, and in a year after, she sent, as a token of gratitude to her native city, the coronal which she had received from the hands of Cherubini, in the singing class of Henri and Blangini. Paer and Bordogni were her next masters, to whom the maturing of her talents and the finish of her style are due.

On leaving the Conservatoire, Mdlle. Dorus was heard at various concerts in Paris, and she then began to travel in the provinces, giving concerts. Her fresh melodious voice, in the management of which she was already skilful, gradually obtained singular neatness and fluency of execution. Her first appearance on the stage was at the Theatre Royal in Brussels, where she met with such complete success that she attracted the notice of Count Lidelkerke, on whose behalf she was offered terms for an engagement at the opera. These she accepted, and for six months she studied lyric declamation with M. Cassel, an artiste of the Theatre Royal. She then made her début in opera and gained much applause.

It will be recollected with what fury the Revolution of September, 1830, flashed on Brussels at a representation of the French opera *La Muette di Portici*. This uproar terrified Mdlle. Dorus, who performed Elvira, and she fled to Valenciennes. However, she did not forget her kind friends, and expressed her feelings of gratitude by giving a concert for the benefit of the victims of the outbreak.

She next obtained an engagement from the directors

of the Académie of Paris, and the 19th November, 1830, she made her début in *Le Comte Ory*, when she was received with marked favour. Her person and her voice were equally agreeable. She was of middle stature, light and graceful in form, and exceedingly pretty, with blue eyes and blonde hair. Her voice was thoroughly French, possessing at once all the beauties and all the defects of the school to which she belonged. Its compass was two octaves, from D to D, but the tone was weak in the lower notes: in the high notes, on the contrary, her voice gained volume, penetrating power, and extraordinary brilliancy. "She shines above all in fioriture and the ornaments of vocalization," says Escudier. "Passages the most eccentric, caprices the most varied, roulades the most daring, offer no obstacle to the marvellous facility of her throat. Mdlle. Dorus is remarkable also for the brilliance and the vigour of her singing. Her voice, of perfect intonation, seizes each note with certainty and a surprising firmness." The highest notes seemed to escape her with as much ease as an ordinary breath; not a sign denoted that the effort cost her a moment's thought, and her singing pleased the eye as much as the ear. It was afterwards laughingly said in Parisian circles that "when once she touches a high note, her audience may lounge into a neighbouring café, eat an ice, and yet be back before she has changed it."

Grisi herself could hardly dwell so long on a note. If Mdlle. Dorus could have combined a little more charm and softness with her brilliancy, she would have been perfect.

She had many beauties, but also many defects. She often regarded with indifference the words of her songs: a grave fault for a singer endowed with a musical feeling so delicate. She was also too apt to consider the melody as a theme whereon she was at liberty to heap a redundance of variations. In flexibility she was surpassed by few singers; she could execute the most difficult passages with extraordinary fluency and rapidity; but for purity of tone and volume, her organ, like most singers of the French school, was throaty, and wanting in the dulcet sweetness of the Italian vocalists. While singing with the ease of a bird, she had a disagreeable habit of forcing up the notes.

She was an admirable musician; one of the best that had appeared on the French stage for years: as an actress she was composed, but inert and indifferent. The impossibility of her attaining tragic or impassioned dignity was owing, perhaps, to her want of physical strength; for she had an ideal of passion in her mind, though she was incapable of embodying it: she was not able even to look a tragic part. There was no deficiency of genuine feeling, but she always appeared to experience an insuperable difficulty in arousing, and, when aroused, exerting with sustained energy, all her powers: an aspect of languor and exhaustion clouded her countenance while on the stage. In light and coquettish characters, where there was not much action required, she was sometimes arch and captivating. Her most advantageous characters were Elvira in *La Muette*, and Mathilde in *Guillaume Tell*. When off the stage, her manner was graceful, unobtrusive, and amiable, if not specially intellectual: the very tones of her voice in conversation spoke of a kind and gentle nature.

At the opening of the Académie in June, 1831, Mdlle. Dorus obtained her first chance of appearing in a prominent part. She was unexpectedly called on to replace Madame Damoreau, who was suddenly taken ill. The piece was *Guillaume Tell*, and Mdlle. Dorus willingly undertook the character of Mathilde. The same month, Auber's *Le Philtre* was ready, but Madame Damoreau was not, and Mdlle. Dorus took the part of Thérèsine. She performed this admirably, with much esprit and coquettish grace, and showed that she had no need of the indulgence claimed for her. The talent of Mdlle. Dorus, it was observed, acquired each day new force.

In 1831, the Opéra came into the hands of Dr. Véron, renowned for his literary, musical, and medical tastes; he determined to make his operatic reign an era in the annals of music, and by a combination of good fortune and good judgment, he certainly succeeded. The prima donnas were Mdlle. Dorus and Madame Damoreau ; the male singers, Adolphe Nourrit and Levasseur, and the dancers, Taglioni and the Elsslers.

Meyerbeer commenced his *Robert le Diable* in 1828, but, interrupted by his frequent journeys, the opera was not completed before the month of July, 1830. Written for the Académie, this work was disposed of by the composer to the Administration, when the Revolution put to flight all ideas of music and harmony. Towards the end of the following year, however, *Robert le Diable* was put in rehearsal. Meyerbeer, an ardent lover of his art, was in a state of feverish agitation, and the critics did their best to extinguish the courage of the composer. At the last general rehearsal, there was the usual number of loungers, who indulged in sneers, suppressed laughter, shrugs, sarcasms and evil prognostications, which circulated on the stage and in the lobbies and boxes : it was said that the piece would not survive ten representations.

At the rehearsal of his operas, Meyerbeer was always timid and nervous, and in his over-anxiety he consulted everybody : the machinist, the prompter, even the very carpenters. One may fancy the unhappy composer, with his small slight figure and dark Jewish countenance, his pensive air and his sparkling eyes, in the midst of his tormentors, a prey to misgivings and apprehensions, and almost to despair. Dr. Véron, however, was confident of the success of the new piece, and although assailed on all sides by spiteful speeches, he strolled hither and thither, listening with smiling serenity to the detractors.

Dr. Véron met Fétis on the stage, and the critic did not conceal his forebodings as to the fate of *Robert le Diable*. "Do not be uneasy," blandly replied the rubicund doctor; "I have listened attentively, and am satisfied that I am not deceived. In this work the great qualities immeasurably transcend its imperfections. The situations are striking, the expression is powerful; the impression cannot fail to be instantaneous and profound. It will make the tour of the world."

Everybody belonging to the theatre exerted themselves to the utmost to ensure the success of the opera. The *mise en scène* was rich and splendid; the orchestra was admirable; the costumes were superb, and the last scene was dazzling. At first, the critics endeavoured to contravene the opinion of the public, but they were obliged to yield and join in the pæans of laudation; "for nobody," as M. Fétis judiciously remarks, "can resist the whole world." Then they came to admit that it was the finest opera, except *Guillaume Tell*, that had been produced at the Académie for years. It certainly made the fortune of the establishment; it placed Meyerbeer, at one bound, on the summit of glory, and it made Julie Dorus a celebrity.

Adolphe Nourrit was an admirable Robert: his voice, his handsome figure, his style of acting, exactly suited the character. His voice had not originally been either light or flexible, but he had resolutely set himself, with the aid of Garcia, to the task of subduing it to his control; and although he did not attain the brilliant fluency or the passionate intensity of Rubini, he could execute rapid passages in a satisfactory manner; while any defects in his vocalization were amply atoned for by his charming method of phrasing, and his exquisite falsetto. He had great tact and discretion in the conception of a character and the expression of dramatic emotion: he seized the most delicate phases of character with quick intelligence, and gave them such an aspect of dramatic truth that it seemed as if the parts he created could not be represented in any other manner. The music of Meyerbeer offered the severest trial to which a singer could be subjected. "Completely different from the Rossinian system, so favourable to the voice, it was a return towards the declaimed opera," observes Fétis; "but in proportions so massive and with an instrumentation so formidable, that success must inflict on individual vocalists serious injury and deterioration." Fortunately Nourrit, by an adroit use of his falsetto, managed to escape with less detriment to his vocal organ than he might have suffered had he constantly employed his chest-voice. Levasseur was a veritable basso, and with Nourrit, Madame Damoreau, and Mdlle. Dorus, completed a group of singers of which France had just reason to be proud.

As Alice, Mdlle. Dorus created the most powerful sensation; it was pronounced to be one of the most exquisite performances ever seen. It was truly "angelic," said Meyerbeer himself, who was hard to please in the matter of *prime donne.* Every one who performed the character after—even Jenny Lind and Pauline Viardot—adopted the model presented by the charming Julie Dorus; and the traditions of her acting and singing in this part have become classical.

Rossini, it is said, was unable to pardon the success of *Robert le Diable;* and his vexation was redoubled on finding that his *Guillaume Tell, Mosè,* and *Siege of Corinth,* were now only fragmentarily performed. Dr. Véron, to propitiate the Italian maestro, proposed to him to compose *Gustave,* with Scribe for his collaborateur; but Rossini shrugged his shoulders, and with a sardonic smile, replied, "I will return to Italy, and will come back when the Sabbath of the Jews is over."

Meyerbeer, it should be remembered, entertained the most profound respect and admiration for Rossini; and was passionately delighted with his operas.

Hérold had, in 1832, just produced his opera, *Le Pré aux Clercs;* but the composer was on his death-bed, and lived only to witness the success of his final opera, which soothed his last moments. Madame Casimir being unexpectedly taken ill after the first representation, the theatre was closed. Hérold sent to Mdlle. Dorus, and begged her, with tears, to undertake the part of the heroine, and Dr. Vércn consented to lend the services of the accomplished artiste; she worked with ardour for three or four days, and on the 21st December 1832, gained a new triumph in the part of Isabelle, which she played for twelve nights consecutively.

Mdlle. Dorus continued her studies with conscientious perseverance, and gradually rendered herself worthy of taking the place of Madame Damoreau. The libretto of *Gustave*, rejected so disdainfully by Rossini, was accepted by Auber, whose genius, light, spirituel, sparkling, was overpowered by it. "The poet kills the music," says a sprightly French writer, "and the ballet kills the opera." The fifth act arrives, and, disembarrassed of Gustave and of M. Scribe, the musician becomes lively. *Gustave* was produced February 27, 1833, with the following cast—Nourrit as Gustave, Levasseur as Ankerstroëm, Mdlle. Falcon as the Countess Amélie, and Mdlle. Dorus as the Page. But the audience dozed through four acts to awake with delight at the fifth; thanks to which, and its gorgeous masquerade, *Gustave* was popular for some time: but the four preliminary acts soon disappeared, and the fifth alone survived.

This year Mdlle. Dorus married M. Gras, first violin of the orchestra at the Opéra, where her brother, M. Dorus, an exquisite flute-player, held an eminent position.

After *Robert,* the next great triumph for Madame Dorus Gras, and for Mdlle. Falcon, the new operatic star at the Académie, was *La Juive.* The great character of Rachel was given to Mdlle. Falcon, and Madame Dorus Gras had the part of Euxodie. Nourrit and Levasseur were the leading male vocalists. All Paris thronged to admire the resplendent scenery and the glittering armour, and applauded vociferously.

At a performance of *Robert le Diable,* Rossini, who was in a box with Meyerbeer, was so pleased with some particular morceau, that he said to his illustrious confrère, "If you write anything better than this, I will undertake to dance upon my head." "You had better then commence practising," responded Meyerbeer, gravely, "as I have just finished the fourth act of *Les Huguenots.*"

M. Véron, knowing the dilatory habits of Meyerbeer, or rather his habit of taking an immense time to elaborate his composition, made an agreement with the composer, by which the maestro engaged to deliver the score of *Les Huguenots* by a fixed day. The day arrived, and the opera was placed in rehearsal; but Madame Meyerbeer having been ordered to Italy on account of her health, her husband determined on accompanying her. He demanded from the Opéra a delay of six months, which was refused; whereupon he took up his score and put it in his pocket. "I and my opera," he said, "are one. I depart; my opera goes with me." And he paid the forfeit of 30,000 francs rather than permit *Les Huguenots* to be rehearsed without his personal superintendence. But he could not forgive the exaction of the forfeit, and he never pardoned M. Véron. He refused to let him have *Les Huguenots* on any terms, and subsequently offered it to M. Duponchel, who succeeded M. Véron in the management, and generously volunteered to repay Meyerbeer the 30,000 francs; but the composer would accept only 20,000.

The success of *Les Huguenots* was neither so brilliant nor immediate as that of its predecessor. At first the public were unable to rightly appreciate the merits of *Les Huguenots*, and by the critics it was placed below *Robert le Diable*. The enthusiasm was shared between Nourrit (Raoul), Falcon (Valentine), and Dorus Gras (Marguerite). It created a great sensation, however.

During the summer, Madame Dorus Gras, with Nourrit, and some other performers, accepted an engagement at the theatre of Lille. She then visited the principal towns of the north of France, and Brussels. In 1836, she was at Toulouse, when the workmen gave her a serenade, surprisingly well performed.

M. Duponchel did not sleep in the midst of his

present prosperity. Dreading lest a cold or other indisposition should incapacitate the first tenor, Nourrit, he sought everywhere, in vain, for another; until one day, on the quay at Rouen, he heard a handsome young cooper, one Poultier, who was singing with all the force of his lungs. Struck with his fine tenor voice, Duponchel brought this young man to Paris, instructed him, and engaged him at a salary of 1,000 francs a month. But Poultier, though he sang very well, was not a substitute for Nourrit, and M. Duponchel had to resume his pursuit of a tenor. At last he heard of Louis Gilbert Duprez, and wrote to him, and in the November following, Duprez arrived in Paris.

A day was fixed when the young tenor was to sing before a kind of musical jury, consisting of Messrs. Duponchel, Halévy, and Ruolz: the latter, at Naples, had written *Lara* for him. Duprez sang, and the future hero of a succession of operatic triumphs was revealed. He was accordingly engaged; Duponchel going through the form of consulting Nourrit on the subject. From that time Duprez' brilliant career began; but the result was fatal to the unfortunate Nourrit. Concealing his grief and mortification at being thus eclipsed and set aside, he left Paris and went to Italy. His melancholy gradually rose to despair and insanity; and at length, after having appeared at Naples, he committed suicide by throwing himself from the window of his room. Duprez, on the other hand, rose at once to the height of Parisian favour. *Guillaume Tell* was revived for his début, Madame Dorus Gras taking the part originally written for Madame Damoreau; and never, it was remarked, had the superb duet in the second act produced such an effect as when sang by Dorus Gras and Duprez.

Halévy's *Guido e Ginevra* was brought forward March 3, 1838, and Mdlle. Falcon was to have been the leading personage in that opera; but she had lost her voice, and was on her way to Italy, so Madame Dorus Gras had to take the part. She could hardly have found one less adapted to her powers than Ginevra, for passionate characters were not suited either to her talent or her person. *Guido e Ginevra* was not received with an ovation, in spite of the singing of Duprez.

In May, 1839, Madame Dorus Gras, accompanied by her brother, appeared in London, at the Philharmonic and other first-class concerts, with Tamburini, Mario, Madame Albertazzi, &c.

During the summer Madame Dorus Gras appeared again in London, singing at concerts. At the close of the fashionable musical season, she undertook a series of concerts around England with Tamburini, Brizzi, M. Laveviere the harpist, and her brother, commencing at York, and finishing, September 6, at Gloucester. In 1842 she received pressing invitations to come to London, which the state of her health compelled her to refuse. From this time, however, she was in the habit of coming almost every year; and in 1844 she went to Dublin.

Modest, unassuming, and never intriguing, Madame Dorus Gras greatly disliked and dreaded the continual cabals and plottings, of which she was not only the witness but frequently the victim, though no rival had ever been able to dethrone her; and she determined to retire from the scene of these mingled triumphs and mortifications. She gave her farewell performance at the Académie, May, 1845, singing for the last time in *Robert le Diable* and *Le Rossignol*. The farewell was brilliant; the public testified their sympathy by unbounded applause and showers of wreaths and bouquets, and the Queen of the French sent her a superb bracelet, accompanied by a flattering letter as a testimony of personal esteem.

After visiting London in 1846, Madame Dorus Gras went to Dijon, Brest, Nantes, and other places. She returned to London in the summer of 1847. In the winter of that year, M. Jullien commenced his attempt at Grand Opera at Drury Lane, and offered an engagement as prima donna to Madame Dorus Gras, with a salary of 2,000*l*. The only impediment to her accepting the offer was that she knew not a word of English; however, she set to work, and contrived to master the libretto of the *Bride of Lammermoor*, in which opera she appeared December 13th, with Mr. Sims Reeves and Mr. Weiss. There was great curiosity to hear this favourite of the concert room, and at first she was much liked for her easy graceful style and brilliant singing, in spite of the perceptible defects of her English pronunciation; but she either would not or could not learn another libretto, and was obliged to withdraw: which was one cause of the ruin of Jullien's Grand Opera scheme.

In 1849, Madame Dorus Gras appeared at the Royal Italian Opera with Mario, Massol, Tagliafico, Salvi, Mdlle. Corbari, etc. She performed in *Masaniello*, *Roberto il Diavolo*, and other modern French operas. She was much admired, though most English critics objected to her tendency to display her extraordinary vocal fluency in extravagant embellishment.

Madame Dorus Gras is at present residing in Paris.

CHAPTER VII.

CORNÉLIE FALCON.

Cornélie Falcon was the daughter of a Parisian tradesman, and having early evinced a taste for music, she was placed in the Conservatoire, where she received instruction from Pellegrini and Bordogni. An earnest, attentive student, she succeeded in carrying off several prizes. On leaving the Conservatoire, she sang at various concerts, where she was but little noticed. At last, through the influence of Adolphe Nourrit, she obtained an opportunity of making her début at the Académie. *Robert le Diable* was revived for the occasion, and she appeared Friday, July 20, 1832, with Nourrit and Mdlle. Dorus.

The lights, the crowd, the buzz, and the novelty of her situation at first alarmed Cornélie. Like every débutante who stepped on the boards of the Grand Opéra, the young songstress trembled as she emerged from the wings in her character of Alice, and her voice faltered; but, gathering courage, she sang her first air with success. Encouraged by this, she became more animated, and at last succeeded in fixing the attention of the audience.

Her voice was full and resonant, especially in the upper and middle notes, and was of great compass, and her intonation was good, though as yet far from perfect. Her accents were touching; for she sang, like Rubini, with *des larmes dans la voix*. Her figure was well formed, tall and slender, and she had the complexion of a Spaniard of pure blood, with black sparkling eyes; her hands were rather large, but finely shaped.

"She indeed was a person to haunt even a passing stranger," says Mr. Chorley, in his *Music and Manners*. "Though the seal of her race was upon her beauty, and it bore the expression of a Deborah or a Judith, rather than of a Melpomene, I have never seen any actress, who, in look and gesture, so well deserved the title of the Muse of Modern Tragedy. Large, dark, melancholy eyes—a form, though slight, not méagre—and, above all, an expressiveness of tone rarely to be found in voices of her register, which was a legitimate soprano—the power of engaging interest by mere glance and step when first she presented herself, and of exciting the strongest emotions of pity, or terror, or suspense by the passion she could develop in action—such were her gifts."

The originality of her style, her fervour, her grandeur, her dignity, her impassioned energy, and the beauty of her voice, raised Cornélie Falcon at one step to a high position. "This little girl from the Conservatoire," says Jules Janin, speaking of her début, "bathed in tears men who have almost grown weary of dramatic emotions. She astonished us."

After some eleven or twelve representations, the performance of *Robert le Diable* was suspended, Mdlle. Falcon having fallen ill. Meyerbeer, who had hastened to Paris, was bitterly disappointed at being unable to see this new Alice. It was not before September that she was sufficiently recovered to resume her performances.

In Auber's *Gustave*, which was produced February 27, 1833, Mdlle. Falcon had the opportunity of creating a new character. Unfortunately the part of the Countess Amélie, with its powder and hoops, and pretty coquetry, was not suited to the dark and mystic style of Cornélie. "Alas, Mdlle. Falcon!" cried Jules Janin; "this young creature, of such great hopes, sang without voice, without expression, without exertion, without energy, without point." She was stifled amidst the mad gaiety, the whirl of the dancers, the glare and splendour of the scenes. The singers in *Gustave* indeed were "nowhere;" the dancers reigned supreme.

"I believe," says Jules Janin, "that never, even at the Opéra, was seen a spectacle more grand, more rich, more curious, more magnificent, than the fifth act of *Gustave*. It is a fairy-land of beautiful women, of gauze, of velvet, of grotesqueness, of elegance, of good taste and of bad taste, of details, of learned researches, of esprit, of madness and of whimsicality, of everything, in a word, which is suggestive of the eighteenth century. When the beautiful curtain is raised, you find yourself in an immense ball-room." The stage of the Grand Opéra, the largest in Paris, is admirably adapted for masked balls, and the side-scenes being removed, the stage was surrounded by a salon, the decorations of which corresponded with those of the boxes. "This salle de bal is overlooked by boxes, these boxes are filled with masks, who play the part of spectators. At their feet, constantly moving, is the circling crowd, disguised in every imaginable costume, and dominoes of every conceivable hue. Harlequins of all fashions, clowns, pedlars, what shall I say? One presents the appearance of a tub, another of a guitar; his neighbour is disguised *en botte d'asperges*; that one is a mirror, this a fish; there is a bird, here is a time-piece: you can hardly imagine the infinite confusion. Peasants, marquises, princes, monks, I know not what, mingle in one rainbow-hued crowd. It is impossible to describe this endless madness, this whirl, this *bizarrerie*, on which the rays of two thousand wax tapers, in their crystal lustres, pour an inundation of soft and mellow light. I, who am so well accustomed to spectacles like this—I, who am, unfortunately, not easily disposed to be surprised—I am yet dazzled with this radiant scene."

Cornélie Falcon took her revenge in *Don Giovanni*, which was produced about June with extraordinary magnificence. She sang with Nourrit, Levasseur, Madame Damoreau, and Mdlle. Dorus. As Donna Anna she was superb, and redeemed herself so far from the failure she had made in *Gustave*, that when *Ali Baba* was brought out in July, Cherubini gave her the part of Morgiana; but here Mdlle. Falcon found herself again hampered with a character unfitted for her, and in which she had nothing to sing. Her great triumph was reserved till February 23, 1835, when *La Juive* was produced. This was the last work M. Véron put on the stage. The scenery of *La Juive* far exceeded in splendour anything that had been brought out at the Parisian Opera. The magnificence of mediæval costume was realized in the richness, variety, and accuracy of the dresses. Mdlle. Falcon was touching in Rachel; she looked the resolved, passionate, pensive Jewish maiden, and transformed the pale sketch of M. Scribe into a beautiful finished picture. Malibran herself applauded Mdlle. Falcon in this part.

But her reputation rests mainly on her performance in *Les Huguenots*, which also combined the talents of Madame Dorus Gras, Nourrit, and Levasseur.

At rehearsal, Nourrit, a keen critic and an intelligent musician, gave Meyerbeer several valuable hints; especially in the fourth act. He counselled the withdrawal of the Queen from the conspiracy scene, as the presence of another woman, he suggested, would weaken the interest attaching to the situation of Valentine. Meyerbeer had terminated the act with the "Bénédiction des Poignards," but Nourrit proposed that this should be followed by a duet. Meyerbeer hesitated: after such a chorus—it was impossible. Nevertheless, Nourrit persisted; and Meyerbeer, vexed and uneasy, went home, and consulted M. Gouin, his landlord and factotum. Could Scribe be induced to make any more alterations? Gouin suggested another plan, to which Meyerbeer agreed. It was eleven o'clock at night, but Gouin rushed off to the Rue Lepelletier, where he discovered Emile Deschamps, the poet, absorbed in a game of dominoes. Emile obligingly left his game, dashed off a set of verses, nodded "Good-night," and returned to his friends.

Meyerbeer, on receiving the verses, flew to the piano, and composed a duo finale, and early next morning he knocked at Nourrit's door, with the music in his hand. Nourrit was delighted, and threw himself into Meyerbeer's arms. Two days after the score was ready, and each musician found on his desk a new duet for Raoul and Valentine. "Then there was another scene," says M. de Mirecourt, one of the biographers of Meyerbeer; "for after the execution of the morceau at rehearsal, frantic applause thundered from the orchestra. Habenech clambered on the stage to congratulate the maestro; Nourrit, Mdlle. Falcon, and all the musicians followed their chief, and Meyerbeer was saluted with acclamations. Never was ovation more magnificent or more spontaneous."

This fourth act of *Les Huguenots* is universally admitted to be one of the grandest successes of the composer. "Save in the two last acts," said George Sand, writing to Meyerbeer, "the character of Raoul, with all your skill, is unable to rise from the weight of commonplace insipidity with which M. Scribe has laden it. Even Nourrit's true sensibility and rare intelligence contend in vain against the sentimental and silly nonentity of the hero, who is 'a thorough victim to circumstances,' as the romance writers phrase it. But how the part rises in the fourth act; how it *tells* in the great scene, which (prudery and objection put aside) I find so pathetic, so intensely mournful, so fearful; so anything rather than Anacreontic! What a duet! What a dialogue! How has the musician wept, implored, raved, and conquered, where the author should have done it? Oh, Maestro! you are a noble, truthful poet, an arch romancer!"

As Valentine, Mdlle. Falcon surpassed herself. Her beauty, her passionate intensity, the life and colour which she threw into the part, elicited universal acclamations. One night, a few weeks after the production of this opera, Malibran quitted her box to embrace Mdlle. Falcon, and thank her, with deep feeling, for the pleasure she had given her in *Les Huguenots*.

March 3, 1837, *Stradella*, by Niedermeyer, was produced, Mdlle. Falcon, Nourrit, and Levasseur taking the first parts. On the 1st April, Nourrit retired from the scene of his triumphs. He selected one act of Glück's *Armide*, and the three last acts of *Les Huguenots*. The farewell was a melancholy one. The house was crowded almost to suffocation, but "the audience was joyless and even sad." One of the most signal proofs of his great talent which Nourrit had ever displayed was in being able, during five hours, to control the profound emotion by which he was agitated.

Soon after this Mdlle. Falcon, who had suffered from fatigue and the exertion she had undergone for five years, found her vocal powers failing her, and one night, in *Stradella*, her voice suddenly left her: the curtain was lowered and the audience dismissed. Her vocal malady excited the most lively sympathy; perhaps the more keen as there was no one to replace her. Every means was suggested to effect a restoration of her vocal powers; and the artiste did not lose her courage: she left her cure to time, and the faculty; hoping against hope that she might yet be able to sing for some time to come. After an absence of some weeks she reappeared with Duprez in *Les Huguenots*. Her voice had never been more pure, more vibrating; the only alteration observable was that it seemed changing from a legitimate soprano to a decided contralto.

Early in 1838, she left for Italy, where her energies revived; but only for a short time. She was beloved by her comrades, and a great favourite with the public; so that when she announced her reappearance for March 14, 1839, there was great rejoicing among her partisans. She chose for her benefit the second act of *La Juive*, and the fourth of *Les Huguenots*, and was supported by Duprez, Massol, and Madame Dorus Gras. The theatre was crowded—it was, a French writer says, like a family gathering to welcome the return of the *voix prodigue*. When the beneficiaire appeared the house rang with acclamations, but the illusion was not of long duration. Some notes, by accident, yet remained pure; but the others were either veiled, stifled, or cracked.

"At first, firm and calm, Mdlle. Falcon assisted without faltering at the spectacle of her own agony," says Charles de Boigne; "but soon the general emotion infected her, her tears gushed forth, and her despair was evidenced in convulsive sobs, which redoubled the applause still more: the last homage to a fine talent which had ceased to exist. Leaning on the shoulder of Duprez, she remained some instants absorbed in grief; but then courageously resumed her duty: as she had commenced her part, she was resolved to finish it. As Rachel she accomplished her painful task, but as Valentine she had yet to drink the bitter chalice of failure to the dregs. When she returned in the fourth act of *Les Huguenots*, the music dragged painfully between the dying gasps of Valentine and the bravos arrested by the sight of so terrible a misfortune." The phrase "Nuit fatale, nuit d'alarmes, je n'ai plus d'avenir," contained an allusion to her situation so poignant that the ill-fated cantatrice was scarcely able to pronounce them.

Such a desperate, agonizing struggle of Art against Nature has seldom been witnessed. The magnificent voice of Cornélie Falcon had fled. Her beauty, her talent, her constant willingness to oblige—these qualities had endeared her to the public. "Add to these the charms of her youth, the love borne to her by all her comrades, and the loss of her voice, followed by the almost desperate efforts made by her to recover it," says Mr. Chorley, "and her disastrous final appearance when no force of will could torture destroyed nature into even a momentary resuscitation, make up one of those tragedies into which a fearful sum of wrecked hope and despair and anguish enters. Hers is a history, if all tales be true, too dark to be repeated, even with the honest purpose, not of pandering to an evil curiosity, but of pointing out the snares and pitfalls which lie in wait for the artiste, and of inquiring, for the sake of art as well as of humanity (the two are inseparable), if there be no protection against them,—no means for their avoidance?"

In 1840 the Home Minister granted to Mdlle. Falcon a pension of sixty pounds a year.

In 1841, it was said that Mdlle. Falcon, with Madame Damoreau, was among the stars who sang at St. Petersburg, and that her reception was most flattering: that she had completely recovered her beautiful voice. The rumour, however, was never confirmed. Some say that Mdlle. Falcon is at St. Petersburg, others that she resides at Paris, others again that she is no longer living.

CHAPTER VIII.

MARIA FELICITA MALIBRAN.

Maria Felicita Malibran, the Gabrielli of modern days, was born March 24, 1808, in the Rue de Marivaux, Paris. Her father, Manuel Garcia, member of a respectable Hebrew family, was a Spaniard, and had been for many years a popular actor and singer at the Prince's Theatre, Madrid. Being ambitious, he left his native country and visited Paris, where his talent as a composer, and a teacher, and an artiste of rare ability were recognized: as Count Almaviva, Otello, above all as Don Giovanni, he was unsurpassed. His wife, Joaquina Sitcher, had under the name of Brionès, obtained much success in the great parts of the Spanish stage.

At the age of four years, Maria accompanied her family to Italy, whither her father was going to study, and at Naples, in 1813, she played the part of the child in her friend Paer's *Agnese*, at the Théâtre des Fiorentini. Two years after, M. Panseron, with whom the family became acquainted in Naples, taught her sol-

feggio, and the composer, Hérold, coming to this city about the same time, gave her the first lessons on the pianoforte. In 1816, Garcia quitted Italy and returned to Paris, having accepted an engagement from Madame Catalani at the Théâtre Italien; but a misunderstanding having arisen, he left Paris and came to London in the spring of 1818.

Maria was a delicate, sickly, sensitive child, and the early years of her life were sad and painful. Shortly after coming to England she was placed for education in the convent at Hammersmith, where, caressed by her teachers and elder schoolfellows, and led away by her vivacity and wilful temper, she would probably have in time been completely spoiled; but her father soon removed her that she might commence her musical education. Already Maria spoke with ease Spanish, Italian, and French; she soon became familiar with English, and afterwards she learnt German.

The temper of Garcia was rough, violent, and irritable, and his behaviour to his own family was not particularly considerate. One day, desiring to give a visitor some idea of a piece which he had recently composed, he roared out with all the strength of his lungs, "La Famiglia!" when his wife, son, and daughter immediately trooped in; then no sooner had the composition been performed than they retired. At a performance at the Catholic chapel in Warwick Street, the Garcia family were to sing an Offertorium composed by the patriarch, "and a fearful wailing the poor things made of it; when the father, unable to endure the noise, broke in and bore all before him with the furious roar of his voice." On another occasion he, with his wife, son, and daughter, sang some quartetts together, when poor Maria, being just in front of her father, was in a position to tempt him to accompany with a cruel blow on the face every fault she committed.

Garcia was determined that no effort should be spared to make his daughter what nature had apparently resolved she should never be—a great vocalist; and on returning to France in November, 1819, he commenced his course of training. He was unable to comprehend how any one could be overcome by doubt, indolence, or timidity; he never could hear the words, "I cannot," without an expression of rage and scorn, and was resolved that his daughter should be reared in thorough contempt for "the weakness of the sex." The child, however, on her part was intelligent, firm, and resolute, and had prodigious instincts for art, but was terribly afraid of her father. Her vocal qualifications, however, seemed very unpromising; her voice was weak, the lower notes imperfectly developed, the upper tones indifferent in quality, hard and thin, and the middle much veiled; above all, her intonation was so doubtful that there was a reasonable apprehension of her ear being defective. Sometimes she would sing so frightfully out of tune that her father would quit the piano precipitately, and run to the farthest corner of the house, while she, distracted with fear, yet feeling within her the sparks of genius which were one day to burst into a flame, would fly after him, and seizing him by the coat, weeping bitterly, would supplicate him to recommence.

"One evening I studied a duet with Maria," says the Countess Merlin, "in which Garcia had written a passage, and he desired her to execute it. She tried, but became discouraged, and said, 'I cannot.' In an instant the Andalusian blood of her father rose. He fixed his flashing eyes upon her: 'What did you say?' Maria looked at him, trembled, and clasping her hands, murmured in a stifled voice, 'I will do it, papa;' and she executed the passage perfectly. She told me afterwards that she could not conceive how she did it. 'Papa's glance,' added she, 'has such an influence upon me that I am sure it would make me fling myself from the roof into the street without doing myself any harm.'"

She was a passionate, wayward child, but generous and ardent; apt to fly into paroxysms of anger, but ever ready to entreat forgiveness, and atone for any injustice she might have inflicted. She was irresistibly charming, frank, bold and original; though impulsive, obstinate, and wilful. "Her proud and stubborn spirit requires a hand of iron to control it," said her father.

"Maria can never become great save at the price of suffering." This was true, for she was a terrible little vixen: though her faults were all inherited from him. By the time she was fifteen, Maria's voice had greatly improved; her chest notes had gained in depth, power, and richness, but the other parts of her organ were still crude and veiled. She left with her family for England, and made her first appearance as one of the chorus at the King's Theatre.

In 1825, when Maria was seventeen, a sudden indisposition of Madame Pasta alarmed Mr. Ayrton, the manager, and Garcia offered the services of his daughter. On the 17th June she appeared as Rosina, in *Il Barbiere di Seviglia*, and gave abundant evidence of talent. "Her extreme youth," said Lord Mount Edgecumbe, "her prettiness, her pleasing voice, and sprightly easy action, gained her general favour." She was immediately engaged for the rest of the season, six weeks, at a salary of 500*l*. On the 23rd July, she sang the part of Felicia in the first representation of *Il Crociato*, by Meyerbeer; which was brought forward by Velluti, the eminent male soprano, at the end of the season, and produced after one month's rehearsal. There was a foolish attempt to force Maria on the public as a prima donna when she was only a very promising débutante, and the most injudicious alterations were made for the purpose; the scena and rondo for Felicia—"Ah! ch'io l'adoro ancor"—was omitted, and a song written by Garcia substituted. This substitution was not made known till the last rehearsal, which took place the night before the opera was produced; and on Ayrton remonstrating, Garcia asserted that the engagement of his daughter gave him the option of changing at pleasure any songs allotted to her.

If her father was ambitious and daring, Maria was so likewise. She had to sing with Velluti a duet in Zingarelli's *Romeo e Giulietta*, and in the morning they rehearsed it together; Velluti reserving his fioriture for the evening, lest the young débutante should endeavour to imitate his ornaments. In the evening he sang his solo part, embroidering it with the most florid decorations, and finishing with a new and beautiful cadenza, which astonished and charmed the audience; Maria seized the phrases, to which she imparted an additional grace, and crowned her triumph with an audacious and superb improvisation. Thunders of applause greeted her, and while trembling with excitement she felt her arm grasped by a hand of iron. "Briccona!" hissed a voice in her ear, as Velluti glared on her, gnashing his teeth with rage.

After performing in London, she appeared in the autumn with her father at the Manchester, York, and Liverpool Festivals, where she sang some of the most difficult pieces from the *Messiah* and the *Creation*. Some said that she failed, others that she sang with a degree of mingled brilliancy, delicacy, and sweetness, that drew down a storm of applause. It is certain that her talents were so little appreciated by her father, and her success was so variable, that she was almost on the point of marrying an orchestral performer of the humblest pretensions.

Garcia at this time conceived a project for establishing an Italian Opera in America; though his company was a miserable one, as he depended chiefly on himself, his wife, his son and daughter. The first opera represented was *Il Barbiere*, on the 29th November, 1825, in which Maria had made her début in London; this was followed by *Tancredi* and *Otello* (Maria playing Desdemona to her father's Moor), by *Il Turco in Italia*, *Don Giovanni*, *Cenerentola*, and two operas composed by Garcia—*L'Amante Astuto* and *La Figlia dell' Aria*. The inefficiency of his corps, vocal and instrumental, nearly drove Garcia to distraction; and one evening, *Don Giovanni* being the opera, he was so transported with fury at the manner in which the orchestra gave the finale to the first act, that he rushed, sword in hand, to the footlights, and compelled them to recommence.

The young Maria's success was extraordinary. The New York writers were in a perfect delirium of admiration. Her fresh lovely voice was declared to be miraculous, and her beauty bewildering, while her amazing vivacity astonished them. The public were delighted, and her popularity was greatly heightened by her execution of English songs, one of which she generally sung every evening. "The demand for these increased to such an extent, that when performing one night in *Otello*, she was called upon by the audience to sing 'Home, sweet home;' and with all the good humour imaginable, she instantly complied with the request."

Shortly after her arrival, M. François Eugène Malibran, a French merchant settled at New York, solicited her hand. He was fifty, Maria seventeen; but the poor girl was already tired of her laborious life, and still more so of her father's temper. Garcia refused his consent; but her stubborn will had been rendered more unmanageable by opposition, and poor Madame Garcia, mild and amiable, vainly strove to act as mediator. One evening *Otello* was to be performed. Maria, of course, was the Desdemona, and her father the Moor. The morning had been a stormy one between father and daughter. At the moment when Othello, his brow lowering, his eyes sparkling with rage, approached to stab Desdemona, Maria perceived that the weapon which glittered in his hand was a real dagger, which her father had bought of a Turk some few days previously; struck with terror and almost frantic, she cried in Spanish, "Papa, papa! for the love of God do not kill me!" Her fear was groundless: the dagger of the theatre having been mislaid,

Garcia had substituted his own. The audience took the matter in good part, and fancied Desdemona's exclamation in Spanish was excellent Italian.

M. Malibran was magnificent in his promises. He assured her she should be independent, and vowed to Garcia that he would make him a present of a hundred thousand francs, in a year or two, for the loss of the services of his daughter. As he was believed to be very wealthy, Garcia yielded; and the ill-matched pair were married on the 23rd March, 1826. A few weeks later, Malibran became bankrupt and a prisoner for debt: his irregularities and imprudences, perhaps his ignorance and incapacity, had brought him to ruin. The young bride immediately and voluntarily resigned, for the benefit of the creditors, any claims which she might have advanced on the strength of the settlements which were made: an act which was highly applauded by the American public.

Garcia was furious, and his rage almost uncontrollable: and he being also involved in pecuniary difficulties, left the United States, going to Mexico with his wife, son, and youngest daughter, Pauline. Alone in a land of strangers, separated from all her relations, chained by the strongest fetters to a man whom she now hated—who was unable to protect her, and who selfishly looked to her musical talents as a means of supplying him with the necessaries of life,—the situation of Maria was pitiable. But, endued with energy of character, Madame Malibran soon resolved on her future course. The Italian company having been disorganized on the departure of her father, she at once commenced the study of English vocal music, and made her appearance on the national stage at New York. She was successful, and each evening a considerable sum of money was sent by the manager of the theatre to M. Malibran. Weary of her hard fate, disgusted with the deceitful man who had thrown such a blight over her young life, Maria determined on separating from her husband. She had not been married to Malibran five months when she took the decided step of quitting him and returning to Europe. She arrived in Paris, September, 1826, when she took up her residence with M. Malibran's sister.

Although she was born in Paris, and had spent some years there, the solitude in which she had pursued her studies had not permitted of her forming many friendships, she therefore found herself on her return completely isolated; but she recollected the friend of her childhood, the Countess Merlin, and sought her out. Hapless, helpless, the young, beautiful, and gifted girl of eighteen appeared before her friend without money and nearly destitute, seeking guidance and protection. That she had brought all this on herself made her case only the more melancholy. Pity, interest, admiration, by turns assailed the heart of her kind friend, who vowed she would spare no effort to make known the genius of poor Maria; and the Countess went about extolling the rare genius and misfortunes of her protégée, until she succeeded in raising an excitement and obtaining for her an engagement.

Madame Malibran made her first appearance at the Grand Opéra of Paris in January, in *Semiramide*, at the benefit of Galli. For the first time in her life she trembled at the ordeal she was about to undergo. She was only nineteen, and had not heard any of the great singers during the most important part of her life; moreover Pasta and Sontag were the great stars of the opera. Thrown entirely on her own resources, she felt that upon the result of that night her future depended. The theatre was larger than any she had ever sung in, and the company was so distinguished, the audience so fastidious and undemonstrative, that a chill struck to her heart, and it was not without a violent effort at self-control that she stepped on the stage.

The sensation she produced was indescribable. At her entrance, her youth and beauty bespoke indulgence for her, and the noble and dignified manner in which she gave the first phrase, "Fra tanti regi e popoli," thrilled through the house, and applause rang from all sides. The difficult phrase, "Frema il empio," proved "a stumbling-block which she could not surmount. Alarmed by this check," says a French critic, "she did not attempt the difficult passage in the da capo, but, dropping her voice, terminated the passage without effect, leaving her audience in doubt and dissatisfaction. On her re-entrance she was coldly received, but she soon succeeded in winning the public to her favour. In the andante to the air 'Bel raggio,' the young singer threw out such powers, and displayed a voice so full and beautiful, that the formal coldness gave way to applause. Encouraged by this, she hazarded the greatest difficulties of execution, and appeared so inspired by her success that her courage now became temerity."

Her half-veiled genius, the novelty of her fioriture, and some flashes of fine dramatic sentiment, showed what she would be when emotion no longer checked her faculties. There were defects in her singing which were only those of inexperience: she multiplied the traits of all styles without considering their relative affinities or their appropriateness in melody, or even in harmony. From that night, however, she was the idol of the Parisians. Some critical observations in the journals, the frequent opportunities she enjoyed of hearing good singers, and above all, her admirable genius, soon gave a better direction to her talent.

The director, who had at first been rather unwilling that she should appear, lest she should interfere with Sontag, now became pressing in his offers. She hesitated a moment between the Grand Opéra and the Italiens, then decided for the latter: wisely, for opera was at that period a very dreary affair at the

Académie. Laurent engaged her at 800 fr. for each night of performance, and a free benefit, and she appeared at the Italian Theatre in May, in *Torvaldo e Dorliska*, with Zuchelli, Donzelli, Pellegrini, and Mdlle. Amigo.

Her voice, like her genius, was thoroughly original, and superior to that of all other artistes of the same class. In character a contralto, it was not precisely beautiful: it had even many defects, especially in the middle tones, which were hard and unequal; to overcome the imperfection of this part of her voice, she was obliged to go through her exercises every day. Her compass extended over three octaves: from D in alt to D on the third line in the bass. In private singing her range was even greater. Her low, soft, sweet, heart-searching tones were the never-failing index of her varying sensibilities. In her choice of ornaments she had a daring which was only justified by the success which almost invariably crowned her flights of fancy. As the pupil of her father, she had adopted a style florid in the extreme; her facility, her fertility of musical inspiration and cultivation of voice, giving her advantages rarely to be found. "Her passages were not only remarkable for extent, rapidity, and complication, but were invariably marked by the most intense feeling and sentiment. Her soul appeared in everything she did." Her extraordinary flexibility enabled her to run with ease over passages of the most difficult character. "In the tones of Malibran," says one of her English admirers, "there would at times be developed a deep and trembling pathos, that, rushing from the fountain of the heart, thrilled instantly upon a responsive chord in the bosoms of all." She was the pupil of Nature. Her acting was full of genius, passion, and tenderness. She was equally grand as Semiramide and as Arsace, and sang the music of both parts superbly. Touching, profoundly melancholy as Desdemona, she was gay and graceful in Rosina; she drew tears as Ninetta, and, throwing off the coquette, could produce roars of laughter as Fidalma. She had never taken lessons in poses or in declamation, yet she was essentially, innately graceful.

In person Maria was a little below the medium height, and the contour of her figure was rounded to a becoming degree of embonpoint. Her carriage was always noble and dignified; her face was more expressive than handsome; her hair—the pride of a Spaniard—was black and glossy, and she wore it always simply parted in the middle, whether she appeared as queen or peasant. Her eyes were dark and expressive; her teeth white and regular; and her whole countenance, with its pensive, and, at times, melancholy aspect, had the charm of indefinable interest and captivation: the mutability of her features was extraordinary, and reflected the most varied emotion and changes of feeling. "She may not have been beautiful," remarks Mr. Chorley, in his *Recollections*; "but she was better than beautiful—in so much as a speaking Spanish human countenance by Murillo is ten times more fascinating than many a faultless angel-face such as Guido could paint. There was health of tint, with but a slight touch of the yellow rose, in her complexion; great mobility of expression in her features; an honest, direct brightness of eye; a refinement in the form of her head, and the set of it on her shoulders."

Fétis often reproached her with employing means of which no one had less need to secure the suffrages of the crowd. "With the degree of elevation to which you have arrived," he would say indignantly, "you should impose your opinion on the public, not submit to theirs." She would shrug her pretty shoulders and laugh. "*Mon cher grognon*, there may, perhaps, be two or three connoisseurs in the theatre, but it is not they who give success. When I sing for you, I will sing very differently."

The Parisian public, transported with such youth, beauty, and talent, threw themselves at her feet, and Maria, feeling herself sustained by the confidence which gives success, and which success gives, often attained the sublime. She appeared as Desdemona, Rosina, and as Romeo, in Zingarelli's opera; characters as diverse as could well be imagined,—two of them, moreover, among the masterpieces of Pasta. It was remarked by a French critic that "if Malibran must yield the palm to Pasta in point of acting, yet she possessed a decided superiority in respect to song." From that time the superiority of Malibran "in respect to song" became each day more indisputable; while, with regard to acting, though no vocal performer has ever equalled Pasta in her own peculiar style of terrible grandeur, yet none has ever surpassed Malibran in grace, originality, vivacity, piquancy, spontaneity, feeling, and those "tender strokes of art" which, coming from the heart, pierce instantly to the heart of every spectator. Her versatility was wonderful: the Semiramide of this evening was to-morrow the gentle Cinderella; the lively, arch Zerlina became the sad Desdemona. A friend once asked her what was her favourite character. "The character I happen to be acting, whatever it may happen to be," she answered.

Pasta, it was justly said, might be called the Siddons of Opera, Malibran the Garrick. Wherever she sang, she animated the orchestra, director, and singers with ardour, by the glow of her genius; and she would voluntarily instruct her fellow performers. She could sing in any school, and in almost any language: Mozart and Cimarosa, Boïeldieu and Rossini, Cherubini and Bellini, she seized on all readily, and presented each in its individual character, while pouring forth the notes as the inspiration of the moment. She had a genius which invents, which reproduces, which imposes types, and which forces others not only to admire, but to imitate. Many contradictory opinions were given of her talent, but none refused to acknowledge her great gifts. Her versatility was extraordinary.

She played the pianoforte remarkably well, and without having taken lessons in drawing, she sketched caricatures, and portraits that were striking likenesses: an amusement in which she often indulged was sketching the profiles of those on the stage while waiting her turn to go on. She could compose with rapidity and felicity romances and songs. In feminine works she excelled, and if she saw a new work, a piece of embroidery, a cap, or a design in tapestry that struck her, she instantly caught the idea, and imitated, often surpassed, the model. Her theatrical costumes and her head-dresses were all invented or made by herself, and she might often be found with the needle in her hand, while exercising her voice. She wrote and spoke four or five languages, and employed them at the same time, without confounding them, in a conversation with different interlocutors; though in the heat of argument her vivacity would sometimes carry her away, so that when at a loss for a word, she would take the first that presented itself. One day, in an animated discussion, a friend reproached her with using language particoloured like a harlequin's suit.

"True," she quickly replied, "it is particoloured like harlequin, but not masked." Her memory was amazing: in four or five hours she could learn an opera in one act well enough to perform it in the evening. She read the music and words, whether in prose or verse, with as much rapidity as clearness. She rode perfectly on horseback, but, like most singers, she danced badly.

Impassioned, vehement, torn by continual excitement, it was sometimes difficult to recal this wayward creature to the commonplaces of ordinary life; but she was very ready to attend to reason, and having the instincts of goodness and justice, was eager in her anxiety to repair any errors into which she might have fallen. She listened with candour and courage to the most severe truths. She was generous, without pomp or ostentation; extravagant and lavish to others, penurious to herself alone. Brusque and original in her frankness, though her unfortunate position needed great tact, she was so ingenuous that she could not conceal her real impressions. She had a child-like simplicity of character and a singular mixture of the most lovable and the most dangerous qualities; she was fond of toys, dolls, trifles, yet she was daring, and devoted to athletic sports and pastimes—riding, skating, swimming, and even shooting. She would often, on returning from an evening spent in going through a long and fatiguing opera, begin jumping over chairs and tables, or up and down stairs like a schoolboy, in the wildness of animal spirits. She herself said, "When I try to restrain my flow of spirits, I feel as if I should be suffocated."

Her habits were not always suited to her sex, but her manners were invariably blameless. Her wild gaiety, her occasional extravagance, her custom of frequently going about in the country dressed like a boy, led to a scandalous rumour that she made an immoderate use of stimulants; whereas she never drank anything but wine mixed with water. Sometimes, when thoroughly exhausted, she would strengthen her nervous system with a glass of Madeira, as she would have employed vinegar, if it would have afforded her the same relief.

Maria was not long before she became discontented with the hostile tutelage of M. Malibran's sister. The necessity of protection, the fear of censure, her youth, and her unfortunate position, compelled her to prolong for many weeks her sojourn with her sister-in-law; but, one fine day, in a moment of irritation, she took "French leave" of her hostess, sent for a hackney coach, packed into it her trunks, jumped in after them, and drove to the house of Madame Naldi, an old friend of the family, a woman of imperious and austere manners, where she installed herself.

To Madame Naldi she was gentle and docile. If by any little fits of ill-humour she offended, she would load her with caresses, and entreat forgiveness with the *abandon* of a child. Madame Naldi saw all her letters, and took all her money, never giving her a sous except in cases of imperative necessity. "It was really touching," says the Countess de Merlin, "to see her yield to the advice, to the petty sacrifices inflicted and exacted by her friend." One day, when her fortune was at its height, Madame Malibran showed a friend a little worn Cashmere shawl. "I use this shawl in preference to any other that I have," she said. "It was the first Cashmere shawl that I ever obtained, and I have pleasure in remembering the trouble I had in coaxing Madame Naldi to permit me to buy it."

In 1828, the principal members of the operatic company at the Italiens were Malibran, Sontag, Donzelli, Zuchelli and Graziani. Malibran appeared in *Otello*, *Matilda di Shabran*, *La Cenerentola*, and *La Gazza Ladra*. The presence of the great German singer was a stimulus, not a check to her talent; but the invidious comparisons which were raised sent many pangs of jealousy to her heart. Every time that Sontag obtained a triumph Maria wept, naïvely saying, "Why does she sing so divinely?" Yet these two exquisite voices were formed for harmony, not for discord. It does not clearly appear how their reconciliation was effected: Madame Merlin says it was at a concert at her house. A kind of plot had been laid by the amateurs, who longed to hear them together;

in the middle of the concert it was proposed to them to sing the duo from *Tancredi*. For some moments they hesitated; at last they agreed, and approached the pianoforte, amid the acclamations of the audience. The enthusiasm which they excited was so lively, that at the termination of the duo, they looked at each other, and, by a spontaneous movement, clasped hands, sealing their triumph with the kiss of peace.

In the midst of these ovations Madame Malibran never lost her simplicity. She was totally ignorant of household affairs: absorbed by her studies, she never had a taste for luxury, nor indulged in superfluous expenses. But if her fellow artistes were in need, she spared no exertion in their behalf. At the house of one of her friends she often met an aged widow, poor and unhappy, and strongly desired to assist her; but the position and character of the lady required delicate management. "Madame," she said at last, "I know that your son makes very pretty verses." "Yes, madame, he sometimes amuses himself in that way. But he is so young." "No matter. Do you know that I could propose a little partnership affair? Troupenas (the music publisher) has asked me for a new set of romances. I have no words ready. If your son will give them to me, we could share the profits." Madame Malibran received the verses, and gave in exchange 600 francs. The romances were never finished.

She performed all these acts of charity with such refined delicacy, such true generosity, that the kindness was doubled. Thus, at the end of this season, a young female chorister, engaged for the opening of the King's Theatre, found herself unable to quit Paris for want of funds. Madame Malibran promised to sing at a concert which some of the leading vocalists gave for her benefit. The name of Malibran of course drew a crowd, and the room was filled; but she did not appear, and at last they were obliged to commence the concert. The entertainment was half over when she came, and approached the young girl, saying to her in a low voice, "I am a little late, my dear, but the public will lose nothing, for I will sing all the pieces announced. In addition, as I promised you all my evening, I will keep my word. I went to sing in a concert at the house of the Duc d'Orleans, where I received 300 francs. They belong to you. Take them."

The Théâtre Italien being closed during the summer months, the principal singers accepted engagements with Laporte, of the King's Theatre; Madame Malibran accepted Laporte's offer of seventy-five guineas for each representation, and left for England with Madame Naldi.

On the 21st April, she appeared at the King's Theatre, in the character of Desdemona. Donzelli was the Moor; Curioni, Rodrigo; Levasseur, Elmiro;

and Madame Castelli, Emilia. Madame Malibran was received by the public with an ovation, but the critics evinced great hesitation. To Madame Pasta was due the idea of reviving this opera, and in the part of Desdemona, a part originally written for Colbran, she had made the first conquest of the Parisians. Sontag had attempted it with diffidence, being unwilling to incur the risk of comparison with Pasta, and determining to adopt a conception entirely different from that of her predecessor. It was difficult to find a medium between the passion of the one actress and the delicate beauty of the other, so Madame Malibran gave a version of the character suited to her individual taste and powers. The critics, who persisted in comparing her with Pasta, objected to her reading.

She was very vehement and impassioned: for example, in the last scene of the first act, during the quintet, "Smanio, deliro, e tremo," she flew from Elmiro to Otello, and from Otello to Rodrigo, in a kind of frantic terror. In the scene where Desdemona endeavours to appease the quarrel of Otello and Rodrigo, she was unnecessarily violent; and when endeavouring to soften the wrath of her father, she fell into a transport of despair, dragging herself on her knees over the stage, tearing her hair, and abandoning herself to uncontrollable grief. Again, in the final scene, when Otello heaps reproaches on her, she called on him to kill her, and satiate his vengeance, in a tone of rage and resolution which was thought to be inconsistent with the gentle character of Desdemona and with the sudden terror she evinced at his murderous purpose. Her explanation was, that she felt as if she were really in the various situations.

"I remember once," says the Countess de Merlin, "a friend advised her not to make Otello pursue her so long when he was about to kill her. Her answer was, 'You are right: it is not elegant, I admit; but when once I fairly enter into my character, I never think of effects, but imagine myself actually the person I represent. I can assure you that in the last scene of Desdemona I often feel as if I were really about to be murdered, and act accordingly.' Donzelli used to be much annoyed by Madame Malibran not determining beforehand how he was to seize her; she often gave him a regular chase. Though he was one of the best-tempered men in the world, I recollect him one evening being seriously angry. Desdemona had, according to custom, repeatedly escaped from his grasp; in pursuing her he stumbled, and slightly wounded himself with the dagger he brandished. It was the only time I ever saw him in a passion."

She next appeared as Rosina, Bordogni being the Count, and Zuchelli Figaro. Her graceful and lively manner, her native simplicity, and her exquisite singing, made this a delightful performance. She also appeared as Ninetta, with Bordogni, Pellegrini and Zuchelli; and it was she who first brought into notice, by her matchless vocalization, the beautiful duo of the prison scene, hitherto generally omitted as of little interest. In July, she performed Tancredi; a character never a favourite with her, for she often declared that he was an insignificant being, with whose feelings she had no sympathy. In her execution of "Di tanti palpiti," it was objected that she covered the air with too great a profusion of ornament. The music of Rossini was, it is true, already sufficiently florid, and Pasta rather diminished than added to the notes of that popular composition.

Madame Malibran performed Semiramide with Madame Pisaroni, and Zerlina to Sontag's Donna Anna. She was very arch and sprightly as the coquettish young peasant, and in the execution of the vocal part she was unapproachable. Malibran's representation of Ninetta and Zerlina gave rise to a good deal of controversy among the contemporary critics. She represented these characters as she imagined they would be in actual life—common country girls, with awkward demeanour and hoydenish manners; thus making them to a certain extent ridiculous rather than interesting. This was undoubtedly a mistake, for the characters are almost entirely ideal: moreover, simple rusticity is not necessarily awkward or vulgar; while to lessen the sympathies of the audience is to impair the dramatic effect, and make the very music they utter in such refined accents appear absurd. Ninetta, as the heroine of a deeply pathetic story, was unlike the generality of peasant wenches; Zerlina, being a true village coquette, would not naturally be either rude or boisterous. "It is by no means rare," argued one critic, "to discover, in the humblest walk of life, an inborn grace and delicacy of nature's own implanting; and such assuredly is the model from which characters like Ninetta and Zerlina ought to be copied." This argument also holds good with regard to the character of Amina. "She mistakes an awkward sprightliness and incessant rapidity of motion," observes another writer, "for the amiable naïveté of an interesting country girl. Nothing could be more out of character than her affected clumsiness in imitating the minuet step in the ball scene with which the first act closes. Country girls are not necessarily clumsy: they are frequently remarkable for grace when moving in their own sphere."

Madame Malibran appeared as Susanna in the *Nozze di Figaro*, for her own benefit, and was irresistible as the arch waiting-maid. It was impossible to choose a part affording greater opportunity of displaying her talent for lyric comedy; and, as far as the acting was concerned, her performance was the best of that kind that had been seen for years on the stage of the King's Theatre. Her vocalization was of course magnificent.

The ludicrous had a strange fascination for Malibran: she had an unaccountable fancy for throwing aside her tragic robe, and donning the most grotesque costume she could find, often declaring she would greatly prefer to play the Duenna in *Il Barbiere*, to Rosina, for the sake of the ridiculous dress: and she actually did perform it in private. In pursuance of this whim, she announced her intention of performing Fidalma, in *Il Matrimonio Segreto*, a part answering to the Mrs. Heidelberg of the *Clandestine Marriage*, and her acting was inimitable: her comic humour was irresistible, and proved a versatility of power rarely, if ever, to be met with. She revelled in the ludicrous situations, and made Fidalma a prominent part by the drollery of her tone and manner: though when she reproached the two sisters alternately with being "un poco insolente," the feeling of mirth was suddenly converted into a burst of admiration by the brilliancy of a roulade on the word "insolente," taken from the C above the lines, and running down the entire range of her voice. Yet at the Birmingham Musical Festival, in the autumn, she sang "Holy, holy Lord," in a style more impressive, as veteran amateurs admitted, than had been heard since the days of Mara.

Madame Malibran had scarcely stepped on French ground ere she learned that her father had unexpectedly returned, with the intention of giving some representations at the Théâtre Italien. This resolution caused much vexation to his daughter, but she did not oppose it. Garcia had lost a part of his voice; his tenor had become a baritone, and he could no longer reach the notes which had in former times been written for him. She knew how much her father's voice had become injured, and knowing equally well his intrepid courage, feared, not without reason, that he would tarnish his brilliant reputation. Garcia displayed even more than ever the great artiste. A hoarseness seized him at the moment of appearing on the stage. "That is nothing," said he: "I shall do very well:" and by sheer strength of talent and of will, he arranged the music of his part (Almaviva) to suit the condition of his voice, changing the passages, transposing them an octave lower, and taking up notes adroitly where he found his voice available; and all this instantly, with an admirable confidence.

In November, having renewed her engagement with Laurent at a salary of 800 fr. for each representation, and a benefit, Madame Malibran appeared as Desdemona. Every day her talent became more resplendent, and her voice was progressing to perfection. The season was unusually brilliant, and the "management" trembled for the health of the darling of the public.

She never rested an instant, but flung herself into all the exertions and pleasures of her fevered life, without calculating the possibility of her strength one day deserting her. She lavished her voice, her time, her energies whenever she was called on to amuse; never hesitating to sacrifice herself to the whim of the moment, or the gratification of her friends.

Having one night promised to sing at the house of Madame Merlin, M. Laurent told her that it was impossible, as it was a benefit night at the theatre. Malibran, after essaying to induce him to alter the performance to another evening, at length observed, in a very bad humour,—"It does not signify. I sing at the theatre because it is my duty; but afterwards I sing at the house of Madame Merlin, because it is my pleasure." And at one o'clock in the morning, after having played Semiramide, she appeared in the Countess' salon, sang there till two or three, supped, waltzed, and did not leave till daybreak.

Thus, after having passed the night at a ball, on the eve of her performance of some arduous character, she rose at twelve, mounted her horse, started off, and did not return till six. As soon as she had dined, she was obliged to be at the theatre, where she would dress hurriedly for her part; but worn out, agitated, and rather oppressed than recruited by a hasty dinner, even her iron will could not bear her through.

One night, after one of these fatiguing days, she fainted at the moment of appearing on the stage;

and was carried into her dressing-room. Twenty vinaigrettes were presented at once, and by some mischance, among the number was one containing a mixture of oil and alkali, which some eager friend held to her lips; half unconsciously she tasted it, and the next moment blisters covered her mouth. What was to be done? She could not appear on the stage; and it was too late to change the performance. The director was in despair. "Stay," said Malibran, rising, "I will arrange it." And taking a pair of scissors lying near, she stepped up to a glass, and without a moment's hesitation, cut off the blisters which swelled her lips! The state in which she remained may be imagined. But she performed the part of Arsace, to the Semiramide of Sontag, and never sang or acted better.

In January, Malibran performed Tancredi for the benefit of Sontag, when for the first time coronals and bouquets were thrown on to the Italian stage in Paris. At the conclusion of the performance, she picked up the floral treasures, and offered them to Sontag; "who," observes a French critic, "in her confusion forgot that a part of these trophies belonged to the fair Tancredi." Malibran was passionately fond of flowers, and when performing Desdemona for her benefit in March, as she lay dead on the stage, watching Othello, in his mad remorse, preparing to stab himself and fall in his turn, she exclaimed in a low tone, "Take care of my flowers! do not crush my flowers!"

In 1830, Madame Malibran became acquainted with M. Charles de Beriot, a native of Belgium, and a distinguished violinist, in whom she felt an interest as much on account of his talents, as because she sympathized with him in a sentimental disappointment. He was in love with Sontag, who did not care for him, and who was, besides, engaged to the Count Rossi. She made no scruple of avowing with child-like candour the predilection she entertained for the young Belgian, and as the surveillance of Madame Naldi became troublesome, because that austere lady combated her passion for De Beriot, she determined to break with her; she therefore took a house in the Rue de Provence, and removed thither.

Madame Malibran reappeared at the King's Theatre in April, in *La Cenerentola*, the music of which afforded her an opportunity for displaying all her resources. Her vocal powers had improved to an extent which tempted her to abuse them by too great a redundancy of ornament, and her style of singing was consequently more florid than it had ever been hitherto; but the ease, the neatness, the rapidity with which she gave all her passages, and the fulness and equality of each of her notes, were not to be surpassed. She also performed in *Otello* and *Il Matrimonio Segreto*. Lablache, who made his first appearance in England in the latter opera, was magnificent as Geronimo. "He looked like a deaf man, and sang like a man possessed of a very fine ear."

Malibran became sincerely attached to Lablache, and to the very hour of her death regarded him as one of her dearest friends. Both were amiable and charitable, and they often united in doing benevolent actions. One day during this season, an Italian émigré addressed Lablache, asking help to return to his own country. The next day, when all the company were assembled for rehearsal, Lablache requested them to join in succouring their unhappy compatriot; all responded to the call; Madame Lalande and Donzelli each contributing fifty francs. Malibran gave the same as the others, but the following day, seizing the opportunity of being alone with Lablache, she desired him to add to her subscription of 50 francs, 250 more: she had not liked to appear to bestow more than her friends, so she had remained silent the preceding day. Lablache hastened to seek his *protégé*, who, however, profiting by the help afforded him, had already embarked; but not discouraged, Lablache hurried after him, and arrived just as the steamer was leaving the Thames; entering a boat, however, he reached the vessel, went on board, and gave the money to the émigré, whose expressions of gratitude amply repaid the trouble of the kind-hearted basso. Another time Malibran aided a poor Italian who was destitute, telling him to say nothing about it. "Ah, madame," cried he, "you have saved me for ever!" "Hush," she interrupted, "do not say that—only the ALMIGHTY could do so. Pray to HIM."

At the close of the opera season, Madame Malibran sang in September and October at Bath and at Bristol, in eight concerts, at a salary of eighty guineas for each concert. She knew no rest; and the fatigues which she voluntarily imposed on herself were scarcely credible. She would fly to Calais, and sing there; then back to England, and anon be on her way to Brussels; where she would sing, and return to England again, gay and light-hearted—singing, dancing and acting at parties for her own amusement: needlessly flinging away the strength and energy she ought to have carefully preserved. It is said, however, that she was haunted by an idea that when she ceased to enjoy existence in this manner, she should die.

Being engaged by the new directors of the Théâtre Italien, Messrs. Robert and Severini, for 1,175 francs for each representation, Madame Malibran presented herself again before her Parisian admirers in November, in the character of Desdemona, when she was welcomed with such enthusiasm that her reception completely unnerved her; but in the second act she recovered herself and sang the duet with Donzelli in the very finest style. She chose for her benefit, at the end of this season, *Otello*, and to render the performance more attractive, she conceived the mad project of playing the rôle of the Moor. She therefore transposed the music, and produced no more effect than did Madame Pasta when she made the same essay in London. The round and delicate form of a woman suited ill the strong and masculine figure of the warlike Moor; and the swarthy complexion she was obliged to assume, enlarged her features and veiled their expression, which was their greatest charm.

Hearing of his wife's success, and of the extraordinary sums she was earning, M. Malibran, who until then had been constantly assisted by her, unexpectedly came over from America. Four years of labour had enabled her to accumulate some savings, and she had therefore just reason to fear that the presence of her husband in Europe would rob her of the fruits of her talents and exertions. Her ill-assorted marriage was full of painful memories; and she prudently declined to see him, while he was equally determined to have his rights. He proposed that they should share equally the emoluments she received, an arrangement which she passionately refused to agree to; eventually, however, through the medium of friends, and at some pecuniary sacrifice on her part, a pacific arrangement was made. But she resolved not to resume her performances while her husband retained the power arbitrarily to seize her earnings; so she hastily retired to Brussels, where she had purchased a château and park. The unpleasant dispute was at last compromised.

In November, Madame Malibran consented to reappear at the Italiens, as Ninetta. Rubini, who had returned to Paris after an absence of six years, sang with her, and the two singers vied with each other, "till," observed a French critic, "it seemed as if talent, feeling, and enthusiasm could go no farther." Unlike Malibran, Rubini was not a finished actor. "He did not trouble himself much about anything but the particular scena which placed him in the foreground. When this was past, he retired, without caring much for the story of the drama, or the conduct of the other performers. In the air, the duet, or the finale, in which he had an active or preponderating part, Rubini would suddenly rouse himself and display all the energy and charm of his incomparable talent. It was in the tone and sonorousness of his organ, in the artistic management of his voice, that all Rubini's dramatic power consisted."

Madame Malibran was now, however, obliged almost immediately to discontinue her performances, as her illnesses became frequent and alarming; she therefore departed suddenly for Brussels, leaving a letter for the director, Severini, informing him of her intention not to return. He was thus reduced to the necessity of closing the theatre. The administration, however, after having devised several expedients, bethought themselves of working on Malibran's feelings, through the influence of a friend. They implored M. Viardot, who possessed her entire confidence, to go to Brussels, and represent to her the disastrous consequences to the theatre of her withdrawal. M. Viardot went, and found her tranquilly prepared to run all risks that she had incurred; but when he had fully impressed on her mind the ruin she would entail on the administration, she started up, exclaiming, "You are right: I did not dream of that. I am so unhappy! Come, I will return." The next day she was on her way to Paris.

But her health was rapidly failing. Often a notice would appear some hours before the opening of the theatre, that the performance was changed in consequence of the sudden indisposition of Madame Malibran; and as on the following day she would be perfectly well, these accidents were attributed to caprice, or to temper. She resented this injustice, when a kind of coolness arose between her and the Parisians, who had hitherto adored her. At last, January 8, 1832, she announced a farewell performance, and appeared as Desdemona in *Otello*. Nothing could surpass her passionate acting, or the touching accents of her voice. The audience, electrified, forgot their former dissatisfaction, and testified their appreciation with fervour; but it was too late: this was her last farewell of the Parisian public, for she felt it impossible to forgive them.

About the middle of July, Lablache passed through Brussels on his way to Naples, and learning by accident that Malibran was there, he went to see her, although obliged to depart within twenty-four hours. She received him with all the joy of a sincere friend, and when Lablache told her that he was going to Italy, she declared that she would go with him. He assured her that he should be compelled to quit the city at dawn the next day, when she laughingly declared that she would be ready; and next morning she was waiting at the door of his hotel before he was awake. It was not till they were on the frontier of Italy that she recollected she had no passport, and she had to remain some days till Lablache could obtain for her permission to enter Lombardy. At Milan she sang at the soirées given by the Governor, and at the house of the Duke Visconti. She did not stay at Milan, but went on to Rome, where she was engaged at the Theatre Valle. The Roman public, however, did not appreciate her merit, because she was so ill-advised as to sing French romances in the lesson scene of *Il Barbiere*, and they chose to resent this innovation.

During her sojourn at Rome, Maria learned the melancholy tidings of the death of her father. She felt the deepest grief, and was ill for some days from one of those nervous attacks to which she was subject.

While at Rome she signed an engagement with Barbaja to give twelve performances at Naples at

1,000 fr. each representation. She appeared in *Otello*, August 6, 1832, at the Fondo, the second theatre, where she sang ten times out of the twelve for which she had been engaged. Her reception by the Neapolitans was at first so cold that she may be said to have failed. But with the impetuosity of their country, they speedily corrected their first mistake, and when she sang, the theatre was crowded at double prices; "notwithstanding the subscribers' privileges were on most of those occasions suspended, and although *Otello*, *La Gazza Ladra*, and Operas of that description, were the only ones offered to a public long since tired even of the beauties of Rossini, and proverbial for its love of novelty."

Her great triumph, however, was on the night when she took her leave in the character of Ninetta. "Nothing can be imagined finer than the spectacle afforded by the immense theatre of San Carlo, crowded to the very ceiling, and ringing with acclamations," says a correspondent of one of the English papers at the time. "Six times after the fall of the curtain, Madame Malibran was called forward to receive the reiterated plaudits and adieux of the assembled multitude, and indicate by graceful and expressive gestures the degree to which she was overpowered by fatigue and emotion.... The scene did not end within the walls of the theatre; for a crowd of the most enthusiastic rushed from all parts of the house to the stage door, and as soon as her sedan came out, escorted it with loud acclamations to the Palazzo Barbaja, and renewed their salutations as the charming vocalist ascended the steps."

She sang at Rome for three nights, then returned to Naples, whence in the autumn she went to Bologna, being engaged to perform for eighteen nights for 1,440*l.*! commencing on the 13th of October with *La Gazza Ladra.* At Bologna she created a furore, which, till then, had been unknown in that quiet city: the Bolognese did not confine the expression of their rapture to shouts and plaudits; they had a bust of their admired songstress executed in marble and placed in the peristyle of the theatre.

In the spring of 1833, Madame Malibran came to London, being engaged to perform in English opera at Drury Lane and Covent Garden, at a salary of 150 guineas for each night, and two benefits (which produced about 2,000*l.*). She appeared May 1, in the *Sonnambula*, which had been transposed expressly for her. After the *Sonnambula*, she performed the part of Count Bellino in the *Devil's Bridge;* this was followed by a new opera written for her by Chelard. In the months of May and June, she appeared for twenty-eight nights at the King's Theatre, for which she received 2,775*l.* She also concluded an engagement with the Duke Visconti, of Milan, for 185 representations—75 in the autumn and Carnival season of 1835–6, 75 in the corresponding season of 1836–7, and 35 in the autumn of 1836, at a salary of 18,000*l*. These were the highest terms ever offered to a theatrical performer since the days of luxurious Rome.

From London the triumphant singer went to Naples, where she appeared at the San Carlo, November 14, in *Otello*. She sang with her sister-in-law, Ruiz Garcia, in a new opera by Pacini, *Irene*, which was performed November 30, and proved a total failure. She then performed Semiramide, January 19, 1834; also played in a new opera by Coccia, composed expressly for her, *La Figlia del Aria*, which did not attain the third representation. Madame Malibran had the ill fortune to have none but bad operas written for her. She performed besides her pet character, Fidalma, in *Il Matrimonio Segreto*, La Sonnambula, February 3, and Norma on the 25th. In these latter parts she excited the enthusiasm of the public to the highest pitch. Her popularity was excessive. Bonnets à la Malibran, caps à la Malibran, everything à la Malibran were the rage; all Italy, in fact, re-echoed her name with enthusiasm. On her arrival at Milan she had to struggle against a party formed by the admirers of Pasta; but as soon as Malibran appeared as Norma, she was proclaimed "la cantante per eccelenza." She performed twenty times at Milan, and obtained an immense success. A medal, executed by the eminent sculptor, Valerio Nesti, was struck in her honour.

Madame Malibran came to London for a few days

only, in order to sing at a concert for the benefit of her brother Manuel. This journey was rapidly performed, and she then went to Sinigaglia, having been engaged by Azzolini to sing from July 15 to August 11, during the season of the fair. During her stay she heard a beggar-girl sing beneath the window of her hotel. Struck with the beauty of the voice, she inquired into the poor girl's history, and finding that it was real want which had driven her to sing in the streets, she placed the girl in a situation where she would receive regular musical instruction.

In August she visited Lucca, where new triumphs awaited her. She made her début in a new opera by Persiani, *Inès de Castro*, which was not successful. She also appeared in *La Sonnambula*, and *I Montecchi ed i Capuletti*, and after her last representation, the people took the horses from her carriage, conducting her home amid an uproar of applause and delight. Returning to Milan, she performed in *Norma*, *La Sonnambula*, *Otello*, *I Montecchi ed i Capuletti*, and the *Maria Stuarda* of Donizetti. When she sang, in the last opera particularly (though the Government caused its immediate withdrawal), the enthusiasm of the public was at its height; bouquets of flowers, and leaves of gold and silver covered her when she reappeared, in answer to frantic shouts, twenty times.

She then went again to Naples. The Neapolitans adored her. On one occasion she specially flattered them: her carriage having been overturned in the morning, she sang in the evening with her arm in a sling, rather than disappoint the audience. At Naples she pursued the same reckless course with regard to her health and strength as she did in all other places: a courageous horsewoman, and a daring swimmer, she alternated her exhausting pleasures with fatiguing studies. She made it a rule to practise music five or six hours a day, and she would go in the evening to parties, where she amused herself in a thousand different ways: making lively caricatures, doggerel verses, riddles, conundrums, *bouts-rimés*, dancing, joking, laughing, singing; and withal she attended to her professional duties with scrupulous punctuality.

On the eve of her departure, Gallo, proprietor of the Teatro Emeronnitio, came to entreat her to sing once at his establishment. He had a wife and several children, and was a very worthy man, on the verge of bankruptcy. "I will sing," answered she, "on one condition—that not a word is said about remuneration." She chose the part of Amina; the house was crammed, and the poor man was saved from ruin. A vast multitude followed her home, with an enthusiasm which amounted almost to frenzy, and the grateful manager named his theatre the Teatro Garcia. On Ash Wednesday, March 13, 1835, Madame Malibran bade the Neapolitans adieu—an eternal adieu. Radiant with glory, and crowned with flowers, she was conducted by the Neapolitans to the faubourgs amid the éclat of vivats and acclamations.

On arriving at Venice, her next appointment, as her gondola approached the quay, fanfares of trumpets announced her arrival, and an immense crowd lined the landing-places; the concourse was so great as she crossed the Place St. Marc, that she became frightened and took refuge in a church, which was soon filled, and it was with much difficulty that a passage could be opened to her hotel. Her powers were highly appreciated by the Venetians, whose enthusiasm amounted to delirium. If their idol paused at a shop on the Place St. Marc, the curious throng pressed round her, so that the police were obliged to interfere; and when she entered her gondola, she was pursued by a flock of other gondolas, which formed a sort of cortège. The city, at her departure, presented her with a diadem. She enjoyed these triumphs with a kind of girlish pleasure, unmixed with pride or exultation.

In March, 1835, the French tribunal granted the divorce from her husband, which she had been long trying to obtain; and ten months after, when the time fixed by French law had elapsed, she married M. de Beriot, March 29, 1836, in the presence of their intimate friends. The day after her marriage, she distributed 1,000 francs among the poor. The

Queen of the French presented her with a superb agraffe adorned with pearls. The couple went to live in Brussels, at the villa which the bride had purchased. Their son, Wilfrid de Beriot, was legalized by this marriage: they had had a daughter, which did not live.

During her sojourn at Milan, she had heard of the premature death of Vincenzo Bellini, on the 23rd September, 1835, and she set on foot a subscription for a tribute to the memory of the young composer, placing her own name for 400 francs at the head of the list. On exactly the same day and month of the following year she herself breathed her last.

When she took her farewell of Milan, the Milanese, as if animated by a presentiment that the parting was for ever, loaded her with marks of distinction. The people conducted her with lighted torches to the Palazzo Visconti, the gardens being brilliantly illuminated to receive her, and military music posted on the canal playing at her approach the most inspiriting melodies.

During the season of 1835 Madame Malibran was engaged by Mr. Bunn to appear at Drury Lane and Covent Garden; and for twenty-six performances, at the rate of three a week, she received no less than 3,463*l*. She performed Isolina in Mr. Balfe's new opera, *The Maid of Artois*, and also appeared in the *Sonnambula*, the *Devil's Bridge*, and in *Fidelio;* a part wherein she was by many considered to surpass even the tender and pathetic Schröder Devrient. "In her English performances," says Mr. Chorley, "her exuberance, not to say extravagance, of style, served the purpose of concealing the mediocrity, and worse, of her play-fellows."

Her labours this season were frightful. She had always been remarkable for activity, but her professional efforts now excited wonder, and even alarm. She rose at five or six in the morning, and practised in her dressing-room for several hours, at the same time inventing attitudes before the looking-glass. It was thus one day the attitude struck her which produced such an effect in *Gli Orazi*, when the news of the death of her lover is announced to the heroine. "While the rehearsals of the *Maid of Artois* were going on from day to day—and Madame Malibran's rehearsals were not so many hours of sauntering indifference—she would, immediately after they were finished, dart to one or two concerts, and perhaps conclude the day by singing at an evening party. She pursued the same course during her performance of that arduous character." She sang at concerts, at royal and noble houses, and at parties for her own amusement.

In April, 1836, just after her marriage, Madame de Beriot came to England again, and soon after her arrival went out one day with a riding-party, when being thrown from her horse, she sustained a serious injury. From this she never recovered; having neglected to attend to herself while the hurt was fresh. Not only did she refuse to be bled, not only did she conceal the affair from her husband, whom she tenderly loved, but she actually sang the same night! She was now at the height of her marvellous talent; having never ceased to improve. Her voice, always wonderful from its extent, had acquired some additional tones in the upper register, and a prodigious facility in certain *tours de force*. She performed at Covent Garden with Templeton, Seguin, and Duruset, chiefly in *Fidelio*.

In September she came again to England. Her agonies from the effects of her fall were sometimes fearful, but she struggled with all the energy of her character, all the power of her mind, against sufferings which would have crushed another; never yielding till death seized her. She was engaged at Manchester, where she was to sing at the Musical Festival. Immediately on arriving there, she went to the hotel where Lablache and the other vocalists were staying. She was then ill; but in a state of unnatural, feverish excitement. The kind-hearted Lablache, shocked at her wild gaiety, spoke to her husband—in vain. At the rehearsals she was either crying or laughing hysterically; but she persisted in going through the rehearsals, lest the public should charge her with caprice: thus exhausting herself unnecessarily when she ought to have taken rest. The day before her first performance at the Collegiate Church, she sang no less than fourteen pieces in her room at the hotel, among her Italian friends. In vain she was cautioned—in vain did her good friend Lablache endeavour to check her insane flights.

The first morning, having been carried out in hysterics, the dying cantatrice insisted on returning and singing the air of Abraham, by Cimarosa. Her profound sadness, the penetrating accents of her voice, the dejection of her aspect, made a deep impression on the audience. In the evening she went to the theatre, and despite her suffering, sang as usual. She attempted again to sing the next day, but fainted, and was carried home. By a powerful effort, she sang in the evening the duet of Andronico, by Mercadante, with Madame Caradori Allan.

Like the expiring flame, which is most brilliant at its last flicker, the voice of Maria Malibran was never more resplendent, never more pure or clear than in these her dying moments. The touching melancholy of her singing, her face, pale and expressive as that of a beautiful spectre, her accents inspired by a soul ready, as it were, to wing its way from earth, awakened an electric thrill of sympathy and admiration in the hearts of the audience. At the end of the duet, the assembly, entranced by such beauty, such genius, and forgetting the condition of the unfortunate vocalist, re-demanded its repetition with enthusiasm. The echoes of applause struck to the heart of the dying singer. Her cheeks were flushed, she raised her head, her eyes shone with preternatural fire, and she recommenced the duet. Her voice was astounding: her soul appeared to be poured forth in each note, and a brilliant shake at the top of the voice concluded this final effort.

She was carried from the theatre to her death-bed. Fainting fits, hysterical attacks, and horrible convulsions terrified those about her. The greatest sympathy was excited in Manchester, indeed all over the country, and in Paris. Bulletins of her health were issued in all the Manchester journals, and people called constantly to make inquiries. The malady made the most rapid and irresistible progress. Her last thoughts were of De Beriot. Recovering from one of her fits of death-like stupor, she anxiously asked if he had performed well, and if the public had applauded him? She died on the 23rd September, 1836, of nervous fever, at the age of twenty-nine. She had always had a presentiment that she should die young.

The death of the gifted, beloved artiste produced a painful sensation throughout Europe. She was universally and deeply regretted, and her loss was felt almost as a public calamity. It was maliciously said at the time that she sank under the mistaken treatment of her own physician, Dr. Belluomini, who was also her intimate friend, and in whom she placed the most implicit confidence. But before he could be summoned she had been treated by some resident physicians, and had been bled. When she saw Dr. Belluomini, she exclaimed, "I am a slain woman; for they have bled me."

Magnificent obsequies were paid to her in Manchester. Her remains were at first interred in the churchyard of the cathedral there, but not long after were exhumed and transported to Brussels, her mother coming to England for that purpose. There was a dispute between De Beriot and the authorities of Manchester as to his right to remove her body.

A circular chapel was raised to her memory at Lacken by De Beriot. A statue of Madame Malibran, in the costume of Norma, sculptured in white marble by Geefs, stands in the centre, faintly illumined by a single ray of light admitted from a dome, and surrounded by masses of shadow. "It appears," says the Countess de Merlin, "like a fantastic thought—like the dream of a poet."

Her first husband, Malibran, died in Paris, November, 1836, of an attack of apoplexy.

In August, 1840, De Beriot married, at Lacken, a young German, Mdlle. Huber, daughter of a magistrate of Vienna, and who, left an orphan at an early age, had been adopted by the Prince Dietrischten Preskau.

A collection of Madame Malibran's compositions was published at Paris after her death by Troupenas.

CHAPTER IX.

GIULIA GRISI.

M. Gaetano Grisi, an officer of engineers in the service of Napoleon under the then existing kingdom of Italy, had two daughters, Giuditta, born in 1802, and Giulietta, born at Milan, July 2, 1812, on the fête of St. Giulia. Their aunt, the once celebrated Grassini, was the only member of the family who was a musician, and from the mother's side they must have inherited the gift of song.

Giuditta was a singer, and enjoyed a good reputation on the Italian stage. She had a mezzo-soprano voice, almost a contralto, of a hard quality, and not very flexible, which she had much difficulty in softening. Her talents developed themselves early. At sixteen she was favourably known as a concert-singer at Milan. Two years later, in 1823, she sang at Vienna, in Rossini's *Bianca e Faliero,* with the already renowned Henrietta Sontag. She afterwards sang at the theatres of Milan, Parma, Florence, Genoa, and Venice. Her

friends considered that the mantle of the great Grassini had fallen on her shoulders, and that being trained in the same grand school, she would be able to tread closely in her aunt's footsteps.

The little Giulia's health was so delicate that her parents did not wish her to enter on the study of music, the least application being injurious to her; she was, therefore, placed for education, at the age of eight, in the convent of Mantellette, in the small town of Gorizia. But she was ambitious of following the career of her aunt, and the nuns, pleased with her childish beauty, took some pains to teach her music; she learned to play the piano very prettily, but did not make much advance in musical training.

After leaving the convent, when fourteen, her home was generally with her sister, either at Milan, or in the places where Giuditta's engagements called her. It was soon remarked that when the elder sister was practising solfeggi or studying her part, the younger would listen attentively. Giulia had an excellent ear, a quick memory, and could repeat fluently and correctly the most difficult passages which she had once heard. She astonished her family by the accuracy with which she imitated the gestures, the carriage, and even the singing of artistes whom she had opportunities of hearing. Giuditta, who appreciated these evidences of vocal and mimetic talent, would listen with delight to the lively efforts of her young sister, and then, clasping her fondly in her arms, prophesy that she would be "the glory of her race." "Thou shalt be more than thy sister, my Giuliettina," she would exclaim. "Thou shalt be more than thy aunt! It is Giuditta tells thee so: believe it." The only defect in Giulia's voice—certainly a terrible one—was a chronic hoarseness, which seemed a bar to her advancement as a vocalist.

Her parents resolved that Giulia should have regular lessons in singing; and she entered the Conservatorio of her native town, where her sister had obtained for her musical training. The early talent she developed, under the direction of the composer Marliani, was remarkable. That she might continue her studies uninterruptedly, she was sent to Bologna, to her uncle, Colonel Ragani, husband of Grassini, by whom she was put under the care of the learned Giacomo Guglielmi, son of the celebrated composer, who during three years devoted himself entirely to her musical education. Gradually the lovely quality of her voice began to be manifest, and its original blemishes disappeared; her tones acquiring depth, power, and richness.

On leaving the Conservatorio, she went to live at Bologna with her sister, who, being much occupied with her own duties, placed Giulia under the tuition of Filippo Celli. He taught her for three months only, as he was obliged to go to Rome to produce his opera of *Amalia e Palmer;* but his instructions, brief as they were, formed a solid basis for her after studies. She also received some lessons from Madame Boccabadati, a near relative of the singer of that name: from her, however, she learned but little.

By continued exertions on her own part, aided by her instructors, her musical education had advanced, and Giulia, encouraged by her friends, proposed to venture on her début on the stage. Giuditta made all the necessary arrangements with the manager of the Teatro Communale, Bologna; and the young girl appeared, 1828, in the little part of Emma, in Rossini's *Zelmira.* She was just seventeen; her voice was then a low mezzo-soprano, and she was in all the freshness of her youthful beauty. Her triumph was complete.

Giuditta shed tears of joy over the brilliant success of her sister; and Rossini, who was then in Bologna, predicted a brilliant future for the young vocalist. The director of the theatre engaged her immediately for the season of the Carnival, and in 1829 she appeared as prima donna in many operas, such as *Il Barbiere, Torvaldo e Dorliska,* and in *La Sposa di Provincia,* which last was composed expressly for her by Milototti.

So dazzling a début drew all the managerial eyes of Italy towards Giulia Grisi, and one of those Italians who are always on the look-out to decoy unwary vocalists,

Signor Lanari, impresario at Florence, flew to Bologna to secure the prize, and induced the young singer, as yet unconscious of her own value, to bind herself exclusively to his service for the term of six years, at a salary which he ought to have blushed to offer to a mediocre performer. Her father was at Milan, and could not be consulted, and the young débutante being inexperienced, the engagement was signed.

Mdlle. Grisi appeared in *I Montecchi ed i Capuletti*, which Bellini, then a young and struggling composer, had just written expressly for her sister at Venice. Few of Bellini's operas enjoyed so great a share of popularity in Italy as this; which, however, he had dashed off without premeditation in fifteen days, at the urgent request of the Venetian manager, to replace a piece which had been condemned. She also performed in *Il Barbiere di Seviglia*, and in the *Giulietta e Romeo* of Vaccai; and she was considered the most charming Juliet ever seen on the lyric stage.

Her triumph was even greater here than at Bologna. She created quite a furore. La bellissima Giulietta was hailed a Queen of Song, and became the topic of conversation amongst the dilettanti. In her second season she sang in an opera composed for her by the maestro Celli, who was charmed with the manner in which she interpreted his work *L'Ezia*, and who gave her some lessons.

In the Carnival of 1830, she appeared as Amenaïde,

in the *Vestale* of Pacini, and in *Ricciardo e Zoraide*, with the celebrated tenor Davide; also in *Tancredi*. This year she sang at Pisa, during the fête of La Luminara, a festival which recurs every five years, when the Pisans for three days illuminate their city most brilliantly. On this occasion the Pisans dedicate festal offerings to all the saints, interchange splendid repasts, and have operas performed twice a day. Giulia Grisi, therefore, sang in *Semiramide* in the morning, and *Otello* in the evening.

Lanari having now made a little fortune by his lucky speculation, coolly transferred his young prima donna, for a handsome consideration, to Crivelli, then director of La Scala. The company included Madame Pisaroni, Giuditta Grisi, and Porto. Giulia first performed in a new opera by Pacini, *Il Corsare*, founded on Lord Byron's poem of the *Corsair*, in which she took the part of Medora.

It was at Milan that Mdlle. Grisi became acquainted with Pasta, whom she ardently admired, and who took a friendly interest in her. Pasta declared, "I can honestly return to you the compliments paid me by your aunt, and say that I believe you are worthy to succeed us." Here she enjoyed the advantage of studying the great lyric tragédienne, with whom she occasionally performed: not a look, a tone, a gesture of her grand model escaped her. She was given the part of Jane Seymour in Donizetti's *Anna Bolena*, which she looked and acted to perfection, Pasta personating the unfortunate Queen. Madame Pasta, struck with the genius displayed by her young rival, exclaimed, "Tu iras loin! tu prendras ma place! tu seras Pasta!" Bellini, who was then in Milan, engaged in the composition of his *Norma*, overwhelmed her with applause and congratulations, intermingled with allusions to the part he had in contemplation for her; that of Adalgisa.

In November, 1831, there was a strenuous rivalry between the two theatres of Milan, La Scala and the Carcano. The vocal company at the latter comprised Pasta, Lina Roser (now Madame Balfe), Elisa Orlandi, Eugénie Martinet, and other ladies; Rubini, Mariani, and Galli being the leading male singers. The composers were Bellini, Donizetti, and Majocchi. At the Scala, which was still under the direction of Crivelli, then a very old man, were Giulietta Grisi, Amalia Schutz, and Pisaroni, with Mari, Bonfigli, Pocchini, Anbaldi, etc. To this company Giuditta Grisi was added, and a new opera by Coccia, entitled *Enrico di Montfort*, was brought out, supported by the talents of the sisters Grisi; but it proved a failure. In December Madame Pasta transferred her services to the Scala, and Donzelli arrived to resume his place as primo tenor. Donzelli was, if not absolutely the first, in the very front rank of tenor singers. His voice was clear, brilliant, and powerful, with a metallic tone of vibrating quality; his conception was vigorous, his manner was energetic or tender as the expression demanded, and his style at once forcible and florid.

Bellini's new opera of *Norma* was immediately put in rehearsal. To Pasta, of course, was assigned the character of the Druid priestess, and to Giulia Grisi was confided the graceful part of Adalgisa; Donzelli was Pollio. Bellini was quite confident of the success of his opera, and during the rehearsals, while seated at the pianoforte in the orchestra, would watch with delight the careful study the singers were making of their parts. Pasta, at the last rehearsal, took much notice of Giulietta, and complimented her both on her voice and on her conception of the character of Adalgisa, frequently turning to Bellini, and exclaiming, in her usual mixture of Italian and French, "Benissima! bene—très bien—pas mal, la piccola!" On the 1st January, 1832, *Norma* was produced. Great expectations were entertained by the public, for the music of Bellini was exceedingly popular, and it was said this would be his masterpiece. The Scala was crowded to the ceiling, and Bellini seated himself at the pianoforte in high spirits.

Norma was the favourite work of its gifted composer. One day when he was in Paris, a lady asked him which of his operas he considered to most nearly approach perfection? The question was certainly rather *broad.* Poor Bellini, naturally modest and sensitive, blushed scarlet. He made some evasive reply, but the lady persisted. "If," said she, "you were at sea with all your *partitions*, and the ship were sinking——".

"Ah!" cried he, without allowing her to finish, "I would leave all to save *La Norma!*"

Strange to say, the first reception of this opera was by no means brilliant. The audience did not care about the chorus of Priests; Donzelli exerted himself in vain to charm them with his cabaletta: the audience shrugged their shoulders and pronounced it to be "commonplace;" and even *Casta Diva* made no impression, though Pasta had never, perhaps, sung so well. Bellini trembled with anxiety. Then Adalgisa appeared, and began "Sgombra è la sacra selva;" the clear resonant tones of Giulia Grisi's voice touched the hearts of the listeners, and they began to applaud. Nevertheless, as the curtain fell on the first act, Pasta regarded the piece as a fiasco, and her forebodings were shared by the other performers. The second act went coldly till the duet between Norma and Adalgisa, "Deh! con te!" which created a furore and was encored. Then Pasta turned to Giulia, and exclaimed in a low tone, "Ecco i conscitori!" The success of the opera, which had been despaired of, was now assured, and *Norma* was performed forty times during the Carnival.

Encouraged by Pasta, Giulia Grisi declared that she, too, would become a great tragedian. "How I should love to play Norma!" she exclaimed to Bellini, one night behind the scenes. "Wait twenty years and we shall see." "I will play Norma in spite of you, and in less than twenty years," she retorted. The young man smiled incredulously, and muttered, "A poco! a poco!" But Grisi kept her word.

Her genius was now fully appreciated, and she had obtained one of those triumphs which form the basis of a great renown. With astonishing ease she passed from Semiramide to Anna Bolena, then to Desdemona, to Donna Anna, to Elena in the *Donna del Lago*. In Semiramide she had that lofty and gracious manner which is peculiar to her.

The young artiste had now learnt her true value, and was aware of the injury she was suffering from remaining in the service to which she had foolishly bound herself; she was now twenty-four, and time was passing away. Her father's repeated endeavours to obtain more reasonable terms for his daughter from Lanari proved fruitless; he urged that, his daughter having entered into the contract without his knowledge, and while she was a minor, it was illegal. "Then if you knew absolutely nothing of the matter, and it was altogether without your cognizance," retorted Lanari, imperturbably, "how did it happen that her salary was always paid to you!"

Intolerant of injustice, and indignant at the advantage taken of her, Giulietta suddenly broke her engagement. Giuditta and her aunt, Madame Grassini Ragani, were in Paris, and to them she resolved to fly.

The Carnival was crowded at Milan, and the manager had engaged Pasta for twenty extra nights, relying on Grisi as seconda donna. Having gained her father's consent to her plan, Giulia went to Marliani, a warm and devoted friend, and begged his assistance; he promised to see her across the frontier, and to provide for her a quick transit through Switzerland to France.

The fugitives started late on a Friday, the Opera being closed on that night, and arrived safely at Bellinzona; when they suddenly discovered, to their horror, that they had forgotten their passports. It was decided that Giulia should make use of her maid's passport to cross the frontier, as she and the girl bore some resemblance in point of height, age, and complexion. Marliani had no resource but to return for the papers; and the fair cantatrice once in safety, was to await him and the femme-de-chambre on the other side the frontier. But urged by fear, she resumed her flight, and for eleven days and nights pursued her solitary journey, through bad roads and over mountain passes covered with snow. It was not until she threw herself into her aunt's arms, half dead with fatigue and terror, that she remembered, too late, her promise to wait for her dear old teacher.

Giuditta and Madame Grassini welcomed her with joy, and it only remained to obtain an engagement. Rossini, Robert, and Severini formed the triumvirate who governed the Opera. Rossini remembered that he had predicted a glowing future for Giulia Grisi some four years previously, and an arrangement was made without any difficulty for her to appear at the Favart; not as a débutante, but with a definite engagement to replace Madame Malibran. She appeared for the first time before a Parisian audience on the 13th October, 1832, in *Semiramide*. She at once became a favourite, and during the season of six months she increased in power and rose higher in the opinion of the public.

In November, 1832, Giuditta Grisi (who had appeared in London during the summer at the King's Theatre,) made her début in Bellini's *La Straniera*. Her sonorous, vibrating voice, so full of charm and beauty, the mingled grace and energy of her singing and acting, her beautiful face, grave and expressive, her gestures replete with truth and originality, her large and noble manner of phrasing the music, obtained for her a triumph. The sisters also sang together in Bellini's *I Montecchi ed i Capuletti*, and Giuditta looked a gallant young cavalier.

Then followed *Don Giovanni*, in which Giulia, as Zerlina, was graceful and charming; but her figure was too commanding, her voice too regal for the village coquette. Rubini was Don Ottavio, Tamburini Don Giovanni. Tamburini was a singer of great brilliancy and power; his voice was a fine baritone, well defined, round, rich, clear, and of wonderful flexibility. He was an accomplished actor, full of spirit and gaiety; he was handsome, his figure was manly, and his air noble and prepossessing.

Immediately after *Don Giovanni*, Giulia Grisi appeared as Anna Bolena, with Madame Tadolini, Santini, and Rubini; when, despite the unavoidable comparison with Pasta, she won an ovation.

Giuditta retired at the end of the season, having amassed a competent fortune, and marrying an Italian gentleman, retired to Italy. She died May 1, 1840, at her country seat at Cremona.

Giulia also retired; but she reappeared on the 1st October, 1833, as Anna Bolena, with Tamburini and two new candidates for public favour, Mdlle. Schutz and the young Russian tenor, Ivanoff. It was remarked that Mdlle. Grisi had improved singularly; she had passed the six months of leisure in the study of her art, and the result was that the once trembling débutante had become a Queen of Song. Her name was now mentioned in the same breath with that of Catalani, Pasta, Malibran. She was no longer Jane Seymour or Adalgisa, but Anna Bolena—Norma!

As a singer, she was to be placed apart from all contemporary artistes. Her gifts, like her beauty, were rare and exceptional. She united the nobleness, the tragic inspiration, of Pasta, with the fire and energy of Malibran. Her voice, a pure soprano of the very finest quality, extended over two octaves; and she could sing without an effort to C in alt. Her low notes were occasionally weak, but the middle ones were full, mellow, and deliciously sweet. Her intonation was exquisitely just, and her execution neat and finished. Not a note escaped her that was not irreproachable. As an actress, she had all the qualities which go to make a great tragedian. She seldom represented the same situation twice in the same manner, yet she was always lofty and noble—a magnificent woman, a superb tragedian, an exquisite singer.

In October, 1833, she appeared as Rosina, in *Il Barbiere di Seviglia*, Tamburini performing Figaro, and Rubini Almaviva. She sang the variations of Rode, in the lesson scene, in a manner which produced an electric effect. This opera was followed by *La Gazza Ladra*, in which the young prima donna obtained a triumph as Ninetta. Tamburini performed the part of her father, and Ivanoff took for the first time the rôle of Gianetto, the betrothed of Ninetta. After this, Bellini's *I Montecchi ed i Capuletti* was performed; Caroline Ungher, who made her début that season, supporting the character of Romeo. Madame Ungher was decidedly clever, but her appearance was woefully against her, being that of "an under-sized, colourless woman," with a plain countenance expressive of nothing in particular. In December, *Don Giovanni* was produced. Giulia Grisi this time took the more appropriate part of Donna Anna. Madame Ungher was Zerlina; Madame Schutz, Elvira; Tamburini performed Don Giovanni; Santini, Leporello.

Bellini's last opera, *I Puritani*, was composed by him at Paris in 1834, and performed for the first time on January 24th, 1835, with Grisi, Rubini, Tamburini, and Lablache—an unrivalled quartett—in the principal characters.

Its production created the utmost enthusiasm, and the duet, "Suona la tromba," especially was echoed by thunders of applause. Rossini, writing of this morceau to a friend at Milan, said, "I need not describe the duo for the two basses. You must have heard it where you are:" a remark very just, but more sarcastic than complimentary. Bellini was made a member of the Legion of Honour, and received the most flattering marks of distinction from Government. He arranged with the Académie to write a French opera, and was already meditating a new work for the San Carlo; but the perseverance with which he pursued his labours was the fatal cause of his death. Eight months after the production of *I Puritani*, he expired, fancying in his last moments of delirium that he was present at a representation of this opera at the Salle Favart.

In 1834, Mdlle. Grisi came to London, and made her début at Her Majesty's Theatre, April 8, in *La Gazza Ladra*. Tumultuous applause greeted this bright musical star. Her charming person, beautiful countenance, fascinating manner, and delightful voice, made her a favourite at once. On April 22, she appeared as Desdemona, in *Otello*. Rubini was the Moor: his Otello was, with the exception of Garcia's, the best ever seen on the stage. Tamburini was Iago; Ivanoff, Rodrigo. Mdlle. Grisi also proved herself a worthy successor of Pasta in *Anna Bolena*.

"Though, naturally enough, in some respects inexperienced on her first appearance in England," observes Mr. Chorley, "Giulia Grisi was not incomplete. And what a soprano voice was hers!—rich, sweet; equal throughout its compass of two octaves (from C to C) without a break, or a note which had to be managed. The voice subdued the audience on her first appearance, ere *Di piacer* was done."

Mdlle. Grisi was an indefatigable concert-singer, and on one occasion she sang at five different concerts, gratuitously, on the same morning. At a grand festival at York, she sang fourteen pieces, of which four had Latin words, and four English. Malibran having received forty guineas each evening at this festival the year before, Mdlle. Grisi refused to accept a lesser sum, and she obtained it; but to show that it was merely a point of principle, she sent to the poor each day the forty guineas which she received. She was made an honorary governor of Westminster Hospital, in acknowledgment of the services which her talents and charity had rendered to that institution.

In December, Mdlle. Grisi appeared as Norma; and thenceforth Norma was her greatest character.

"In this character, Grisi," observes a writer in the *Musical World*, "is not to be approached, for all those attributes which have given her her best distinction are displayed therein in their fullest splendour. Her singing may be rivalled, but hardly her embodiment of ungovernable and vindictive emotion. There are certainly parts in the lyric drama of Italy this fine artiste has made her own: this is one of the most striking, and we have a faith in its unreachable superiority—in its completeness as a whole—that is not to be disturbed. Her delivery of 'Casta Diva' is a transcendent effort of vocalization. In the scene where she discovers the treachery of Pollio, and discharges upon his guilty head a torrent of withering and indignant reproof, she exhibits a power, bordering on the sublime, which belongs exclusively to her; giving to the character of the insulted priestess a dramatic importance which would be remarkable even if entirely separated from the vocal pre-eminence with which it is allied. But in all its aspects the performance is as near perfection as rare and exalted genius can make it, and the singing of the actress and the acting of the singer are alike conspicuous for excellence and power. Whether in depicting the quiet repose of love, the agony of abused confidence, the infuriate resentment of jealousy, or the influence of feminine piety, there is always the best reason for admiration, accompanied in the more tragic moments with that sentiment of awe which greatness of conception and vigour of execution could alone suggest."

From 1834, Mdlle. Grisi continued to sing alternately in Paris and in London. "In 1834," to again quote Mr. Chorley, "she commanded an exactness of execution not always kept up by her during the after years of her reign. Her shake was clear and rapid; her scales were certain; every interval was taken without hesitation by her. Nor has any woman ever more thoroughly commanded every gradation of force than she—in those early days especially;—not using the contrast of loud and soft too violently, but capable of any required violence, of any advisable delicacy. In the singing of certain slow movements pianissimo, such as the girl's prayer on the road to execution in *La Gazza*, or as the cantabile in the last scene of *Anna Bolena* (which we know as 'Home, sweet Home'), the clear, penetrating beauty of her reduced tones (different in quality from the whispering semi-ventriloquism which was one of Mademoiselle Lind's most favourite effects) was so unique as to reconcile the ear to a certain shallowness of expression in her rendering of the words and the situation.

"At that time the beauty of sound was more remarkable (in such passages as I have just spoken of) than the depth of feeling. When the passion of the actress was roused—as in *La Gazza*, during the scene with her deserter father—with the villanous magistrate, or in the prison with her lover, or on her trial before sentence was passed—her glorious notes, produced without difficulty or stint, rang through the house like a clarion, and were truer in their vehemence to the emotion of the scene than were those wonderfully subdued sounds, in the penetrating tenuity of which there might be more or less artifice. From the first, the vigour always went more closely home to the heart than the tenderness in her singing; and her acting and her vocal delivery—though the beauty of face and voice, the mouth that never distorted itself, the sounds that never wavered, might well mislead the generality of her auditors—were to be resisted by none."

In February, 1836, during the performance of Donizetti's *Marino Faliero*, at the moment when Giulia Grisi was entering her box in the course of the third act, she perceived near the door, as if in ambuscade, an individual whose declarations of love had already annoyed her for some months. She uttered an exclamation, and M. Robert, who accompanied her, requested the intruder to retire. He bowed, murmuring some unintelligible excuses, when Colonel Ragani, Grisi's uncle, joined the party, and attempted to remonstrate on his unbecoming conduct. The intruder drew a sword from the cane which he carried, and menaced all who surrounded him; a scuffle ensued, and the *mêlée* was ended by the arrival of the commissary of police. The brawler, whose name was Dupuzet, was condemned to one month's imprisonment and a fine of sixteen francs. M. Dupuzet, who was some thirty-five years of age, was known as the author of the *Legende of Jehanne la Lucelle,* and the *Démon de Socrate.*

On Sunday, April 24, 1836, Giulia Grisi was married to M. Auguste Gérard de Melcy, a French gentleman of independent fortune. On her marriage she went with her husband to reside at the fine Château de Vaucresson, which she had purchased some time previously. The admired prima donna did not leave the stage, but continued to perform during the summer in London, and during the winter at Paris.

In 1837 she appeared in London in *Semiramide,* with Rubini and Tamburini. The most remarkable performance of the season, however, was *Don Giovanni.* The excitement to hear her as Donna Anna was intense. Long ere the doors were opened both entrances of the theatre were surrounded by crowds; and, owing to one of the doors not being properly opened, several persons were slightly hurt. Many ladies turned back frightened; some, bolder, reached the pit, or the entrance to the pit, with no greater misfortune than a very considerable derangement of their dress. After some laughing and some disputing, as many as possible of the unfortunates who could not penetrate farther than the lobbies, were accommodated on the stage: there were more than a hundred persons at the wings; and it was supposed that the audience altogether consisted of more than four thousand people.

Madame Grisi realized the highest expectations of the crowded assembly. Madame Albertazzi was the Zerlina; Tamburini, Don Giovanni; Lablache, Leporello; and Rubini, Ottavio.

At the last representation of *Otello* this season, Madame Pasta, who was then in England, proved the sincerity of her friendship, for she many times applauded her young rival; who, after the opera, went to the box of the Queen of Lyric Tragedy to thank her for such homage.

Don Giovanni was performed at the Théâtre Italien, January 14, 1838, with the strong cast of Mesdames Grisi, Persiani, and Albertazzi; with Rubini, Tamburini, and Lablache. About an hour after the doors were closed, the Opera House was discovered to be on fire, and was very shortly reduced to a heap of ruins—an accident supposed to have arisen from some of the fireworks used in the infernal gulf into which the commandant hurls the profligate. Severini leaped from a window near the top of the building, and was instantly killed. Robert only saved himself by means of a ladder-rope; and Rossini, who had an apartment in the theatre, escaped by simply being absent: but the whole of his musical library, said to be valued at upwards of 200,000 francs, was destroyed, with many rare manuscripts.

In 1838, M. Duponchel, the director of the Opéra, was looking for another tenor to replace Duprez, as he had replaced Adolphe Nourrit by that admirable singer, and at last his eager eyes lighted upon a handsome young refugee officer of two-and-twenty, named Candia. M. Candia, who was the son of a Piedmontese general, and had been, besides, an officer in the Piedmontese guard, had for some time been the cynosure of attention in certain Parisian circles. As he moved in aristocratic society, his expenses were necessarily heavy; and he dared not ask his father for pecuniary assistance, the old gentleman being a severe disciplinarian, and very angry with his son.

M. Candia had been often told that he had a hundred thousand francs of income in his throat, and Duponchel volunteered to give him fifteen hundred francs a month to begin with, if he would appear at the Opéra. He hesitated, on account of his aristocratic birth and his patrician father, and could not make up his mind to sign the name of Candia to a theatrical contract; but dining one day at the house of the Countess de Merlin with the Prince Belgioso, M. Duponchel, and many others, M. Candia was induced to accept the proposal of M. Duponchel, and he compromised with his family pride by signing his Christian name only—that of Mario.

On the 2nd December, 1838, after a severe course of study under the direction of Michelet, Ponchard, and Bordogni, Signor Mario appeared in the part of Robert le Diable. In spite of his agitation, he was triumphantly successful. "What a delicious voice!" was the cry. "Why, he will replace Rubini!" Higher praise could not have been bestowed.

The season of 1839 in London was chiefly remarkable for the production of *Lucrezia Borgia*, in which Madame Grisi presented a splendid contrast to her equally truthful conceptions of such parts as Elvira and Norma: it served also to introduce to the English public Signor Mario, who appeared as Gennaro. Such characters as Lucrezia Borgia seemed created for Grisi. The more elevated the character the more suited to her. The most fleeting touches, the most massive shadows, were boldly portrayed with a powerful yet light hand. Love in all its phases she delineated as no other artiste had the skill to do. Dramatic, impassioned as Desdemona, she pictured love in all its ardour, its unsullied purity, its despair; as Anna Bolena, she softly shadowed forth "love in its melancholy and its regrets," and as Norma, she painted love in tints of fire: love in its jealousy, its guilt, its scathing fury; as Lucrezia, she displayed love in all its maternal intensity, its vengeful cruelty.

In 1840, Madame Grisi won fresh laurels from her English admirers in *Roberto Devereux*, and also in *Il Barbiere di Seviglia*, with Mario. "The Five"—Mesdames Grisi and Persiani, Signori Rubini, Tamburini, and Lablache—came to England as usual in 1841; but in 1842 Madame Grisi did not appear at Her Majesty's Theatre.

In January, 1843, *Don Pasquale*, one of the sprightliest and pleasantest operas ever written, was placed in rehearsal by Donizetti at the Théâtre Italien. Its reception at rehearsal was ominous: despite the beauty of the music, which was in his happiest vein, the orchestra kept a dead silence. Not a sound of satisfaction, not a token of approbation, was afforded by the musical jury. The two directors stood by trembling for its success; but Donizetti listened and shrugged his shoulders, and taking the arm of his friend M. Dormoy, the publisher, quietly left the theatre. "Let them alone," he coolly said; "they know nothing about it. I know what *Don Pasquale* wants. Come with me." On reaching home, Donizetti hurried upstairs to his bedroom, and in a drawer beneath an old battered pianoforte, he pulled out from amidst a quantity of music what appeared to be a song.

"Take this," said he to M. Dormoy; "this is what *Don Pasquale* requires. Carry it at once to Mario, that he may learn it without delay, and tell him that he must rehearse it this evening." This song was

"Com' è gentil." The serenade was sung with the accompaniment of a tambourine, the accompanyist being Lablache himself, who was concealed from the eyes of the audience.

It is needless to say that *Don Pasquale* was a success. The same year it was produced in London. This season also Madame Grisi appeared as Ninetta before the audience of Her Majesty's Theatre.

In 1847 the memorable operatic schism took place, which led to the formation of "the Royal Italian Opera" at Covent Garden Theatre. The principal members of the company of Her Majesty's Theatre who seceded from that house and joined the new establishment were Madame Grisi, Madame Persiani, Signor Mario, and Signor Tamburini; and the company was strengthened by the addition of several eminent performers previously unknown in England, of whom Mdlle. Alboni was the chief. The lessee of Her Majesty's Theatre endeavoured to make head against this defection by engaging the services of Jenny Lind, who became the great support of the old house, as Grisi was of the new. The Royal Italian Opera opened, in the beginning of the season of 1847, with *Semiramide*, Grisi appearing as the Assyrian Queen, and Alboni as Arsace. The vast theatre was crowded to the doors; the representation was splendid, and the excitement of the public was extreme. In all the subsequent vicissitudes of the

Royal Italian Opera, Grisi steadily adhered to it, and it was on its boards that she took her final leave of the English public.

Madame Grisi, probably alarmed by the Revolution of February, abandoned the Opera of Paris in 1848. During the season of that year in London, she added the part of Leonora in *La Favorita* to her repertoire.

In 1851, Madame Grisi repaired to St. Petersburg with Signor Mario. Her benefit, in February, 1852, was a perfect ovation: the opera was *Lucrezia Borgia*, during which she was recalled twenty times; and after the performance the Czar presented her with a Cashmere shawl worth 4,000 roubles (about 800*l*.), a tiara of pearls and diamonds, and a ring of great value.

In 1854, after more than twenty years of uninterrupted triumph, Madame Grisi, with Signor Mario, gave what were announced as "farewell performances." The operas in which she appeared included *Norma*, *Lucrezia Borgia*, *Don Pasquale*, *Gli Ugonotti*, *La Favorita*. The first, given June 1, was *Norma*, Madame Grisi performing Norma; Mdlle. Maria, Adalgisa; Tamberlik, Pollio; and Lablache, Oroveso; the last performance, given August 7, consisted of the first act of *Norma*, and the three first acts of *Gli Ugonotti*, in which Mario sustained the principal tenor part.

"Rarely in her best days," said one critic, "had Grisi been heard with greater effect, and never were her talents as an actress more conspicuously displayed." At the conclusion of the performance, the departing singer received an ovation. Bouquets were flung in profusion, vociferous applause rang through the theatre, and when she reappeared the whole house rose: the emotion which was evinced by her admirers was evidently shared by herself.

Madame Grisi then left Liverpool with Signor Mario, for New York. The terms of the engagement were 17,000*l.* for six months. The two artistes made their début at Castle Garden, August 18, in *Lucrezia Borgia.* Their arrival created the greatest excitement; nothing else was talked of for the moment. They performed seventy times altogether in America. The manager, Mr. Hackett, declared at a farewell dinner given to the two celebrated singers, that he had gained nearly 12,000*l.* by their engagement.

On returning from New York, Madame Grisi was prevailed on to postpone her resolve of retiring, and to reappear in London, May, 1855, as Leonora in *La Favorita.* *Don Pasquale* was given in June, having the attraction of being performed by the four singers for whom it was originally written. Grisi next appeared at the Théâtre Italien, in 1856 and 1857. She was coldly received by the Parisians in *Semiramide* and *Lucrezia Borgia,* but conquered the sympathies of the public in *Norma,* in which she supplied by dramatic energy the obvious failure of her voice.

During 1856 she was singing at Drury Lane Theatre, with Madame Gassier, Madame Rudersdorff, and Herr Formes; in 1857 she was performing with a fine company in Dublin; in March, 1858, she was again in Paris, having been engaged by Calzado, director of the Théâtre Italien; from Paris she returned to London.

Madame Grisi performed at Madrid in 1859. The Theatre Royal opened Thursday, October 6, with great éclat, under the direction of Signor Mario. The house was crowded, and among the audience were many of the most distinguished persons of the Court of Spain. Grisi appeared as Norma, and Mario as Pollio. During the first act, some of the audience, influenced by an unaccountable impulse, insulted Madame Grisi in a most disgraceful manner: she was obliged to make a written appeal to the Spanish public, which had the effect of propitiating the audience on her second appearance; but on this occasion Mario was ill, and the performance came to an abrupt termination.

The season of 1861 witnessed the final retirement of the great prima donna, who gave some farewell performances at the Royal Italian Opera in *Norma*, and some other favourite operas.

"A quarter of a century," says Mr. Chorley, "is a fair length of reign for any Queen—a brilliant one for an Opera Queen of these modern times, when 'wear and tear' are so infinitely greater than they used to be. The supremacy of Madame Grisi has been secured and prolonged by a combination of qualities rare at any period. In our day there has been no woman so beautiful, so liberally endowed with voice and with dramatic impulse as herself—Catalani excepted. In many respects Madame Grisi has been more satisfactory than her gorgeous predecessor—more valuable to her public, because less exacting. . . . . As an artiste, calculated to engage and retain the average public, without trick or affectation, and to satisfy, by her balance of charming attributes—by the assurance, moreover, that she was giving the best she knew how to give—she satisfied even those who had received much greater pleasure, and had been impressed with much deeper emotion, in the performances of others. I have never tired of Madame Grisi, during five-and-twenty years;—but I have never been, in her case, under one of those spells of intense enjoyment and sensation which make an epoch in life, and which leave a print on memory never to be cancelled by any later attraction—never to be forgotten so long as life and power to receive shall endure."

CHAPTER X.

CLARA ANASTASIA NOVELLO.

WITH the name of Novello there are many art-associations. Vincent Novello was a distinguished composer of vocal music, chiefly for the service of the Papal Church. He was even more eminent as an editor, his arrangement of the masses of Haydn and Mozart being in use in every Roman Catholic chapel throughout the kingdom, while his name is distinguished by his noble edition of the sacred works of Purcell. He was one of the original members of the Philharmonic Society, and in the old days, before the "Conductor" of musical performances became a separate branch of the profession, Vincent Novello used, alternately with his brother members, to preside at the pianoforte at the Society's concerts: he subsequently became the responsible director.

All his family have shown themselves to possess talent and energy, and some have become distinguished for their abilities. His son Alfred, himself a musician, has earned the gratitude of the lovers of music by the publication of classical music arranged by his father in a cheap form; another son, Edward, who died young, evinced no ordinary talent as an artist: in which pursuit Miss Emma Novello also made some proficiency. Miss Sabilla Novello made a favourable impression as a vocalist, resigning the arduous career to devote herself to the production of theoretical works on the art. Mrs. Cowden Clarke, devoted to literature, is a writer of tales and essays, and has gained world-wide celebrity as the compiler of a *Concordance to Shakspeare;* and another sister, who was a singer at the English Opera House when it was under the direction of Mr. Arnold, retired from the stage on her marriage with Mr. Serle, a dramatic author and actor, and a political writer.

The brightest star in the cluster is Clara Novello, born June 10, 1818, in Oxford Street, London. Her gifts, which were developed early, came to her by inheritance. When almost an infant she commenced her preparatory studies under the care of Miss Hill, of York, and then under the direction of Mr. John Robinson, also of that city. In 1824 she returned to London.

Her "clear childish treble" was admired by all her friends; she could sing, amongst other difficult songs, "The Soldier tir'd," that trying air in the *Beggar's Opera,* "Cease your funning," and many pieces of a similar kind requiring brilliant execution. "Her father's house," says one of her biographers, "was a gathering-place of many of the most eminent literary men of that notable literary period. Leigh Hunt, Hazlitt, Keats, Shelley, were more or less frequent guests of her paternal home, and others, not less renowned for wit and wisdom, were members of the brilliant circle; Charles Lamb, for one, as unmusical as he was humorous, enjoyed the meetings, though he had no sense for the occasional music, which was the chief attraction; and, in his wonderful *Chapter on Ears,* he describes these very reunions."

The year of her return home, the little Clara went with her parents to France. There was a vacancy for a candidate in the Conservatoire de Musa Sacra, at Paris, and Fétis, who was charmed with the little English warbler, advised her father to apply. The instruction being gratuitous, there was of course great competition; Mr. Novello, however, went to M. Choron, who was at the head of the establishment, and laid before him the claims of his daughter Clara. It was necessary that the youthful candidate should undergo a trial and examination previously to admission, and the child, young as she was—only six years—sang courageously before M. Choron. The worthy musician was not a man to frighten anybody, it is true: he was a little round personage, with fine delicate features, an animated, benevolent physiognomy, and a man of infinite wit and of varied acquirements. M. Choron did not understand or appreciate "The Soldier tir'd," and he required another specimen of her ability, in a style with which he was more familiar. The child, nothing daunted, sang the "Agnus Dei" from Mozart's Mass in F, in the execution of which she displayed such genuine musical feeling, and so much promise, that she was unhesitatingly preferred over nineteen competitors.

The little girl's studies in the seminary were principally directed to sacred music, in which she made such rapid progress, that she was soon capable of sustaining a part in the performances of the pupils. At one of the public exhibitions, Clara had the honour of singing before the King, Charles X., and the Royal family. Prince Polignac, who was present, paid her some kind and encouraging compliments. She was so young at the time that she had to be placed on a stool that she might be seen by the audience. It was in this academy that Clara acquired her solid and firm sostenuto, from singing, without instrumental accompaniment, the choral pieces of Palestrina, Leo, Handel, and other composers.

For six years she continued the course of instruction afforded by the Conservatoire. In the Revolution of July, however, the institution, being dependent on the Government, was broken up; and Clara was of course immediately removed. As she was hurried through the turbulent streets, "meeting in her progress the wounded and dying, the horrors of the scene produced so strong an effect upon her nervous system, that upon her arrival at her friend's house, she sank into a sleeping stupor, in which she remained thirty-six hours; and thus, in all probability, was saved from an attack of brain fever."

In 1833, when she was only fourteen years old, an age when most singers are only commencing their studies, Clara Novello made her début before an English audience at a benefit concert given by Mrs. Sewell, at Windsor, where she took part in the duet, "Forsake me not," from Spohr's *Last Judgment*, and sang a little ballad, "Chagrin d'Amour." She sang at the Ancient Concerts, and at the Philharmonic Concerts—being the youngest vocalist that ever appeared at the performances of this society; also at many provincial musical festivals. And at the great Musical Festival held in Westminster Abbey in 1834—from which may be dated the progress, if not the origin, of the Sacred Harmonic Society—Clara Novello was one of the principal singers.

In August, 1836, Mr. John Barnett's opera, the *Mountain Sylph*, being revived at the English Opera House, Clara Novello appeared as Jessie, Miss Shirreff taking the part of the Sylph. Clara acquitted herself extremely well, especially in the concerted music. At the great Musical Festival in Manchester, in the next month, to which a melancholy interest is attached in consequence of the death of Madame Malibran, Clara Novello was one of the vocalists. She was even then thought highly of, though singing by the side of that gifted performer. Her lovely voice, her refinement of style, were beginning to make a profound impression. The other singers were Madame Caradori Allan, Mrs. Shaw, Mrs. Bishop, Signori Ivanoff and Lablache, Braham, Phillips, &c.

"Tuesday evening preceding the Festival," says Mrs. Novello, "Malibran not only gave Clara Novello some excellent advice upon her appearance in public (doubly valuable from her acknowledged superior style of effective costume, both on the stage and in private), but actually took down and re-dressed my daughter's hair, and, with her accustomed freedom from envy, kept admiring the long silky tresses as they passed through her fingers, finishing the friendly operation by inserting a double-headed silver pin in the plait, of which she begged her acceptance, kindly adding, 'You will not like it the less because I have worn it in Amina.' The delight experienced by the young aspirant may be imagined, who doted upon her as a woman and an artist. 'It is a talisman,' she exclaimed, 'and I shall sing better from this night.'"

Clara had many pieces to sing, all of which she executed admirably, both airs and concerted music. In the beautiful duet by Marcello, "Qual anelante" (on Wednesday morning), she sang with the dying Malibran. The unrivalled prima donna "had set her mind upon its producing a great effect," says Mrs. Novello, "and when she arranged with Clara the cadence they were to introduce, she refused to write it down, saying in her kind tone of encouragement, 'You will follow me; I am quite sure of you, and of its being encored.' The effect was, indeed, as if both singers had been inspired. When requested to repeat it, Malibran exclaimed, 'I will sing it fifty times; and as to Clara, she is a good-natured little thing, and will do anything you require of her.' Just before they began it a second time, her eye caught mine, and she whispered, 'Clara, how pleased mamma looks!'"

Malibran was inspired by a strong affection for her young friend. Mrs. Novello nursed her in her dying moments, and in the course of many confidences, poor Maria spoke of her husband, De Beriot, and of her old comrade, Lablache, with the warmest admiration and affection; and of Clara in the same manner. "I love very few persons," she energetically exclaimed; "but those I do love, I *love*," and her eyes beamed with intense devotion and fervency. "You need not be anxious for your daughter. She is in the right way. She cannot fail of obtaining the highest rank in the profession, with her voice and the education she has received."

Clara was strenuously advised by Malibran, it is said, to go at once to Italy and study for the stage. Certain existing engagements, at the Worcester Festival and elsewhere, however, detained her at home for some months. Her style was already formed to a great extent, and she wisely refrained from forcing her voice. As a favourite with the public her position was established, and for it she was indebted to nothing but her own merit. Never did vocalist owe less to favouritism or personal efforts to win applause.

"Her style is purely correct and rational," says a critic of the period. "She takes no unwarrantable liberty with her author, and what graces she introduces are never redundant or at variance with the character of her music. Her *sostenuto* is remarkable for firmness, equality, and steadiness. This valuable qualification in her singing is attributable to her early practice of the long suspensions that constantly occur in the choral music of Palestrina, and which formed part of her almost daily lessons while in Paris. The chief characteristic of her singing is sweetness and equability, without effort; indeed, whether executing a Tyrolean ballad, or that exceedingly arduous scene, *Tu m'abbandoni*, of Spohr, her manner is equally composed."

Her voice was a high soprano, two octaves in compass, from D to D, pure, open, brilliant, clear, and liquid as a well-tuned silver bell, and extremely sympathetic, combining the fulness and richness of the contralto with the compass of the mezzo-soprano. In the upper register some of the tones were wonderfully touching. Not a trace of affectation or display was ever perceptible in her singing.

About this time the rising young vocalist received a pressing request from Mendelssohn to sing at Leipzig. The maestro, in his first visits to England, had constantly joined the social gatherings at the house of Mr. Vincent Novello, and had then learned to appreciate the young Clara. "It is said that in summer weather, parties were frequently formed, of which he was one and Malibran another, for excursions in the fields round London. On these occasions, as on all others, music was essential to the day's enjoyment; accordingly, the masterpieces of the great Italian and English composers would form the necessary baggage of the caravan of pleasure; and with these spread out before them, seated on the grass beneath the shade of the hedgerows, and beyond the chance of interruption, the cheerful group would sing the madrigals or the motets, the part songs or anthems, which delighted their forefathers." Mendelssohn, having thus had every opportunity of discovering the rich musical gifts of Miss Novello, and fully estimating them, now invited her to sing at the famous Gewandhaus Concerts, which were under his direction.

In October, 1837, Clara Novello left London for

Rotterdam, on her way to Leipzig, accompanied by her father, mother, and sister, and made her first appearance at the Leipzig Concerts on the 2nd November. Her reception was most flattering. Her beautiful voice, good style, pure intonation, perfect expression, and admirable aplomb, especially at the termination of the phrases, won instant applause for her. The German critics were in ecstasies. Clara Novello's efforts at these concerts were pronounced by Mendelssohn to be a real service to the lovers of music, and the maestro described her in a letter to Mr. Alfred Novello, her brother, as a confirmed favourite of the Leipzig public. Replying to a request of our Philharmonic directors, that he would recommend them some singer for their series of concerts, Mendelssohn wrote, "The greatest singers in Germany are Miss Clara Novello and Mrs. Alfred Shaw." The benefit concert of the young English artiste in February, 1838, was one of the most successful ever known in Leipzig.

From Leipzig, Clara went to Berlin, when the Philharmonic Society of that city elected her an honorary member. From Berlin she proceeded with her family to Italy, but again her intention of preparing for the stage was diverted; she having so many engagements to sing at the various musical festivals then being celebrated in Milan in honour of the Emperor of Austria's coronation as King of Lombardy. The spring of 1838 was spent by Miss Novello in

Vienna; and a series of engagements in the principal cities of Germany occupied her time and attention during the season of 1838–39. She was at Berlin in January, 1839, and the King of Prussia, Frederick, was so delighted with her rendering of "I know that my REDEEMER liveth," that he took a paternal interest in her, and wrote an autograph letter to his sister the Empress of Russia, for the young vocalist, who was going to St. Petersburg. Indeed, she was the *enfante chérie* of the Berlinese.

In no place is music more warmly appreciated, or its exponents more liberally rewarded, than in Russia, as Miss Clara Novello could have attested. After remaining a short time there, she returned to Berlin, giving her first concert in the hall of the King's Theatre. Every place was taken, and the applause was loud and vehement. Her pure style and beautiful intonation were deservedly admired throughout the Continent. She also appeared at the Dusseldorf Festival, with Mdlle. von Fassmann, who was a celebrity in Germany, and whose voice—at least when she had one, some years before 1839—had been a powerful soprano, "the natural toughness of which," says Mr. Chorley, "had never been wrought out of it by practice. In all passages of the least volubility she was totally inaudible, or so languidly heavy as to destroy every idea of tone."

From 1839, no obstacles opposed the projected

dramatic studies of Clara Novello; and remembering the kindness of Rossini, when they had met on the occasion of the Coronation fêtes at Milan, she determined to visit him at Bologna with her father and brother. The great master, charmed with her talent, and enraptured with her voice, gave her friendly counsels. His advice was that she should relinquish public life for a year, and study for the stage, frequent the theatre regularly, and give her undivided attention to operatic music. She accordingly went to Milan, where she became the pupil of Micheroux, the master of the greatest Italian theatrical singers of the day, and under his direction she studied diligently for a whole year.

Having accepted an engagement to perform at several theatres in Italy for three years, Miss Novello made her début in opera, at Padua, July 6, 1841, choosing the ambitious part of Semiramide for her first essay. She was then one-and-twenty. Her success was complete; and as she increased in experience, she attained more command of the special requirements of the stage, and gained every day greater success. She subsequently appeared at Rome, Fermo, Milan, and other places, where her performances were a succession of triumphs. The critics were at a loss for language wherein to express their admiration and delight: the rich Italian tongue was ransacked by poets, even, for epithets to embody their ideas of the exquisite talent of the fair Inglesina. From November, 1841, to the following March, Clara Novello was singing at Bologna, under the immediate auspices of Rossini. The Bolognese were enchanted with "la bella Inglese."

In the summer, Clara Novello was singing at Modena. At her departure, on the 28th July, after a triumphant season, the crowd surrounded her carriage, and accompanied her home with shouts and choruses, filling the coach with bouquets and wreaths of the choicest flowers. She then returned to Bologna for the autumn. Her next engagement was at Rome.

In Italy all theatrical engagements are effected by means of correspondents—agents, who devote their talents to negotiating arrangements between managers and the composers and singers; and it was through one of these agents that Miss Novello entered into an engagement for the Carnival season of 1842, at Rome. But when she prepared to start for the imperial city she found, to her surprise, that she was eagerly and confidently expected by the director of the theatre of Genoa. This was an unexpected and awkward dilemma; each impresario demanded the fulfilment of the agreement, and it was impossible to comply with the requisitions of both.

It so happened that when Miss Novello made the unpleasant discovery of her awkward situation, she was singing at Fermo, which is within the

Papal territory, and consequently under the jurisdiction of the Roman authorities. "She could not quit the place without a passport," says one of her biographers, "which document the manager of the Opera House at Rome had the power to prevent her obtaining; he thus held the lady in such firm possession as would effectually bind her from appearing at the other theatre, though it did not compel her to sing at his own. The Minister of Police at Fermo, Count Gigliucci, communicated to the lady the restraint imposed upon her by the Roman manager, whereof he, the Count, was the unhappy instrument; adding also that he was under the sad necessity of placing the lady under arrest till she should have made arrangements satisfactory to the impresario, whose interest he protected." Being quite unwilling to become a heroine at such a price, Miss Novello wrote to the Earl of Aberdeen, then Secretary for Foreign Affairs, who promptly informed the Roman Government that "such proceedings could not be sanctioned towards a British subject." The matter was then settled by arbitration. The Carnival season of 1842 was to extend over twelve weeks, and for six weeks the songstress was to perform at Rome, while for the other moiety of the time she was to be at the service of the impresario at Genoa.

The courtly Count Gigliucci, in making a captive of the charming English vocalist, found himself bound in fetters stronger than ever were forged by the hand of man, and from which he had no wish to be free; in short, he refused to let the lady depart, until she had blushingly confessed that he was not disagreeable to her. It was eventually arranged that when her present professional engagements had been fulfilled, she should become the Countess Gigliucci.

Miss Novello was almost worshipped as a tenth Muse at Rome; the theatre was crowded whenever she appeared, and on the 19th January, 1843, when she took her benefit, she received an ovation such as had not been equalled for years. A shower of verses and bouquets, waving of handkerchiefs, and a storm of applause, greeted her appearance as Norma; and when she sang "Casta Diva," the furore was at its height: bouquets and coronals (the camellias of which latter alone, it was confidently asserted, were estimated at 100 scudi—twenty-five guineas English!) were flung at her feet, and the audience recalled her twenty-nine times! At the conclusion of *Norma*, she went into a box to hear Moriani in an act of *Lucia*. The audience, catching sight of her, rose, and, regardless of Moriani, sprang upon the benches and applauded for nearly ten minutes. When she stepped into her carriage, she found herself surrounded by the *élite* of Rome, bearing upwards of a hundred wax torches, while all the way home flowers were showered upon her, and vivas rent the air. Arrived at home, her house was beset with carriages, from which ladies of the first rank and quality waved their handkerchiefs, while the military band played her most popular airs, and the shouts continued of "Viva la Novello, evviva!" The hall and staircases were filled with her admirers, who, as she ascended, kept up exclamations of "Come back to us, Novello: don't forget the Romans!" &c. &c. By degrees the streets were cleared, but a serenade came to disturb the slumbers earned by fatigue. The Philharmonic Society of Rome voted her a free diploma, constituting the talented English prima donna an honorary member.

Her reception at Genoa offered a painful contrast to this triumph, for when she appeared in *I Puritani*, with Ivanoff, she was violently hissed. At the first indication of disapprobation, Miss Novello quitted the stage, and it was only by the most earnest entreaties that she could be persuaded to return. She reappeared before her old admirers, pale as a statue, and absolutely speechless from emotion; but her appearance and manner soon reduced the audience to silence, and she had an opportunity of explaining to the dissatisfied audience the cause of the failure of her powers. "Signori," she said, calmly, "to make me sing at present is an outrage! The Genoese received me with so much kindness last year, that I exhausted my strength in my journey to be with them at the earliest moment. It would be an insult to them, for whom I feel so much gratitude, were I to continue to sing any longer. I have done all I could to content them." Miss Novello appeared in February in a new opera, written expressly for her, on the story of Virginius. She arrived in London in March, 1843.

Mr. Macready, the eminent tragedian, had undertaken the management of Drury Lane Theatre, with the view of raising the English drama from the depressed state into which it had fallen; and a part of his plan was to bring forward first-class musical pieces, to be performed by English artistes. His operatic company consisted of Miss Clara Novello; Mrs. Alfred Shaw, one of the most popular of English soprani; Mrs. Serle, Mr. Henry Phillips, Mr. Allen, &c. The choice of the opera which was to open the campaign was rather unfortunate. Pacini's *Sappho*, a "grand," weak, pretty, somewhat insipid work, was selected; this being the first time of its production in this country. To Miss Novello was assigned the passionate character of Sappho, Mrs. Alfred Shaw appeared as Climene, and Mrs. Serle as Dirce; Messrs. Phillips, Allen, Stretton, and Reeves, took the parts of Alcander, Phaon, Lysimachus, and Hippias. The public evinced a great desire to hear their favourite on her return from Italy, and to ascertain how far she had improved; consequently the theatre was crowded on the 1st April.

The opera was elegantly mounted; the opening scene, in particular, the entrance of the stadium at Olympia in Elis, where the Olympic games are being celebrated and Sappho wins the lyric crown, was beautiful and classic. Clara Novello's acting was energetic, though by some thought to be wanting in delicate light and shade; but the impassioned character of the Greek songstress needed chiefly vehement feeling. Her voice, it was noticed, had wonderfully improved, and in that large and bold style of ornament which was the fashion of the newest Italian school, she was an adept. The duet between Sappho and Climene was admirably sung. Mrs. A. Shaw was a charming singer, and remarkable for distinctness and expression. *Sappho* was only successful on account of its pretty melodies and the graceful performance of Clara Novello and Mrs. Shaw.

It was followed by Handel's *Acis and Galatea*, the production of which forms an epoch in modern theatrical annals. The scenery of Stanfield, and the instrumentation of Mr. T. Cooke, assisted in creating a splendid effect. The character of Galatea was, of course, undertaken by Miss Novello, and Mr. Allen was the Acis, a part which had been rendered popular by Miss P. Horton.

The character of Polyphemus was sustained by Herr Staudigl, the celebrated baritone, who by the force of his genius made a magnificent impersonation of a most arduous part. His representation of the gigantic monster was only too kindly; he sang so genially, so heartily, that the idea of his "hideous love" was lost—he was no longer the brutal ogre, but a large-hearted, ill-fated lover, who had the misfortune to be horribly ugly; at the same time, he enlisted the sympathies of the audience, and humanized the repulsive aspect and ferocious character. Staudigl was a noble-minded and kind-hearted man, as well as a great artiste. Young Emery this season applied to him to know his terms for singing at his benefit. "You are the son of a great actor," replied the German basso, almost reproachfully; "my terms are nothing: you may announce me to sing, or act, or whatever you please. I shall feel it a duty as well as a pleasure to appear."

Clara Novello sang the lovely melodies of Handel infinitely better than the graceful inanities of Pacini. Her clear pure tones were heard in this serenata to the utmost advantage, especially in the last air. *Sappho* was performed again, Staudigl replacing Henry Phillips as Alcander, the High Priest; a most distasteful character, to which was attached the weakest music in the opera. Staudigl "electrified" the audience, and gave his part character and colour, delivering the words clearly and distinctly, without any defect of foreign utterance; but no genius could infuse life and vigour into such insipid music. The season terminated somewhat abruptly, Mr. Macready's efforts to redeem the drama having met with unbounded applause, but no more solid proofs of the public approval.

Miss Novello sang at the leading provincial musical meetings, gathering fresh laurels at every step. At the Birmingham Musical Festival, where she sang with Miss Rainforth, Mrs. Knyvett, Mrs. Alfred Shaw, Henry Phillips, Fornasari, and Signor Mario, she was greatly admired. When she appeared in *Norma*, her acting and singing created a multitude of conflicting opinions.

Having completed her engagements, Clara Novello was married on October 22, 1843, to the Count Gigliucci, and, without any formal leave-taking, quitted public life. Immediately after the ceremony the happy couple left London, going first to Paris, then to Naples. Madame Clara Novello was the fourth English vocalist who gained a title and marriage in modern days, the others being Miss Stephens (Countess of Essex), Miss Foote (Countess of Harrington), and Miss Bolton (Lady Thurlow). To this list must now be added the name of Victoire Balfe (Lady Crampton). The political hurricane which swept over Europe in 1848 destroyed the fortunes of many a noble house; and the Countess Gigliucci, like her sister artiste, the amiable Countess Rossi, was rudely aroused from her tranquillity by the storm, and like her, too, again entered into the art-arena to retrieve her husband's losses.

In 1850, Madame Novello reappeared in the musical world as unostentatiously as she had left it. She presented herself first at Rome; in December she appeared at Lisbon, where she obtained a triumph in *Beatrice di Tenda*. She appeared at our musical festivals in 1852, and thenceforth, in England, she restricted herself to singing at concerts and festivals. She is, therefore, best known here as the interpreter of the works of the great masters of sacred song. Her voice had gained in power, brilliancy, and refinement during her retirement; and her style was noble, and, above all, thoroughly English. While capable, as she had from girlhood proved herself, of singing the masterpieces of foreign music, she sang British ballads as no one else could sing them; she could render the grand oratorio music of Handel, Haydn, and Mozart, and with equal beauty sing the simple strains of "John Anderson" and "Auld Robin Gray." But the beauty and purity of her voice, the exquisite delicacy of her style, and the refinement of her manner, were eminently adapted to sacred music, and the exaltation of her feeling was most apparent in devotional music.

Her voice, "so available, it would seem for all purposes, so capable, so beautiful, and so telling, is toned down and sobered," says an able writer, "to a religious feeling that lends it its peculiar characteristic, and makes it almost sombre in expression and colouring. From this peculiarity, this sombreness of tone,

Madame Novello derives her special power in sacred music. Of the demonstrative quality, so indispensable to the dramatic singer, she exhibits but little, and is seldom outwardly energetic or forcible. Intensity without display, and earnestness arising from a manner full of repose and always absorbed, constitute the specialities which distinguish Madame Novello from all other singers of sacred music. So rapt, indeed, is she at most times in her performance, that, even when singing, could our ears deceive us so, she might stand as an exemplification of Wordsworth's Nun, 'breathless with adoration.' Whether this be pure instinct, or the most consummate art, we cannot say. In either case the result is the same, and the wonderful influence of the vocalist is made manifest."

At a concert given by Signor Puzzi at Drury Lane Theatre, July 5, 1853, Madame Novello appeared in *I Puritani*, with Signori Gardoni, Marchesi, and Burdini, creating a deep sensation by the "fervour of her acting and the excellence of her singing." This was her last dramatic display in England.

Madame Novello concluded an engagement for three years with La Scala, Milan, and commenced, January, 1854, with Verdi's *Rigoletto*. As Gilda, the favourite character of Madame Bosio, our charming English vocalist created a furore, and throughout she sustained her reputation in Italy as a dramatic singer. The Carnival of that year opened somewhat inauspiciously, and she had some difficulties to contend with; a new opera by Puzzi, *Il Convito di Baldassare,* disappointed the Milanese, who expected something unusually excellent from the composer; it was produced with great splendour, but the singers vainly exerted themselves to bear up against the tame, hastily-written score.

Apart from her beautiful voice, Madame Novello was invaluable in an operatic company, from her steady and correct intonation, and thorough musical knowledge. Miss Sabilla Novello, in her work on *The Voice and Vocal Art,* mentions a most interesting example of her sister's unfailing surety of intonation. At the rehearsal of a new opera at La Scala, Madame Novello, in the finale, consisting of a double quartet and chorus performed without orchestral accompaniments, kept the pitch, notwithstanding the chorus sank and dragged the other solo voices down with them. The first violin, fancying the prima donna might be getting sharp, sounded her note on his instrument, and found her perfectly in tune, although the chorus and other solo voices had sunk half a note! After repeated rehearsals, this finale had to be changed into a quintet, from the impossibility of keeping the chorus up to the pitch.

At the Norwich Festival, in 1854, Madame Novello sang with Madame Bosio, Lablache, Gardoni, and Mr. Sims Reeves. For four days' performances she received three hundred guineas. The following year, her admirers at Birmingham were greatly disappointed and angered by the non-appearance of their favourite. The committee objected to her demand of three hundred guineas, and offered only the terms she had received in her girlish days; which they must have known she would not accept. This was the only occasion on which any of the festivals suffered from her absence.

But it was in June, 1859, that Madame Novello achieved her grandest triumph, on the occasion of the Handel Festival at the Crystal Palace, where she sang with Miss Dolby, Madame Sherrington, Mr. Sims Reeves, Mr. Weiss, and Signor Belletti, and an accompanying host of nearly three thousand vocal and instrumental performers, in the presence of twenty-seven thousand auditors. The clear, pure tones of her voice, full, rich, brilliant, and perfectly distinct, penetrated to every corner of the enormous structure; —a place anything but favourable to the transmission of sound. That magnificent display of beautiful and impressive singing is indelibly stamped on the memory of all who heard it.

Unlike her great predecessor, Mara, Madame Novello resolved to withdraw from the arena of public life in the fulness of her powers. Never had she gained such triumphs as in the year which she fixed for her final retirement; for time had added to the purity, delicacy, and refinement of her style.

The Queen of English Soprani took her leave at the

Crystal Palace, in the *Messiah*, but she also gave, November 24, 1860, a farewell concert at St. James's Hall. Her farewell, it was justly remarked, was in admirable harmony with her pure and spotless career. "It was a manifestation of pure unadulterated art from beginning to end," observed a leading musical journal; "and at the termination of the concert the vast assembly dispersed with the most intimate conviction that music had lost one of its most gifted and justly distinguished representatives"—one who for ten years, with Mr. Sims Reeves, had maintained the English school at a lofty standard of excellence. Madame Novello's voice, though she was evidently suffering from indisposition, was as clear, bright, penetrating, flexible, and vigorous, as unerringly modulated as ever. It was only just that Clara Novello's adieu should be sung to Mendelssohn's music, therefore she selected that master's unfinished *Loreley* as the principal feature of the concert; the second part of the programme consisting of Benedict's *Undine*, in which the departing prima donna was assisted by Miss Palmer, Mr. Wilbye Cooper, and Mr. Weiss. Her final display was a solo verse of "God Save the Queen"—that piece in which she had so often electrified thousands at the Crystal Palace.

The Countess Gigliucci is now residing in Italy with her family.

CHAPTER XI.

PAULINE VIARDOT GARCIA.

Pauline, the second daughter of the famous singer and musician Garcia, was born in Paris on the 18th July, 1821. Her elder sister, Maria, then thirteen, was painfully studying under the direction of her father, standing pale and timid behind his chair and learning the way to sing steadily while the tears were streaming down her cheeks. Her brother, Manuel, then a lad, was also studying, to assist his father as a teacher. On the 29th August the child was presented for baptism in the parish church of St. Roch, having for sponsors the celebrated Ferdinando Paer and the Princess Pauline Prascovie of Galitzin (Countess of Schonvalsh), and was named Michelle Ferdinande Pauline. At the age of three, Pauline left Paris with her family, her father being engaged at the Opera House in London, and Maria having been pronounced by him a finished singer, fully qualified to take an engagement. The next year Garcia being struck with the happy notion of esta-

blishing an Opera in America, the whole family started for New York.

The company had been performing for some time, when Garcia lost his prima donna, Maria, who unfortunately accepted the hand of M. Malibran. When the crash came which made Maria worse than widowed, Garcia abruptly quitted New York, going with his wife and youngest child to Mexico, where he commenced a series of operatic performances. Little Pauline here received some lessons on the pianoforte from Marcos Vega, organist of the cathedral. She was singularly clever, and at the age of six could speak with equal facility four languages—French, Spanish, Italian, and English. To these she subsequently added German, in which she became a proficient; and she learned, before she was eight-and-twenty, to read Latin and Greek. Her lessons were suddenly interrupted, however. Civil war broke out in Mexico immediately after the declaration of independence, and the scenes of conflict were dreadful to witness. Garcia, fearing that he should lose all his earnings, resolved to return to Europe. Maria was in New York, and Manuel had left the preceding year (1826) to visit France. Turning his money into ingots of gold and silver, Garcia started at once.

The little party, perfectly aware of the dangers of the way, were travelling rapidly on their road over the mountains leading from Mexico to Vera Cruz, when a band of brigands waylaid and robbed them. There was some dry humour about these wretches, for though they stripped the famous tenor, intending to leave him bound, with a guard to prevent his raising an alarm, on discovering that he was a singer, they were determined to have some fun. Untying him, they roughly placed him, naked as he was, on a rock, and ordered him to sing for their amusement. Manuel Garcia was not exactly the kind of man to submit quietly to this treatment, even at the muzzle of a gun, and he refused to obey their command. They persisted, and began to threaten; so, thinking that perhaps they might be as good (or as bad) as their word, Garcia commenced; but fatigue and agitation combined to choke his voice, and he sang so vilely that his strange audience hissed violently. Astounded and enraged at such an indignity—an outrage to which he had never before been subjected—the great tenor raised his head with a haughty gesture, and, gathering strength and courage, burst into one of his most magnificent flights of song. "This so charmed his hearers, that they drowned his voice with cries of 'bravo!' and a loud clapping of their hands, took him down from his elevation, restored to him his clothes and a portion of his money, and gave him an escort to the coast."

By this catastrophe, which Pauline, child as she was, never forgot, her father lost upwards of 600,000 fr., (about 21,000*l.*), the product of his labours and travels. He managed, however, to embark safely, and found consolation for his disaster in teaching Pauline during the long and dreary voyage. It was on their passage that he gave her her first vocal instructions; composing little pieces expressly for her, with words from all languages. "We have seen these curious polyglot vocabularies," says a writer in the *Musical World*, "which must have been of excellent effect in training the infant ear and voice in the art of part singing, and furnishing it with a diversity of idiom." Her father was very fond of this mild darling, whom he preferred to the brilliant, wilful Maria. "Pauline," he would say, "can be guided by a thread of silk; Maria needs a hand of iron."

At seven, Pauline could play the pianoforte sufficiently well to accompany her father's pupils, and Garcia, seeing the taste she evinced for this instrument, confided her to the excellent master, Meysenberg, under whose care she made rapid progress. Conscious herself of a decided talent for the pianoforte, she devoted three years to finger-exercise alone. She was then placed under the direction of the eminent Franz Liszt, one of whose most distinguished pupils she became. It was probably under the care of this master that she gained that accuracy and brilliancy of musical conception which afterwards shone forth in her admirable vocal performances. Liszt, with whom she executed the most difficult and complicated works of Bach, wished very much that she should, like himself, aim at celebrity as a pianist. Her health, however, was not equal to the fatigue caused by so sedentary a study, and she could give only so much attention as would enable her to accompany herself; but she was so far finished that when she was fourteen or fifteen she was able to perform at the concerts of her sister Maria. Garcia thought her voice and talents far transcended those of Maria, and when a buzz of ecstatic admiration about the voice of Madame Malibran met his ear, he would rejoin, "There is a younger sister, who is a greater genius than she."

Pauline lost her father when she was only eleven, and shortly after the death of her husband, Madame Garcia visited Paris. The good lady took up her residence with Adolphe Nourrit, one of Manuel's most eminent pupils; and Nourrit, a man of kind disposition, took the keenest interest in the young Pauline. He strove to cheer and advise the widow of his old master, and, with mistaken zeal, was very anxious to persuade Rossini to become the teacher of Pauline. The maestro consented, and Nourrit brought the news to Madame Garcia with a face beaming with delight. What was his amazement when she quietly declined the offer. He could hardly believe that she was in earnest to reject such a teacher as the master-spirit of the age! and he was still more astounded when she added that her son Manuel should be Pauline's instructor, and that should her son not be able to come from Italy for the purpose, she would take Pauline in hand herself. Nourrit was not aware of the vast difference between the systems pursued by Rossini and the Garcias. Professional engagements detained Manuel in Italy; so, confident in her own resources, and that soundness of principle on which the school of Garcia was founded, the widowed lady applied herself to her labour of love.

It may be said, however, that in reality Pauline educated herself: certainly she gained nothing from her sister Maria, for the wandering life of the latter gave few opportunities for them to meet; and as her mother removed to Brussels, Pauline, even when her brother came to Paris, was unable to profit by his instructions. What she acquired was the result of her own spontaneous studies, guided by the taste and judicious counsels of her mother. Pauline was eager, quick, enthusiastic, and, above all, industrious. She had a fixed point to aim at, and now commenced her studies with earnestness. Previously she had learned in a desultory manner, though her intelligence enabled her to appreciate fine music; and she was so smitten with the beautiful melodies of Schubert, that she copied them all with her own hand. "A remarkable instance," says some one, "of solitary and spontaneous enthusiasm." She entered upon a course of laborious vocal training; and having exhausted the solfeggi which her father had written for her sister Maria, the happy idea crossed her mind that she might compose some for herself. She was thus obliged to bring into actual exercise the principles of harmony and counter-point which she had learned from Reicha. She also acquired other accomplishments besides music. Without any master she learned, like her sister, to draw and to paint in water-colours; she sketched portraits, caricatures, and costumes. Living in retirement at Brussels, entirely devoted to her studies, and assisted by the advice of her mother, Pauline rapidly neared the goal which she was determined to reach. She was just sixteen when, flushed with conscious genius, she exclaimed, "Ed io anchè son cantatrice."

Her voice, originally somewhat harsh and unmanageable, had been tutored into perfect pliancy and beauty. Like the organ of her sister in quality, it combined the two registers of soprano and contralto, from low F to C above the lines; but the upper part was formed chiefly by art. Like that exquisite voice, too, it had the soul-stirring tone, the sympathetic and touching character which penetrates to the heart. It was pure and mellow, though not of the most powerful order. Her singing was expressive, "descriptive," thrilling, full, equal and just, brilliant and vibrating; especially in the medium and in the lower chords. Capable of every style of art, it was adapted to all the feelings of nature, but particularly to outbursts of grief, joy, or despair. "The dramatic colouring which her voice imparts to the slightest shades of feeling and passion is a real phenomenon of vocalization which cannot be analyzed," says Escudier. "No singer we ever heard, with the exception of Malibran," says another critic, "could produce the same effect by means of a few simple notes. It is neither by the peculiar power, the peculiar depth, nor the peculiar sweetness of these tones that the sensation is created, but by something indescribable in the quality which moves you to tears in the very hearing."

Her first public appearance was worthy the future of Pauline Garcia. It was at Brussels, on the 15th December, 1837, that she sang at a concert for the benefit of the poor; and on this occasion De Beriot made his first appearance after the death of his wife. The King and Queen, the Prince de Ligne, the corps diplomatique, and many persons of celebrity were present. This concert opened nobly the career of the young artiste. The Philharmonic Society caused two medals to be struck for De Beriot and Mdlle. Garcia, the mould of which was immediately broken.

After some other performances equally brilliant, Pauline quitted Belgium for Germany, with her mother and De Beriot. Her name, her talent, gained for the young débutante a warm welcome everywhere. The

Queen of Prussia sent her a splendid suite of emeralds. At Frankfort she sang a duo with Mdlle. Sontag, who was on the eve of departing for St. Petersburg. Probably Henrietta recalled the days of her glorious rivalry with the dead sister of Pauline, when they had walked on flowers to receive the ovations offered by Paris and London. In the summer of 1838, Pauline and her mother left Germany, and after a short stay in Brussels, finally arrived in Paris.

The 15th December, the anniversary of the Brussels concert, Pauline appeared in public with De Beriot at the Théâtre de la Renaissance, and a crowded andience greeted her with loud applause. She sang an air by Costa, difficult both from its compass and from the recollection evoked of her sister; an air by De Beriot, and the "Cadence du Diable," imitated from "Tartini's Dream," which she accompanied on the piano with infinite grace and skill. Her second appearance was at a concert given by "La France Musicale," in the saloon of M. Herz, when she was supported by Rubini, Lablache, and Ivanoff. Her admirable performance on this occasion confirmed her rising fame, by revealing the precision, firmness, boldness, and brilliancy of her style.

England, however, was the country selected by Pauline Garcia for her theatrical début. She was eighteen years of age when, on Thursday, May 9, 1839, she made her first appearance at Her Majesty's

Theatre, in the same opera in which her sister Maria had made her début before an English audience—*Otello.* Undismayed by traditionary impressions, by the recollections of Malibran, of Pasta, and of Sontag, Pauline gave to the part a new reading. The public were intensely anxious to hear this gifted sister of their lost favourite, and listened eagerly to any account of her genius. At the rehearsal, her voice, style, execution, expression, manner—in short, everything but external appearance—bore so strong a resemblance to Maria, that the performers were affected, and tears were seen to steal down the cheeks of the most veteran artiste. Nothing, save a little more physical power, was needed to complete the singular likeness.

Every one noticed the singular resemblance existing between her voice and that of her sister Maria. One day a young lady was taking a lesson from Lablache, who lodged in the same house with Mdlle. Garcia. The great basso was explaining to her the manner in which Malibran gave the air from *Norma*, which she was about to try; when, at the moment the pupil seated herself at the piano, a voice was heard in the adjoining room singing this cavatina: it was Mdlle. Pauline; but the young girl, struck with superstitious terror, imagined that a phantom had come to give her a lesson, and she fainted.

In person there was but a slight resemblance between the sisters. Pauline's figure was tall and elegant, occasionally commanding, her physiognomy noble, expressive, and full of character; but her features were far from being handsome, the outline of her face being somewhat harsh and irregular; her forehead was broad and intellectual; her hair was of a rich black, her complexion pale, contrasting charmingly with large black eyes, ardent, and full of fire. Her walk was grave and dignified, and her carriage majestic and easy. "She looked older than her years," Mr. Chorley says (in his *Reminiscences*); "her frame (then a mere reed) quivered this way and that; her character dress seemed to puzzle her, and the motion of her hands as much. Her voice was hardly settled, even within its after-conditions; and yet—paradoxical as it may seem—she was at ease on the stage, because she had brought thither instinct for acting, experience of music, knowledge how to sing, and consummate intelligence. There could be no doubt with any one who saw Desdemona on that night, that another great career was begun."

Her singing created a marked sensation. The high and low notes seemed to be produced without effort, yet were sufficiently powerful to fill the house with a flood of clear, sweet, rich melody. Her powers were, however, still immature; though her acting, like her singing, was full of promise, and her conception surprising. "By the firmness of her step and the general confidence of her deportment," observes a contemporary critic, "we were at first induced to believe that she was not nervous, but the improvement of every succeeding song, and the warmth with which she gave the latter part of the opera, convinced us that her powers must have been confined by something like apprehension." Rubini was the Otello; Tamburini, Iago; and Lablache, Elmiro. June 15, Mdlle. Garcia appeared in *La Cenerentola* with the same great singers. As Angelina she was even more admired than as Desdemona. Her pure taste, her unexaggerated truth, her perfect facility of execution combined to render her performance nearly faultless, despite her youth and inexperience of the stage. "She has," says one writer, "more feeling than Madame Cinti Damoreau in the part in which the greater portion of Europe has assigned to her the pre-eminence, and execution, even now, in very nearly equal perfection." Every note was clear and distinct as a clarionet, and she was rewarded by "thunders of applause."

M. Viardot, an eminent literary man, was then director of the Italian Opera of Paris, and being in London, he offered Mdlle. Garcia the position of prima donna for the approaching season. She had already received similar offers from the theatre, but, young and inexperienced, she shrank from undertaking a responsibility which she felt was too much for a girl of eighteen; she, however, consented to appear for a few nights. Great was the impatience of the Parisian public to hear the young cantatrice in opera, and every box was taken at the Italiens for the performances. Her début took place on the 8th October, and was long remembered as the brightest triumph on the French lyric stage, since Malibran made her début. She appeared as Desdemona, with Rubini, Tamburini, and Lablache, and realized the most sanguine expectations. The audience were struck with the wonderful extent of her voice, her admirable musical knowledge, and the perfect correctness of her costume. The only drawbacks were her youth and inexperience; but the critics assured her, almost apologetically, that this slight disadvantage would disappear but too soon. Her second character was Angelina, in *La Cenerentola;* her third part was Rosina, in *Il Barbiere.* An accidental failure of memory, although disguised by brilliant improvisations, was injurious to the effect of the first representation of *Il Barbiere.* Rosina, notwithstanding her dazzling vocalization, perhaps even owing to it, proved not the Rosina that the audience had anticipated. She achieved a triumph, but it was rather a tribute to her great musical skill, which enabled her to conceal beneath the splendour of extempore melody the failure of her memory. On her second appearance she made a glorious atonement, and the part of Rosina has ever been played and sung by her with an exquisite perfection. For her benefit she appeared, with Madame

Persiani, Rubini, and Tamburini, in *Tancredi;* and for the benefit of Fanny Elssler, February, 1840, she performed in the last act of *Otello*, with Duprez.

Mdlle. Garcia and M. Viardot were married, April 18, 1840, when they left for Italy; M. Viardot resigning his post at the Opéra, being charged with an important mission by the Minister of the Interior relative to the fine arts. The following year Madame Viardot reappeared in England. Her Majesty's Theatre opened, March 16, with *Gli Orazi ed i Curiazi.* Madame Viardot performed Orazia, and confirmed the favourable impression she had made the preceding season. In several parts of the opera, her singing and acting were superb, and many concurred in awarding the crown of Pasta and Malibran to the young vocalist. Mario was the Orazio, and a Miss Alicia Nunn made her début as Curiazio.

The health of Madame Viardot was not strong, and her physical energies were quite unequal to the strain upon her ardent nature; she was, therefore, obliged to decline the offers both of the London and Paris managers, preferring to travel and visit Spain, the native land of her mother. In June, 1841, she was singing at Madrid, and on her second appearance, as Desdemona, the audience so eagerly testified their ecstasy that the amiable songstress, flattered probably by such unrestrained expressions of delight, voluntarily sang the rondo finale from *La Cenerentola.* Spell-bound, the audience found it impossible to tear themselves away, and called the charming songstress again and again to receive their repeated applause. The curtain fell and the band disappeared, but the crowd would not go; so at a sign from Madame Viardot, the pianoforte was wheeled on the stage, when she sang with electrical effect a French romance and two Spanish airs, accompanying herself. When she was at length permitted to leave the theatre, a crowd of amateurs attended her carriage to the gates of her hotel, amid a hurricane of vivas! On her way to Paris through Grenada, at the close of her tour, Madame Viardot performed twice in *Il Barbiere*, in a style of artistic perfection, both musical and dramatic, quite unprecedented in that part of the world. She also performed *Norma* twice, a character in which she was fully equal to her sister.

In October, 1842, Madame Viardot made her reappearance at the Théâtre Italien, as Arsace, with Madame Grisi and Tamburini. Pauline Viardot, Giulia Grisi, and Fanny Persiani, formed a trio of singers such as had not often been heard at the same theatre; each possessing voice and talent of the highest order, yet perfectly distinct. In 1843, Madame Viardot published five songs and romances, in an album, entitled *L'Oiseau d'Or*. She declined the offers made from London that year, and at the close of the Paris season, about Easter, went to Vienna, where her powers were highly appreciated. In August, she was at Berlin, and Meyerbeer, who was then writing his *Prophète*, arranged a concert in order that the King might have an opportunity of hearing her. Madame Viardot had a brilliant success in Berlin, and aroused quite an Italian furore among the staid citizens. In 1844 she was singing at Vienna, with Ronconi, and she formed one of the crowd of distinguished visitors who attended the Beethoven fête, at Bonn, in 1845.

After singing at Paris with Mesdames Grisi and Persiani, the next engagement of Madame Viardot was at Berlin, where she sang at the end of 1846 and the beginning of 1847. In March she took the Berlin critics by storm, in a German version of *La Juive*. She was called before the curtain at the termination of every act, and at midnight the members of the orchestra executed a serenade under her windows; indeed, the enthusiasm with which she was greeted proved that the mantle of her illustrious sister had fallen on her.

She showed herself, also, to be as amiable as she was gifted. One evening she had been announced as Alice, in *Robert le Diable;* when, unfortunately, Mdlle. Tuezck, the Isabelle of the evening, was taken ill. The manager was in despair: there was no singer to substitute for her, and the opera must be set aside. The part of Alice taxed the powers of the most vigorous singer; but Madame Viardot smilingly declared that, rather than disappoint the audience, she would play *both characters!* And she actually did so, changing her costume with every change of scene, and representing in one opera the two opposite rôles of the princess and the peasant! The enthusiasm of the audience was such that she was vociferously called for at the end of every act, and when the curtain dropped, the house rose *en masse*, and greeted her with a storm of applause.

From Berlin she went to Dresden, where Robert Schumann heard her as Rosina, and pronounced Rosina to be "her finest rôle." When Mdlle. Lind quitted the German Opera at Berlin, Madame Viardot took her place, and created an unparalleled enthusiasm in Hamburg, Dresden, Frankfort, Leipzig, etc. Her repertoire then consisted of Desdemona, Cenerentola, Rosina, Camilla (in *Gli Orazi*), Arsace, Norma, Ninetta, Amina, Romeo, Lucia, Maria di Rohan, Leonora (in *La Favorita*), Zerlina and Donna Anna, the Iphigenia of Glück and the Rachel of Halévy, the Alice and Valentine of Meyerbeer.

As Alice, Madame Viardot completely identified herself with the creation of the poet; and in the character of Valentine she was irreproachable. This part was for her what Medea was to Pasta, Fidelio to Malibran, or Norma to Giulia Grisi. In the severe and classic school of singing Madame Viardot has no superior, perhaps no equal; and in the music of

Glück, of Handel, of Beethoven, she shone pre-eminently. "The florid graces and embellishments of the modern Italian school," says one writer, "though mastered by her with ease, do not appear consonant to her genius. So great an artiste must necessarily be a perfect mistress of all styles of singing, but her intellect evidently inclines her to the severer and loftier school."

In 1848 Madame Viardot was engaged at our Royal Italian Opera by Mr. Delafield. By that time the great genius of Madame Viardot had matured, and a volume might be filled with the criticisms written on her voice, her acting, her original conception. Even those judges ordinarily most stern seemed to have scarcely anything but praise to offer to Madame Viardot. She was admitted to be, as one able critic acknowledges, "a woman of genius peculiar, inasmuch as it is universal." Never was prima donna more fortunate in satisfying even the most exacting.

The announcement of her first appearance (May 9), "created an immense sensation in all musical circles." She had to contend against a combination of the most unfortunate circumstances that ever surrounded any singer. The house was crowded by those anxious to witness her appearance as Amina, the Dowager Countess of Essex, Madame Grisi and Mdlle. Alboni being among the most eager expectants. Despite her nervousness—"her trembling was apparent to all parts of the house," as one journal recorded—her success was undoubted from the commencement of the Opera. "She proved herself equal to Malibran," says a writer in the *Musical World*, speaking of this performance; "there was the same passionate fervour, the same absorbing depth of feeling: we heard the same tones whose naturalness and pathos stole into our very heart of hearts: we saw the same abstraction, the same abandonment, the same rapturous awakening to joy, to love, and to devotion. Such novel and extraordinary passages, such daring flights into the region of fioriture, together with chromatic runs ascending and descending, embracing the three registers of the soprano, mezzo-soprano, and contralto, we have not heard since the days of Malibran."

On her second appearance, being no longer trammelled by the circumstances which had previously harassed her, Madame Viardot's triumph was complete. "Madame Viardot's voice grows unconsciously upon you," observes one critic, "until at last you are blind to its imperfections. The voice penetrates to the heart by its sympathetic tones, and you forget everything in it but its touching and affecting quality. You care little or nothing for the mechanism, or rather for the weakness of the organ; you are no longer a critic, but spell-bound under the hand of genius, moved by the sway of the enthusiasm that comes from the soul: abashed in the presence of intellect."

From that time, Madame Viardot appeared almost every season in London, in all the great parts in which she had distinguished herself on the Continent. Her most memorable achievement was her performance in 1849 of the character of Fides in *Le Prophète*. This opera was then a novelty, having been recently produced at Paris. Meyerbeer had kept it long in his portfolio, determined not to bring it out till Fides could be represented by the performer for whom it had been expressly written. Madame Viardot's appearance in it on the Parisian boards created an immense sensation; and equally great was the impression made by her reappearance in it at Covent Garden. It has since been sustained by other performers of the greatest eminence; but it has been unanimously admitted that none have attained the standard given by Viardot.

Her last season in England was that of 1858. There was an Italian Opera at Drury Lane, for which she was engaged, and where she appeared in several of her principal parts. In this, as in previous years, she sang at the leading concerts in the metropolis, and at the great provincial festivals. Her last appearances in England were at the Birmingham festival of the above year.

From England she went to Poland. In December, Prince Gortschakoff entertained in his palace all the rank and fashion of Warsaw with a concert, at which she was the chief attraction. She sang the grand air from *L'Italiana*, two pieces from *Le Prophète*, and some Russian airs. The performance of *Le Prophète* being prohibited at Warsaw, Madame Viardot made her début two days after in *Norma;* she next appeared in *Il Barbiere*, when her reception was, if possible, even more brilliant. After the performance, Prince Cantacuzene was sent by Prince Gortschakoff to invite Madame Viardot to tea in the Governor-General's house, where she was met by an assembly of the *élite* of the Court and the nobility. The January and February of the following year found Madame Viardot at Berlin. Her success, it is unnecessary to add, was immense: the theatre was always crowded at double prices. In March, 1861, this incomparable artiste created a great sensation by singing in a selection from Glück's *Alceste*, at the Paris Conservatoire, where she had not sung for many years. She appeared again in Paris in 1862.

Madame Viardot, in private life, is loved and esteemed for her pure and cultivated mind, her amiable temper, the suavity of her manner, and her high principles; as she has been admired by the public for her genius, her voice, and her dramatic power, and respected for her punctuality and willingness to oblige. She had never ceased to be a favourite, but always retained her supremacy, spite of the most attractive novelty, or the most brilliant rivalry.

CHAPTER XII.

FANNY PERSIANI.

NICOLAS TACCHINARDI, who was the great star of the Odéon under the Empire, was one of the most admired tenors of his day. He was not by nature formed for a stage hero, being short, with a large head sunk in his shoulders, and a repulsive face; but he had an exquisite voice and irreproachable taste, and was as capricious as he was ugly. Nor did his demeanour on the stage lessen the unfavourable impression of his person; for he would march down to the orchestra with his hat in one hand, and his cane in the other, and then, without the least gesture or action, sing his song, and walk off again. Being perfectly conscious that his personal defects operated against him in the estimation of those who were not familiar with his beautiful voice, he would beg those who wrote for him to give him parts which permitted him to sing at the side-scenes before entering on the stage, that thus he might be heard before being seen. This expedient was not always easy to manage, however, so he invented another stratagem for concealing from the spectators some portion of his unfortunate figure ; he would come on the stage standing in a triumphal car, looking even then a victor whose aspect terribly belied his supposed deeds. At his first appearance on the boards of the Odéon, he was saluted with the most insulting outburst of laughter and smothered ejaculations of "Why, he's a hunchback!" Being accustomed to this kind of greeting, Tacchinardi tranquilly walked to the footlights, and bowed. "Gentlemen," he said, addressing the pit, "I am not here to exhibit my person, but to sing. Have the goodness to hear me." They did hear him, and when he ceased, the theatre rang with plaudits: there was no more laughter. His personal disadvantages were redeemed by one of the finest and purest tenor voices ever given by Nature and refined by Art, by his extraordinary intelligence, by an admirable method of singing, an exquisite taste in fioriture, and a marvellous facility of execution.

After the events of 1815, Tacchinardi left France and returned to his native Italy; and when at Rome he had a second daughter, Fanny, born October 4, 1818. She was passionately fond of music; and while yet a child, her father gave her lessons. At nine she could play on the piano, and sing with grace, though in a thin, uncertain voice, her father's ariettas and duettini, with her elder sister, Elisa; who was an excellent pianist, and a good musician and composer. At eleven, Fanny performed, as a childish amateur, the part of prima donna at a little theatre which her father had fitted up in his country-house near Florence (his native city), for the use of his pupils. Despite her decided talent and predilection for the stage, however, her father was averse to her adopting it as a profession.

But she sang in public when fourteen, with much success, at the concerts of amateurs and of artists, and at some theatrical representations for the benefit of her father; and in 1828 and 1829, she sang many times in the concerts which were given during Lent at the Court of the Grand Duke of Tuscany, where Tacchinardi had been *chanteur du chambre* since 1822. Nature had given to Fanny a voice of great extent, but wanting, in some parts, flexibility, sweetness, and power: defects which subsequent hard study and untiring efforts only to a certain degree remedied.

In 1830, Fanny Tacchinardi married Joseph Persiani, a composer of several operas of more or less merit, and resided with him in her father's house, far from the musical world. But she was, like Mara and our own Billington, like Malibran, Pauline Viardot, and many others, a *musicienne de race*, and as such her gifts could not be kept in obscurity.

A French amateur, a M. Fournier, a rich merchant established at Leghorn, had composed an opera entitled *Francesca di Rimini*, the subject being taken from the tragedy of Pellico. The Frenchman was one of those musical enthusiasts who are ready to do anything, if only their pieces are publicly represented, and he was prepared to pay for everything—the scenery, the singers, the musicians. The first vocalists were accordingly engaged, Madame Pisaroni and Rosalbina Caradori being the contralto and soprano. On the day of rehearsal, June, 1832, all the singers responded to the call, with the exception of Madame Caradori, who was detained at Florence by the public. M. Fournier was in despair, and the manager in a fidget. What was to be done? Suddenly some one recollected the distinguished dilettante, Madame Persiani, who resided some leagues from Leghorn, and might perhaps be induced to undertake the part of the heroine on this occasion. Accordingly, a deputation of the friends of M. Fournier, amongst whom were some friends of Tacchinardi, came to represent the case of the poor composer in want of a soprano singer, and implored her aid. After some hesitation, and having obtained the consent of her husband and father, Madame Persiani signed with a trembling hand the engagement which was offered her, and made her début in the *Francesca di Rimini* of the merchant-musician.

It must be confessed that her début was *not* brilliant: it did not even presage future successes. Having commenced her career, however, she was too valorous to relinquish it. Passing to the theatre of Milan, she there laid the foundation of her renown, which rose rapidly at Florence, where she sang with Duprez and Porto. Donizetti, who was then in that city, wrote for these three artistes his *Rosmonda d'Inghilterra*.

Madame Persiani was next engaged at Vienna, where the impression which she made was all the more honourable to her, as the great theatre of that capital is the rendezvous of the élite of Viennese society. She was afterwards engaged at Padua, and at Venice, where, in 1833, she played chiefly in *Romeo e Giulietta*, *Il Pirata*, *La Gazza Ladra*, and *L'Elisir d'Amore*. Madame Pasta was singing here, and Madame Persiani, who performed with her in *Tancredi* and *L'Elisir d'Amore*, did not hesitate to enter into competition with this illustrious rival. The Venetians were charmed with the blonde Persiani, and unanimously designated her "la petite Pasta;" though in her talent she did not resemble the great tragedian in the remotest degree. At Milan, where the echo of her Venetian successes had preceded her, she appeared in *Beatrice di Tenda* and *La Sonnambula*. In the autumn of the same year (1833), she left for Rome, and during her stay in that city, two operas, *Misantropia e Pentimento*, and *I Promessi Sposi*, were written for her. She also performed with Ronconi, in *Il Pirata*. At Pisa, in *Otello*, she met with equal admiration, and she sang at the Teatro Carlo Felice, at Genoa, during the Carnival.

The next year she was at the San Carlo, at Naples, with Duprez, Coselli, and Lablache. Donizetti, who was charmed with her voice, resolved to write another opera for her, and as with him there was not much delay between conceiving an idea and carrying it into execution, being furnished with an interesting libretto, the last act of which he wrote himself, he set to work, and in the space of six weeks produced one of the most beautiful operas he had ever written,—*Lucia di Lammermoor*. Duprez, then in the zenith of his power, was a singer of the first order, and it is thought that the large and severe style of this vocalist exerted a favourable influence on the inspiration of the composer, who wrote for him the character of Edgardo. As the gentle Lucy, Madame Persiani was soft, pathetic, sentimental, and impassioned. She performed with ease, intelligence, and expression. This part always remained her favourite.

In appearance, Madame Persiani was small and thin, with a face somewhat long and colourless, and though interesting and pleasing, on the stage she looked older than she really was. Her eyes were soft and dreamy, her smile piquant, her hair exquisitely fair and unusually long. Her manner was lady-like and unassuming, and her actions were graceful. "Never was there woman less vulgar, in physiognomy, or in manner, than she," says Mr. Chorley, describing Madame Persiani; "but never was there one whose appearance on the stage was less distinguished. She was not precisely insignificant to see, so much as pale, plain, and anxious. She gave the impression of one who had left sorrow or sickness at home, and who therefore (unlike those wonderful deluders, the French actresses, who, because they will not be ugly, rarely *look* so) had resigned every question of personal attraction as a hopeless one. She was singularly tasteless in her dress. Her one good point was her hair; which was splendidly profuse, and of an agreeable colour."

As a vocalist, it was agreed that her singing had the volubility, ease, and musical sweetness of a bird: her execution was remarkable for velocity. Her voice was rather thin, but its tones were clear as a silver bell, brilliant and sparkling as a diamond: it embraced a range of two octaves and a half (or about eighteen notes, from B to F in alt), the highest and lowest notes of which she touched with equal ease and sweetness. She had thus an organ of the most extensive compass known in the register of the true soprano. Her facility was extraordinary; her voice was implicitly under her command, and capable not only of executing the greatest difficulties, but also of obeying the most daring caprices—scales, shakes, trills, divisions, fioriture the most dazzling and inconceivable. She only acquired this command by indefatigable labour. Study had enabled her to execute with fluency and correctness the chromatic scales ascending and descending, and it was by sheer hard practice that she learnt to swell and diminish her accents; to emit tones, full, large, and free from nasal or guttural sounds, to manage her respiration skilfully, and to seize the delicate shades of vocalization. In fioriture and vocal effects, her taste was faultless; and she had an agreeable manner of uniting her tones by the happiest transitions, and diminishing with insensible gradations. She excelled in the effects of vocal embroidery, and her passion for ornamentation tempted her to disregard the dramatic situation in order to give way to a torrent of splendid fioriture, which dazzled the audience without always satisfying them.

She excelled in Lucia, Amina, Ninetta, and Zerlina: characters which require placidity, feminine grace, softness, and appeal to the sympathies of the spectators, were best adapted to her style and talent. That she was not incapable of tragic emotion, however, her mad scene in *Lucia di Lammermoor* attested. "It is not only the nature of her voice which limits her," remarks Escudier, "it is also the expression of her acting; we had almost said the ensemble of her physical organization. She knows her own powers perfectly. She is not ambitious, she knows exactly what will suit her, and is aware precisely of the nature of her talent."

Her style was all her own—graceful and gentle. As Zerlina, she was the bewitching Spanish girl, in all her native beauty and picturesqueness; her innovations were rare; every touch was in the finest taste, and since the days of Fodor, no one invested the character of Zerlina with so much truth and grace as Madame Persiani. Yet she shone less in Mozart's music than in the compositions of other masters; her light and brilliant voice, her airy style, fitting her more for the modern Italian than the severe German school. As an actress, Madame Persiani, although not very animated, was natural, often touching. She possessed much versatility, and in comedy was easy and elegant; her best parts being Rosina and Adina. She belonged to the same school as Sontag.

On the occasion of her second visit to Naples, in 1835, an incident occurred which afforded Madame Persiani deep gratification. During the representation of *Lucia*, she was one evening changing her costume between the acts, when a lady entered her dressing-room, and after a few general compliments on her singing, took in her hands the long fair tresses which floated in wild profusion over the shoulders of the cantatrice, asking if they were really her own. Madame Persiani laughingly invited her to satisfy herself on this point, when the visitor said, with a smile, "Allow me, Signora, since I have no wreath of flowers to offer you, to twine you one with your own beautiful tresses;" and she did so. Madame Persiani's heart beat with pride and joy, for it was Malibran who spoke.

From Naples she went to Genoa. Here Severini heard her and offered her an engagement for the Théâtre Italien. She accepted it, provisionally, being unable to go immediately to France, in consequence of her numerous engagements.

In the same year, coming from Naples to Leghorn, to fulfil an engagement at Florence, she fell seriously ill during the voyage, in consequence of a dreadful storm which broke over the vessel. On her arrival in the Tuscan capital, she presented herself weak and exhausted before the impresario, who nevertheless insisted on enforcing the terms of her engagement, and on compelling her to appear in *I Puritani.* She remonstrated in vain, and went on in a nearly dying condition, hoping for the indulgence of the audience. Scarcely had the first few notes escaped her quivering lips, when she was borne down by a storm of angry hisses. But so far from crushing Madame Persiani, this unexpected salutation gave her an impetus, and seeing the audience thus pitiless, she continued her part with the most imperturbable coolness, careless whether they were pleased or not. A few weeks later, when she had recovered her strength and voice, the popular admiration became boundless; but she was as insensible to praises as she had been to reproaches:

she replied to the enthusiasm by a disdainful, icy smile, and at the expiration of her engagement left Florence never to return.

At Vienna she was named chamber-singer to the Emperor. At Venice, in 1837, the ever industrious Donizetti, who wrote more operas than he had lived years, composed for her and Ronconi his *Pia Tolomei*, which was performed at the Apollo Theatre.

Madame Persiani was at length free to undertake her Parisian engagement. As she approached the French capital, her fears grew almost insupportable; and when at last the day was fixed irrevocably for her début, an involuntary shivering seized her, and her limbs bent under her as she stepped on the stage, November 7, 1837. The opera was *La Sonnambula*, and Rubini, Tamburini, and Mdlle. Assandri were the performers with the débutante. The aristocratic audience of the theatre was not tardy in sanctioning with its high approval the great renown which had preceded the candidate for their favour; but her début was not so brilliant as might have been expected. Timidity, perhaps, was the cause that obscured the beauty of her talent, and until she appeared in *Il Matrimonio Segreto*, she was not rightly appreciated. "Since the retirement of Madame Fodor," said one critic, "the part of Carolina has never been comprehended, sung and rendered with the same mixture of sweetness and power." Rubini, Tamburini, Mdlle.

Assandri, and Madame Albertazzi took the other characters. In December she appeared as Lucia, and from this time she was the idol of the Parisian public, who placed her above even Grisi herself, for the same reason that they placed Duprez above all tenors, even above Nourrit.

In 1838, Madame Persiani appeared in London, at Her Majesty's Theatre, in *La Sonnambula*. "It is no small risk to any vocalist to follow Malibran and Grisi in a part which they both played so well," observed one critic, "and it is no small compliment to Persiani to say that she succeeded in it." She next appeared as Lucia, with Rubini, Tamburini, &c. By the close of the season she had established herself as an undoubted favourite, and she continued, with little intermission, to sing alternately in London and Paris, for many years. In 1839, she performed at Her Majesty's Theatre with Grisi, Lablache, Tamburini, and Mario.

In 1841, after the close of the London season, she sang for twelve nights at Brussels, with Rubini; and it was said that the two artistes received each 100*l.* nightly. In October they were at Wiesbaden, and during the tour they had undertaken, they were everywhere received with the warmest acclamations; but at Wiesbaden the "enthusiasm" was greatest. Princes, ministers and diplomats crowded round M. Metternich, who had come from his château of Johannisberg, to be present at the concert given by the two eminent vocalists; and at the conclusion of the performance, the Prince took Rubini by the arm, and walked up and down the salon with him for some time. They had become acquainted at Vienna. "My dear Rubini," said Metternich, "it is impossible that you can come so near Johannisberg without paying me a visit there. I hope you and your friends will come and dine with me to-morrow." The following day, therefore, Rubini, Madame Persiani, etc. went to the château, so celebrated for the produce of its vineyards, where M. Metternich and his Princess did the honours with the utmost affability and cordiality. After dinner Rubini, unasked, sang two of his most admired airs; and the Prince, to testify his gratification, offered him a basket of Johannisberg, "to drink my health," he laughingly said, "when you reach your château of Bergamo." Rubini accepted the friendly offering, and begged permission to bring Madame Rubini, before quitting the north of Europe, to visit the fine château. Metternich immediately summoned his major-domo, and said to him, "Remember that if ever M. Rubini visits Johannisberg during my absence, he is to be received as if he were its master. You will place the whole of the château at his disposal so long as he may please to remain." "And the cellar also?" asked Rubini. "The cellar also," added the Prince, smiling: "the cellar at discretion."

In 1842 Madame Persiani was again in London. In Paris she was more admired every day. This year, being in Vienna, Donizetti wrote for her his pathetic opera of *Linda di Chamouni*. As the unfortunate Linda, she almost equalled her performance of Lucia, and displayed great taste and feeling. She did not come to England in 1845, but in 1846 she was warmly welcomed. It was observed that her voice was brilliant and clear as ever, and that she had, if possible, improved in the mechanical resources of her art.

In 1847, Covent Garden Theatre, converted into a superb, spacious opera-house, was opened under the title of the Royal Italian Opera; and it was understood that several of the principal performers had invested large funds in the undertaking, which was directed by Signor Persiani. It was, according to the announcement of the proprietors, "established for the purpose of rendering a more perfect performance of lyric drama than hitherto in this country." The principal members of the company, who had quitted Her Majesty's Theatre, were Mesdames Grisi and Persiani, and a young singer named Mdlle Alboni, who had gained a reputation in Italy; Signori Mario and Tamburini, Salvi and Ronconi, Rovere and Marini. The orchestra, which was under the superintendence of Signor Costa (formerly chef d'orchestre of Her Majesty's Theatre), was of extraordinary strength and excellence. The chorus was numerous and efficient, while the costumes, scenery, and decorations were magnificent.

In October, Madame Persiani reappeared at the Italiens, with Tagliafico and Gardoni; but she vanished from the stage at Paris, terrified, like many other songstresses, by the thunders of the Revolution, and accepted an engagement at a salary of 640*l.* for the season of 1848, from Mr. Delafield, who was just embarking on his rash speculation as an operatic manager. In 1849 she sang again, receiving 500*l.*; when she performed Zerlina and other favourite characters. After this year Madame Persiani took leave of the London stage, although she continued to sing at concerts.

In March, 1850, Madame Persiani, with Tamburini and Gardoni, signed an engagement to appear at the Theatres Royal of Amsterdam and the Hague; she was subsequently engaged with Mario and Tamburini for the Imperial Theatre of St. Petersburg, where she appeared in *La Sonnambula*, *Il Barbiere*, etc., and in *Il Fantasma*, an opera by her husband. She was greatly admired in this capital; and the Czar Nicholas, with the members of the Imperial family, gave her the most gratifying proofs of approbation. Quitting St. Petersburg, she went to Moscow, where she gave several representations and concerts. She afterwards visited Prussia, Germany, Saxony,

Belgium, Holland, Spain, Ireland, Scotland, and the principal cities of France. In 1854, she was engaged to sing for fifteen nights at the Teatro Communale of Bologna; she also sang at concerts in London the same year, and in 1856, she was singing at Bordeaux. In 1858, she accepted, after some hesitation, an engagement from Mr. E. T. Smith to sing in opera at Drury Lane, and appeared in *I Puritani*, *Don Pasquale*, *Linda di Chamouni*, and *Don Giovanni*. She was greeted with the old familiar plaudits. One of her pupils, Miss Laura Baxter, also appeared. In December, 1858, Madame Persiani fixed her residence at Paris, with the view of devoting herself entirely to musical tuition. There she has since remained.

In 1859, when Mario was about to take his benefit (March 14), at the Théâtre Italien, Calzado, director, entreated Madame Persiani to undertake the character of Zerlina. The part of Don Giovanni having been transposed for Mario, the part of Zerlina was also necessarily altered, especially the passages which she has to sing with the Don. Madame Persiani at first refused to enter on so daring a task as performing this version of Zerlina almost without a rehearsal; but Signor Mario pleaded his own cause so eloquently that she yielded. She was anxious, in fact, to pay her debt of gratitude to the Parisians, whose idol she had been, and she felt that she could not do so more gracefully than by appearing for the last time in her life in a part with which her name was so pleasantly associated. "My career," she said, "began almost in lisping the divine music of *Don Giovanni*; it will be appropriately closed by the interpretation of this chef-d'œuvre of the master of masters, the immortal Mozart." Her voice was found to be singularly fresh and clear, her talent had lost nothing of its piquancy, and she was applauded to the echo.

On leaving the theatre after this performance, she learnt the death of her father, the celebrated Tacchinardi.

CHAPTER XIII.

CATHERINE HAYES.

The shades of a summer evening were beginning to gather over the city of Limerick, so famed for its gloves, its races, and its lasses; parties of pleasure were floating down the Shannon, passing, one after another, the picturesque gardens attached to the mansion of the Earl of Limerick and to the See house of the Bishop, which stretched to the river's edge, when the silence of evening was broken by a delicious childish warbling, as if some little Loreley had emerged from the stream. Song after song was poured forth in quick succession, and more than one boat crept under the shadow of the trees, that its occupants might listen to the unseen songstress; who, hidden in a woodbine bower, unconscious of the audience she had attracted, continued singing till, at the conclusion of the *Lass of Gowrie,* she broke into a prolonged and thrilling shake. The listeners, carried away by their admiration, made the welkin ring with a rapturous shout of applause, startling the timid child, who fled, half blushing, half frightened.

The singer was little Catherine Hayes, then some ten years of age, a native of Limerick, born in 1828, at No. 4, Patrick Street. A gentle, reserved girl, delicate and quiet, shrinking from the rough sports of other children, her great enjoyment was to sit alone in the woodbine arbour at the end of the garden of the Earl of Limerick (an aged female relative being in the service of that nobleman); and here she would warble all the Irish ballads she caught up from time to time. Among the listeners on this particular evening, was the Hon. and Right Rev. Edmond Knox, Bishop of Limerick, whose correct taste and refined judgment enabled him to immediately discern the budding talent of the little songstress. From that evening her open-air practice ceased, and little Kitty found herself a musical wonder. She was invited to the See house, and became the star of a series of musical réunions given by her new patron, and directed by the Messrs. Rogers, musicians of much promise—one of whom afterwards became organist of Limerick Cathedral.

Catherine was also noticed by a lady of the city, a highly accomplished amateur, who, pleased with the youthful talent of the child, invited her to her house, and voluntarily taught her to sing simple ballads, being amply repaid by the quick intelligence of her little pupil. One day the lady asked her to execute a shake; the blushing girl modestly shrank from the difficulty, although urged most pressingly; her ambition being awakened, however, she determined to try if she really could manage it, and returning to the solitude of her woodbine bower she began to imitate the shake played for her by her friend, and discovered, with a thrill of joy, that she could absolutely give it in perfection. Timid, and unable to quite credit that she was indeed gifted with this valuable grace, Catherine did not acknowledge that she had achieved the difficulty, but a few days after, placing herself at the piano beside her friend, she lost her timidity completely on the termination of a ballad, and broke into a shake so brilliant, so ringing, so finished, that her hearer was astonished, and uttered an exclamation of delight, which penetrated to the heart of Catherine: amid all the triumphs of her professional career the "surprise, affection, and gladness," with which her shake on this occasion was greeted by her friend was never effaced from her mind. It was from this lady that Miss Hayes gained the first elementary knowledge of music.

The Bishop, pleased at the rapid progress of his protégée, and anxious to give her an opportunity of making her talents available for her support, consulted with some friends in Limerick, who concurred in advising him to place Catherine with some eminent musical professor; and her mother being unable to defray the expenses, a subscription was raised, and a large sum soon collected. Signor Antonio Sapio was selected as the master for Miss Hayes. The Bishop accordingly wrote to him, and the little Catherine, bidding adieu to her mother and sister Henrietta, went to Dublin, and took up her residence with Signor Sapio, April 1, 1839.

Her voice was then a soprano, with a full, clear, silvery tone; her natural taste was pure and refined, but her knowledge of music was very limited. She was earnest, however, and eagerly applied to study with the view of perfecting herself as a concert singer, and she studied so assiduously that in a few weeks there was a visible improvement. On May 3, 1839, scarcely a month from the time of her arrival in Dublin, she appeared with her master at his annual concert in the great room of the Rotunda, before a crowded and fashionable audience. She was welcomed with Irish cordiality, and, although timid, she sang with some confidence. Even the professional friends of her master were surprised at her rapid improvement. She sang with great sweetness, and was encored in the duet, "O'er shepherd pipe," with Signor Sapio. Her second appearance took place the 8th December at a concert given by the Anacreontic Society; her style, naturally pure, had been cultivated with the utmost care, and her execution of "Qui la voce," from *I Puritani*, and "Come per sereno," showed the excellence of her tuition.

The following month the young singer paid a visit to her native city, where her patrons were greatly astonished and gratified by her singular progress. The Bishop gave a private concert expressly in her honour, and her performance richly rewarded those friends who had taken so kind an interest in her welfare. Before quitting Limerick she sang in public at a musical entertainment, for the joint benefit of herself and Signor Sapio.

On returning to Dublin and resuming her studies, her ardour required to be checked, lest her health should suffer from too constant application. She sang again in public, June 12, 1841, at a concert given by Mr. J. P. Knight, at which she was introduced to Liszt, who was so charmed with her voice and style that he wrote in terms of congratulation to Mrs. Knox, daughter-in-law of the Bishop of Limerick. During the remainder of this year Miss Hayes was one of the leading singers at the Anacreontic, Philharmonic, and other Dublin concerts. She was soon in a position to command terms, and increased her demand from five to ten guineas; a prosaic method of proving that she was becoming a favourite with the public. She visited Belfast (singing at the opening of the Anacreontic Hall), Limerick, Parsonstown, and other places, in the course of the summer and autumn.

On September 12, Catherine was introduced to Lablache, the mighty basso; she was rather alarmed at the idea of singing before this veteran judge, and it was with much difficulty that she could be persuaded to venture on "Qui la voce." Lablache heard her with attention; and when she had finished, instead of offering any opinion, he simply asked her to try another and more difficult solo. Then he proposed that they should sing a duet together, then another, till the trial terminated in a day's practice. At last Lablache smiled, and with some flattering words predicted a most glowing future for her. He advised that she should turn her attention to operatic singing, and, as a preliminary step, suggested that she should go to see Grisi and Mario perform in *Norma*. The height of Catherine's ambition had previously been to become a concert singer; but these remarks changed the direction of her ideas.

Lablache's opinion was conveyed in the following letter to Signor Sapio: "I have heard with infinite pleasure your pupil, Miss Hayes, and I find she possesses all the qualities to make a good singer. With your instruction she can but gain every day, and I am certain she will end by becoming a perfect vocalist in every sense of the word." Mr. Benedict was also present at this interview.

The next night Catherine went to hear Madame Grisi; and from that night her aim was to become an operatic singer. She remained under the tuition of Signor Sapio until August, 1842, when she returned home; one of her last performances in Dublin being at a private concert given by the Countess de Grey. Her great desire was now to go immediately to Paris, in order to take finishing lessons from Manuel Garcia; and she succeeded in obtaining the consent of her friends to her departure. It was suggested that she might wait until a family, about to go to France in October, should leave Ireland, when she could accompany them; but the thought of the delay fretted the impatient girl, and she became so feverish that her friends were fain to permit her to start alone. In October, Catherine arrived in Paris with a letter of introduction to Mr. George Osborne, the pianist, by whose amiable wife she was warmly received.

Miss Hayes at once commenced her studies with Garcia, whom she declared to be "the dearest, the kindest, and the most generous of masters." At the end of eighteen months, Garcia said he could not add a single grace or charm to her beautiful voice, and advised her to proceed immediately to Italy, where alone she could obtain the requisite finish and practice for the lyric stage. In accordance with this counsel she went to Milan, and placed herself under the instruction of Signor Felice Ronconi (brother of the celebrated baritone), professor of singing to the Conservatorio. While studying with him, her clear, pure voice and already admirable style caused her to be invited to numerous musical réunions; at one of which she met Grassini, who sincerely congratulated her on the possession of an organ so beautiful, and on the bright future which awaited her. The Signora also gave a more substantial proof of her disinterested admiration, by writing to Signor Provini, impresario of the Opera at Marseilles, telling him of this young star, and advising him in a friendly way not to lose an opportunity of securing a valuable addition to his company. Signor Provini accordingly came to Milan, and having heard Miss Hayes, offered her terms which seemed to her a fortune, and she joyfully accepted an engagement for two months.

The 10th May, 1845, Catherine Hayes stood trembling at the wings in the Opera House of Marseilles, as Elvira, in *I Puritani*. The house was crowded, and she felt a kind of faintness, and a dreadful sinking of the heart; indeed, when she stepped on the stage, she thought her failure was almost certain, and she afterwards said that the agony of that thought was nearly insupportable. The audience received her with some slight encouragement; but the trying scene between Elvira and Giorgio passed off in silence: not a sound of approval was heard until the eighth scene opened, when, in her bridal array, the agitated Elvira, her lips blanched with fear, again appeared. She was faint and frightened, and the failure which she had anticipated on her first entry now seemed certain. But on commencing the polacca, "Son Vergin," she felt suddenly inspired, and, her very despair lending her courage, she sang this beautiful air with sweetness, tenderness, and expression. "The ice was at once thawed," says one of her biographers; "a general burst of approbation startled her from almost despair into a perfect rapture. A flattering encore then further bewildered her with a new and exquisite joy, and at its termination, as the shouts of applause followed her from the stage, she wept with pleasure to know that the dream of her life's ambition had begun to be realized, and she *felt* she had succeeded. The curtain fell amid the most enthusiastic plaudits, renewed again and again, till the agitated but delighted girl reappeared, when numbers of the passionate music-loving audience who had rushed *en masse* from the theatre, and returned loaded with artificial flowers, literally filled the stage with their graceful offerings, making a perfect garden around the embarrassed débutante."

She next appeared in *Lucia di Lammermoor*, when she confirmed the favourable impression which she had created; and afterwards she performed Zora in *Mosè in Egitto*. During her three months' stay in Marseilles, her popularity increased so rapidly that Signor Provini actually offered her an engagement at the Opera in Paris. Fearing, however, to encounter such an ordeal while she had yet so much to learn, she wisely declined the brilliant offer and returned to Milan, where she resumed her studies under the direction of Signor Ronconi. The young singer next appeared at the annual concert of Ricordi, the music publisher, where she met the manager of La Scala, Signor Morelli, who offered her an engagement, which she accepted. She was then only seventeen, being the youngest artiste who ever filled the position of prima donna at that vast theatre.

Three months after she made her début at La Scala in Donizetti's *Linda di Chamouni*, but without success. Her timidity, perhaps, was the reason. She then appeared as Desdemona, and "made a decided fiasco." But she courageously persevered, and at last created a great sensation in *La Sonnambula*. In *Otello* she also achieved a triumph, the character of Desdemona being well adapted to her delicate, girlish style of beauty, and her clear, pure soprano: she represented this gentle heroine so admirably that the Milanese unanimously gave her the flattering designation of "la Perla del Teatro." She remained at Milan during the autumn of 1845 and the Carnival of 1846, when Madame Bishop was engaged. In the spring of 1846, Miss Hayes went to Vienna, where, she laughingly wrote home, she was quite "spoilt." "She was afraid," she said, "that her head would be turned with the intoxication of such unexpected success."

On the first night of the Carnival of 1847, Miss Hayes made her appearance in Venice, in a new opera composed expressly for her by Malespino, a young Italian nobleman, entitled *Albergo di Romano*. The music was indifferent, and the singers worse. The audience received the opera with chilling silence, and when Cattarina entered in the middle of the first act, she found the house in a horribly bad humour. At sight of her fair young face, however, and on hearing the clear tones of her sweet soprano, the anger of the audience gradually dissipated; and although Catherine could not save the piece from condemnation, she rescued it for this one night. She then appeared as Lucia, with great success. During the rondo of the third act, the audience was so silent, that (said the *Figaro* of Venice) the buzzing of a fly might have been heard; and at the close of the opera Miss Hayes was called twice on the stage, and applauded for nearly ten minutes. In *Linda di Chamouni*, she was not only completely successful, but was the cause of a little theatrical uproar. At Venice, the law regulating theatres prohibits any artiste, at any theatre, from appearing before the curtain more than thrice, in compliance with a call from the audience; but when Miss Hayes had retired at the end of the opera, on this occasion, the excited crowd shouted for her to come forward a fourth time. The young prima donna dared not venture to disobey the police regulations;

and the excitement then became terrific, the audience asseverating that if she did not appear as many times as they chose to call for her, they would tear down the theatre; it was judged advisable to yield to their wishes, and, when she finally appeared, she was covered with flowers.

She also performed in a new opera, *Griselda*, by Frederico Ricci, and then visited Vienna, where Ricci wrote for her his *Estrella*. She then returned to Italy, appearing first at Milan, where she sang in Mercadante's *Giuramento*, and also in *Mortedo*, an opera composed expressly for her. Thence she went to Bergamo, where she met Rubini, at a banquet given by the Podesta. She had always greatly desired to hear this illustrious tenor, and having intimated her wish, he very kindly sang for her his celebrated air from *Il Pirata;* asking her afterwards to accompany him in the duet, "Su la Tomba," from *Lucia di Lammermoor*. Anxious to give this great master a favourable idea of her powers, Miss Hayes exerted herself to the utmost, and surpassed herself. Rubini said the most flattering things to her, and assured her of undoubted success. For her benefit at Bergamo, she gave a miscellaneous concert, which was largely attended.

From Bergamo she went, in September, 1847, to Verona, where she sang during the Carnival in Verdi's *I Masnadieri*, and was received with a tempest of applause. Thence she went to Florence, where she met Madame Catalani, who always welcomed her as a visitor. One day, Catherine having sung in the salon before a large company, the ex-Queen of Song kissed her affectionately, and exclaimed, "What would I not give to be in London when you make your début! Your fortune is certain: and remember my doors are always open to you." Mercadante, the composer, also expressed the highest admiration for Cattarina's talents.

At the Carlo Felice, Genoa, she performed Maria di Rohan and other leading parts in Verdi's works with distinguished success. On the occasion of her farewell benefit, when the curtain fell, the aristocratic ladies left their boxes, and went behind the scenes to present the young donna with enormous bouquets, expressing at the same time the warmest wishes for her success in England.

Mr. Delafield, who had offered engagements to almost every prima donna in existence, had engaged Catherine Hayes at a salary of 1,300*l.* His company consisted of Mesdames Grisi, Persiani, and Brambilla, Signori Mario, Salvi, the two Lablaches, and Tamburini. On Tuesday, April 10, 1849, Catherine Hayes made her début at the Royal Italian Opera, in Donizetti's *Linda di Chamouni*, with Tagliafico, Salvi, Tamburini, and Mdlle. de Meric, a new contralto. Her voice had now become a clear and beautiful soprano, of the sweetest quality, fresh, mellow, and pure, and of good compass, ascending with ease to D in alt.

The upper notes were limpid, and like a well-tuned silver bell up to A; thence up to D flat they were less liquid, and slightly veiled, betraying signs of having been strained by her exertions on the Italian stage. The middle register had not yet gained that fulness and sonorous sweetness which afterwards constituted its greatest charm; but the lower tones were the most beautiful ever heard in a real soprano. Her style, unpretendingly pure, was artistic and graceful. She never forced her voice, although she had abundance of energy at command; nor ever exaggerated, though she had deep sensibility and strong dramatic feeling. Her intonation was invariably correct, and she had great facility of execution, notwithstanding that her voice was not remarkable for flexibility. She had faults, it is true, but these were atoned for by many beauties.

Her conception of character was fine, energetic, and earnest, though she failed in the physical strength requisite for embodying her ideas; she never trifled on the stage, but as far as her powers would admit, threw herself into the dramatic situation with spirit. She was a touching actress in parts such as Amina, Lucia, or Linda—innocent, plaintive, and charming; and in such characters the pathos of her singing was very touching. She was tall, with a fine figure, and delicately marked, perfectly feminine features; her manner was graceful and lady-like, and her movements unconstrained.

The audience received her with rapturous welcome, which took her by surprise, and at first rendered her so nervous that she could scarcely command her powers. Her acting in the last scene, when Linda gradually recovers her reason and recognizes her lover, her parents, and her friends, was beautiful—pathetic and forcible in the highest degree. Towards the close of the performance, those who observed her narrowly saw that she was affected by some overpowering emotion; and when the curtain fell, she was to be seen kneeling in a private box, sobbing at the feet of her first and dearest friend, the Bishop of Limerick. She had noticed him among the assembly, and at the first opportunity flew to pour out her joy and gratitude, ascribing to him every honour and reward she had gained. All the London papers pronounced eulogiums on her performance, and her success was undoubted.

Her second performance (May 4) was *Lucia di Lammermoor*, with Mario and Tamburini. She made a still more favourable impression in this opera, in which she was not only pathetic, but original. *Roberto il Diavolo* was represented for the first time at the Italian Opera May 12, with great splendour, when Catherine Hayes took the part of Alice, for the first time. The cast, though including one or two favourites, was not sufficiently strong, and the opera not proving beneficial to the treasury, was withdrawn after two representations. Madame Dorus Gras, in defiance of a severe cold, took the character of Alice at the second performance, in consequence of the sudden indisposition of Miss Hayes.

The Irish prima donna had the honour of singing at Buckingham Palace towards the close of the season, when her Majesty condescended to enter into conversation with her, complimenting her on what she was pleased to term her "deserved success," and anticipating for her future honours and rewards. Prince Albert and the Duke of Cambridge also paid her the most flattering compliments.

The announcement of the engagement of Miss Hayes by the Dublin Philharmonic Society, after an absence of seven years, drew an unusually full audience to the concert-room, including the Earl and Countess of Clarendon. The welcome home of the "Irish Lind," as she was called, was truly Hibernian in its warmth and enthusiasm, and her singing created an extraordinary sensation. She made her second appearance at the Theatre Royal. The opera was *Lucia di Lammermoor*, the Edgardo of the evening being Signor Pagliere, an unknown performer. "His ludicrous inefficiency," says a writer in the *Dublin University Magazine*, "elicited shouts of laughter, with a variety of ingenious mimicries from the wags among the audience—the manifestations of disapprobation for him being blended with loud applause for the frightened débutante. In the midst of this uproar and noise, a more glaring break-down than before on Edgar's part was followed by a hurricane of 'catcalls.' Miss Hayes, with wonderful self-possession, curtsied to that unfortunate gentleman, and left the stage.

The curtain was then rung down; and an indescribable scene of tumultuous excitement followed; cheers, groans, laughter, and hisses, forming a very Babel of discord. Mr. Sims Reeves, who, with Mr. Whitworth, Miss Lucombe, and an English opera company, had terminated an engagement the day of Miss Hayes' coming, occupied a private box, and sat, during all this turmoil, full in view of the audience. He was quickly recognized, and shouts of "Reeves! Reeves!" arose from nearly every part of the house. The lessee, Mr. Calcraft, on this, came forward, and intimated that "he had then no control over Mr. Reeves, whose engagement had terminated, and who, on being asked to sing on this emergency, had positively declined." Mr. Reeves instantly sprang to his feet, leaned out of the box, and on obtaining a partial silence, said, in no very temperate tones: "Ladies and Gentlemen, I will sing to oblige you, but not to oblige Mr. Calcraft;" on which the lessee, in the blandest tones, concluded the first act of unpleasantness in these words: "I am not angry, I assure you, that Mr. Reeves has declined to sing to oblige me; but I am gratified to find that he has consented to do so to please the audience, and doubly gratified because, under the untoward circumstances, he will support your gifted and distinguished young countrywoman."

"After the necessary delay of dressing, &c., the curtain again rose, and the opera proceeded, Mr. Reeves performing Edgar better than on any former occasion in this city, and Miss Hayes nerving herself so fully for her task that no trace of tremulousness, no shadow of the agitating scene through which she had passed, marred the beauty of her singing and acting. At the termination of each act they were both called before the curtain; and when the opera concluded, their presence was again and again demanded, amid the almost furious waving—not only of hats and handkerchiefs, but of canes and umbrellas. The curtain having finally descended, the lessee came forward, Mr. Reeves also appearing at the wing, and still in the costume of Edgardo: this occasioned a renewal of the uproar; but mutual explanations ensued, and the singer and manager shook hands upon the stage. This unfortunate disturbance had nearly proved fatal to the success of the first appearance of Catherine Hayes in the metropolitan theatre of her birth-place; that success being thus suddenly imperilled, and so nearly marred, it is not surprising that Miss Hayes should refer to this incident as the most painful throughout her entire career."

The following evening she appeared in *Norma;* and she concluded her brief engagement by performing in *La Sonnambula*, completing her visit by two concerts given in her native city. Her second appearance in Dublin took place in February, 1850. The 11th and 12th March she was engaged to sing at Limerick in *Linda di Chamouni* and *Lucia di Lammermoor*, being accompanied by Miss Poole, Mr. Travers, Signor Polonini and Herr Menghis. From Limerick she went to Cork and Waterford, and her reception was everywhere most gratifying.

Having accepted an engagement from Mr. Lumley, Catherine Hayes made her first appearance in Her Majesty's Theatre the 2nd April, with Sims Reeves, and Signori Belletti and F. Lablache. Her début in *Lucia di Lammermoor* was a great success. The London critics, without a single exception, spoke in ecstasies of her vocal and dramatic excellence; yet she was afforded very few opportunities of appearing. Ill health may, perhaps, have interfered with her performances; for in June Madame Frezzolini was obliged, at a few hours' notice, to undertake her part of Lucia.

During the winter of 1850–51 she went on a tour through Ireland, creating a furore scarcely inferior to the "Lind mania" of '47. She then went through the English counties, singing at Manchester, Liverpool, Birmingham, &c. At the Carnival in Rome in 1851, she was engaged at the Teatro d'Apollone, and performed in *Maria di Rohan*, which she sustained for twelve successive nights. Nothing could exceed the delight which her singing and acting created. She also performed in *I Puritani*, and was announced to appear in many other operas, which were abruptly forbidden by the police authorities. She was treated with the greatest respect and attention by the most exclusive circles in Rome, as much on account of her irreproachable personal character as through admiration for her talents. She was honoured with the diploma of the "Accademia di Santa Cecilia," one of the oldest and most respected musical societies in Italy.

From Rome she returned to London, where during the season of 1851 she was the star of the concert-room in London, and of the performances of the Sacred Harmonic Society, where she sang in the oratorios of Handel, Haydn, and Mendelssohn. May, 1851, she sang at the Philharmonic Concerts, Liverpool; and in June she was at Cork. She was more suited for the concert-room than for the stage, and her ballad singing was incomparable: indeed in the execution of the ballads of her native land she was not to be surpassed. She threw her whole soul into them, with an ardour which seemed to English ears somewhat exaggerated; and through her magical interpretation of their national airs, she exercised an extraordinary spell over the feelings of her Irish audiences: since the days of Catherine Stephens, no vocalist had ever given ballads as Catherine Hayes gave them. In July and August Miss Hayes visited Trouville and Havre; then returned to England to sing at concerts in Manchester and Liverpool. Her final appearance in England for many years was at the Theatre Royal, Liverpool.

She then commenced one of the most singular journeys round the world ever undertaken by artiste. She left Liverpool in September, with Mr. Augustus Braham and Herr Menghis, for New York. Her commencement at New York was threatened with failure, in consequence of inefficient management; but fortunately, Mr. W. Evory Bushnell, a famous electioneering agent, seeing what might be done, boldly proposed to rescue her, and volunteered to carry her triumphantly through the length and breadth of the Union. She accordingly, by his advice, forfeited 3,000*l.*, and permitted him to undertake the management of her tour.

December, 1851, she was at Philadelphia; she arrived at San Francisco November, 1852, and was singing at California in 1853. Her success in this region was marvellous: fabulous sums were paid for the choice of seats, and one ticket sold for 1,150 dols. She then departed for South America, and after visiting the principal cities, embarked for the Gold Fields of Australia. She gave concerts in the Sandwich Islands, and arrived in Sydney, January, 1854. From Sydney she went to Melbourne and Adelaide. At

Melbourne she became such a favourite that when she announced her departure a petition, most numerously signed, was presented to her, begging her to continue her performances for some time. From Adelaide she went to India, giving concerts in Calcutta and Singapore. March, 1855, she gave, in aid of the Patriotic Fund, a concert which realized upwards of 200*l.* She then went to Batavia, and in the capital of Java she created an immense sensation. From thence she turned her steps to Port Philip, revisited Melbourne and Sydney, appeared at the Bendigo Gold-fields, and sang at Hobart Town and Launceston. She then re-embarked for England in the *Royal Charter*, arriving at Liverpool, August, 1856, after an absence of five years, and in October she was married to Mr. Bushnell (the manager of her tour), at St. George's, Hanover Square.

Catherine Hayes (for she retained her maiden name in public) continued to sing at concerts, her voice having gained in power and lost nothing in sweetness during her lengthened absence. After fulfilling an engagement with M. Jullien, Mrs. Bushnell went on provincial tours, and visited the south of France and Spain, whither her husband had been ordered by his physicians for his health. Mr. Bushnell was the victim of a hereditary malady, and they fixed their residence at Biarritz, hoping that the mild climate would completely restore him: he died, however, July 3, and his widow returned to England, occupying herself professionally in singing at concerts in London and the provinces.

On Sunday, August 11, 1861, she died at Sydenham, in the zenith of her fame. In private life she had been a most amiable, kind-hearted Irishwoman, ever ready to assist the distressed; by her friends she was idolized; by the public she was respected for the purity of her life, and admired for her talents. She left property to the value of 16,000*l.*, and bequeathed legacies to her relatives and friends.

CHAPTER XIV.

MARIETTA ALBONI.

MARIETTA ALBONI was born at Cesena, a little town of the Romagna, the 10th March, 1822. Her father, one of a most respectable Italian family, was a captain in the customs department of Cesena; and he bestowed on all his children a very good education. Marietta, evincing a taste for music, besides a faculty for acquiring languages, was placed with Signor Bagioli, a music teacher of her native town, who took such care of her that at eleven she could read music at sight. Having studied solfeggio with Bagioli, Marietta was sent to Bologna to take lessons from Madame Bertolotti. She had the good fortune at the same time to receive instructions from Rossini, and the great maestro had a very clear idea of her future. Some one asked his opinion of her talents. "At present," he is reported to have answered, "her voice is like that of an itinerant-ballad singer, but the town will be at her feet before she is a year older."

Shortly afterwards Morelli, director of many theatrical agencies in Italy and Germany, engaged her for the Teatro Communale of Bologna, and she appeared there as Maffeo Orsini, in *Lucrezia Borgia*, in 1842. She was then transferred to La Scala, where she performed in Donizetti's *Favorita*. Rossini himself signed her two first engagements. "I am," said he, "a subscribing witness to your union with renown. May success and happiness attend the union." Her success was attested by the fact that the manager of La Scala renewed her engagement for four successive seasons.

From Milan, Marietta proceeded to Vienna, where she won fresh laurels, being the prima donna for three years. She then repaired to St. Petersburg, where she sang for two seasons; returning thence to Vienna, she travelled through Holland, giving concerts. She sang also in Berlin. When she arrived in that city, she was asked if she had waited on M——? "No," she replied. "Who is this M——?" "Oh," answered her friend; "he is the most influential journalist in Prussia." "Well, how does this concern me?" "Why," rejoined the other, "if you do not contrive to ensure his favourable report, you are ruined." The young Italian drew herself up disdainfully. "Indeed!" she said, coldly: "well, let it be as heaven directs; but I wish it to be understood that, in *my* breast, the woman is superior to the artist, and though failure were the result, I would never degrade myself by purchasing success at so humiliating a price." The anecdote was repeated in the fashionable saloons of Berlin, and so far from injuring her, the noble sentiment of the young débutante was appreciated. The King invited her to sing at his court, where she received the well-merited applause of an admiring audience; and afterwards his Majesty bestowed more tangible evidences of his approbation.

At the commencement of the summer of 1846, Marietta was singing at Dresden, in *Il Barbiere*, with Tsitatschek, and early in 1847 she sang at Rome.

Mr. Beale having heard her at Milan, and being charmed with her voice, consulted Signor Costa, and offered her an opportunity of being heard in England. She was engaged in 1847, at the Royal Italian Opera, Covent Garden. Unheralded by the trumpet of fame, and almost unknown, she appeared under most disadvantageous circumstances. It was the season when the "Lind mania" was at its height, and the blaze of the Swedish Nightingale's popularity threatened extinction to any star which might come too near her. Nevertheless, one night Alboni appeared on the stage, and in the morning found herself famous.

She appeared Tuesday, April 6, as Arsace, in *Semiramide*, with Madame Grisi and Tamburini; and the success she achieved then she never lost. The audience were astounded at the wonderful sweetness and capacity of her organ. In place of a timid débutante, they found before them a highly-finished vocalist, unrivalled since the days of Pisaroni; and when she poured out her voice in a grand volume of rich melody, the crowded house was electrified. In the magnificent duet, "Giorno d'Orrore," her tones rose with a luscious power which was responded to by thunders of applause. To her we are indebted for that beautiful air, "In si barbara," hitherto suppressed for want of a contralto of sufficient compass to give it full effect.

Her voice was a superb contralto, yet embracing almost three octaves, from E flat to C sharp: its tones were rich, full, sonorous, mellow, liquid; in truth, the vocabulary of epithets might be exhausted in a vain endeavour to convey an idea of its beauty. Its quality throughout was equally pure, beautiful, flexible and sympathetic. Her articulation was clear; her notes came, even in the most difficult and rapid passages, with the fluency and precision of a well-played instrument. The purity of her intonation was absolutely faultless; the rapidity and certainty of her execution no one can imagine who has not heard her. Her style and method were models of perfection, her taste was refined, her skill consummate. She displayed the utmost reverence for the ideas of the composer whose works she interpreted; and even in the music of Rossini she did not interpolate a note. But her singular ease was the greatest matter of wonder: she smiled as she ran over the most intricate scales; and her singing enchanted the connoisseur as much as the merest amateur. Yet it gave the hearer the idea of being purely spontaneous, not acquired by art or labour.

In person she was large, and "frankly inclined to embonpoint;" yet albeit portly, she was exceedingly feminine in aspect. Her figure was symmetrical, graceful, and commanding; her features, without pretensions to regular beauty, were highly agreeable and full of vivacity and kindliness. Her physiognomy was genial; her eyes, when lighted by the passion of her part, flashed with extraordinary brilliancy; her smile was "bewitching;" and when she laughed, she not only revealed the whitest teeth, but her laugh was so infectious, it was impossible to resist echoing her gaiety. She was not a tragedian, like Pasta or Grisi: on the contrary, she was always a little cold as an actress, and her manner indolent and apathetic; though her "stage deportment" was not without grace. Her resplendent voice, however, sufficed to redeem any personal imperfections; and although at first some critics were inclined to disparage the young débutante, they acknowledged that an artist of high order had appeared.

Mdlle. Alboni went from triumph to triumph. Her Malcolm, in *La Donna del Lago*, was pronounced unequalled since the time of Pisaroni; in Orsini she created a furore. As De Gondi (*Maria de Rohan*), she was admirable; and as Pippo, inimitable. She undertook, at very brief notice, to play Persiani's part in *Il Barbiere di Seviglia*, in consequence of the sudden illness of that popular vocalist; and at no time was Alboni seen to greater advantage. There was a vivacity and lively humour in her performance which won every heart.

M. Duponchel, who, with M. Roqueplan, had succeeded M. Pillet in the management of the Opéra in Paris, came to England to offer her an engagement. In October, therefore, the young singer, now a world-wide celebrity, appeared at four concerts in Paris, with Alizard and Barroilhet. The programme of these concerts was not much varied: the cavatina of Arsace, the duo of Arsace and Assur, the cavatina of Isabella in *L'Italiana in Algieri*, the duo from *Il Barbiere*, the Brindisi from *Lucrezia Borgia*—these composed the list of pieces.

As in London, Mdlle. Alboni's appearance in Paris was not announced with a flourish of trumpets. "Many persons, artists and amateurs," said Fiorentino, "absolutely asked on the morning of her début, Who is this Alboni? Whence does she come? What can she do?" And their interrogatories were answered by some fragments of those trifling and illusory biographies which always accompany young vocalists. There was, however, intense curiosity to hear and see this redoubtable singer who had held the citadel of the Royal Italian Opera against the attraction of Jenny Lind, and the theatre was crowded to suffocation by rank, fashion, beauty, and notabilities on the night of her first concert, October 9. When she stepped quietly on the stage, dressed in black velvet, a brooch of brilliants on her bosom, and her hair cut *à la Titus*, with a music-paper in her hand, there was just one thunder-clap of applause, followed by a silence of some seconds. She had not one acknowledged advocate in the house; but when Arsace's cavatina, "Ah! quel giorno," gushed from her lips in a rich stream of melodious sound, the entire audience was at her feet, and the critics could not command language sufficiently glowing to express their admiration.

"What exquisite quality of sound, what purity of intonation, what precision in the scales!" cried the *Revue et Gazette Musicale*. "What finesse in the manner of the breaks of the voice! What amplitude and mastery of voice she exhibits in the Brindisi; what incomparable clearness and accuracy in the air from *L'Italiana*, and the duo from *Il Barbiere!* There is no instrument capable of rendering with more certain and more faultless intonation the groups of rapid notes which Rossini wrote, and which Alboni sings with the same facility and the same celerity. The only fault the critic has in his power to charge the wondrous artiste with is, that when she repeats a morçeau, we hear exactly the same traits, the same turns, the same fioriture; which was never the case with Malibran or Cinti Damoreau."

"This vocal scale," says Scudo, speaking of her voice, "is divided into three parts, or registers, which follow in complete order. The first register commences at F in the bass, and reaches F in the *medium*. This is the true body of the voice, whose admirable timbre characterizes and colours all the rest. The second extends from G in the *medium* to F on the fifth line, and the upper part, which forms the third register, is no more than an elegant superfluity of Nature. It is necessary next to understand with what incredible skill the artiste manages this instrument; it is the pearly, light, and florid vocalization of Persiani joined to the resonance, pomp, and amplitude of Pisaroni. No words can convey an idea of the exquisite purity of this voice, always mellow, always equable, which vibrates without effort, and each note of which expands itself like the bud of a rose—sheds a balm on the ear, as some exquisite fruit perfumes the palate. No scream, no affected dramatic contortion of sound attacks the sense of hearing, under the pretence of softening the feelings."

"But that which we admire above all in the artiste," observes Fiorentino, "is the pervading soul, the sentiment, the perfect taste; the inimitable method. Then what body in the voice! What largeness! What simplicity of style! What facility of vocalization! What genius in the contrasts! What colour in the phrases! What charm! What expression! Mdlle. Alboni sings as she smiles—without effort, without fatigue, without audible and broken respiration. Here is art in its fidelity! here is the model and example which every one who would become an artiste should copy."

"It is such a pleasure to hear real singing!" says Hector Berlioz. "It is so rare; and voices at once beautiful, natural, expressive, flexible, and *in tune*, are so very uncommon! The voice of Mdlle. Alboni possesses these excellent qualities in the highest degree of perfection. It is a magnificent contralto of immense range (two octaves and six notes—nearly three octaves—from low E to C in alt.), the quality perfect throughout, even in the lowest notes of the lower register, which are generally so disastrous to the majority of singers who fancy they possess a contralto, and the emission of which resembles nearly always a rattle, hideous in such cases, and revolting to the ear. Mdlle. Alboni's vocalization is wonderfully easy; few sopranos exhibit equal facility. The registers of her voice are so perfectly united, that in her scales you do not feel sensible of the passage from one to the other; the tone is *unctuous*, caressing, velvetty, melancholy, like that of all contraltos, though less sombre than that of Pisaroni, and incomparably more pure and limpid. As the notes are produced without effort, the voice yields itself to every shade of intensity; and thus, Mdlle. Alboni can sing from the most mysterious piano to the most brilliant forte. And this alone is what I call singing *humanly*—that is to say, in a fashion that declares the presence of a human heart, of a human soul, of a human intelligence. Singers not possessed of these indispensable qualities should, in my opinion, be ranged under the category of mechanical instruments. Mdlle. Alboni is an artiste entirely devoted to her art, and has not up to this moment been tempted to make a trade of it; she has never, hitherto, given a thought to what her delicious notes—precious pearls, which she lavishes with such happy bounty—might bring her per annum. Different from the majority of her contemporary singers, money questions are the last with which she occupies herself: her demands have hitherto been extremely modest. Added to this, the sincerity and trustworthiness of her character, which amounts almost to singularity, are acknowledged by all who have any dealings with her."

The first night of Mdlle. Alboni's appearance some of the boxes were not filled; on the succeeding nights there was not a place to be had. "Two theatres as large as the Opéra might have been easily crammed." At the last, more than a thousand persons were refused admission. The excitement was extraordinary. Alboni surpassed herself, and was almost smothered with roses and camellias, and deafened with applause; the stage was literally transformed into a flower-garden with the profusion of bouquets.

The morning after her second appearance, she was seated quietly in her hotel on the Boulevard des Italiens, reading the feuilletons of Berlioz and Fiorentino in the *Journal des Débats* and *Le Constitutionnel*, with a kind of childish delight; entirely unconscious, apparently, that she was the sole theme of conversation in all Parisian circles. A friend came in, when she asked, "in the most unaffected tone of sincerity," whether she had sung "assez bien" on Monday night, and broke into a fit of merry laughter at the answer: "Très bien pour une petite fille." "Alboni," writes this friend, "is assuredly, for a great artiste, the most unpretending and simple creature in the world. She has not the slightest notion of her position in her art in the eyes of the public and the musical world."

It was said that M. Vatel, manager of the Italiens, was driven nearly frantic at her unprecedented success; for, by the advice of Lablache, he had declined to engage her, although he might have done so at no great sacrifice.

On the termination of the four concerts, Alboni went to Pesth, and then returned to Vienna. At Pesth she performed Orsini in *Lucrezia Borgia*, and De Gondi in *Maria de Rohan*, and gave a concert besides. At Vienna, she gave a concert the 20th

November, in the Theater an der Wien, and obtained "a prodigious success." From Vienna, she returned to Paris. She made her début as Arsace, in *Semiramide*, Thursday, December 2, with Madame Grisi, Coletti, Cellini, and Tagliafico.

The theatre was crowded with fashionable, literary, and artistic celebrities, princes, ministers of state, dilettanti, and women of fashion and wit. A subdued murmur circled round the house; some prognosticated a triumphant success, others a partial one—if not a complete failure; and a universal buzz of whispers betrayed the lively interest felt by the audience.

The curtain rose. Grisi came on, and was received with a burst of applause. At length, a sudden and unbroken silence fell on the assembly; the orchestra played the long symphony which preludes the contralto air, "Eccomi alfin in Babilonia," and, with a tranquil step, Alboni issued from the side-scenes, and slowly walked up to the footlights. "There was a sudden pause," says one who was present; "a feather might almost have been heard to move. The orchestra, the symphony finished, refrained from proceeding, as though to give time for the enthusiastic reception which was Alboni's right, and which it was natural to suppose Alboni would receive. But you may imagine my surprise and the feelings of the renowned contralto, when not a hand or a voice was raised to acknowledge her! I could see Alboni tremble; but it was only for an instant. What was the reason of this unanimous disdain, or this unanimous doubt?—call it what you will. She might perhaps guess, but she did not suffer it to perplex her for more than a few moments. Throwing aside the extreme diffidence that marked her entrée, and the perturbation that resulted from the frigidity of the spectators, she wound herself up to the condition of fearless independence for which she is constitutionally and morally remarkable, and with a look of superb indifference and conscious power, she commenced the opening of her aria. In one minute the crowd, that but an instant before seemed to disdain her, was at her feet! The effect of those luscious tones had never yet failed to touch the heart and rouse the ardour of an audience, educated or uneducated." Alboni's triumph was instantaneous and complete; it was the greater from the moment of anxious uncertainty that preceded it, and made the certainty which succeeded more welcome and delightful. From this instant to the end of the opera, Alboni's success grew into a triumph. During the first act she was twice recalled; during the second act, thrice; and she was encored in the air "In si barbara," which she delivered with pathos, and in the cabaletta of the second duet with Semiramide.

She next performed in *La Cenerentola* with the same success.

In 1848 Mdlle. Alboni again appeared before an

English audience at Covent Garden, at a salary of 4,000*l*. She commenced with Tancredi, Madame Persiani being the Amenaïde. She was, if possible, more captivating than ever, and her voice seemed to have gathered power and volume. Her natural ease and freedom from mannerisms were enchanting; it was only to be regretted that she had not more dramatic energy. The chief event of the season was her performance in *La Cenerentola*, in March. She also performed in *Anna Bolena*, with Madame Grisi, Tamburini, Tagliafico, and Mario; and (in July) in *Gli Ugonotti*, with Madame Viardot and the aforesaid Signori; then in *La Gazza Ladra*. In the autumn she returned to Paris, when her success was as brilliant as before.

In 1849, on the retirement of Jenny Lind, Mdlle. Alboni became the prima donna of Her Majesty's Theatre, performing with Calzolari, a young tenor of great excellence, Lablache, Colletti, Moriani, and Ronconi. She performed the parts of Rosina, Ninetta, Zerlina in *Don Giovanni*, and Norina in *Don Pasquale*, astonishing the public by the facility with which she sang music so opposed to her own genre; but it was regretted that the superb contralto had quitted her proper realm.

In March she abruptly disappeared. Before leaving Paris she had promised to sing at the annual concert of poor old Filippo Galli, and her name was announced in the bills for Friday, the 23rd March.

In the hurry of her departure she had omitted to warn him that she would not be able to return before the very hour at which the concert was to begin; and the suspense and anxiety of the unfortunate Filippo were to be more easily imagined than described when, asked if Alboni would sing, he could not answer definitively—"Perhaps yes, perhaps no." He sold very few tickets, and the rooms (in the Salle Herz) were thinly occupied. She, however, had not forgotten her promise: at the very moment when the matinée was commencing she arrived, in time to redeem her word, and reward those who had attended; but too late to be of any service to the veteran. Galli was in despair, and was buried in reflections neither exhilarating nor profitable, when, some minutes after the concert, the comely face and portly figure of Alboni appeared at the door of his room. "How much are the expenses of your concert?" she kindly inquired. "Mia cara," dolorously responded the bénéficiaire, "cinque centî franci (500 francs)." "Well, then, to repair the loss that I may have caused you," said the generous cantatrice, "here is a bank note for a thousand francs. Do me the favour to accept it." This was only one of the many kind actions she performed.

From Paris she went to Italy, where she was called by family affairs, and then she returned to England to resume her engagement. The autumn found her again at the Théâtre Italien, performing in *La Cenerentola*, etc., with Lablache, Bordas, and Ronconi, director of the establishment.

In April, 1850, after a tour of unprecedented brilliancy in the provinces of France, Mdlle. Alboni returned to Paris, "with new laurels and rolls of bank notes." The principal operas in which she performed during her trip were *La Favorita* and *La Reine de Chypre.* Her success had been so great that the directors of the Grand Opéra (Théâtre de la Nation) immediately engaged her for sixteen represenations of Madame Viardot's great character of Fides in *Le Prophète.* She commenced in May. To attempt this part was regarded as an act of singular daring; but, as Madame de Staël observes, "there is nothing so successful as success." Meyerbeer himself not only offered no objection, but, being present at the first performance, went behind the scenes, and warmly congratulated her on her triumph. From Paris Mdlle. Alboni went to Madrid, where she sang in *La Favorita* and *La Sonnambula* with Madame Frezzolini, Gardoni, Herr Formes, and Ronconi. In September she reappeared at the Théâtre Italien in *La Favorita,* and was received with overwhelming enthusiasm. She returned soon after to Madrid.

The following May she quitted Madrid and returned to Paris, when Auber's *Corbeille d'Oranges,* written for her, was produced. Although the character of Zerlina was a charming one, it did not suit her; and having sung this part for two months she came to London—returning to Paris in September. December, 1851, she commenced a course of representations and concerts in the provinces in England.

In 1852 Mdlle. Alboni paid a visit to the United States, where she was enthusiastically received. If she did not raise the furore which Jenny Lind had created, she was none the less admired; and her departure on the conclusion of her tour was universally regretted. She gave her farewell concert in New York at the Metropolitan Hall, the 2nd May. The hall was crowded in every corner, and the applause was vehement, regret for her departure being loudly expressed. This concert was for the benefit of Signor Arditi, who had been the conductor of her performances during her sojourn in America.

In July, 1853, Marietta Alboni married the Comte de Pepoli, at Paris; and it was rumoured that she was about to withdraw from the stage; but she effectually disproved this by appearing, in 1854, in Paris, performing in *La Donna del Lago* and others of Rossini's operas. In the spring of 1855 she was performing in Barcelona, from whence she came direct to England. On her appearance before her London admirers, the reputation of her youth was revived, and her popularity was undiminished. In May she went with Ernst and other artistes on a provincial tour, under the management of Mr. Beale, returning then to London.

In July, 1855, she was at the Grand Opéra in Paris, performing in *Le Prophète*, etc., with Roger, having contracted an engagement for three years. In 1856 she was at Her Majesty's Theatre with Mdlle. Piccolomini, and made her first appearance in the character of Azucena in *Il Trovatore*. Her performances were not confined to the Opera-house; she sang at the Crystal Palace and in the Surrey Music Hall. In October she was again at the Italiens, commencing with *La Cenerentola*. She then, in conjunction with Mario, Graziani, and Madame Frezzolini, began performing in the works of Verdi. *Il Trovatore* was performed in January, 1857, and was followed by *Rigoletto*, which was produced in defiance of the protestations of Victor Hugo, from whose play, *Le Roi s'amuse*, the libretto had been taken. Victor Hugo declared that the representation of the opera was an infringement of his rights, as being simply a piracy of his drama, and he claimed that the Théâtre Italien should be restrained from performing it. The decision of the court was, however, against the irascible poet, and he had to pay the costs of the action.

The winter of 1857 was passed by Madame Alboni in Madrid. In the spring of 1858 she was singing at the Théâtre Italien of Paris. Among the operas in which she performed during the London season of 1858 was *Luisa Miller*. In order to render the ensemble as perfect as possible, she undertook, with real artistic feeling, a minor character—the Duchess. After a lapse of some years, too, she resumed her original part of Maffeo Orsini. She also appeared with Mdlle. Tietjens, the new prima donna, in *Il Trovatore*.

In 1859, Madame Alboni was again at the Italian Opera, Paris, performing Isabella in *L'Italiana in Algieri*, etc. No living singer is more thoroughly imbued with the traditions of the school to which she belongs. *Il Giuramento*, disinterred the preceding season for the gratification of the dilettanti, was reproduced, Alboni, Madame Penco, and Graziani being its chief support.

In 1860, after an absence of two years, Madame Alboni reappeared, May 19, at Her Majesty's Theatre, as Maffeo Orsini.

In 1861, Verdi's *Ballo in Maschera* was brought out at the Théâtre Italien, Mesdames Alboni, Battu, and Penco, Signori Mario and Graziani, forming the cast. In the summer Madame Alboni undertook a musical tour through England. In the present season, 1863, she is a member of the powerful company of Her Majesty's Theatre.

In private life Alboni is amiable, gay, generous—full of that charming insouciance which characterizes the Italian artiste. She is perfectly good-humoured, with the simplicity of a child, and whenever her immense success caused the envy of her rivals she was the first to laugh and disarm jealousy by some bon mot. She is distinguished, moreover, by many eccentricities, and for the independence of her disposition. She bought a very fine hotel at the Cours de la Reine, richly furnished, and installed therein her sisters and brothers. Her brothers were among the bravest soldiers of the band of Garibaldi.

CHAPTER XV.

ANGIOLINA BOSIO.

ANGIOLINA BOSIO belonged to a family of Italian artists who have cultivated with much credit music and the drama. She was born at Turin, August 22, 1830, and educated at Milan; her singing-master being the excellent teacher Cataneo. The impresario Barocchi divining her budding talent, offered her a modest engagement, and at the age of sixteen she made her début, July, 1846, at the Teatro Rè, Milan, in *I Due Foscari*. After a brief engagement she went to Verona, where she confirmed the best hopes of her friends, and excited great interest among the frequenters of the opera. She then suddenly appeared in Copenhagen, where she was applauded and caressed: so popular did she become, indeed, that no effort was spared to retain her for six years; but the climate was not suited to her, and she was obliged to leave the country. Her farewell is described as something extraordinary. She was next engaged at the Circo Theatre, in Madrid, and created an immense enthusiasm among the Spaniards, the director of the theatre being compelled, by the universal voice, to engage her for the season following. In 1848, Angiolina appeared in Paris, at the Théâtre Italien, in *I Due Foscari*, etc., with Bordas and Morelli, but did not create even a passing remark. She went immediately to Havana, as a member of Marti's troupe, going thence to New York, Philadelphia, and Boston. She was ardently admired by the Americans.

She returned to Europe in 1851, and shortly after married a Greek gentleman, named Xinda Velonis. She was engaged for the season of 1852 by Mr. Gye, for the Royal Italian Opera, and on Tuesday, June 15, 1852, Madame Bosio made her début in the opera of *L'Elisir d'Amore*. She did not create by any means a favourable impression; her voice appeared "worn," and her intonation sharp. She walked the stage with ease, but beyond this did not display any talent as an actress, and she was pronounced to be "a good second-rate singer, nothing more;" but for the Dulcamara of Ronconi, the opera would have proved a failure. The public remembered how Madame Persiani, Mdlle. Lind, Madame Viardot, even Madame Castellan, had treated the light and brilliant character of the coquettish Adina. Her next appearance was in *Ernani*, when it was admitted that she was certainly a tolerable singer—a pretty good substitute in case of necessity.

Accident, however, revealed her genius. On the conclusion of the season, three extra performances were given at reduced prices. M. Jullien's *Pietro il*

Grande, produced the same year, was announced, but the illness of Tamberlik compelled the manager to substitute *I Puritani,* and Madame Grisi having declined to sing, Bosio was requested to undertake the part of Elvira: feeling sure of success she did not hesitate.

"Madame Bosio was extremely nervous in the first scene," says one who was present. "The duet with Giorgio was ineffective throughout; the polacca created no impression. The curtain fell on the first act with scarcely a hand of applause. Many left the house. The audience were listless and apathetic; still they were not unkind, and listened, when, under other circumstances, they would have expressed dissatisfaction. The curtain rose on the second act, and when Elvira came on in the mad scene, and commenced the favourite cavatina, 'Qui la voce,' the audience were strangely inattentive. Perhaps their indifference inspired the singer with determination; perhaps, from her very fear there grew a courage. Whatever the cause, Madame Bosio began to sing in reality, and the slow movement was followed by 'bravas' from all parts of the house. Now came the artiste's revenge. The cabaletta literally took the house by storm, and created an immense furore. A more sudden and enthusiastic sensation was never witnessed. Madame Bosio was encored with acclamations, and recalled several times; and, what was more to the purpose, her singing indicated no falling off in the third act. This performance was in reality the turning point of Madame Bosio's fortune."

Her success was talked of with wonder in all fashionable and musical circles; and Mr. Gye immediately engaged her for three years.

Madame Bosio was the prima donna of that winter in Paris. She took the leading part when Verdi's *Luisa Miller* was produced at the Grand Opéra. She then appeared in *Il Barbiere di Seviglia*—a very different work. She also sang six times successively in Rossini's fine but tiresome opera, *Mosè in Egitto*. She also appeared at the Théâtre Italien, in Rossini's *Matilda di Shabran*, an opera in which she was seen to great advantage.

In the programme of the Royal Italian Opera for 1853, Madame Bosio was announced to sustain the principal characters in three new operas—Rossini's *Matilda di Shabran*, Verdi's *Rigoletto*, and Spohr's *Jessonda*. She appeared first in *Il Barbiere*, then as Adina (*L'Elisir d'Amore*) with Ronconi and Luchesi, a new tenor.

Rigoletto was produced for the first time in England, May 14. None of Verdi's works, with the exception of *Ernani*, had gained such a reputation, and at the time of its production in England, it was being performed at twenty or thirty theatres on the Continent. It was regarded by Verdi himself as his chef-d'œuvre. It created great interest and curiosity among the patrons of the Royal Italian Opera; the story being dramatic and full of bustle, the characters striking and well coloured, the scenic effects superb, the dresses and decorations costly and magnificent; it naturally, therefore, created a furore. Mesdames Bosio and Nantier Didiée, Signori Mario, Ronconi, Tagliafico, and Polonini, constituted the cast. Madame Bosio surpassed herself, and carried off the suffrages of even those who had previously refused to acknowledge her talent. Her impersonation of Gilda was so exquisite as to remove any doubt of her title to be considered a performer of the first class. She also appeared as Marguerite de Valois in *Gli Ugonotti*, the new prima donna, Madame Julienne, being indisposed.

Her voice, a high, silvery soprano, was of the finest timbre, limpid, flexible, vibrating, and of great extent. She had a perfect method, and irreproachable good taste; and she was one of the most finished vocalists of her time. She had dramatic feeling as profound as truthful; but her style, original, yet tempered by judgment, never reached the expression of passion. She could not divest herself completely of her individuality, nor abandon herself to the emotions of the character; but she possessed a subtle intellectual charm indefinable, yet impossible to resist. She belonged to the school of singers, who, while shining equally in the works of Mozart, Rossini, Bellini, Donizetti, even of Verdi and Mercadante, yet preserve the traditions of the fine school of Italian singing. She was, above all, supereminently graceful in her person, deportment, and acting. She was by no means handsome—her features were irregular and ill-formed; yet, on the stage she looked a most beautiful woman.

In May, 1854, Madame Bosio reappeared in *Il Barbiere*, with Mario, Tagliafico, Ronconi, and Lablache. The critics had now no words sufficiently glowing to express their admiration: she was charming—exquisitely delightful. She performed in *I Puritani* during this season; and with the exception, always, of Grisi, she was the best Elvira ever seen. There was a fluent ease in her performance of the most difficult and trying passages which was perfectly captivating. Rossini's *Matilda di Shabran*, promised the preceding year, was also produced. Madame Bosio was an admirable Matilda; and if she had not the exhaustless variety in ornament possessed by Madame Persiani, she was yet fully capable of executing fluently the most light and florid music: her voice was invariably pure, true, and deliciously sweet, her style most finished, and she seemed to improve every day. She never appeared in a part which suited her more admirably than Matilda; and in it she sealed her reputation as a florid soprano singer of the highest class. The music of this opera, though composed in haste by Rossini (in ten days, it is said, for the Carnival at Rome in 1821) is brilliant and spirited, if careless and irregular; but the plot is very stupid. May 11th, Madame Bosio appeared with Sophie Cruvelli, Mdlle. Marai, Ronconi the inimitable, Lablache, Tamberlik, Tagliafico, etc., in Mozart's *Don Giovanni*. She was a most captivating Zerlina—sweet, interesting, and elegant. She performed also in *L'Elisir d'Amore*, with Ronconi. She sang in *Il Barbiere*, June 26th, when Mario, as the Count, made his first appearance for the season, and Lablache, as Bartolo, his first appearance at the Royal Italian Opera; Ronconi being the Figaro. As Rosina, Madame Bosio was "charming," her acting being graceful and animated, and her singing, though deficient in power, exquisitely sweet and full of expression. In *Rigoletto*, Madame Bosio represented Gilda with increased reputation both as an actress and singer. In *Rigoletto*, Signor Ronconi had a part which brought out all his versatile talents and high artistic powers.

During the winter of 1854, Madame Bosio performed at the Italiens, in Paris, then under the management of Signor Ragani, uncle of Giulia Grisi. The following year she again made her appearance at the Royal Italian Opera, in *Ernani*, with Tamberlik, Tagliafico, etc. The ringing quality of her voice was displayed to perfection in this opera. She performed shortly afterwards in *Le Comte Ory*, with

Mdlle. Nantier Didiée, Mdlle. Marai, Tagliafico, and Gardoni. As the Contessa she was seen to great advantage, for her best performances were those in which the singing was of more importance than the acting, and in which neither tragic power nor comic humour was needed. *Le Comte Ory* is full of lively, luxuriant melodies, and skilfully constructed harmony; but the plot is absurd and trashy. Of all modern soprani, Madame Bosio most understood and appreciated the music of Rossini; and instead of regarding the melodies of the great maestro as simply themes for the purpose of displaying the richness of her own fancy, she sang them conscientiously and with due deference.

She sang at the Festival at Norwich, with Clara Novello, Lablache, Gardoni, Sims Reeves, and others, receiving 300*l*. for four days.

This year Madame Bosio accepted an engagement at St. Petersburg. The terms were 100,000 francs for four months, and a guaranteed benefit of 15,000 francs more, with permission to sing at private soirées and concerts. Her success in St. Petersburg was extraordinary. The Théâtre Italien of that city has been, for many years, one of the most brilliant in Europe. From the time of Catherine II. composers and Italian vocalists have been cordially welcomed at the Court of Russia, and largely remunerated. Cimarosa, Paisiello, Sarti, Boïeldieu, and Adolphe Adam have written operas and ballets for the Théâtre Italien and the Théâtre Francais of that capital: Rubini spent the last six years of his professional career in the empire of the Czar; and Lablache, and many other great artistes, found themselves richly repaid for daring the rigours of the climate.

After a delay of some months, caused by the illness of Madame Bosio, *L'Etoile du Nord* was produced, January 4, 1856, at the Italian Theatre, St. Petersburg: Signor de Bassini was Peter the Great; Calzolari, Danilowitz; Bettini, Ismailoff; Lablache, Gritzenko; Mdlle. Marai, Prascovie; Mesdames Rossi and Tagliafico, the Vivandières, and Madame Bosio, Cattarina. The action of the piece was altered: to suit the prejudices of his Imperial Majesty, the characters were changed, and the scene was transferred to Dalecarlia in Sweden, King Eric taking the place of the Czar. So great were the expectations of success, and such the demand for places, that the prices were raised; yet the house was crowded to suffocation, and the opera was the most indubitable triumph ever achieved at the Théâtre Italien. October 1st, she appeared in *La Traviata*. From St. Petersburg she went to Moscow.

In 1856, Madame Bosio (with Signor Mario) rescued the Royal Italian Opera by the brilliancy of her performances at the Lyceum Theatre, whither the Italian company had been removed on the destruction by fire of the establishment in Covent Garden. Never did she sing or act more captivatingly than during this season. Her most remarkable performance was in *La Traviata,* which she then appeared in for the first time in England. Her personation of the unhappy Violetta, in almost every respect different from the reading of Mdlle. Piccolomini, was most touchingly beautiful.

Having rested at Florence, after her labours in Paris, she returned to the Lyceum in 1857, with Signor Mario; and appeared again in *La Traviata,* with Mario and Tagliafico. Her exquisitely refined, bewitching impersonation of the ill-fated Violetta created a singular excitement. Her Zerlina, in *Fra Diavolo,* was also much admired.

The performance of *La Traviata,* February, 1858, terminated the season of the Théâtre Italien of St. Petersburg, when Madame Bosio (who sang with Calzolàri and Bartolini) was received with acclamations; and at the end of the first act, a deputation waited upon her in her box to offer her a princely gift—a splendid bouquet formed of three stars surrounded by magnificent turquoises and diamonds. During the evening the public lavished tokens of their admiration on their favourite, and at the termination of the opera the greater part of the audience escorted her carriage to the door of her hotel. The Emperor and Empress also made her superb presents.

In the May following, Madame Bosio made her first

appearance for the season in *La Traviata*, with Signor Gardoni, at the new theatre, Covent Garden. She was more brilliant and more admirable than ever during this—alas! her last—season in London; and surpassed all her former efforts. From London she returned to St. Petersburg, when the Czar nominated her première cantatrice, and Signor Tamberlik the premier chanteur to their Imperial Majesties—an entirely exceptional favour. Signor Tamberlik also received the gold medal, surrounded with diamonds, suspended to the cordon of St. Andrew, which had been accorded to three artistes only—Rubini, Tamburini, and Lablache. Madame Bosio was the first who obtained the honour of being named première cantatrice to the Imperial Court.

Suddenly her admirers were startled by the news that Angiolina Bosio was DEAD. The melancholy intelligence reached England from Paris in April, 1859, and "filled all musical London with consternation and regret." She had died on the 12th of that month, at St. Petersburg. Always of a delicate and frail constitution, suffering, too, from an affection of the lungs, the rigorous climate of Russia had in all probability hastened her death. Her loss, a serious one to the lovers of music, was sincerely lamented by the public. So gifted a singer, so amiable a woman, so elegant an actress, in the prime of life—she was scarcely thirty,—in the flush of her powers and reputation,—could not but be regretted by all who had heard her. Her remains were transported to the vaults of the cathedral church, April 15, through an immense crowd: the Nevskoï Perspective being so thronged with a dense mass of spectators, from the house of mourning to the church, that it was with difficulty the coffin, carried by bearers, could reach its destination. Persons of all classes pressed round with garlands, flowers, crowns. It was a troublesome task to clear the stairs and corridors of the house where she had lived, which was invaded by the crowd for an hour before the ceremony.

The obsequies took place the following day. The cathedral church of Saint Catherine was filled long before the time; though they had been obliged, in consequence of the crowd which besieged it, to admit only those who had tickets. Members of the corps diplomatique, the highest grades of the administration and of the army, ladies of rank and fortune, pressed to pay a last mark of respect to the gifted being whom they had so admired and applauded in her lifetime. The arts, the sciences and letters delegated their most noble representatives: the pupils of the University and of the schools mixed in the crowd of officers of all ranks and of all regiments, and *employés* of divers departments. The coffin, covered with crowns and flowers, had, the previous evening, been placed before the choir on an elevated estrade. At eleven o'clock the mass commenced, the requiem of Mozart being sung by the artistes of the German Opera and of the chapel of the cathedral. The comrades of poor Bosio had already left two weeks before she died, or they would have taken part in the ceremony. About half-past twelve the funeral cortège began to move, and leaving the church, proceeded towards the cemetery of Sainte Marie. The crowd was enormous, and it did not diminish till it reached the gates of the cemetery, where the cortège was met by many ladies, weeping and praying. The choristers of the Italian Opera sang a funeral chant; and after the prayer of the clergy, the coffin was lowered into the grave, where wreaths and bouquets were flung, and one of the persons present then pronounced a funeral oration. "All eyes were full of tears," says the *Journal de St. Petersbourg*. Never, indeed, was songstress more sincerely regretted.

CHAPTER XVI.

JENNY LIND GOLDSCHMIDT.

There lived in the city of Stockholm, a quiet, almost humble couple, named Lind; the husband taught languages, and the wife kept a school for children. They were Protestants, members of the Lutheran Church. They had two children, a pale, delicate, sickly girl, named Jenny, and a boy named John. Frau Lind had had another girl by her first marriage, but lost her by an early death.

Jenny, born October 6, 1821, was a lonely child: her chief consolation was her voice, which she was perpetually exercising, when at work, or at her solitary play. At three years old singing was her ruling passion: every song that she heard she could repeat with fluency and perfect accuracy; and during her frequent illnesses, she would solace herself with some favourite melody. Thus she attained her ninth year; a shy, timid, sickly child.

She then happened to attract the notice of Frau

Lundberg, an actress, who heard her sing; and, struck with her pure, silvery tones and correct enunciation, told Jenny's parents of the treasure they possessed, urging them to devote their child to the stage. Jenny's mother, entertaining the common prejudice against theatres, was at first horrified by the idea; but Frau Lundberg succeeded in conquering her dislike, and the good mother at last consented to leave the decision of the matter to her child. The little girl at once declared herself determined to devote herself to all the studies requisite to prepare herself for the stage; and she was conveyed by the kind actress to Croelius, a music-master well-known in Stockholm.

This old man became enthusiastic about the abilities of his new pupil, whom he introduced to Count Pücke, manager of the Court Theatre, requesting the Count to hear her, and to patronize her. Rough in speech and morbid in temper, the Count was not remarkable for a gentlemanly reserve: he always said exactly what he thought, and his thoughts were not invariably of the kindest or most charitable nature. When Jenny was brought before him, he regarded her slight figure with astonishment. "You ask a foolish thing," said he, looking disdainfully at the gentle, pale little child, in her simple gown of black bombazine. "What shall we do with that ugly creature. See what feet she has! and then her face! She will never be presentable. No, we cannot take her. Certainly not." Nothing daunted, Croelius insisted, almost indignantly, and at last exclaimed, "Well, if you will not take her, I, poor as I am, will take her myself, and have her educated for the stage." The Count relented, and condescended to hear the child sing. Already her voice possessed that heart-searching quality by which it afterwards exercised so irresistible a spell. The result was that the plain little child was admitted into the school, and placed under the care of an able master, Herr Albert Berg, director of the singing school of the Opera, who was assisted by the composer Lindblad.

Two years later, when Jenny was eleven, at a comedy performed by the pupils of the theatre, several of the audience were struck by the spirit and animation with which a very young pupil performed the part of a beggar-girl in the play. This young pupil was Jenny Lind, who then began to appear in children's characters; exciting a sensation similar to that with which Leontine Fay, in her early career, moved all Paris. Vaudevilles were written expressly for her: the truth of her conception, the originality of her style, gained for her the reputation of being a prodigy; while the modesty and amiability of her demeanour secured for her love and regard.

When she was twelve, the sunny aspect of her future was suddenly clouded, and her ambitious hopes crushed; for her voice began to lose somewhat of its silvery tone, and the upper notes vanished. In vain she tried to recover them. The hope of training her as a singer for the grand opera was therefore abandoned. She had outgrown her childish parts without becoming qualified for more advanced ones, and was soon forgotten by the public which had once admired her. Forbidden to exercise her voice, the only consolation to the unhappy girl was continuing her instrumental and theoretical musical studies, to which she devoted herself for the space of four years.

It happened towards the close of this painful period that a grand concert was given at the theatre; and the fourth act of Meyerbeer's *Robert le Diable* formed the chief feature of the programme. The part of Alice in that act, consisting of one solo only, was very unpopular among the singers, and Herr Berg remembering the unlucky Jenny, offered to her the objectionable *rôle*. She meekly consented to appear; though with a nervous agitation which threatened to destroy what powers she yet possessed; and with a heart palpitating with mingled hope and foreboding, she began to study her part. On the evening of the concert, she presented herself almost unnoticed. She was in a state of nervous excitement and trepidation; though nobody noticed the obscure singer who took the despised character of Alice. But when she sang the air allotted to her, it seemed as if a miracle had been wrought in her favour, for every note of her register had recovered its beauty and sweetness. A burst of applause saluted her: every eye was directed towards her, and the young vocalist became the heroine of the evening. No one was more astonished than Berg, who, the next day, informed Jenny that she was considered qualified to undertake the *rôle* of Agatha, in Weber's *Der Freischütz.*

Towards this character the secret ambition of Jenny Lind had long yearned; for it was the one which first awakened her artistic sympathies. To study it deeply had been with her a labour of love, and she looked forward with joy to be able to represent it worthily one day. Her discouragements and disappointments were now all forgotten, and the dream of her hopes seemed to be at length realized. At the rehearsal preceding the representation of the evening, she sang in such a manner that the members of the orchestra laid down their instruments and clapped their hands with rapturous applause. "I saw her at the evening representation," says Frederika Bremer. "She was then in the spring of life, fresh, bright, and serene as a morning in May; perfect in form; her hands and her arms peculiarly graceful, and lovely in her whole appearance. She seemed to move, speak, and sing without effort or art. All was nature and harmony. Her singing was distinguished especially by its purity and the power of soul which seemed to swell in her tones. Her 'mezzo voice' was delightful. In the night-scene where Agatha, seeing her lover coming, breathes out her joy in rapturous song, our young singer, on turning from the window at the back of the stage, to the spectators again, was pale for joy. And in that pale joyousness she sang with a burst of outflowing love and life, that called forth not the mirth, but the tears of the auditors."

Jenny Lind has always regarded the character of Agatha as the keystone of her fame. From the night of this performance she was the declared favourite of the Swedish public, and continued for a year and a half the star of the Opera of Stockholm; performing in *Euryanthe*, *Robert le Diable*, *La Vestale*, of Spontini, and other operas. She laboured meanwhile with indefatigable industry to remedy certain natural deficiencies in her voice. Always pure and melodious in tone, it was originally wanting in elasticity; she could neither hold her notes to any considerable extent, nor increase nor diminish their volume with sufficient effect; and she could scarcely utter the slightest cadence. But, undaunted by difficulties, she persevered, and ultimately achieved that brilliant and facile execution which, it is difficult to believe, was partially denied her by nature.

Gradually, however, to the surprise and alarm of the young girl, her voice, overstrained and exhausted, lost somewhat of its freshness. The public, who no longer sought to hear her for the sake of novelty, came no more to the theatre even when she sang delightfully as Pamina (*Die Zauberflöte*), or as Anna Bolena; in short, the Opera was almost deserted. Jenny Lind's voice had need of further training, and she felt the necessity of higher teaching than she could obtain in her native city. She desired, also, to be enabled to behold those great artistes whom she had heard praised so much; and her anxious wish was to become the pupil of Garcia, who had formed so many eminent singers. A formidable money difficulty presented itself—that stumbling-block which impedes so many artists in pursuit of ideal perfection: the difficulty of defraying the expenses of her journey, and of her residence in France, seemed an insuperable bar to the realization of her wishes. She resolved to trust to her own resources alone; accordingly, during the recess when the Opera was closed, accompanied by her father, she visited the principal towns of Sweden and Norway, giving concerts, and thus amassed a fund adequate to her probable necessities. Having obtained leave of absence from the manager of the Opera in Stockholm, and bade farewell to her parents, whose avocations did not permit them to accompany her, she started alone for Paris, full of enthusiasm for her art and eagerly anticipating a successful course of study.

Arrived in Paris, her first visit was to Garcia, to whom she presented her letters of introduction. Garcia gave her a kind reception, and listened, without a word or gesture, to her singing. When, fluttered with feverish anxiety, she awaited his dictum, he said, calmly: "My good girl, you have no voice; or, I should rather say, that you had a voice, but are now on the point of losing it. Your organ is strained and worn out; and the only advice I can offer you is to recommend you not to sing a note for three months. At the end of that time come to me again, and I will do my best for you." Poor Jenny departed in the deepest dejection, and passed the three wearisome months in the strictest retirement. "I lived on my tears and on the recollection of my home," she herself said, pathetically. At the expiration of three months of solitude and silence, she paid her second visit to Garcia, who pronounced her voice greatly improved, and susceptible of continued culture. Although she profited immensely by the teaching of this great master, and composed cadences and ornaments which he himself considered worthy of copying, yet he never anticipated for his young Swedish pupil any particular distinction in the musical world. Jenny Lind has frequently remarked that, next to herself, Garcia was the person who, of all others, would have been most surprised at her triumphs had he lived to witness them.

At this period, Garcia was teaching a country-woman of Jenny's, a Mdlle. Nissen, who possessed a very powerful, full-toned voice, but lacked mental abilities. Jenny Lind confessed that it often brought her to despair to hear Garcia hold up this lady to her as an example, while she felt that she understood more, and was pursuing loftier aims, than would ever be attained by her sister student. Garcia was wont to say, "If Jenny Lind had the voice of Nissen, or the latter Lind's intelligence, one of them would become the greatest singer in Europe. If Lind had more voice at her disposal, nothing would prevent her from becoming the greatest of modern singers; but as it is," he would add, "she must be content with singing second to many who will not have half her genius."

The following year, a Swedish composer was sent to Paris, in order to summon the young singer home to resume her station at the Opera in Stockholm. By this gentleman she was introduced to Meyerbeer, and the well-practised judgment of the composer of *Robert le Diable* soon recognized the pearl of great price. His only doubt was whether the flute-like purity of her delicate organ would be sufficiently telling in a large space. To test this, he arranged a rehearsal with a full orchestra, in the salon of the Grand Opéra, when Jenny Lind sang the three great scenes from *Robert le Diable, Norma,* and *Der Freischütz.* Her success was triumphant; but through the jealousy of a powerful prima donna, M. Léon Pillet was dissuaded from engaging the young Swede.

Shortly after, in the spring of 1843, Jenny Lind

reappeared in her native city in *Robert le Diable*, where she reaped the rich reward of her persevering efforts. Her voice had acquired astonishing flexibility and strength; she could warble like a nightingale; her tones were fresh, beautiful, and clear; she had become a perfect mistress of her art, and was an excellent actress. The good people of Stockholm received her with a rapturous welcome.

At this time Jenny Lind was perfectly unknown out of her native country. Many entreaties had been addressed to her to appear at Copenhagen; but the idea of making a début in that city frightened her: she expressed the greatest dread of accepting the offers of the Danish manager. "I have never made my appearance out of Sweden," she observed; "everybody in my native land is so affectionate and kind to me, and if I made my appearance in Copenhagen, and should be hissed! I dare not venture on it!" However, the temptations held out to her, and the entreaties of Burnonville, the ballet-master of Copenhagen, who had married a Swedish friend of Jenny Lind's, at last prevailed over the nervous apprehensions of the young singer, and Jenny made her first appearance at Copenhagen as Alice, in *Robert le Diable*. "It was like a new revelation in the realms of art," says Andersen (*Story of my Life*), "the youthful fresh voice forced itself into every heart: here reigned truth and nature; and everything was full of meaning and intelligence. At one concert she sang her Swedish songs; there was something so peculiar in this, so bewitching, people thought nothing about the concert-room; the popular melodies uttered by a being so purely feminine, and bearing the universal stamp of genius, exercised the omnipotent sway—the whole of Copenhagen was in a rapture." Jenny Lind was the first singer to whom the Danish students gave a serenade; torches blazed around the hospitable villa where the serenade was given, and she expressed her thanks by again singing some Swedish airs impromptu. "I saw her hasten into a dark corner and weep for emotion," says Andersen. "'Yes, yes,' said she, 'I will exert myself; I will endeavour: I will be better qualified than I now am, when I again come to Copenhagen.'"

"On the stage," adds Andersen, "she was the great artist who rose above all those around her; at home, in her own chamber, a sensitive young girl with all the humility and piety of a child. Her appearance in Copenhagen made an epoch in the history of our opera; it showed me art in its sanctity—I had beheld one of its vestals."

Jenny Lind was one of the few who regard Art as a sacred vocation. "Speak to her of her art," says Frederika Bremer, "and you will wonder at the expansion of her mind, and will see her countenance beaming with inspiration. Converse then with her of

God, and of the holiness of religion, and you will see tears in those innocent eyes: she is great as an artist, but she is still greater in her pure human existence!"

"She loves Art with her whole soul," observes Andersen, "and feels her vocation in it. A noble, pious disposition like her's cannot be spoiled by homage. On one occasion only did I hear her express her joy in her talent and her self-consciousness. It was during her last residence in Copenhagen. Almost every evening she appeared either in the opera or at concerts; every hour was in requisition. She heard of a society, the object of which was to assist unfortunate children, and to take them out of the hands of their parents, by whom they were misused and compelled either to beg or steal, and to place them in other and better circumstances. Benevolent people subscribed annually a small sum each for their support; nevertheless, the means for this excellent purpose were very limited. 'But have I not still a disengaged evening?' said she; 'let me give a night's performance for the benefit of those poor children: but we will have double prices!' Such a performance was given, and returned large proceeds. When she was informed of this, and that, by this means, a number of poor children would be benefited for several years, her countenance beamed, and the tears filled her eyes. 'It is, however, beautiful,' said she, 'that I can sing so.'"

From Copenhagen Jenny Lind returned to Stockholm, where she was received most flatteringly by her countrymen, although it was the wish of her admirers and friends that she should remain in Sweden. But Jenny was desirous of extending her reputation, and she wrote to Meyerbeer, asking him to obtain for her an engagement at Berlin. The kind-hearted composer, who had admired her so much at Paris, and who was pleased to be able to show his interest, answered her letter in less than a week, offering her the position of second soprano at the Theatre Royal. Jenny accepted it, bade her parents farewell once more, and departed for Berlin in 1843. Her departure was a scene of triumph, and the streets were crowded with thousands of persons to bid her adieu.

At Berlin Jenny made no sensation at first. She appeared in secondary characters, Mdlle. Nissen being the prima donna. Adalgisa, in *Norma*, was the best of those with which she was favoured. She was noticed very slightly by the critics; some said she was a tolerable actress, others, that she had a cultivated voice, but no power. She, however, became a favourite with the manager and with her comrades, from her industry, her modesty, her amiability, and good temper. One evening, when she had been at the theatre some four months, there was a large concert given in behalf of some charity. The fourth act of *Robert le Diable* was announced, and again, by a strange coincidence, the solo of Alice was assigned to Jenny. Again a spell was wrought: she electrified the audience by the manner in which she sang the few bars of this despised air; as her notes rang full and clear through the theatre, the wings filled with listeners, and when she ceased, the entranced audience broke into a long and continued tempest of applause.

The genius of Jenny Lind was now revealed to the Berlinese, and for four months she was their idol. At the end of 1843, M. Belinaye went to Berlin, and, through the medium of Lord Westmoreland, was presented to the young singer, and offered her terms from Mr. Lumley; but no engagement was entered into.

In August, 1844, she went to Dresden. Meyerbeer was then writing his *Camp of Silesia*, and he offered Jenny Lind the first part, Vielka. She knew nothing then of the German language; but two months of application enabled her to speak it with purity. The characters which she sustained during her stay in Dresden were, in addition to Vielka, Norma, Amina, and Maria in *La Figlia del Reggimento*.

At the request of the manager of Stockholm, however, she returned to her native city, to assist at the coronation of the King of Sweden. With each performance her fame extended more widely: throughout all the districts of Germany, and far beyond its bounds, her reputation spread, and the managers of

London and Paris vied in striving to win the Northern songstress. From Stockholm she made a tour through Vienna, Berlin, Copenhagen, and other cities; in Hamburg a silver laurel-wreath was presented to her on her departure, and her entire journey was a constant succession of triumphs. During the following summer she was invited to the fêtes on the Rhine, given by the King of Prussia in honour of our Queen; she also visited Frankfort and Cologne. The Countess of Rossi (Henrietta Sontag) pronounced her to be the first singer of her time.

From November, 1845, till the end of March, 1846, she fulfilled her engagement for five months at the Theatre Royal, Berlin. She then proceeded to Vienna, where she made her début as Norma, April 22, in the Theater an der Wien. The reports which had preceded her, the exaggeration of the so-called Lind-enthusiasts, and the unprecedentedly high prices of admission, had raised to such a degree the anticipations of the public, that Jenny Lind expressed her doubt of succeeding, and declared that, but for having given her word, she would not consent to perform at all. With visible nervousness, with the elevation and dignity of a priestess, but yet with a feeling of humbleness, she ascended the Druid altar, and, amid a silence of hushed expectation, commenced to sing. Scarcely had her tones resounded than the whole house burst into one simultaneous cheer, decisive of her success in Vienna.

Soon after this she returned to her native city, and then reappeared in Berlin. She received a liberal offer of an engagement with Mr. Bunn, manager of Drury Lane Theatre, and an agreement was signed in presence of Lord Westmoreland (British Minister at Berlin) and M. Meyerbeer. M. Belinaye just then renewed Mr. Lumley's offers; and Jenny Lind, being now better acquainted with the management of the London theatres, found that she had made a great mistake in consenting to make her début in London at Drury Lane. She therefore wished to break off her engagement with Mr. Bunn, and volunteered to pay him 2,000*l.* on receiving the paper signed by her; Mr. Bunn at first refused, but the dispute was finally settled February 22, 1848, by his being awarded 2,500*l.* damages in a court of justice.

So enthusiastic were the people of Berlin, that on the close of her engagement the manager was obliged to re-engage her, at the rate (it is said) of 4,000*l.* per annum, with two months of congé. The "enthusiasm" was almost beyond conception. The difficulty of gaining admission into the theatre, even when she had appeared upwards of a hundred nights, was so great that it was found necessary, in order to prevent the practice of jobbing in tickets, which was becoming very prevalent, to issue them according to the following directions, which were put forth by the manager: "Tickets must be applied for on the day preceding that for which they are required, by letter, signed with the applicant's proper and Christian name, profession, and place of abode, and sealed with wax, bearing the writer's initials with his arms. No more than one ticket can be granted to the same person; and no person is entitled to apply for two consecutive nights of the enchantress's performance."

In June, 1846, Mdlle. Lind was principal vocalist of the Niederheinische Musicfest, held at Aix-la-Chapelle, Mendelssohn being the conductor. He was delighted with her, and thus expressed his opinion of her—"There will not in a whole century be born another being so largely gifted as Jenny Lind."

At this period Jenny Lind received a profusion of offers of engagements. It is said that his Majesty the Czar offered her as much as 56,000 francs per month, for five months, making in all about 11,200*l.* sterling—a sum unparalleled in musical history.

She appeared the following September at Frankfort, where triumphant success awaited her. The enthusiasm and excitement were unprecedented. "Dine where you would," said a correspondent of the *Athenæum*, "you heard of Jenny Lind!—when she was coming—what she would sing—how much be paid—who had got places—and the like. So that what with the exigeant English dilettanti flying at puzzled German landlords with all manner of Babylonish protestations of disappointment and uncertainty, and native High

Ponderosities ready to trot in the train of the enchantress where she might please to lead, with here and there a dark-browed Italian prima donna louring, Medea-like, in the background, and looking daggers whenever the name 'Questa Linda!' was uttered—nothing, I repeat, can be compared to the universal excitement, save certain passages ('green spots' in the memory of many a dowager Berliner) when enthusiasts rushed to drink champagne out of Sontag's shoe. . . In *La Figlia del Reggimento*, compared with the exhibitions of her sister songstresses now on the German stage, Mdlle. Lind's personation was like a piece of porcelain beside tawdry daubings on crockery."

Mdlle. Lind then reappeared in Vienna, where she was received with the same enthusiastic delight. She was treated with marked attention by the Empress and the Archduchess Maria. The sensation caused previous to her departure for England was extraordinary, and during her last performances at the great theatres, the stalls, ordinarily sold at two florins, rose to fifty; yet three thousand persons were unable to procure admission. The last night, not content with calling her forward innumerable times, with plaudits, cheers, and deafening shouts, the audience joined the crowd which attended her home. Thirty times she was summoned to her window, and the crowd cried urgently, "Jenny Lind, say you will come back again!" At length Jenny Lind, bathed in tears, took asunder the heaped bouquets lying on her table, and scattered from the balcony the separated flowers, which were snatched up by the eager crowd.

Her departure from Stockholm for London was signalized by a demonstration most unusual for so cold a people as the Swedes. Between fifteen and twenty thousand persons were assembled on the quay to take leave of their beloved countrywoman; military bands were stationed at intervals, and she embarked amid cheers, music, good wishes, and sobbing adieux. The rigging of the vessels in the harbour was manned, and the hurrahs and waving of handkerchiefs continued as long as the steamer which bore her away was in sight. Her last performance in her native city was in aid of the funds of a charitable institution she had founded, and the tickets of admission on this occasion were sold at immense prices by auction.

Mdlle. Lind arrived in London April 17, 1847. Her first days were passed with her friend Mrs. Grote, wife of the historian and member of Parliament; but she subsequently took a furnished house at Brompton, where she lived in strict seclusion from society during her engagement.

One of the first who heard the Nightingale was Lablache. The mighty basso was in raptures with her voice; every note, he said, "was like a pearl." This comparison quite took the fancy of Jenny, and one morning, during rehearsal at Her Majesty's Theatre, she tripped up to the great Italian, and politely asked him to lend her his hat. He readily complied, though surprised at the oddity of such a request; she took the hat with a graceful curtsey, and retired to a distant part of the stage, where she commenced singing a French air with her lips to the edge of the broad-brimmed chapeau. Having concluded her performance she returned to Lablache, and ordered him to fall on bended knee, as she had a valuable present for him, returning him his hat, with the declaration that she had made him exceedingly rich, according to his own showing, insomuch as she was giving him a hatfull of "pearls." Her simplicity and innocent gaiety delighted all, and as for Lablache, he could scarcely have been more gratified if she had filled his hat with diamonds.

Jenny Lind's début took place the 4th May. The opera was *Robert le Diable,* thus cast: Robert, Fraschini; Raimbaud, Gardoni; Bertram, Staudigl; Isabelle, Madame Castellan; Alice, Mdlle. Jenny Lind. The house was crowded to suffocation. The Queen, Prince Albert, and numbers of eminent personages were present. The accounts of the débutante's brilliant triumphs in Germany, and the extraordinary enthusiasm which she had everywhere created, had rendered the musical world most anxious to see and hear her. She had been the subject of conversation in all circles; her name was in everybody's mouth ere she set foot on the English shore. Always, at the commencement of an opera, Mdlle. Lind suffered from a nervousness which she only mastered in the course of performance. Before the opera began a shudder would seize her; she stepped falteringly on the stage, and sang her first notes timidly, only conquering her agitation by degrees. How, then, must she have felt on this all-important evening?

"The curtain went up, the opera began, the cheers resounded, deep silence followed," says a writer in the *Musical World,* "and the cause of all the excitement was before us. It opened its lips, and emitted sounds. The sounds it emitted were right pleasing, honey-sweet, and silver-toned. With this there was, besides, a quietude that we had not marked before, and a something that hovered about the object, as an unseen grace that was attired in a veil of innocence, transparent as the thin surface of a bubble, disclosing all, and making its own presence rather felt than seen."

The appearance of Jenny Lind in her pilgrim's garb was the signal for an enthusiastic outburst of applause. The delicious sustained notes which commenced her first cavatina, *Va, dit-elle,* full, clear, and bell-like, then dying off into the faintest whisper, were exquisite: they were followed by thunders of applause, above which rose the stentorian brava of Lablache, who was sitting in his box enraptured. Each verse of the charming little romance, *Quand je quittai la Normandie,* was encored. "At the conclusion of the last she gave the roulade, *à pleine voix*, limpid and deliciously sweet, and finished with a shake so delicate, so softly executed, that each one held his breath to listen, and the torrent of applause at the end baffled description." At the conclusion of the opera, Jenny Lind was called before the curtain three distinct times—shouts, waving of hats and handkerchiefs, every sign of rapturous delight being displayed by the audience.

Her performance, both dramatic and vocal, transcended the most highly-wrought expectations. Combining the rustic simplicity of the low-born maiden with the lofty purity of her holy mission, Jenny Lind's Alice was a sublime as well as a captivating creation; while she showed every quality of vocal art—a voice whose tone penetrated to every heart, style and execution the most exquisitely finished, and those powers of expression which render music the most eloquent language of sentiment and passion. Her voice, a high soprano, neither powerful nor of great compass, possessed much suavity and delicious lightness, and was singularly brilliant, clear, and silvery in the upper register, though a little throaty in the middle.

"It is wanting in that roundness and mellowness which belongs to organs of the south," observes a very able musical critic. "When forced it has by no means an agreeable sound, and falls hard and grating on the ears. It is evident that, in the greater part of its range, acquired by much perseverance and study, nature has not been bountiful to the Swedish nightingale in an extraordinary degree. But art and energy have supplied the defects of nature. Perhaps no artiste, if we except Pasta, ever deserved more praise than Jenny Lind, for what she has worked out of bad materials. From an organ, neither naturally sweet nor powerful, she has elaborated a voice capable of producing the most vivid sensations. In her mezzo-voce singing scarcely any vocalist we ever heard can be compared to her. The most delicate notes, given with the most perfect intonation, captivate the hearers and throw them into ecstasies of delight. This is undoubtedly the great charm of Jenny Lind's singing, and in this respect we subscribe ourselves among her most enthusiastic admirers. . . . She sustains a C or D in alt with unerring intonation and surprising power. These are attained without an effort, and constitute another charm of the Nightingale's singing.

"In pathetic music, Jenny Lind's voice is heard to much advantage. Indeed, her vocal powers seem best adapted to demonstrate the more gentle and touching emotions. For this reason her solo singing is almost that alone in which she makes any extraordinary impression. In ensemble singing, excepting in the *piano*, her voice, being forced beyond its natural powers, loses all its beauty and peculiar charm, and becomes, in short, often disagreeable. . . . Her voice, with all its charm, is of a special quality, and in its best essays is restricted to a particular class of lyrical compositions. . . . . As a vocalist, Jenny Lind is entitled to very high, if not the highest commendation. Her perseverance and indomitable energy, joined to her musical ability, have tended to render her voice as capable and flexible as a violin. Although she never indulges in the brilliant flights of fancy of Persiani, nor soars into the loftiest regions of fioriture with that most wonderful of all singers, her powers of execution are very great, and the delicate taste with which the most florid passages are given, the perfect intonation of the voice, and its general charm have already produced a most decided impression on the public mind. By the musician, Persiani will be always more admired, but Jenny Lind will strike the general hearer more."

Another critic thus speaks of Jenny Lind's voice. "Her voice is a pure soprano—of the fullest compass belonging to voices of this class, and of such evenness of tone that the nicest ear can discover no difference of quality from the bottom to the summit of the scale. In the great extent between A below the lines and D in alt, she executes every description of passage, whether consisting of notes 'in linked sweetness long drawn out,' or of the most rapid flights and fioriture, with equal facility and perfection. Her lowest notes come out as clear and ringing as the highest, and her highest are as soft and sweet as the lowest. Her tones are never muffled or indistinct, nor do they ever offend the ear by the slightest tinge of shrillness—mellow roundness distinguishes every sound she utters. As she never strains her voice, it never seems to be loud; and hence, some one who busied themselves in anticipatory depreciation, said that it would be found to fail in power: a mistake of which everybody was convinced who observed how it filled the ear, and how distinctly every inflection was heard through the fullest harmony of the orchestra. The same clearness was observable in her pianissimo. When, in her beautiful closes, she prolonged a tone, attenuated it by degrees, and falling gently upon the final note, the sound, though as ethereal as the sighing of a breeze, reached (like Mrs. Siddons' whisper in Lady Macbeth) every part of the immense theatre. Much of the effect of this unrivalled voice is derived from the physical beauty of its sound, but still more from the exquisite skill and taste with which it is used, and the intelligence and sensibility of which it is the organ. Mdlle. Lind's execution is that of a complete musician. Every passage is as highly finished, as perfect in tone, tune, and articulation, as if it proceeded from the violin of a Paganini or a Sivori, with the additional charm which lies in the human *voice* divine. Her embellishments show the richest fancy and boundless facility; but they show still more remarkably a well-regulated judgment and taste."

As an actress she was easy, natural, and perfectly

original. "Following her own bland conceptions," remarks one writer, "she rises to regions whence, like Schiller's maid, she descends to refresh the heart and soul of her audience with gifts beautiful and wondrous. Her individuality entirely disappears in her dramatic assumptions; her whole soul is melted into and vitalises the creations of the poet, while the high art stamps perfection on her impersonation." Her by-play was exquisite: she never spared herself in seeking to please her audience. The truth of her acting was once exemplified strangely in Germany, when a singer who performed Elvino to her Amina, declared that he could not act with her, as he was unable to approach her with the wrath the part required, much less spurn her from him—her pathetic delineation of anguish and innocence piercing his heart.

She was not handsome, but of very pleasing aspect. Her face was peculiarly placid, her features well-marked and expressive, her complexion pale, her cheek-bones high, her eyes light grey or blue, "dove-like" in their sweetness; her hair was a pale flaxen, very abundant and wavy. In figure she was slightly above the middle size, and very slender, but her movements were full of grace. She had an air of simplicity and goodness; she looked cold, reserved, modest, and timid.

Robert le Diable was repeated the following Thursday, when her Majesty was again present. The struggle for admission was even greater than on her first appearance; and the theatre was crowded to the roof. Mdlle. Lind was recalled three times, and overwhelmed with tumultuous plaudits and showers of bouquets. The enthusiasm of the public increased daily, and was beyond description. Enormous sums were paid for boxes, and multitudes travelled from the most distant parts of the country to obtain a single hearing of the Swedish Nightingale. Three gentlemen came from Liverpool, for the purpose of hearing her; but after staying a week in London, they were not fortunate enough to obtain admission, and returned home disappointed. Any number of hours were spent by her devoted admirers before the doors of the Opera-house on the chance of obtaining a seat in the pit. From twenty to twenty-five pounds were paid for a single box on her night of performance—while four or five guineas were commonly paid for one stall. Articles of furniture were called by her name; portraits and memoirs innumerable of the famous artiste were published.

During the season Mdlle. Lind performed Amina, in *La Sonnambula*, Maria in *La Figlia del Reggimento*, etc. She also performed in Verdi's new opera, *I Masnadieri*, which work was by no means a success. Her chef-d'œuvre was Amina, in which she was simple, graceful, and touching. At the conclusion of her first performance of *La Sonnambula*, there was an unprecedented scene of excitement. The pit rose *en masse*, hats and handkerchiefs were waved on all sides, even the ladies in the boxes joining in the demonstration. Jenny Lind was vehemently called for, and when she came tripping on, the scene baffled description.

At the desire of the Queen, the Swedish songstress undertook to perform *Norma*. Though she did not equal Grisi, she gained fresh laurels, and heaps of bouquets, to which her Majesty condescended to add one. During the season, Mdlle. Lind sang, in conjunction with Mdlle. Alboni, Madame Grisi, Herr Staudigl, and other leading artistes, at the Queen's private concerts.

At the close of the season, a handsome "testimonial" was presented to her by Mr. Lumley—of pure silver, nearly three feet in height, representing a pillar wreathed with laurel, at the feet of which were seated three draped figures, Tragedy, Comedy, and Music.

The Swedish Nightingale went into the provinces under an engagement with Mr. Lumley, and everywhere created an electrical sensation. The excitement of London was repeated. She then visited Scotland and Dublin. At Edinburgh, fifteen guineas were actually paid for the privilege of hearing her. In this city two concerts were given by Mr. Howard Glover and his brother, who gave Mdlle. Lind 1,000*l.* for her services, Lablache 200*l.*, Gardoni 150*l.*, yet they realized above 1,200*l.* by the speculation. In Dublin Mdlle. Lind was received with an uproar of delight.

She then returned, by way of Berlin, to Stockholm, where she passed the winter. Such was the eagerness to witness her performance at Stockholm, that the places at the theatre were put up at auction, and brought immense prices. With her share of the proceeds, Mdlle. Lind established an asylum for the support of decayed artists, and a school for young girls who were studying for the musical profession. One girl so quickly profited by this opportunity, that she was considered by her benefactress sufficiently promising to be sent to Paris to complete her studies, with a provision of 6,000 francs for her expenses. When Mdlle. Lind left Stockholm to return to London, the quays were crowded by the people of the city; all the ships in the harbour were manned; and amid the playing of bands of music, she was conducted to the steamer, in which she embarked in presence of the Queen of Sweden and her Court.

The "Lind mania" raged in 1848 without diminution. The public were dazzled, enchanted. They heard with delight, too, of her munificent deeds of charity, and the many traits of her amiability, her piety, and her goodness. To her repertoire she added this season Lucia, Susanna, and Elvira (*I Puritani*). In June she appeared for the first time as

Adina, in *L'Elisir d'Amore*, with Lablache, Belletti, and Gardoni. She continued in England after the termination of the season, probably on account of the unsettled state of the Continent; and during the autumn and winter, she undertook extensive provincial tours, sometimes appearing in her dramatic characters, but more frequently singing at concerts and in oratorios. She went on a trip to Dublin, where she received a tumultuous ovation. At Birmingham, Manchester, Norwich, there was one fever of delight. At Manchester, she gave two concerts in aid of the Infirmary of the city, and, as an acknowledgment of her kindness, the people of Manchester presented her with a superb dressing-case and a necklace of pearls. In the city of Norwich, she formed the acquaintance of the excellent Bishop, who remained one of her most cordial and attached friends. On leaving Norwich she was presented by the Bishop with a Bible, while the Mayor, on behalf of the city, offered her a splendidly-illustrated edition of Milton's *Paradise Lost*.

The following April, Jenny Lind re-appeared at Her Majesty's Theatre for a limited number of nights, having resolved finally to take leave of the stage. Her last operatic performance in opera was given May 10, in her original character of Alice. Even in the first flush of the public excitement never was there a more striking scene than the Opera-house presented on the night of her farewell. The crowd was dense: boxes, stalls, pit—every nook was filled. Her Majesty, Prince Albert, the Duchess of Kent, and all the rank and fashion of London assembled to pay a last tribute of admiration. At the fall of the curtain the vast assembly rose with a burst of cheers, and the shouts of delight were deafening. In a few moments Jenny Lind came forward, led by Gardoni, and bowed respectfully to the audience. She was visibly affected, yet shrank from all open expression of her feelings. Scarcely had she retired when another storm arose, and again Jenny Lind came forward, led by Belletti. Bouquets were showered on the stage, and the applause was louder if possible than ever. A third time she was called; when she came on alone, trembling with suppressed emotion, bowing lowly, and looking an eloquent farewell. This time the enthusiasm was so irrepressible, so prolonged, so spontaneous, so overwhelming, that she was no longer able to control her feelings, and tears of gratitude flowed over her pale cheeks.

The close of 1849 found her in Germany. At Lubeck she concluded a treaty with Barnum, the exhibitor of General Tom Thumb, which resulted in her visiting America under his auspices. The terms were 80,000 dollars, 200*l*. for each of the 150 concerts at which Mdlle. Lind was to sing; the entire personal expenses of her party being paid. She was accompanied by Signor Belletti and Jules Benedict, the former of whom received 12,500 dollars, the latter 1,000 dollars.

The time between signing her American engagement and her departure was employed by Jenny Lind in giving concerts on the Continent, mostly for charitable purposes. She sang at Berlin, Bremer, and Göttingen, with her unvarying success. At the two latter places, the students formed a procession by torchlight in her honour, gave her a serenade, and formed an escort for her to Nordheim.

Her last songs on this side the Atlantic were given at Liverpool, in the splendid new hall of the Philharmonic Society. There were, including the orchestra, upwards of 3,000 persons present. The appearance of the Swedish Nightingale was the signal for a demonstration that cannot be described. The audience stood up to welcome her, and such a volley of cheers as rent the air was, perhaps, never before heard within the walls of a theatre or concert-room; three times was the salvo repeated, and it was almost with difficulty that Mdlle. Lind, who seemed quite overpowered by her reception, was enabled to obtain silence. She sang some English airs. Her pronunciation of English was exceedingly pure and articulate, "with just so much of accent as gave it a special and fascinating quaintess." In the ballad style she excelled quite as much as in the florid and bravura school: there was a simplicity, an earnestness of declamation, a peculiar charm, which thrilled the hearer.

Her arrival at New York, in September, being expected, the dock and landing were crowded with persons curious to obtain the first glimpse of the great songstress. Amid cheers and acclamations from the hundreds gathered around the carriage in waiting for her, Mdlle. Lind disembarked, and was driven to the Irving House Hotel. At midnight 30,000 persons assembled, and at one in the morning, 130 musicians came up to serenade her, led by 700 firemen. The excitement was extraordinary: it became a distinction even to have a probability of hearing her sing. The papers actually published the names of those who bought tickets, and printed a fac-simile of the card which was to admit the public to hear her: they were not ashamed to fill their columns with stories of the most ridiculous nature. The anxiety to see Mdlle. Lind whenever she happened to take a drive was almost frantic. Public "reception days" were arranged for her, and throngs of ladies attended her drawing-rooms. Presents of all kinds poured in upon her, the donors thereof anticipating that she would give them rings, pins, bracelets, brooches, etc. etc., in token of gratitude. The first three days, innumerable bouquets and other testimonies of esteem were sent, which she declined to receive. On the day of the first concert, spite of torrents of rain, there were 5,000 persons in the office buying tickets; and the first ticket for the first concert was sold for 600 dollars (45*l.*) On the morning of Mdlle. Lind's first appearance, September 11, at Castle Garden, there was nothing else talked of from one end of New York to the other. The building was crowded to excess in the evening, though there were very few ladies. Shouts from 7,000 throats saluted the Swedish songstress as, pale and agitated, she stepped timidly forth, dressed simply in white; the applause surpassing everything that had previously been offered her. She sang "Casta Diva," a duet, with Belletti, from Rossini's *Il Turco in Italia*, the Trio Concertante with two flutes from Meyerbeer's *Camp of Silesia*, accompanied by herself—a most exquisite performance, her voice perfectly echoing the notes of the flutes. She sang also two national airs of Sweden.

The first concert realized 26,000 dollars. Mdlle. Lind gave her share, 10,000 dollars, to the benevolent institutions of New York, and on learning that some of the members of the New York orchestra were in indigent circumstances, she generously made them a substantial gift. Her beneficent actions during her entire stay in America are too numerous to detail. She helped numbers, and gave largely of the enormous sums which she received. Frequently would she flit away from her house, quietly, as if about to pay a visit, and then she might be seen disappearing down back lanes or into the cottages of the poor. She was warned to avoid so much liberality, as many unworthy persons took unfair advantage of her bounty; but she invariably replied, "Never mind; if I relieve ten, and one is worthy, I am satisfied." She had distributed 30,000 florins in Germany; she gave away in England nearly 60,000*l.*; and in America she scattered in charity no less than 50,000 dollars. Making a certain provision for her own future support, as well as that of her beloved parents, who resided in Sweden, her desire was to devote the proceeds of her visit to America to promoting education among the poor of her native land.

Her second début in the States was in Boston, October 1, at the Tremont Temple, where she had the same stupendous success. October 7, she sang in Providence. The next concert which she gave in Boston was appropriated to charitable purposes. She then went to Philadelphia, back to New York, again to Philadelphia, then to Baltimore, Washington, Richmond, Charleston, Havanna, and other places. At Baltimore, while standing at a balcony, bowing to the loud and enthusiastic applause of the multitude, at the close of a serenade, she had the misfortune to drop her shawl; in less than a minute it was torn into fragments, which were distributed to all who were in the immediate vicinity, as mementoes of the songstress.

In June, 1851, Mdlle. Lind availed herself, after the 95th concert, of an article in the agreement with Mr. Barnum, which enabled her to prematurely conclude her engagement, and by a sacrifice of some 30,000 dollars, to break the partnership. She then continued the series herself.

Some time after this she married Mr. Otto Goldschmidt, a pianist, son of a wealthy merchant of Hamburg. He was twenty-four, small, but good-looking. His graceful and finished style of playing had obtained for him much applause in London at the concerts of the Musical Union in 1849.

Madame Lind Goldschmidt returned to Europe in 1852. After a brief tour through England en route to Germany, declining every proposition for a public appearance, she settled in Dresden, employing in good works, and in piously founding schools, etc. a part of her immense fortune. Excepting on the occasion of concerts given at Vienna, Hamburg, and a few other German cities, she confined herself strictly to the retirement of private life up to December, 1856; when she reappeared in London, at Exeter Hall, and by her admirable rendering of the finest sacred music revived her former popularity. For her first appearance, the *Creation* was chosen; the music of this Oratorio being especially suited to the marvellous fulness and purity of her voice. "The wonder is," said one critic, "that the notes should issue forth with such sustained ease from a frame so comparatively gentle." The beautiful airs, "With verdure clad," and "On mighty pens," were warbled with a charming clearness of intonation; and all the other pieces were delivered with an extraordinary beauty and finish. Her second appearance was in *Elijah*, in which she sang with splendid effect. Her intensity of feeling, her faultless skill, her exquisite taste, were irreproachable.

From that to the present time, Mr. and Mme. Goldschmidt have lived almost entirely in England, having apparently determined to make this country their permanent home. She has occasionally appeared in public, generally for benevolent purposes; and, whenever she appears, she is received with as much enthusiasm as ever. In private society she meets with the esteem and regard due to her virtues and talents.

CHAPTER XVII.

SOPHIE CRUVELLI.

Sophie Cruvelli, the daughter of a Protestant clergyman named Cruwell, was born, 1830, at Bielefeld in Prussia. Her family, though by no means rich, possessed some little property, and intended to endow Sophie with a moderate fortune when she should marry. Her parents resolved to educate her with care, and finding that she had a decided taste for music, her mother took her to Paris when she was fourteen that she might obtain finishing lessons.

Permarini and Bordogni were the masters from whom she received instruction. The latter, at once perceiving the intuitive genius of the girl, spared no trouble, and would not allow her to spare herself labour. He made her practise solfeggio four hours a day, setting her the most difficult exercises he could invent; and during two years of severe application and tedious labour, he would not permit her to sing anything but vocal scales. At the end of that time her mother came to take away Sophie, thinking that she must by this time have acquired a sufficient mastery of French and music, and might very well return home. But Bordogni protested against robbing the musical world of such a treasure as the Fräulein Cruwell would prove, after two or three years more of study: it was foolish, it was wrong, he declared, to prevent her from following what was obviously her destiny. Madame Cruwell saw the justice of Bordogni's representations. "If my daughter devotes herself to the stage," she said, "and freely embraces the career of an artiste, we may endeavour to submit to further sacrifices; but if merely destined to bring up a family, she has learnt quite enough of solfeggio: her little fortune will be all consumed by her singing lessons." Sophie was consulted, and declared that she must become a prima donna; so it was settled that she should complete her studies in Italy, and the family left for Milan. Before quitting Paris, however, she appeared at a concert given by the *Revue et Gazette Musicale*, September 12, 1847.

At Milan, she was preparing to commence operations with spirit, when a dreadful discovery was made. She could not sing at all! When she opened her lips, not a sound came forth; her voice was absolutely gone! The despair of the family, the anguish of Sophie, are not to be depicted. Nothing remained to be done but to return to Bielefeld. While making their preparations for departure in mournful sadness, Signor Lamberti, an experienced professor, to whom they had been recommended, was announced. They described to him their misfortune, at which Lamberti was very much surprised; however, he began talking to Sophie, and soon ascertained what he had suspected to be the truth, that her voice had simply been exhausted by the fatigue of her journey. He therefore advised the family to defer their departure for a few days. They did so, and when he called again, Sophie's voice had returned clearer and more beautiful than ever: the high notes had gained additional purity and strength, and the lower were more rich and mellow than they had ever been before. Lamberti assisted the young German with advice and instruction, and at last, at the end of 1847, Sophie made her début at La Fenice, under the Italianized name of Cruvelli, in the part of Doña Sol (*Ernani*). She next performed Norma, and was most favourably received.

Deserted by his original company, Mr. Lumley was roving all over Europe in quest of another, and having heard Mdlle. Cruvelli at Venice, he immediately engaged her for the ensuing season. The company at Her Majesty's Theatre in 1848 consisted of Mesdames Persiani and Viardot, Mesdemoiselles Alboni and Cruvelli, Signori Cuzzani, Belletti, Gardoni, and Polonini.

Mdlle. Cruvelli was then only eighteen, and her voice and style were still unfinished; yet although she was unaided by any extraneous interest, and the "Lind mania" was raging, Mdlle. Cruvelli made a decided sensation. She appeared Saturday, February 19, in *Ernani*, with Cuzzani, Gardoni, and Belletti. She possessed much enthusiasm, spirit, and animation, though as yet deficient in physical power, and often led into mistaking violence for energy. Her voice, in compass from F to F, was a clear silvery soprano, the low notes of which had something of the contralto quality; her tones were vigorous, fresh, and bell-like. In appearance she was youthful and engaging. Her figure, of the middle height, was fine and well-moulded, her face of the Teutonic type. Her manner was particularly dramatic, and her style energetic. The audience were prepossessed in her favour,. and gave her the kindest reception; in fact, she was entirely successful.

Mdlle. Cruvelli made a further advance as Odabella, in *Attila*, and as Lucrezia in *I Due Foscari;* her performances were acknowledged to be of high order, both vocally and dramatically. She also gained much credit by her personation of Lucrezia Borgia; acting with great intelligence, earnestness, and energy. She appeared in *Ernani* five times; as Abigaile, in *Nino*, twice; as Lucrezia Borgia, thrice; as Rosina in *Il Barbiere*, and the Countess in *Nozze di Figaro*, to Jenny Lind's Susanna, several times. Her Rosina was a pretty, piquant performance, modest and unpretending, and not deficient in dramatic truth.

Unfortunately, Sophie was driven away by the Lind

fever, and she retreated to Germany, where she commenced a musical tour. She was at Berlin when the revolution broke out, and was obliged to quit the city. She left Berlin for Trieste, where, during the Carnival, she performed in *Attila*, *Norma*, *Don Pasquale*, *Macbeth*—in short, anything and everything, old and new, serious and comic, classical and sensational. Early in 1850 she was at Milan, where the patrons of La Scala offered her the most extravagant ovations. She then went to Genoa, where she had an unlucky difference with the young habitués of the parterre, in consequence of a misunderstanding. She sang in *Lucrezia Borgia*, *Norma*, *Nabucco*, and *Attila*, and her success was so great that it was impossible to obtain a place without securing it several days in advance. Her last part was in an opera by Signor Chiaramonte, a Neapolitan composer, which added greatly to her fame, and she was eulogized in the most rapturous terms by the Italian journalists.

The second week in April, 1850, she made her first appearance at the Théâtre Italien, in Paris, then under Mr. Lumley's direction, as Elvira, to Mr. Sims Reeves' Ernani. She was received with enthusiasm which surpassed even that excited at Venice, Trieste, or Milan, and she repeated the character several times to crowded houses. She appeared for a second time at Her Majesty's Theatre, May 20, 1851, in *Fidelio*, with Mr. Sims Reeves.

Her improvement had been marvellous. Although scarcely more than twenty, she had now become a most admirable artiste. The sculpturesque beauty of her physiognomy, the profound dramatic sentiment of her acting, the incomparable brilliancy of her voice, elicited universal admiration. Her Leonora was an exquisitely finished, an entrancing performance; and her acting and singing in the prison scene was forcible, intense, yet delicately shaded. "From the shuddering expression given to the words, 'How cold it is in this subterranean vault,' spoken on entering Florestan's dungeon," said one critic, "to the joyous and energetic duet, in which the re-united pair give vent to their rapturous feelings, all was inimitable. Each transition of feeling was faithfully conveyed, and the suspicion growing by degrees into certainty that the wretched prisoner is Florestan, was depicted with heart-searching truth. The internal struggle was perfectly expressed."

"With Mdlle. Cruvelli," says this writer, "Fidelio is governed throughout by one purpose, to which everything is rendered subservient. Determination to discover and liberate her husband is the mainspring not only of all her actions, and the theme of all her soliloquies, but even when others likely to influence her design in any way are acting or speaking, we read in the anxious gaze, the breathless anxiety, the head bent to catch the slightest word, a continuation of the same train of thought, and an ever living ardour in the pursuit of the one cherished object. In such positions as these, where one gifted artist follows nature with so delicate an appreciation of its most subtle truths, it is not easy for a character occupying the background of the stage picture to maintain (although by gesture only) a constant commentary upon the words of others without becoming intrusive or attracting an undue share of attention. Yet Cruvelli does this throughout the first scene (especially during the duet betwixt Rocco and Pizarro, in which Fidelio overhears the plan to assassinate her husband) with a perfection akin to that realized by Rachel in the last scene of *Les Horaces*, where Camille listens to the recital of her brother's victory over her lover ; and the result, like that of the chorus in a Greek drama, is to heighten rather than lessen the effect. These may be considered minor points, but, as necessary parts of a great conception, they are as important, and afford as much evidence of the master mind, as the artist's delivery of the grandest speeches or scenes."

"Mdlle. Cruvelli," observes another critic, "has the power of expressing joy and despair, hope and anxiety, hatred and love, fear and resolution, with equal facility. She has voice and execution sufficient to master with ease all the trying difficulties of the most trying and difficult of parts."

Norma was Sophie's second performance. "Before

the first act was over, Sophie Cruvelli demonstrated that she was as profound a mistress of the grand as of the romantic school of acting, as perfect an interpreter of the brilliant as of the classical school of music." She represented Fidelio five times, and Norma thrice.

Her features were most expressive, and well adapted to the lyric stage; her manner also was dramatic and energetic. She was highly original; and always thought for herself. Possessing a profound insight into character, her conception was always true and just, while her execution continually varied. "The one proceeds from a judgment that never errs, the other from impulse, which may possibly lead her astray. Thus, while her Fidelio and her Norma are never precisely the same on two consecutive evenings, they are, nevertheless, always Fidelio and Norma. . . . She does not calculate. She sings and acts on the impulse of the moment; but her performance must always be impressive, because it is always true to one idea, always bearing upon one object—the vivid realization of the character she impersonates to the apprehension of her audience." So much was she the creature of impulse, that even when she would spend a day, a week, a month, in elaborating a certain passage—a certain dramatic effect—perhaps on the night of performance she would improvise something perfectly different from her preconceived idea.

Her sister Marie made her début in Thalberg's *Florinda*, in July, with Sophie. She was a graceful and charming contralto; but her timidity, and an over-delicacy of expression, did not permit her then to display her talents to the greatest advantage. The brother of the sisters Cruvelli was a fine baritone.

At the close of 1851, Sophie went again to the Théâtre Italien; and the following year she returned to London, making her appearance, April 17, as Norma, with Lablache and Gardoni. She had established herself as a welcome favourite, and performed during the season in *La Sonnambula*, *Il Barbiere*, etc. Her improvement was remarkable even in her acting, always so energetic and impulsive. Before the termination of the season, the whimsical young lady suddenly disappeared, without giving any reason for her extraordinary proceeding, or vouchsafing any subsequent explanation. She was heard of in August at Wiesbaden, from whence she repaired to Aix-la-Chapelle, where she performed in *Le Prophète*. Then she was on the banks of the Rhine, and afterwards she reappeared at the Théâtre Italien.

There was unwonted excitement among the frequenters of the Grand Opéra in Paris on January 16, 1854, for Sophie Cruvelli was to make her début there, the opera selected for this occasion being *Les Huguenots*. She was to receive 100,000 francs for six months. Meyerbeer was very much pleased, and set to work once more on his long-promised opera, *L'Africaine;* the principal character in which he destined for Mdlle. Cruvelli, of whose talents he entertained the highest opinion. The house was crowded to the ceiling. A fortnight in advance, orchestra stalls were sold for 200 francs, and boxes were scarcely to be obtained. The Emperor and Empress arrived some time before the hour of commencing; and the number of notabilities among the audience was striking. Meyerbeer, pleased by the renewed impetus given to his pet opera, was present; as also were Auber, Benedict, Berlioz, Alboni, Madame Viardot, Mario, Tamburini, Vivier, Théophile Gautier, Fiorentino; "it was scarcely possible to direct an opera-glass to any part of the house without bringing the face and figure of some notable person into view." It was unanimously agreed that such a Valentine had never been seen or heard; and Meyerbeer himself, who is not easily satisfied, especially in his own works, expressed the warmest approbation.

In March, Spontini's *Vestale* was reproduced. As many years had elapsed since its performance last in Paris, the greatest curiosity was manifested to hear it. Nevertheless, it did not obtain the triumphant success that had been anticipated; for, although Mdlle. Cruvelli sang with great power and sometimes with almost terrible energy, the opera was executed very carelessly by the orchestra and the chorus. Mdlle. Cruvelli's performance was praised on all sides. "She is, in fact, almost the only cantatrice who acts as well as sings. She would have made an excellent tragedian," says one writer. Roger and Bonnehée took the other parts in this opera, and were much applauded.

Having been engaged at the Royal Italian Opera, Sophie Cruvelli appeared Thursday, April 27, as Desdemona, with Tamburini and Ronconi. She received, it was said, 250*l.* a night for eight nights. May 3, she appeared in *Fidelio*, in which she was not to be surpassed; and on May 11 (for the first time at the Royal Italian Opera), in *Don Giovanni*. As Donna Anna she achieved a new success, displaying unexpected intensity and variety of passion, and delivering some of the fine recitatives and airs in a superb style.

June 21, *Robert le Diable* was revived with great splendour at the Grand Opéra in Paris, in presence of a brilliant and overflowing audience. Sophie Cruvelli was magnificent as Alice, and her voice was pure and fresh. In October, an extraordinary sensation was created in the musical circles of Paris by the sudden disappearance of Sophie. She was announced to perform in *Les Huguenots*, but when the evening arrived, she was not to be found. She had left Paris by the Northern Railway, without any intimation of where she was gone. The previous season, at the Théâtre Italien, she had more than once played a trick of the same kind, not being regularly paid; but it created great surprise that she would relinquish such an enormous salary—4,000*l.* for a season consisting of eight months, for singing only twice a week—abandon everything, injure the manager, M. Fould, and insult the public—all for a whim. Every imaginable reason for her departure was guessed at. Her furniture, and the money at her bankers', were seized upon as a security for the forfeit (4,000*l.*), which she had incurred by this breach of her engagement, and her private letters and papers were opened and read. In November, she "demanded and obtained permission" to return to the Grand Opéra, when the cause of her eccentric flight appeared to be a "misunderstanding." She presented herself again in *Les Huguenots*, and the audience testified their displeasure by receiving the truant in solemn silence; but she ultimately succeeded in winning their pardon, and continued to be the great attraction, for some time, in *Les Huguenots.*

In 1855, Verdi's *Vêpres Siciliennes* was produced, Mdlle. Cruvelli taking the part of Hélène, the other characters being performed by Bonnehée, Gueymard, and Obin. The mise-en-scène was splendid, and the opera was completely successful. "The audience was electrified by the tones of her magnificent voice, which realized with equal effect those high inspirations that demand passion, force, and impulse; and those tender passages that require delicacy, taste, and a thorough knowledge of the art of singing. No one could reproach Mdlle. Cruvelli with exaggeration, so well did she know how to restrain her ardent nature." "Cruvelli is the Rachel of the Grand Opéra!" exclaimed a French critic.

Rumours of her approaching marriage now began to circulate, and it was understood that she was about to finally quit the stage; and on January 5, 1856, Sophie Cruvelli married the Baron Vigier, a wealthy young Parisian, the son of Baron or Count Vigier, whose father endowed the city of Paris with the immense bathing establishments upon the Seine, which bear his name, and who, under Louis Philippe, was a member of the Chamber of Deputies, and afterwards Peer of France.

In July, 1857, a concert was given for the poor at Vannes, at which Madame la Baronne Vigier (Sophie Cruvelli) sang, and which produced the sum of 4,000 francs (160*l.*).

In 1860, Madame Vigier was residing with her husband at his baronial mansion at Nice, and sang on many occasions in the salons of the élite of the official and fashionable world. She sang her own compositions among others—one of which consisted of variations on a well-known Tyrolienne, showy, replete with traits as eccentric, and eccentricities as defiant of rule as herself. She continued to sing frequently at charity concerts.

CHAPTER XVIII.

MARIETTA PICCOLOMINI.

During the Carnival of 1856, a stranger would have imagined that the inhabitants of the little town of Sienna had suddenly become frantic; for they were rushing hither and thither, from church to theatre, from the duomo to balls and dancing parties. They were mad with joy at having received permission to wear masks, which had been prohibited for more than eight years.

They were deliriously dancing, shouting, singing, ogling, laughing, screaming, with the most hilarious gaiety and frolicsome good-humour, pelting each other with roses, violets, and camellias, confetti, or bon-bons; doing everything by turns, and nothing long, and finishing the day by going to the opera, to weep over the woes of the unhappy Violetta, heroine of *La Traviata*, personated by Marietta Piccolomini. Next to the rapture of being allowed to resume their masks, there was nothing they were more infatuated with than the performance of this young prima donna; and an Italian audience, when it takes a fancy to a singer, behaves in a manner incomprehensible to people not accustomed to such vehement demonstrations.

Marietta Piccolomini was the idol of the Siennese that season, and the opera of *La Traviata*, condemned in the other theatres of Italy, but triumphantly revived by her, was the favourite piece of the Carnival. Marietta, who had been born in Sienna, in 1834, was a descendant of the Piccolomini family, which, transplanted by Charlemagne among the Gauls, and replanted in fertile Italy, had bloomed with clusters of illustrious men. One of the principal personages of the family was Pope Pius II., and one of Marietta's uncles was a Cardinal.

Marietta, though the descendant of a noble line, had taken it into her head that she would like to become a singer. She was allied to the most distinguished families in the kingdom, and was to have a respectable dowry, and her parents were horrified at her wish to become a vocalist. From the age of four years, Marietta had amused herself at playing at mock representations; she used to sing duets with her mother, a skilful amateur; and she had been instructed by Romani, one of the first professional teachers in Italy. Long did she implore her father to allow her to appear on the stage; at last her entreaties prevailed, she was permitted to follow her own fancies, and she made her début at Rome, November, 1852, in the operas of *Poliuto* and *Don Bucefalo*, under the guidance of her teacher, Romani. Then she appeared at her native town of Sienna, from whence she went to Florence, where she performed in *Lucrezia Borgia*, with immense success. She was scarcely sixteen, and being naturally of a juvenile aspect, she appeared then a mere child. However, although she had not the commanding presence of the haughty Lucrezia, she sang very captivatingly, and the opera was applauded. In the scene where, in the interview with her consort, the Duchess exclaims, "Tremble, Duke Alfonzo! Thou art my fourth husband, and I am a Borgia!" this portentous threat, from the lips of a child, was so irresistibly droll that the audience were seized with an uncontrollable fit of laughter. Nevertheless, she performed the character for twenty nights successively. From Florence, Marietta ran all over Italy, like an *enfant gatée*, intoxicated with the pleasure of having crowded audiences at her feet. She was free to choose her engagements; she had only to present herself for everybody to fly in ecstasy to hear her.

At Turin, where Ristori had first made herself famous, Mdlle. Piccolomini appeared in November, 1855, for the first time in *La Traviata;* which, in spite of her youth and inexperience, she interpreted with so much talent that, on the second night of her performance at the Teatro Carignano, a vast concourse of people assembled to greet her as she came forth, and were about to unharness the horses from her carriage. But Marietta started up, her cheeks flushed, her eyes sparkling, and said, indignantly, that "men should not put themselves in the place of beasts. Italy had other and nobler uses for her sons." Then, seeing that they were determined on paying her this objectionable homage, which she was equally determined not to accept, she hurried through the stage door, and made her way on foot to her hotel. On another occasion her house was surrounded at midnight by an excited crowd, "bent on manifesting their frantic delight at her musical power," when she came forward, and "sternly rebuked the young men of Italy for their levity, and pointed out how they could more nobly fulfil the great object of their existence."

On her benefit night, December 16, 1855, the scene was more like a festival and a public triumph than a theatrical representation. The doors were opened at half-past three o'clock; in a few minutes the theatre was filled by a dense crowd, which waited patiently four hours for *La Traviata* and the darling Piccolomini, whom they had heard for thirty-five successive nights already. Their pet singer was hailed with an uproar of delight; flowers were showered on the stage, and, every moment, every phrase was followed by the most enthusiastic applause. The performances over, there was a frantic shout for the vocalist, and such fanaticized excitement has rarely been paralleled. The crowd waited till their idol had quitted the theatre, and when she appeared at the stage door, they gave her a wildly enthusiastic reception. "Everybody pressed round her, to bid her adieu, to shake hands with her, even to touch her dress; and when at last she got into her carriage, the crowd followed her to the hotel, shouting, 'Viva la Piccolomini!' She had scarcely entered her apartment, when the shouts recommenced, and the enchantress was compelled to show herself in the balcony, again to thank the crowd which completely thronged the street."

The next day there was a benefit at the Teatro Carignano for M. Bianchi, first violin, and M. Anglois, first contra basso, when Marietta was to sing again. The prices were raised, and the same pieces were performed as on the preceding day; nevertheless every seat was occupied. The brindisi, in *La Traviata*, sung by Mdlle. Piccolomini and Signor Massimiliani was encored, and she was recalled at least ten times after each morçeau. Signor Massimiliani, the tenor, was presented by the public with a coronal of gold, as a souvenir of his success in *La Traviata* with Mdlle. Piccolomini. At the end of the performance all the artistes were recalled, and when la Piccolomini appeared, the audience rose and waved their handkerchiefs as a farewell. The ovation of the previous evening was renewed—men and women ranged themselves in a double line in the corridors and passages, and a group of young men detached the horses from her carriage in order to draw it in triumph to her hotel; but she declined this honour, and passed slowly through an almost impenetrable crowd, which accompanied her the whole way to the door of her own apartment. They began cheering again when she disappeared from view, but she was obliged to present herself several times to thank them. "This evening," she said, in thrilling accents, "will be ever remembered as the happiest of my life."

The proceeds of her fourteen nights' representations were divided among the poor.

The reports of Marietta's triumphs at last attracted the attention of the manager of Her Majesty's Theatre, who engaged the charming young prima donna, and she appeared for the first time before an English audience in *La Traviata*, Saturday, May 24, 1856.

She is agreeable, sprightly, *petite*, with a vivacious grace of manner perfectly bewitching. Her figure is slender and extremely elegant; her features are bright, and capable of expressing the rapid transitions of varying emotion, from archness and coquetry to tender pathos and deepest sorrow. Her voice is a high soprano, fresh and youthful, but in range perhaps a little more than two octaves, crisp and flexible, pretty fluent, and rather sweet than powerful. Her musical declamation is excellent, her taste pure. Her début was a decided success.

May 5th, she appeared as Lucia di Lammermoor. There was great curiosity to see how she would treat this character; the demand for stall tickets was unprecedented, and extravagant prices were extorted; not a box was unoccupied, and every portion of the theatre was crowded. The ordeal was a trying one; but Mdlle. Piccolomini passed through it with éclat. By the fascination of her manner, her perfect appreciation of the requirements of the stage, her undoubted talent, and by a peculiarly skilful means of managing her somewhat limited voice, she showed herself a most excellent performer, and her Lucia was a veritable triumph. Some passages were inverted, however, to bring them within the compass of her voice, and others materially altered to suit the capabilities of her vocalization.

June 26th, Mdlle. Piccolomini appeared for the first time as Maria, in *La Figlia del Reggimento*, and July 26th, *Don Pasquale*. In both she was charming. She was considered to resemble Sontag more nearly than any other singer. Her small, slight figure, her graceful manner, her coquettish style, bore a certain similitude to the great German singer, though in point of vocalization she was very inferior. She also performed Zerlina, in which she was bewitching, though her conception and singing were undoubtedly faulty.

"Mdlle. Piccolomini's Zerlina is one of the prettiest things witnessed or conceivable," exclaims one critic. "When she frisked on to the stage with the 'Giovinette,' she was greeted with a storm of applause, and her deliciously coquettish singing and acting of 'La ci darem,' with Signor Beneventano, produced a peremptory demand for its repetition. The other well-known songs, 'Batti, batti,' and 'Vedrai carino,' were sung to perfection."

With very few exceptions, Marietta won the applause of the London critics, who found it impossible to find fault, even with her numerous imperfections. "If this or that passage in *La Figlia* or *Don Pasquale* was not delivered with the magnificence of voice of a Grisi, a Persiani, a Sontag, or a Lind," says one, "and clothed, as by these artistes, with an abundance of fioriture, perhaps the pen was inclined to record that the vocal powers of the performer were insufficient for the important position of prima donna; but the ink would not flow till the writer was resolved to pass over such shortcomings, and to render generous tribute to dramatic powers more intense, and yet more refined, than were ever witnessed in so young a candidate for European fame."

At the close of the London season, Mdlle. Piccolomini went to Dublin. Her first appearance on the stage there was hailed with "one unanimous burst of welcoming plaudits." At the fall of the curtain the young prima donna was vociferously called for, and then nearly buried in heaps of flowers, while "peal after peal of cheering echoed through the house." So cordial a greeting was rarely accorded to a débutante on the Dublin stage.

The reception which she had met with in England was faint compared to that which awaited her in Paris, where she appeared Saturday, December 6, in *La Traviata*, which was then performed for the first time in the French capital.

Verdi, who did not like his operas to be represented at the Italiens, because he was not paid for the right by that theatre, tried his best to deprive the Parisians of hearing the charming Sardinian in his *Traviata*, as he had already tried to prevent them from having *Il Trovatore*. He demanded, it was said, 20,000 francs from the director of the Italian Opera (M. Calzado) for "permission" to perform *Rigoletto* and *La Traviata*, which the director refused to agree to. When M. Calzado announced *La Traviata*, M. Boyer, director of the Vaudeville Theatre, applied to the President of the Civil Tribunal for an order on M. Calzado not to perform the piece, on the ground that the libretto was taken from the *Dame aux Camélias*, by Alexandre Dumas, junior, which is the property of the Vaudeville Theatre. But on hearing M. Calzado, the President declined to interfere in the matter.

There was an unusually brilliant and fashionable

audience assembled to witness the début of the Sardinian Nightingale. The youth, beauty, and fascinating manner of the piquant little prima donna were dilated on in the warmest terms by those who had had an opportunity of hearing and seeing her, and her reception was all that could have been expected by the most sanguine. The audience were enraptured with her. Some, indeed, who had unreasonably anticipated seeing a Grisi or a Malibran, were disappointed when they beheld this simple young girl of twenty summers, with a moderate voice, whose chief attributes were her bewitching manner and perfectly original style of acting.

The Parisian journalists were for some time irresolute as to the terms in which they should speak of the petite artiste. One says, "She at one time has the air of a child; at another, all the appearance of mature age. She sings, but is not a cantatrice; she plays with talent, yet she cannot be called an actress. At one moment she appears inexperienced and simple; the next, one would think she had been ten years on the boards. She is an enigma—a problem." "Mdlle. Piccolomini is pleasant, *petite*, slender, sprightly, and bounds on the stage like a gazelle," says Scudo. "Everything speaks with her: her piquant physiognomy, her expressive eyes, her natural attitudes, her gestures, everything—to the coquettish way she tosses her charming head. She is an Italian, but an *Italienne de race*, who is happy to pass through life like a butterfly, joyous and free. Her voice is a thin soprano, without extent, without timbre or brilliancy; one might say that it was one of those French voices which may be heard at the Opéra Comique: but she sings with such intelligence the words which are confided to her, she sings with a feeling so true and so marked, that we almost forget her faults. It will not do to analyze too rigorously the talent of Mdlle. Piccolomini; but listen without prepossession, see her walk with grace, turning in her hand a bouquet of violets, and do not think whether she is an accomplished vocalist or not. She is an *enfant bien douée*, who has much to learn; but with no radical faults, and possessing an indefinable charm which attracts and delights you, spite of your better judgment. After certain legitimate reservations, we may say that Mdlle. Piccolomini is not an ordinary artiste, and we can only say of this charming child, *Elle est charmante*."

The Empress was so much disappointed at being prevented from hearing La Piccolomini on her début, that an Imperial order was sent to M. Calzado for an extraordinary performance, which accordingly took place the following Monday, when their Majesties attended. Piccolomini performed *La Traviata* in Paris nineteen times in the course of two months.

April 21, 1857, Mdlle. Piccolomini made her reappearance in London in *La Figlia del Reggimento.*

Her reception was an ovation—there were showers of bouquets, storms of applause. She also performed in *Don Giovanni*, *Lucia di Lammermoor*, *Le Nozze di Figaro*, etc. Her répertoire, became more extended this season; she was determined not to be satisfied with the negative reputation she had already gained, but was anxious to improve; being conscious of the real defects under which it could not be denied she laboured, though she had decidedly advanced in knowledge and practice during her absence. On the occasion of her benefit, in July, there was a most extravagant demonstration; not only were applause and bouquets rained on her, but among other offerings of admiration was a white dove, which, attached to a wreath, fell fluttering from one of the boxes on to the stage!

Her Majesty's Theatre being closed, Mdlle. Piccolomini made a provincial tour, and was received with great éclat at Liverpool, Manchester, Birmingham, Glasgow, Edinburgh, Bath, Bristol, Cheltenham, Brighton, and other places. Then she repaired again to Dublin. In November and December she went with Giuglini on a "starring" tour through Germany.

February, 1858, Marietta reappeared again at Her Majesty's Theatre, as Arline, in Balfe's opera, *La Zingara* (*The Bohemian Girl*), with Belletti, Vialetti, and Giuglini. She was received with frantic rapture, and literally pelted with bouquets; so also was Signor Giuglini: this being the first instance of floral offerings being made to a gentleman. The charming little prima donna already contemplated withdrawing from the scene of her triumphs; and April 18, she appeared as Violetta, this being the first of a series of six farewell performances, previous to her final retirement into private life. She did not excite the same enthusiasm as formerly, though she had still many ardent admirers. On the 26th, a new opera, by Signor Campana, entitled *Almina,* written expressly for Mdlle. Piccolomini, was produced, but it created hardly any sensation. In *Almina,* which was performed three times, Mdlle. Piccolomini took her leave of the stage. It was regretted that her last appearances were not devoted to the character of Violetta, with which she had become so identified.

In October, ten thousand persons were attracted to the Crystal Palace by the announcement of the farewell benefit of Marietta Piccolomini previous to her departure for the United States. Every reserved seat was occupied—a rare occurrence in that vast hall. The concert, apart from its exceptional interest, was not very remarkable. The programme was composed entirely of pieces from well-known operas by Verdi, Mozart, and Donizetti. Mdlle. Piccolomini, who sang alone and with Signor Giuglini, was received with overwhelming plaudits. She sang in her best manner, and in addition to many airs from foreign operas (including the famous *Libiamo*) she gave, in English, the once favourite song, "I dreamt that I dwelt in Marble Halls." At the conclusion of the concert, the entire audience rose, and waved hats and handkerchiefs with the wildest enthusiasm.

Before leaving England, Mdlle. Piccolomini went on her customary provincial tour. In August she went to Dublin, where she performed in *Don Giovanni* with Madame Viardot Garcia. Her Zerlina, although not one of her finest characters, and though her voice was somewhat overtaxed by the music of the part, was applauded with rapture. The furore of delight which the enchanting Marietta created was extraordinary. The "gallery gods" spontaneously composed, set to a popular tune, and sang in her honour and praise, an address wherein they described their admiration and pleasure. In October, she appeared at New York. The fevered expectations of the public caused the seats to sell at a high premium, and the Americans were in raptures with the charming little cantatrice.

In 1859 (June 20), Mdlle. Piccolomini reappeared in London, at Drury Lane, in *La Traviata*, with Signor Giuglini. She appeared also in *La Figlia del Reggimento*, in *Don Giovanni*, the last act of *I Martiri*, and the *Bohemian Girl*. Altogether she performed some sixteen or seventeen nights; but nobody cared much about her. From London she went to the provinces.

Mdlle. Piccolomini, in 1860, married the Marquis Gaetani, and in June, 1861, she sang for the benefit of the sufferers from the earthquake in Central Italy.

In private life, the piquant, sparkling little heroine of *La Traviata* is one of the most delightful, sportive creatures in existence. It is charming to see her with those whom she loves. Her kindness of heart has been lately shown by her coming to London expressly for the purpose of singing at the three complimentary performances at Her Majesty's Theatre, for the benefit of Mr. Lumley, who offered her her first London engagement.

CHAPTER XIX.

LOUISA PYNE.

Louisa Pyne was scarcely five years of age when she astonished her parents and friends by the beauty of her voice, her love for music, and the fluency with which she could repeat airs that she heard. Such gifts were not to be neglected, and some of her relatives being in the musical world, were well qualified to judge of her promise. Her uncle, Mr. Pyne, was the well-known tenor singer.

Miss Pyne was placed with Sir George Smart; and so quickly did she profit by the instruction of that master, that at the age of ten she made her début at the Queen's Concert Rooms, Hanover Square. Her voice was even then very clear and powerful, and amidst the crash of more than fifty orchestral performers it was heard distinctly. She was rewarded with the most enthusiastic plaudits. During 1841 and 1842, the concerts of the "Misses Pyne" in London were very fashionably attended, and the rapid improvement of the sisters, Susan and Louisa, was especially noticed.

In 1847, the young Louisa appeared in Paris, and was received with great favour. A pleasing incident marked this sojourn. The secretary of a society for the education of homeless children remarked to the sisters that he "feared it must break up for the want of funds." "Oh!" replied the kind-hearted girls, "let us sing for them." They did so, and the institution was saved.

In August, 1849, Miss Louisa Pyne essayed, for the first time, the performance of opera, at Boulogne. She appeared as Amina in *La Sonnambula*, and was completely successful. Two months later, Mr. Maddox commenced an operatic season at the Princess's Theatre, and Miss Louisa Pyne was engaged as prima donna, Madame Macfarren, wife of the eminent composer, being the contralto, Mr. Harrison the tenor, and Mr. Weiss basso. The theatre opened October 1, with *Don Giovanni* (in English), Miss Pyne performing Zerlina. Her voice was a lovely soprano, remarkable for sweetness, compass, flexibility, and resonance, deliciously true and beautiful in quality, though slightly veiled. Her intonation was correct, her method and style fine; she had the utmost fluency, and though fond of indulging in the most dazzling embellishments, all her ornaments were admirably placed and appropropriate. In appearance she was, as everybody knows, petite and blonde, with a most agreeable expression and a peculiar piquancy, her face sparkling with liveliness and intelligence. At that period she was but a novice on the stage, and deficient in dramatic energy; yet, disdaining all stage trickery, she evinced an original conception and irreproachable taste: there was a simplicity and elegance in all she did.

Miss Pyne's second performance at the Princess's was Amina; and her charming and intelligent style and beautiful voice made this personation most striking.

Mr. Macfarren's *Charles the Second* was produced October 27, when Miss Pyne, as Fanny, the innkeeper's daughter, her first original character, achieved a triumph; more than redeeming the promise of her début. She sang with the purest taste, and warbled florid passages with bird-like ease and facility. "Miss Louisa Pyne has taken the town by storm," it was said. This character completed the triad of successes, of which Zerlina and Amina constituted the supporting figures. She was encored in each of her four songs, and also in her duet with Madame Macfarren, who performed Julian. The voice of Madame Macfarren was a contralto of considerable compass, round and sweet. Messrs. Harrison, Weiss, and Corri performed the leading male characters.

In the summer of 1850, Miss Louisa Pyne was singing at Liverpool, in opera, performing in *La Sonnam-*

bula, etc., with Mr. Harrison and Mr. and Mrs. Weiss. Her Amina was very much admired. She represented with simple truth the gentle, loving village maiden, first joyous in her happy affection, and then crushed with undeserved grief. The principal feature of the conception was its quiet, subdued mildness. "Miss Pyne's representation is, in fact, one of repose," observes a writer of the period. "It is a personation which charms by its simplicity, though it never overwhelms by its intensity. We cannot, perhaps, give a better idea of Miss Pyne's peculiarities of singing and acting, than by saying that she is somewhat of an English Sontag; though, of course, we do not intend to insinuate that she can pour out the fluent and unapproachable graces of that delightful vocalist. She resembles her, however, in the graceful delicacy of her action, and also in the surprising elegance of her vocalization."

In the spring and summer of 1851 Miss Pyne was at the Haymarket Theatre, Mr. Webster having engaged an excellent operatic troupe to perform on alternate nights with the dramatic company. Miss Pyne was supported by Mrs. Harriet Cawse, and Messrs. Donald King, Corri, Weiss, James Bland, etc. The conductor was Mr. Mellon. The company commenced their campaign in May with *The Crown Diamonds*, when Miss Pyne, as Cattarina, sang brilliantly. Other operas of a similar character were performed during the season. On August 14 of this year Miss Pyne sang at the Royal Italian Opera, in *Il Flauto Magico*, with the Italian company, before her Majesty and Prince Albert. She next sang at Windsor Castle, and afterwards at Buckingham Palace on several occasions. Every year she sang at the various musical festivals. In the course of the season of 1852 she sang at different concerts, the Philharmonic, etc., and she continued to appear at concerts until, in August, 1854, she embarked at Liverpool for America with her parents and her sister Susan, accompanied by Messrs. Harrison and Borrani.

She made her début before an American audience at the Broadway Theatre, October 9, in the *Sonnambula* in English. The house was crowded in every part, the tickets being only half a dollar, and the success of the young English prima donna was decided. She took New York by storm, and presents of every imaginable kind, and of great value, were showered on her. The *Sonnambula* was followed by the *Bohemian Girl* and by *Maritana*, the latter being personally directed by Mr. Wallace. The American journalists were horrified at the bad moral of *Maritana*, but captivated with the music and with the talent of the prima donna.

At the termination of her engagement in New York Miss Pyne was serenaded at her private residence, and throughout the Union she met with the same flattering reception. New Orleans was bewitched, and Cincinnati was unable to express its delight; altogether, the tour was highly satisfactory in every respect.

With the exception of Jenny Lind's engagement, Miss Pyne's farewell performances at New York were unexampled for enthusiasm. After her last appearance on the stage a deputation of ladies and gentlemen waited upon her at her hotel, and presented her with a magnificent gold bracelet, as a token of "admiration for her talent, and esteem for her private virtues." In America Miss Pyne's bounty was spontaneous and generous; the Blind and the Lunatic Asylums, the High Schools of New York, and many other charitable institutions, were all largely benefited by the free and unsolicited exercise of the talents of our English prima donna.

After an absence of more than three years, she presented herself once more before her London admirers; having, in conjunction with Mr. Harrison, taken the Lyceum Theatre for a season of three months. On September 21, 1857, she appeared in *The Crown Diamonds*, which was performed alternately with the *Huguenots*; both operas being well put on the stage. It was noticed that Miss Pyne's Transatlantic experiences had given her much confidence and knowledge of the stage, both in singing and acting, while her voice, though it had lost somewhat of its power, had gained in mellowness and richness. The *Rose of Castile*, a new opera by Mr. Balfe, was produced October 29.

Miss Pyne sang and acted, from the beginning of this opera to the end, with a fire, force, and finish which won for her the highest applause, and justified her in taking the first rank in her art. In 1858, the Pyne and Harrison Company were at Drury Lane. The operas performed were the *Rose of Castile*, Flotow's *Martha*, *Maritana*, *Crown Diamonds*, the *Bohemian Girl*, the *Trovatore*, and the *Daughter of the Regiment;* the last being for the benefit of Miss Pyne, who appeared as Maria for the first time in London. She sang the music of the Vivandière with exceeding brilliancy and admirable taste.

In 1859, the English Opera company was at Covent Garden, commencing October 9 with Meyerbeer's *Dinorah*. Emboldened by the success of the preceding season, the management considerably increased the strength of their company, and made extensive arrangements in every department. In producing *Dinorah* on the English stage and as an English opera, the original modelling of the Opéra Comique was restored, and the Italian recitatives were replaced by dialogue. Miss Pyne surprised even her most enthusiastic admirers by her performance of the graceful heroine. "That Miss Louisa Pyne would make Dinorah one of those brilliant and marvellous feats of vocalism that she alone of all English singers can accomplish, was expected by every one," says a critic, noticing the performance; "but that she should have so greatly eclipsed all her previous realizations was scarcely to have been anticipated: yet she has done so; and her rendering of Dinorah will place her foremost amongst living artistes, whether native or foreign. Meyerbeer has so studded the part with difficulties of the most elaborate character, and written the pitch so high that scarcely any voice can touch it; but when accomplished—and accomplished as it is by Miss Louisa Pyne—the effect is truly marvellous. Her singing of the opening *berceuse* was truly exquisite, but in the Shadow song she achieved her greatest success; for anything more truly beautiful, finished, and exquisite in the execution it is impossible to imagine—it was the perfection of florid singing. . . . In every respect we may congratulate Miss Louisa Pyne upon a great and brilliant triumph, not alone as a singer, but also as an actress."

The English version of *Il Trovatore* was also produced, and later in the season *Satanella* and *Bianca* by Mr. Balfe. Mr. Wallace's *Lurline* was brought out February 23, 1860, and created a great sensation. Miss Louisa Pyne sang most brilliantly. In 1861, the operas performed were *Bianca*, the *Daughter of the Regiment*, the *Domino Noir*, *Hiawatha*, *Lurline*, *Maritana*, Mr. Glover's *Ruy Blas*, *Robin Hood*—a new opera by Macfarren—*Satanella*, Mr. Linley's operetta the *Toymaker*, and Mr. Alfred Mellon's *Victorine*. Early in 1862, Mr. Benedict's *Lily of Killarney* was produced; and a new operetta, *Court and Cottage,* by an amateur composer, Mr. Frederick Clay, was brought out on Miss Pyne's benefit, March 22.

Miss Louisa Pyne's performance in *Le Nozze di Figaro,* when she took the place of the American prima donna, Mdlle. Kellogg, at Her Majesty's Theatre, during the season of 1862, was universally admired, and was no minor triumph. Of the successes achieved by Miss Pyne during the past season of the English Opera Company it is perhaps hardly necessary to speak, inasmuch as they are fresh in the memory of all her admirers.

Miss Louisa Pyne is twenty-eight years of age, having been born in 1835.

CHAPTER XX.

TERESA TIETJENS.

TERESA TIETJENS is descended from an ancient and noble family. Her parents, who were of Hungarian extraction, resided in Hamburg, where Teresa was born in June, 1834.

Like most great lyric artists, Teresa displayed an early taste for music. Her parents lost no time in obtaining for her the best instruction, and when she was twelve years old she was under the care of an eminent professor. When only fourteen, she possessed a voice of remarkable power and marvellous sweetness; and as it became developed, it was found to be a high soprano of extensive register, ranging from C below the line to D in alt, and of superb quality—clear, resonant, and perfectly pure. Such a voice required nothing but cultivation to yield fame and fortune; and Mdlle. Tietjens was accordingly sent to Vienna, to study under the best masters in Germany. With an enthusiastic passion for the profession she was about to enter, she applied herself with ardour to her studies, and, in a very short time, she had acquired sufficient science to commence her career.

On her return to Hamburg, she readily obtained an engagement at the principal theatre in that city, and made her first appearance before a public audience in April, 1849. With the daring confidence of youth she seized on the splendid, seductive *rôle* of Lucrezia Borgia, without reflecting on the difficulties it presented—difficulties which only the powers of a Grisi could conquer. At that time Teresa was little more than fifteen, and although of a tall, commanding figure, she was, of course, very girlish in aspect. It may easily be conjectured that her first assumption of the character of the haughty Duchess was not a complete success; yet it was far from proving a failure: she won applause, and was encouraged to persevere. On her second representation she was more confident, and her voice more under her control; she consequently met with the most flattering reception. She appeared night after night in the same opera, with incredible success, until at length her reputation became firmly established. To perform Lucrezia Borgia successfully at fifteen, was an augury of future triumph.

Her first appearances were marked by a romantic interest. Mdlle. Tietjens happened to captivate a rich young gentleman, who offered her his hand, but required her to relinquish the stage. She refused to comply with this requisition, and rejected his offer of marriage. Her father being dead, the young artiste was then under the care of a guardian, and this gentleman strenuously urged the lover's suit. At last Teresa consented to retire for a time, on the understanding that if her inclination for the profession should be as ardent as ever at the end of nine months, she should be permitted to reappear in public. On the expiration of the term of probation, the fair songstress again presented herself before the footlights, and her luckless lover disappeared.

The director of the Royal Opera, Frankfort-on-the-Maine, having heard Mdlle. Tietjens at Hamburg, was so delighted with her splendid voice that he made her an offer to sing at his theatre; she accepted his proposal, and went to Frankfort early in 1850. Her success in that city was brilliant and decided, and her reputation increased so greatly that she received offers of engagement from various European capitals. The director of the Imperial Theatre of Vienna undertook a journey to Frankfort-on-the-Maine expressly to hear the new singer, and, if possible, to secure the prize; and her engagement with the Opera of Frankfort being about to expire, Mdlle. Tietjens gladly availed herself of the opportunity of singing in Vienna, where she made her début at the Imperial Theatre in 1856. Her reception by a crowded audience was most enthusiastic. She appeared in the part of Donna Anna (in German); and at the fall of the curtain she was recalled no less than four times. The manager, finding that she was a success, at once secured her services for three consecutive seasons, and she became a great favourite in Vienna. Before the conclusion of the second season, Mdlle. Tietjens had appeared in a number of leading operas: *Norma, Les Huguenots, Lucrezia Borgia, Le Nozze di Figaro, Fidelio,* and *Il Trovatore;* and, on the sudden indisposition of another singer, she appeared in a light comic part, when she won golden opinions.

Mr. Lumley hearing of Mdlle. Tietjens, and the sensation she was creating, started without delay for Vienna, and made such regal propositions that no one could have resisted his overtures. Unfortunately the youthful cantatrice had signed an agreement with the director of the Vienna theatre for a term extending over three years, of which two only had then expired. Mdlle. Tietjens was therefore unable to accept Mr. Lumley's tempting offer; but a negotiation was entered into, and an arrangement eventually made which permitted her to come to England for three months, with the express understanding that she was not to exceed that limit.

Her Majesty's Theatre opened the 13th April, 1858, with *Les Huguenots,* when Mdlle. Tietjens made her first appearance in London as Valentine, Giuglini taking the part of Raoul for the first time. A difficulty presented itself to Mdlle. Tietjens in studying her part, as she did not understand Italian; but she nevertheless learnt her part by rote, and nobody would have suspected that she was not perfectly conversant with the meaning of every syllable she uttered. It was a dangerous experiment, but it proved successful. There was a crowded and fashionable audience, and the Queen and Prince Consort were present.

The voice of Mdlle. Tietjens is a pure soprano, fresh, penetrating, even, and powerful; it is unusually rich in quality, extensive in compass, and of great flexibility; it has a bell-like resonance, and is capable of expressing all the passionate and tender accents of lyric tragedy. Teresa Tietjens is, in the truest, fullest sense of the word, a lyric artist, and she possesses every requisite needed by a cantatrice of the highest order—personal beauty, physical strength, originality of conception, a superb voice, and inexhaustible spirit and energy. Like most German singers, Mdlle. Tietjens regards ornamentation as merely an agreeable adjunct in vocalization; and in the music of Valentine she sang only what the composer had set down: neither more nor less—but that was accomplished to perfection. Her performance of Valentine is irreproachable.

As an actress, her tall, stately, elegant figure is admirably calculated to personate the tragic heroines of Opera. Her face is beautiful, her large eyes flash with intellect, and her classical features are radiant with expression; her grandeur of conception, her tragic dignity, her glowing warmth, and *abandon*, render her worthy of the finest days of lyric tragedy. She is thoroughly dramatic; her movements and gestures are noble, and entirely free from conventionality; her walk is easy, while her attitudes are classical without being in the least constrained.

Her second part was that of Leonora, in *Il Trovatore*, which she has made her own. When she appeared as Donna Anna in *Don Giovanni*, she took the house by storm by the magnificence of her singing and the intense dramatic force of her acting. The music of this opera suited her exactly.

In June, she appeared as Lucrezia Borgia. The qualities which this part demands are precisely those with which Mdlle. Tietjens is endowed—tragic power, intensity, impulsiveness. Her commanding figure and graceful bearing gave weight to her acting, while in the more tender scenes she was exquisitely pathetic and displayed great depth of feeling. "Com' é bello" was rendered with thrilling tenderness, and the allegro which followed it created a furore: it was one of the most brilliant *morceaux* of florid decorative vocalism heard for years, the upper C in the cadenza being quite electrical. At the end of the first and second acts, the heart-rending accents of a mother's agony, wrung from the depths of her soul, and the stern, haughty, scornful courage, and vengeful fierceness of the Borgia, were contrasted with consummate genius and harrowing truthfulness. Grisi herself never portrayed this great character with more power.

Mdlle. Tietjens also appeared as the Countess in *Le Nozze di Figaro*, but with less marked success.

To the regret of the London public, Mdlle. Tietjens was obliged to return to Vienna early in the autumn, to complete her engagement there; the manager refusing to extend her congé. From Austria she went to Italy, with the object of acquiring facility in the Italian language, and she was there met by Mr. E. T. Smith, who instantly engaged her for his Italian Opera at Drury Lane Theatre. Mdlle. Tietjens inaugurated her second London season by appearing May 3, 1859, in the part of Lucrezia Borgia; and having acquired a complete command of the Italian language, she sang and acted more magnificently than ever.

Mdlle. Tietjens then appeared successively in *Il Trovatore*, *Don Giovanni*, *Les Huguenots*, and *Norma*; which last she performed for the first time in England, achieving a triumph: though her performance was too much imbued with Teutonic stiffness to be unreservedly approved by the lovers of Italian opera. By her splendid singing, and the sustained grandeur and impassioned energy of her acting, she gained, however, the plaudits of the unprejudiced. July 26th, she appeared in Verdi's *Vêpres Siciliennes*. In this opera she "sang magnificently, and acted with extraordinary vigour and passion." At the close of the fourth act, when Hélène and Procida are led to the scaffold, the conflicting emotions that agitate the bosom of the heroine were pictured with wonderful truth and intensity by Mdlle. Tietjens.

On the termination of the season, Mdlle. Tietjens, with Signori Giuglini, Badiali, etc. appeared in Dublin, then at Manchester, Liverpool, Leeds, Glasgow, Edinburgh, and other places. Wherever she sang she met with the same brilliant success which had attended her in London and at the various musical festivals in England. Her fame increased every year, with the development of her talents and skill. The season of 1860 at Her Majesty's Theatre opened, under the direction of Mr. E. T. Smith, with Flotow's *Martha*, April 10th, when the principal characters were sustained by Mdlle. Tietjens, Madame Lemaire, Giuglini, and Vialetti. This opera was not very successful, and it was replaced by *Il Trovatore*, in which Mdlle. Tietjens was supported by Madame Borghi Mamo, Giuglini, and Vialetti. April 17th, Mdlle. Tietjens appeared as Lucrezia Borgia. She was grander, and sang more superbly than ever in this part. May 5th, she performed Donna Anna, Madame Borghi Mamo being the Zerlina. *Norma* was brought out three days later.

The wondrous German cantatrice had singularly improved in this character, and her singing of "Casta Diva" was surprising. She essayed the part of Semiramide for the first time, May 22nd. Although her excessive anxiety to acquit herself well in her difficult task impeded the full exercise of her powers, her performance of the character was splendid. Her singing, though at times gorgeous and magnificent, was not always perfect; but her acting was grand, powerful, and picturesque in the extreme.

"In Tietjens' Semiramide," says a critic, "her intellectuality shines most from its contrasting with the part she impersonates: a part which, in itself, nowise assists her; but, as in a picture, shadow renders a light more striking. In the splendid aria, 'Bel raggio,' the solfeggi and fioriture that she lavished on the audience were executed with such marvellous tone and precision that she electrified the house. The grand duet, with Alboni, 'Giorno d'orrore,' was exquisitely and nobly impressive, from their dramatic interpretation of the scene." Mdlle. Tietjens performed also in *Les Huguenots* and in *Oberon*.

It is hardly necessary to advert to the triumphs of Mdlle. Tietjens at the Crystal Palace Concerts. In 1861 Mr. Mapleson took the Lyceum Theatre for a short season, commencing, June 8, with *Il Trovatore*. Mdlle. Tietjens was the prima donna, Madame Alboni the contralto, Signor Giuglini the tenor. "Tietjens is the most superb Leonora, without a single exception, that the Anglo-Italian stage has witnessed," observes one admiring critic. Verdi's *Un Ballo in Maschera* was produced June 15, for the first time in this country, and was a triumphant success. Mdlle. Tietjens appeared to the utmost advantage as the energetic heroine, Amelia. She sang and acted her part magnificently, and her singing throughout the entire of the third act was pronounced one of her greatest achievements. This season was a very arduous one for Mdlle. Tietjens, as well as for her comrade, Signor Giuglini; for they had to sing at the Lyceum three, and sometimes four, times a week, besides singing at the Crystal Palace on Fridays, and at various morning and evening concerts. The principal operas were *Il Trovatore, Lucrezia Borgia, Martha, Les Huguenots, Norma,* and *Don Giovanni.*

Mdlle. Tietjens was now accepted as the successor of Grisi, though no two artists could be more unlike in many respects than the Italian and German singers. "But," one critic justly remarks, "in passionate feeling, energy, power of voice, and grandeur of style, a comparison may be established. In certain characters Grisi has left no one to fill her place. These will be found mostly in Rossini's operas, such as Semiramide, Ninetta, Desdemona, Pamira (*L'Assedio di Corinto*), Elene, etc., to which we may add Elvira in *I Puritani*, written expressly for her. In not one of these parts has anybody created an impression since she sang them. They all belong to the repertoire of pure Italian song, of which Giulietta Grisi was undoubtedly the greatest mistress since Pasta. That Mdlle. Tietjens could not contend with her on her own Ausonian soil no one will deny. Her means, her compass, her instincts, all forbade. There is, however, one exception—Norma, in which the German singer may challenge comparison with the Italian, and in which she occasionally surpasses her. In the French and German répertoire the younger artiste has a decided advantage over the elder, in possessing a voice of such extent as to be enabled to execute the music of the composers without alteration of any kind. Everybody knows that Mdlle. Tietjens has not only one of the most magnificent and powerful voices ever heard, but also one of the most extraordinary in compass. To sing the music of Donna Anna, Fidelio, Valentine, etc., without transposition or change, and to sing it with power and effect, is granted to few artistes. Mdlle. Tietjens is one of these great rarities, and therefore, without any great stretch of compliment, we may assert that, putting aside the Rossinian repertoire, she is destined to wear the mantle of Grisi."

In no previous season was Mdlle. Tietjens so popular, or so much admired, as during the season of 1862. Her most remarkable performance was the character of Alice, in Meyerbeer's *Robert le Diable.*

"Mdlle. Tietjens' admirable personation of Alice," observes the critic of a leading daily paper, "must raise her to a still higher rank in public estimation than that she has hitherto so long sustained. Each of the three acts in which the German soprano was engaged, won a separate triumph for her. We are tired of perpetually expatiating on the splendid brightness, purity, and clearness of her glorious voice, and on the absolute certainty of her intonation; but these merely physical requisites of a great singer are in themselves most uncommon. Irrespectively of the lady's clever vocalization, and of the strong dramatic impulse which she evinces, there is an actual sensual gratification in listening to her superb voice singing with immoveable certainty in perfect tune. Her German education, combined with long practice in Italian opera, peculiarly fit Mdlle. Tietjens for interpreting the music of Meyerbeer, who is equally a disciple of both schools."

All the journals agreed in praising with rapture this superb performance. From the delicious romance, "Va, dit-elle," to the final trio, her singing and her acting were unrivalled since the days of Jenny Lind. Her glorious voice thrilled through the house in a flood of rich melody, and never was her intonation more unerring, more faultless. Her Norma was more splendid than ever. The rendering of "Casta Diva" was exquisitely refined, and in the final duet with Pollio she produced a sensation unequalled since the golden days of Giulia Grisi. During the present season—1863—the popular German prima donna has performed at Her Majesty's Theatre.

In private life, Mdlle. Tietjens is much beloved and esteemed. She is exceedingly kind and generous in disposition, and amiable in character.

CHRONOLOGICAL LIST OF OPERAS,

AND THEIR COMPOSERS.

LULLI.

Cadmus. Paris, July, 1673
Alceste. January, 1674
Thesée. February 3, 1675
Atys. January 10, 1676
Isis. January 5, 1677
Bellérophon. January 29, 1679
Proserpine. 1680
Psyché. 1682
Phaéton. April 17, 1683
Amadis. January 15, 1684
Roland. March 8, 1685
Armide. February 15, 1686
La Grotte de Versailles. 1701
Iphigénie. May 6, 1704

PURCELL.

Dido and Eneas. 1677.
The Tempest. 1690. King Arthur; The Indian Queen; Tyrannic Love; The Prophetess. 1691. Bonduca; Don Quixote. 1695.

SCARLATTI.

L'Onestà nell' Amore. Rome, 1680
Pompeo. Naples, 1684
Teodora. Rome, 1693
Odoacre. Naples, 1694
Pirro e Demetrio. Naples, 1697
Il Prigioniero Fortunato. 1698
Il Prigioniero Superbo. 1699
Gli Equivochi nel Sembiante. 1700
Le Nozze co'l Nemico
Il Mitridate Eupatore
Laodicea e Berenice. Naples, 1701
Il Figlio delle Selve. 1702
Il Trionfo della Libertà. 1707
Il Medo. 1708
Il Martirio di Santa Cecilia. 1709
Il Teodoro. Naples, 1709
Ciro Riconosciuto. Rome, 1712
Porsenna. Naples, 1713
Scipione nelle Spagne. Naples, 1714
L'Amor Generoso. Naples, 1714
Arminio. Naples, 1714
Il Tigrane. Naples, 1715
Carlo, Re d'Allemagna. 1716
La Virtù trionfante dell' Odio e dell' Amore. Naples, 1716
Il Trionfo dell' Onore. Naples, 1718
Il Telemacco. Rome, 1718
Attilio Regolo. Rome, 1719
Tito Sempronico Gracco. 1720
Turno Aricinio. Rome, 1720
La Principessa Fedele. Rome, 1721
Griselda. Rome, 1721
Didone Abbandonata.
La Caduta dei Decemviri. 1723

HANDEL.

Almira. Hamburg, 1704
Nero. Hamburg, 1705
Daphne; Florida; Roderigo. 1706

Agrippina. Venice, 1707
Pyrrhus. 1708
Silla.
Rinaldo. London, 1710
Pastor Fido. 1712
Teseo. 1713
Amadigi. 1715
Radamisto. 1720
Muzio Scaevola. 1721.
Floridante. 1721
Ottone; Giulio Cesare. 1723
Tamerlane.
Rodelinda. 1725
Alexander; Scipio. 1726
Admetus; Ricardo Primo. 1727
Siroe; Tolomeo. 1728
Lothario. 1729
Parthenope. 1730
Poro. 1731
Acis and Galatea. London, 1731
Ætius (or Ezio). London, 1732
Sosarme; Orlando. 1732
Arianna. 1734
Ariodante; Alcina. 1735
Atalanta.
Giustino; Arminio; Berenice. 1737
Faramondo; Serse. 1738.
Jupiter in Argos. 1739
Imeneo. 1740
Deidamia. 1741

VINCI.

La Silla Dillatore. 1719
Le Feste Napolitane. 1721
Semiramide Riconosciuta, Rome; Rosmira Fedele; Siroe. 1723
Farnace, Venice; Caduta de' Decemviri. Naples, 1724
Astianatte; Ifigenia in Tauride. Venice, 1725
Catone in Utica; Asteria. 1726
Il Sigismondo, Rè di Polonia, 1727
Alessandro nell' Indie, Naples; Didone Abbandonata, Rome. 1729

HASSE.

Antigone. Brunswick, 1723
Sesostrate. Naples, 1726
Attalo, Rè di Bitinia. Naples, 1728
Dalisa. Venice, 1730
Artaserse. Venice, 1730
Arminio. Milan, 1731
Cleofide. Dresden, 1731
Cajo Fabrizio. Rome, 1731
Demetrio. Venice, 1732
Alessandro nell' Indie. Milan, 1732
Catone in Utica. Turin, 1732
Euristeo. Warsaw, 1733
Asteria. Dresden, 1734
Senocrita. Dresden, 1736
Atalanta. Dresden, 1737
La Clemenza di Tito. Dresden, 1737
Alfonso. Dresden, 1738
Irene. Dresden, 1738
Demetrio. Dresden, 1739
Artaserse. Dresden, 1740
Olimpia in Eruda. London, 1740
Numa Pompilio. Dresden, 1741
Lucio Papirio. 1742
Didone Abbandonata. 1742
L'Asilo d'Amore. 1743
Antigono. 1744
Arminio. 1745
La Spartana; Semiramide. 1747
Demofoonte. 1748
Il Natale di Giove. 1749
Attilio Regolo. 1750
Ciro Riconosciuto. 1751
Ipermestra; Leucippo. 1751
Solimanno. 1752
Adriano in Siria. 1752
Arminio. 1753
Artemisia. 1754
L'Olimpiade. 1756
Nitetti. 1759
Il Trionfo di Clelia. Dresden, 1761
Siroe. Vienna, 1763
Zenobia. Vienna, 1763
Romolo ed Ersilia. Innspruck, 1765
Partenope. Vienna, 1767
Ruggiero. Milan, 1770

GALUPPI.

Gli Amici Rivali. 1722
La Fede nell' Incostanza
Dorindo. 1729
Odio Placato. 1730
Argenside. 1733
Ambizione Depressa. 1735
Elisa, Regina di Tiro. 1736
La ninfa Apollo
Tamiri
Ergilda
Avilda. 1737
Gustavo I. Rè di Swieza. 1740
Aronte, Rè de' Sciti
Berenice. 1741
Madame Ciana. 1744
L'Ambizione Delusa
La Libertà Nociva
Forze d'Amore. 1745
Scipione nelle Spagne. 1746
Arminio. 1747
Arcadia in Brento. 1749
Il Page della Cucagna. 1750
Arcifanfo, Rè di Matti
Alcimena, Principessa dell' Isole Fortunate
Il Mondo della Luna
La Mascherata. 1751
Ermelinda. 1752
Il Mondo alla Rovescia
Il Centi Caramela
Le Virtuose Ridicole
Calamità de' Cuori
I Bagni d'Abono. 1753
Il Filosofo di Campagna. 1754
Antigona
Il Povero Superbo
Alessandro nell' Indie. 1755
La Diavolessa
Nozze di Paride. 1756
Le Nozze
Sesostri. 1757
Adriano in Sirio. 1760
L'Amante di Tutti. 1761
Artaserse
I tre Amanti Ridicoli
Ipermestra
Antigono. 1762
Il Marchese Villano
Viriate
L'Uomo Femmina
Il Puntiglio Amoroso
Il Rè alla Caccio
Cajo Mario. 1764
La Donna di Governo. 1764

PORPORA.*

Ariana e Tesco. Naples, 1717
Eumène. Rome, 1722
Issipele. Rome, 1723
Germanico. Rome, 1725
Imeneo in Alene. Venice, 1726
Siface. Venice, 1726
Meride e Selinunte. Venice, 1727
Ezio. Venice, 1728
Semiramide Riconosciuta; Tamerlano. Dresden, 1730
Alessandro nelle Indie; Annibale; Arbace. Venice, 1732
Polyphème; Ifigenia in Aulide; Rosalba. 1737
Statira. 1742
Temistocle. 1742
Le Nozze d'Ercole e d'Ebe. 1744
Il Trionfo di Camilla. Naples, 1760

LEONARDO LEO.

Sofonisba. 1718
L'Olimpiade. 1735
La Clemenza di Tito. 1735
Achille in Sciro. 1740

(English Ballad Opera.)

The Beggar's Opera. (*Gay.*) London, January, 1728

---

* Porpora produced (according to Dr. Burney) more than fifty operas altogether; but the titles have not been preserved.

RAMEAU.

Hippolyte et Aricie. Paris, 1733
Castor et Pollux. 1737
Dardanus. Paris, November 19, 1739
Pygmalion. 1747
Samson. 1747
Zorastre. 1749
Acante et Céphise. 1752
Les Surprises de l'Amour. 1757

ARNE.

Rosamond. 1733
Opera of Operas. 1733
Zara. 1736
Comus. 1738
The Blind Beggar of Bethnal Green
Fall of Phaeton
King Pepin's Campaign
The Temple of Dulness. January 17, 1745
Don Saverio. 1749
Britannia
Elisa. 1750
Cymon
Artaxerxes. February 2, 1762
Elfrida
King Arthur
The Guardian Outwitted
L'Olimpiade. April 25, 1765
The Birth of Hercules. 1766
Achilles in Petticoats
Thomas and Sally
The Ladies' Frolick. 1770

PERGOLESE.

Il Maestro di Musica
Il Geloso Schernito
L'Olimpiade. Rome, 1735
La Contadina
La Serva Padrone. Paris, 1752
Amor fà l'Uomo Cieco.
Recimero

JOMELLI.

L'Errore Amoroso. Naples, 1737
Odoardo. Naples, 1738
Ricimero. Rome, 1740
Astiannasse. Rome, 1741
Il Frastullo
Sofonisba
Ciro Riconosciuto
Achille in Sciro. Vienna, 1745
Didone. Vienna, 1745
Eumene. Naples, 1746
Merope. Venice, 1747
Ezio. Naples, 1748
L'Incantato. Rome, 1749
Ifigenia in Tauride. Rome, 1751
Talestri. Rome, 1751
Attilio Regolo. Rome, 1752
Semiramide
Bajazette
Demetrio
Penelope. Stuttgart
Enea nel Lazio. Stuttgart, 1755
Il Rè Pastore. Stuttgart
Alessandro nell' Indie. Stuttgart
Nitetti. Stuttgart
La Clemenza di Tito. Stuttgart
Demofoonte. Stuttgart
Il Fedonte. Stuttgart
L'Isola Disabilita. Stuttgart
Endimione. Stuttgart
Vologeso. Stuttgart
L'Olimpiade. Stuttgart
La Schiava Libertà. Stuttgart
L'Asilo d'Amore. Stuttgart
La Pastorella Illustra. Stuttgart
Il Cacciator Deluso. Stuttgart
Il Matrimonio per Concorso. Stuttgart
Armide. Naples, 1771
Ifigenia in Aulide. Naples, 1775

GLÜCK.

Artaxerxes. Milan, 1742
Demetrio. Venice, 1742
Fall of the Giants.* London
L'Arbre Enchanté. Paris, 1745
La Cythère Assiégée. Paris, 1745
Telemaco.
Orfeo ed Euridice. Vienna, Oct. 5, 1762
Iphigéne en Aulide. Paris, 1774
Orphée. Paris, April 19, 1774
Alceste. Paris, April 23, 1776
Armide. Paris, January 17, 1779
Iphigénie en Tauride. Paris, May 18 1779
Echo et Narcisse. Paris, Sept. 24, 1779

SARTI.

Pompeo in Arminia. 1752
Il Rè Pastore. 1752
Medonte. Florence
Demofoonte
L'Olimpiade
Ciro Riconosciuto. Copenhagen, 1756
La Figlia Ricuperata
La Giardiniera Brillante. 1758
Mitridate. Parma, 1765
Il Vologeso. 1765
La Nitetti. 1765
Ipermestra. Rome, 1766
I Contratempi. Venice, 1767
Didone. 1767
Semiramide Riconosciuta. 1768
I Pretendenti Delusi. 1768
Il Calzolajo di Strasburgo. Modena, 1769
Cléomène. 1770
La Clemenza di Tito. Padua, 1771
La Contadina Fedele. 1771
I Finti Eredi. 1773
Le Gelosie Villane. 1776
Farnaçe. 1776
L'Avaro. 1777
Ifigenia in Aulide. 1777
Epponima. Turin, 1777
Il Militare Bizzarro. 1778
Gli Amanti Consolati. 1779
Fra i due litiganti il terzo gode. 1780
Scipione. 1780
Achille in Sciro. Florence, 1781
L'Incognito. Bologna, 1781
Giulio Sabino. Venice, 1781
Alessandro e Timoteo. 1782
Le Nozze di Dorina. 1782
Siroe. Turin, 1783
Idalide. Milan, 1783
I Rivali Delusi. London, Tuesday, Jan. 6, 1784
Armida e Rinaldo. St. Petersburg, 1785
La Gloire du Nord. 1794

MONSIGNY.

La Servante Maîtresse. 1754
Aveux Indiscrets. Paris, 1759
Le Maître en Droit. Paris, 1760
Le Cadi Dupé. Paris, 1760
On ne s'avise jamais de tout. Sept. 17, 1761
Le Roi et le Fermier. 1762
Rose et Colas. 1764
L'Ile Sonnante. 1768
La Reine de Golconde. Paris, July 4, 1779

* In addition to the *Fall of the Giants*, Glück composed about forty-five operas during his stay in London (1745 to 1763).

Le Deserteur. 1779
Le Faucon. 1772
La Belle Arsène. 1775
Le Rendezvous bien Employé. 1776
Felix; ou, l'Enfant Trouvé. 1777

PAISIELLO.

La Pupilla. Bologna. 1763
Il Mondo alla Roverscia. Bologna
La Madama Umorista. Modena
Demetrio. Modena
Artaserse. Modena
Le Virtuose Ridicole. Parma
Il Negligente. Parma
I Bagni di Abano. Parma
Il Ciarlone. Venice
L'Amore in Ballo. Venice
Le Pescatrici. Venice
Il Marchese Tulipano. Rome
La Vedova di Bel Genio. Naples
L'Imbroglio delle Ragazze. Naples
L'Idolo Cinese. Naples
Lucio Papirio. Naples
Il Furbo mal accorto. Naples
Olimpia. Naples
L'Innocente Fortunato. Venice
Sismanno nel Mogola. Milan
L'Arabo Cortese. Naples
La Luna Abitata. Naples
La Contessa dei Numi. Naples
Semiramide. Milan
Il Montesuma. Milan
Le Dardane. Naples
Il Tamburo Notturno
Andromeda. Milan
Annibale in Italia. Turin
I Filosofi. Turin
Il Giocatore. Turin
La Somiglianza dei Nomi. Naples
Le Astuzie Amorose. Naples
Gli Scherzi d'Amore e di Fortuna. Naples
Dom Chisciotta della Mancia. Naples
La Finta Maga. Naples
L'Osteria di Mere-Chiaro. Naples
Alessandro nell' Indie. Modena
Il Duello Comico. Naples
Done Anchise Dampanone. Naples
Il Mondo della Luna. Naples
La Frascatana. Venice
La Discordia Fortunata. Venice
Il Demofoonte. Venice
I Socrati Imaginari. Naples
Il Gran Cid. Florence
Il Finto Principe. Florence
Le Due Contesse. Rome, 1777
La Disfatta di Dario. Rome, 1777
La Serva Padrona. St. Petersburg
Il Matrimonio Inaspettato. St. Petersburg
Il Barbiere de Seviglia. St. Petersburg
I Filosofi Imaginari. St. Petersburg
La Finta Amante. Poland
Il Mondo della Luna. Moscow
La Nitetti. St. Petersburg
Lucinda ed Artemidoro. St. Petersburg
Alcide al Birio. St. Petersburg
Achille in Sciro. St. Petersburg
Il Rè Teodoro. Vienna
Antigone. Naples
L'Amore Ingenioso. Rome, 1785
La Grotta di Trofonio. Naples
Le Gare Generose. Naples
L'Olimpiade. Naples
Il Pirro. Naples
Gli Schiave per Amore. London, April 24, 1787
I Zingari in Fiera. Naples
La Fedra. Naples
Le Vane Gelosie. Naples
Catone in Utica. Naples
Nina; o, la Pazza d'Amore
Zenobia di Palmira. Naples
La Locanda
La Cuffiara. Naples
La Molinara. Naples

La Modista Raggiratrice. Naples
Elfrida. Naples
Elvira. Naples
I Visionari. Naples
L'Inganno Felice. Naples
I Giuochi d'Agrigente. Venice
La Didone. Naples
L'Andromacca. Naples
La Contadina di Spirito. Naples
Proserpina. Paris, 1803
I Pittagorici. Naples

SACCHINI.

Semiramide. Rome
Eumene. Rome
Andromacca. Naples
Artaserse. Rome, 1762
Alessandro nelle' Indie. Venice, 1768
Scipione in Cartagine. Padua, 1770
Ezio. Naples
Nicostrate
Alessandro Severo
L'Adriano in Siria
L'Eroe
Cinese. Munich, 1771
Callirhoe. Stuttgart, 1772
Armida. Milan, 1772
Il Gran Cid. Rome, January, 1773
L'Amore in Campa
Tamerlano. London, February, 1773
Vologeso. Naples, 1773
La Contadina in Corte. Rome
L'Isola d'Amore
L'Olimpiade. Milan
Lucio Vero. Naples, December, 1773
Nitetti. London, 1774
Perseo. London, 1776
L'Amore Soldato. London, 1777
Creso. London, January 2, 1778
Erifile. London, February 6, 1778
Il Calandrino. London, 1778
Enea e Lavinia. 1779
Renaud, Chimène (adaptations of former operas)
Armide. Paris, March, 1783
Dardanus. Paris, 1784
Œdipe à Colonne. Paris, 1785
Arvire et Evelina. Paris, 1787

(English Ballad Opera.)

Love in a Village. (*Bickerstaff.*) London, December 3, 1763

GOSSEC.

Le Faux Lord. 1764
Les Pêcheurs. 1766
Toinon et Toinette. 1767
Le Double Déguisement
Sabinus. Paris, 1773
Alexis et Daphné. 1775
Philémon et Baucis. 1775
Hylas et Sylvie. 1776.
La Fête du Village. 1778
Thesée. Paris, March 1, 1782
La Reprise de Toulon. 1786

GRÉTRY.

Le Vendemiatrice. Rome, 1765
Les Mariages Samnites
Le Huron. Paris, August 20, 1768
Lucile. Paris, 1769
Le Tableau Parlant. Paris, 1769
Isabella et Gertrude. Geneva, 1769
Zemire et Azor. November, 1771
Céphale et Procris. 1775
Le Seigneur Bienfesant. Paris, 1780
Andromaque. Paris, June 6, 1780
La Double Epreuve; ou, Colette à la Cour. Paris, January 1, 1782
L'Embarras des Richesses. Paris, November 26, 1782
La Caravane. 1783

Panurge. Paris, January 25, 1785
Amphytrion. 1786
Denis le Tyran. 1794
Anacréon. 1797
Richard Cœur de Lion

ARNOLD.

The Maid of the Mill. January 31, 1765
Rosamond. 1767
The Castle of Andalusia. 1782
Peeping Tom. 1784
Here, There, and Everywhere. 1784
Two to One. 1785
Turk and no Turk. 1785
The Siege of Curzola. 1786
Inkle and Yarico. Saturday, Aug. 4, 1787
The Enraged Musician. 1788
Battle of Hexham. 1789
New Spain. 1790
The Basket Maker. 1790
The Surrender of Calais. 1791
The Children in the Wood. 1793
Auld Robin Gray. 1794
Zorinski. 1795
The Mountaineers. 1795
Who Pays the Reckoning? 1795
Bannian Day. 1796
The Shipwreck. 1796
The Italian Monk. 1797
False and True. 1798
Cambro-Britons. 1798
The Veteran Tar. 1801

MOZART.

Mitridate. 1767
Lucia Silla. Salzburg, 1773
Zaide
La Finta Giardiniera. Munich, 1775
Idomeneo, Rè di Creta. Munich, 1780
Die Entführung. Vienna, 1782
Le Nozze di Figaro. Vienna, April 28, 1786
Don Giovanni. Prague, Nov. 4, 1787
Così fan Tutte. 1790
Die Zauberflöte. 1791
La Clemenza di Tito. 1791

ANFOSSI.

Cajo Mario. Venice, 1769
La Clemenza di Tito. Rome, 1769
Il Visionari. Rome, 1771
Il Barone di Rocca. Rome, 1772
L'Incognita per Seguitata, Rome; Antigono, Venice; Demofoonte, Rome. 1773
Lucio Silla, Venice; La Finta Giardiniera, Rome. 1774
Il Geloso in Cimento, Rome; La Contadina in Corte; L'Avaro. 1775
Isabella e Rodrigo, o la Costanza in Amore; La Pescatrice Fedele; L'Olimpiade, Rome. 1776
Il Curioso Indiscreto; Lo Sposo Disperato; Cleopatra. Milan, 1778
Il Matrimonio per Inganno. Paris, 1779
La Forza delle Donne. Milan, 1780
I Vecchi Burlati. London, 1781
I Viaggiatori Felici, London; Armida. 1782
Gli Amanti Canuti, Dresden; Il Trionfo d'Ariana, Prague; Il Cavaliere per Amore, Berlin; Chi cerca trova, Florence. 1784
Didone Abbandonata. Naples
La Vedova Scaltra. 1785

La Fiera dell' Ascensione; L'Imbroglio delle tre Spose, Padua. 1786
La Pazzia de' Gelosi; Creso, Rome; La Villanella di Spirito, Rome. 1787
Artaserse, Rome; L'Orfanella Americana, Venice; La maga Circe, Rome; Le Gelosie Fortunate. 1788
La Gazetta ossia il Baggiano deluso. Rome, 1789
Zenobia in Palmira. Florence, 1790
Issifile. 1791
Il Zottico incivilito. Dresden, 1792.
L'Americana in Olanda; La Matilda ritrovata; Gli Artigiani
Cublai, Gran Cân de' Tartari. 1788
Il Pastor Fido. 1789
La Princesse de Babylone. Paris, 1789
La Cifra. 1789
Sapho. Paris, 1790
Catalina. 1792
Il Mondo alla Rovescia. 1794
Palmira. 1795
Il Moro. 1796
Falstaff. 1798
Danaus. 1800
Cesare in Farmacusa. 1800
Angiolina. 1800
Annibale in Capua. 1801
La Bella Selvaggia. 1802
Die Neger. 1804

SALIERI.

Le Donne Letterate. 1770
L'Amore Innocente. 1770
Armida. 1771
Il Don Chisciotte. 1771
Il Barone di Rocca Antica. 1772
La Fiera di Venezia. 1772
La Secchia Rapita, 1772
La Locandiera. 1773
La Calamità de' Dori. 1774
La Finta Scema. 1775
Delmita e Daliso. 1776
Europa Riconosciuta. 1776
La Scuola de' Gelosi. 1779
Il Talismanno. 1779
La Partenza Inaspettata. 1779
La Dama Pastorella. 1780
Der Rauchfangkehrer. 1781
Les Danaïdes. 1784
Semiramide. 1784
Il Ricco d'un Giorno. 1784
Eraclito e Democrito. 1785
La Grotto di Trifonio. 1785
Les Horaces. 1786
Tarare. 1787
Axur, Rè d'Ormus. 1788

HAYDN.

Le Diable Boiteux. Vienna
La Cantarina. 1769
Philémon et Baucis. 1773
Geneviève de Brabant. 1777
Didon. 1778
Le Voleur des Pommes. 1779
Le Conseil des Dieux. 1780
L'Incendie
Der Zerstreute.
Goetz de Berlichingen
L'Incontro Improviso
Lo Speziale
La Pescatrice. 1780
Il Mondo della Inna
L'Isola Disabitata
Armida. 1782
L'Infedeltà Fedele
La Fedeltà Premiata
La Vera Castanza. 1786
Acide e Galatea
Orlando Paladino
L'Infedeltà Deluso
Orfeo. London, 1794
Didone Abbandonata. London

JOHN CHRISTIAN BACH.

Catone. Milan, 1758
Orione. London, 1763
Zanaide. London, 1763
Berenice. London, 1764
Adriano in Siria. London, Jan. 26, 1765
Ezio. London, 1765
Carattaco. 1767
L'Olimpiade. 1769
Orfeo. 1770
Temistocle
Siface
Lucio Silla
La Clemenza di Scipione
Amadis de Gaule. Paris, Dec. 14, 1779

MARTINI.

L'Amoureux de Quinze Ans. 1771
Le Fermier Cru Sourd. 1772
Le Rendez-vous Nocturne. 1773
Henri IV.; ou, la Bataille d'Ivry. 1774
Le Droit du Seigneur. 1783
L'Amant Sylphe; Sapho. 1794
Annette et Lubin. 1800

NAUMANN.

Achille in Scirp. Palermo, 1767
Alessandro nell' Indie. Venice, 1768
La Clemenza di Tito. Dresden, 1769
Le Nozze disturbate; Venice; Solimanno. 1772
L'Isola disabitata; Armida, Padua; Ipermestra, Venice; Il Villano Geloso, Dresden; L'Ipocondriaco, Dresden; Elisa, Dresden; Osiride; Tutto per Amore, Dresden; Amphion, Stockholm; Cora
Gustavus Vasa, Stockholm. 1780
La Reggia d'Imeneo, Dresden; Orphée et Eurydice, Copenhagen. 1785
La Dama Soldato. Dresden, 1791
Amor Giustificato. Dresden, 1791
Protesilao. Berlin, 1793
Andromeda; Acis e Galatea, Dresden, 1801.

REICHARDT.

Hanschen und Gretchen; La Lanterne Magique de l'Amour
Le Bucheron. 1775
Le Sesse Galanti, Potsdam
La Gioia dopo il duolo. Berlin, 1776
Ariencisia; Andromeda; Protesilao. Berlin, 1778
Ino. 1779
Procris et Céphale. 1780
L'Amour seul rend heureux. 1781
Panthée. 1786
Brenno. Berlin, 1787
Claudine de Villa Bella. 1788
Lilla; L'Olimpiade; Ervin et Elmire. 1790
Tamerlan, Berlin; L'Ile Sonnante, ou des Esprits. 1799
Rosamunda, Berlin; Amour et Fidélité, Berlin; Jery et Bately; L'Art et l'Amour. 1801
Le Château Enchanté. 1802
L'Heureux Naufrage, Cassel; Bradamante, Vienna. 1808

CIMAROSA.

Il Pittor Parigino. Rome, 1776
I Due Baroni. Rome, 1776
I Finti Nobili. Naples, 1777.
L'Armida Immaginaria. Naples, 1777

Gl' Amanti Comici. Naples, 1777
Il Ritorno di Don Calandrino. 1779
Cajo Mario. Rome, 1779
Il Mercato de' Malmantile. 1779
L'Assalonte. 1779
La Giuditta. Florence, 1779
L'Infedeltà Fedele. 1780
Il Falegname. 1780
L'Amante combattuto dalle Donne Dispunto. Naples, 1780
Alessandro nell' Indie. Rome, 1781
Artaserse. Turin, 1781
Il Conovito di Pietra. Venice, 1782
La Ballerina Amante. 1783
Nina e Martuffo. 1783
La Villana Riconosciuta. 1783
Oreste. 1783
L'Erre Cinese. Naples, 1783
Olimpiade. Vicenza, 1784
I Due Supposti Conti. 1784
Giannina e Bernadino. Naples, 1785
Il Marito Disperato. 1785
Il Credulo. 1785
La Donna al peggior si appigli. 1786
Le Trame Deluse. 1786
L'Impresario in Augustie. 1786
Il Fanatico Burlato. 1786.
Il Sacrifizio d'Abramo. Naples, 1786
Il Valdomiro. Turin, 1787
La Vergine del Sole. Milan, 1787
La Felicità Inaspettata
La Locandiera. London, Jan. 15, 1788
Atene Edificata.
Ninetta. London, January 16, 1790
Il Matrimonio Segreto. Vienna, 1792
La Calamità de' Cuori. 1792
Amor Rende Sagace. Vienna, 1792
I Traci Amanti. 1793
Astuzie Feminili. 1793
Penelope. Naples, 1793
L'Impegno Superato. Naples.
Il Capricio Dramatico. London, March 1, 1794
I Nemici Generosi. Rome, 1796
Gl' Orazi ed i Curiazi. Venice, 1797
Achille all' Assedio di Troia. 1798
L'Apprensivo Raggirato. Naples, 1798

SHIELD.

The Flitch of Bacon. 1778
Rosina. January 1, 1783
The Poor Soldier. 1783
Robin Hood; or, Sherwood Forest. April, 1784
The Noble Peasant. August 4, 1784
Fontainebleau; or, Our Way in France. Nov. 16, 1784
The Nunnery
Love in a Camp; or, Patrick in Prussia. February 22, 1786
Marian. Thursday, May 22, 1788
The Farmer. January, 1788
The Prophet. December 13, 1788
The Crusade. 1790
The Woodman. 1791.
Hartford Bridge. 1792
Midnight Wanderers. 1793.
Travellers in Switzerland. 1794
Mysteries of the Castle. 1795
Arrived at Portsmouth. January 13, 1796.
Lock and Key. Tuesday, Feb. 2, 1796.
The Lad of the Hills; or, the Wicklow Gold Mine. April 9, 1796
Abroad and at Home. November, 9, 1796
Italian Villagers. 1797.
Two Faces under a Hood. 1807

PICCINI.*

Le Donne Dispetose. Florence
Le Gelosie. Florence
Il Curioso del Proprio Danno. Florence
Zenobia. Florence, 1756
Alessandro nell' Indie. Rome, 1758
Cecchina. Rome
L'Olimpiade
Roland. Paris, Tuesday, Jan. 27, 1778
La Sposa Collerica. Paris, Oct. 20, 1778
Le Fat Meprisé. 1779
Lucette
Atys. Paris, Tuesday, February 22, 1780
Didon. 1783
Le Dormeur Eveillée. 1783
Le Faux Lord. 1783
Diane et Endymion. 1784
Pénèlope. 1785
Le Mensonge Officieux. 1787

CHERUBINI.

Quinto Fabio. 1780
Armida. Florence, 1782
Messenzio. Florence, 1782
Adriano in Siria. Leghorn, 1782
Lo Sposo di tre Femine. Rome, 1783
L'Idatide. Florence, 1784
Alessandro nell' Indie. Mantua, 1784
La Finta Principessa. London, May 2, 1785
Giulio Sabino. London, March 30, 1786
Ifigenia in Aulide. Turin, 1788
Démophoon. Paris, 1788
Lodoiska. Paris, 1791
Elisa. Paris, 1794
Medée. Paris, 1797
L'Hôtellerie Portugaise. Paris, 1798
La Punition. Paris, 1799
La Prisonnière. Paris, 1799
Les Deux Journées. Paris, 1800
Anacreon. 1803
Achille à Syros. Vienna, 1806
Pimmalione. Paris, 1809
La Crescendo. 1810
Les Courses de Newmarket. 1810
Les Abencerrages. Paris, 1813
Bayard à Mezières. 1814
Blanche de Provence. 1821
Ali Baba. Paris, July, 1833

VOGLER.

Der Kaufmann von Smirna; Albert der Dritte von Bayerk. Munich, 1781
Eglé. Stockholm, 1787
La Karmesse. Paris, 1783
Castor et Pollux, Mannheim; Gustave Adolphe, Stockholm. 1791
Samori. Vienna, 1804

ZINGARELLI.

Montezuma. Naples, 1781
L'Alsinda. Milan, 1785
Il Telemacco. Milan, 1785
Recimero. Venice, 1785
Armida. Rôme, 1786
Ifigenia in Aulide. Milan, 1787
Annibale. Turin, 1787
Antigone. Paris, 1789
La Morte de Cesare. Milan, 1791
L'Oracolo Sannito. Turin, 1792

* Before his arrival in Paris (1776) Piccini had already composed one hundred and thirty-three operas.

Pirro. Turin, 1792
Il Mercato di Monfregoso. Turin, 1793
La Secchia Rapita. Turin, 1793
Artaserse. Milan (*La Scala*), 1794
Gl' Orazi ed i Curiazi. Turin, 1794
Apelle e Campaspe. Venice, 1794
Il Conte di Saldagna. Venice, 1795
Romeo e Giuletta. Milan, 1796
Mitridate. Venice, 1797
Meleagro. Milan, 1798
Carolina e Menzicoff. Venice, 1798
Edipo a Colona. Venice, 1799
Il Ritratto. Milan, 1799
Il Ratto delle Sabine. Venice, 1800
Clitemnestra. Milan, 1801
Il Bevitore Fortunato. Milan, 1803
Inès de Castro. Milan, 1803
Tancredi al Sepolcro di Clorinda. Naples, 1805
Baldovino. Rome, 1810
Berenice. Rome (*Th. Valle*), 1811

PERSUIS.

Estelle. 1783
La Nuit Espagnole. 1791
Phanor et Angola. 1798
Fanny Morna, 1799
Le Fruit Défendu. 1800
Marcel. 1801
Léonidas. 1799
Le Triomphe de Trajan. 1807
Jerusalem delivrée. 1812
L'Heureux Rétour. 1815
Les Dieux Rivaux.

DALAYRAC.

L'Eclipse totale. 1782
Le Corsaire. 1783
Les Deux Tuteurs. 1784
La Dot; L'Amant Statue. 1785
Nina. 1786.
Azemia; Renaud d'Ast. 1787
Sargines. 1788
Raoul de Créqui; Les Deux Petits Savoyards; Fanchette. 1789
La Soirée Orageuse; Vert-Vert. 1790
Philippe et Georgette; Camille ou le Souterrain; Agnès et Oliver. 1791
Elise Hortense; L'Actrice chez elle. 1792
Ambroise, ou Voilà ma Journée; Roméo et Juliette; Urgande et Merlin; La Prise de Toulon. 1793
Adèle et Dorsan. 1794
Arnill; Marianne; La Pauvre Femme. 1795
La Famille Américane. 1796
Gulnare; La Maison isolée. 1797
Primerose; Alexis, ou l' Erreur d'un bon Père; Le Château de Monténéro; Les Deux Mots. 1798
Adolphe et Clara; Laure; Le Leçon, ou la Tasse de Glace. 1799
Catinat; Le Rocher de Leucade; Maison à Vendre. 1800
La Boucle de Cheveux; La Tour de Neustadt. 1801
Picaros et Diego. 1803
Une Heure de Mariage; Le Pavillon du Califé; La Jeune Prude. 1804
Gulistan. 1805.
Lina, ou le Mystère. 1807
Koulouf; ou, les Chinois. 1808
Le Poète et le Musicien. 1811

LESUEUR.

Telemaque. Paris, 1787
La Caverne. February 16, 1793.
Paul et Virginie. 1793
La Mort d'Adam. 1793.
Les Bardes. July 10, 1804

STORACE.

L'Equivoci. Vienna, 1786
La Cameriera Astuta. London, March 4, 1788
No Song no Supper. London, May 3, 1790
The Siege of Belgrade. January 1, 1791
Dido, Queen of Carthage. May 23, 1791
The Pirates. 1792
The Prize. 1793
The Haunted Tower. January 3, 1794
The First of June. 1794
Cherokee. 1794
Lodoiska. 1794
My Grandmother. 1795
The Iron Chest. 1796
Mahmoud; or, the Prince of Persia. April 30, 1796

PAER.

La Locanda de' Vagabondi. Parma, 1789
I Pretendenti Burlati. Parma, 1790
Circe. Venice, 1791
Saïd ossia il Seraglio. Venice, 1792
L'Oro fà Tutto. Milan, 1793
I Molinari. Venice, 1793
Laodicea. Padua, 1793
Il Tempo fà Giustizia à Tutti. Pavia, 1794
Idomeneo. Florence, 1794
Una in Bene ed Una in Male. Rome, 1794
Il Matrimonio Improviso. 1794
L'Amante Servitore. Venice, 1795
La Rossana. Milan, 1795
L'Orfana Riconosciuta. Florence, 1795
Ero e Leandro. Naples, 1795
Tamerlano. Milan, 1796
I Due Sordi. Venice, 1796
Sofonisba. Bologna, 1796
Griselda. Parma, 1796
L'Intrigo Amoroso. Venice, 1796
La Testa Riscaldata. Venice, 1796
Cinna. Padua, 1797
Il Principe di Taranto. Parma, 1797
Il Nuovo Figaro. Parma, 1797
La Sonnambula. Venice, 1797
Il Fanatico in Berlina. Vienna, 1798
Il Morto Vivo. Vienna, 1799
La Donna Cambiata. Vienna, 1800
I Fuorusciti di Firenze. Vienna, 1800
Camilla. Vienna, 1801
Ginevra degli Almeri. Dresden, 1802
Il Sargino. Dresden, 1803
Tutto il male vien dal Buco. Venice, 1804
L'Astuzie Amorosa. Parma, 1804
Il Maniscalco. Padua, 1804
Leonora ossia l'Amore conjugale. Dresden, 1805
Achille. Dresden, 1806
Numa Pompilio. Paris, 1808
Cleopatra. Paris, 1810
Didone. Paris, 1810
I Baccanti. Paris, 1811
L'Agnese. Parma, 1811
L'Eroismo in Amore. Milan, 1816
Le Maître de Chapelle. Paris, 1824
Un Caprice de Femme. Paris, 1834
Olinde et Sophronie. Paris, 1834

The Magician no Conjuror. (*Count Mazzinghi.*) 1790

DIBDIN.

Damon and Phillida. 1768.
The Padlock. 1768
Lionel and Clarissa; The Jubilee; The Blackamoor. 1770
The Wedding Ring. 1773
The Waterman; The Christmas Tale. 1774
The Seraglio. 1776
The Quaker. 1777
Poor Vulcan. 1778
Liberty Hall. 1785
Harvest Home. 1787
The Cobbler; Rose and Colin; Annette and Lubin; The Wives' Revenge; The Graces; The Saloon; The Shepherdess of the Alps; The Barrier of Parnassus; The Milkmaid; The Land of Simplicity; The Passions; The Statue; Clump and Cudden; The Benevolent Tar; The Region of Accomplishments; The Lancashire Witches; The Cestus; Pandora; Long Odds; Tom Thumb; The Deserter.

MÉHUL.

Hypsipilie. 1787
Alonzo et Cora
Euphrosine et Corradin. 1790
Stratonice
Horatius Coclès
Le Jeune Sage et le Vieux Fou
Doria
Phrosine et Mélidor
La Caverne. 1795
Adrien
Le Jeune Henri. 1797
Timoléon
Ariodant. 1799
Joanna
L'Heureux malgré lui
Hélène
L'Irato.
Une Folie.
Uthal.
Gabrielle d'Estrées
Le Prince Troubadour
Valentine de Milan
La Journée aux Aventures
Arminio. 1794
Scipion. 1795
Tancrède et Clorinde. 1796
Sésostris
Agar dans le Désert
Les Amazones. 1812

KREUTZER.

Jeanne d'Arc à Orleans. 1790
Paul et Virginie; Lodoïska. 1791
Charlotte et Werther; Le Franc Breton. 1792
Le Deserteur de la Montaigne de Hamon; Le Congrès des Rois; Le Siège de Lille; La Journée de Marathon. 1793
Astianax. 1801
Aristippe; Le Petit Page; François Premier; Jadis et Aujourd'hui. 1808
Antoine et Cléopatre. 1809
La Mort d'Abel. 1810
Le Triomphe du Mois de Mars. 1811
L'Homme sans Façon. 1812
Le Camp de Sobieski; Constance et Théodore. 1813
Les Béarnais; L'Oriflamme. 1814
La Princesse de Babylone. 1815
Les Deux Rivaux; La Perruque et la Redingote; Le Maître et le Valet. 1816
Le Négociant de Hambourg. 1821
Ipsiboé. 1823
Matilde

KUNZEN.

Holger-Danske. 1790
Les Vendangeurs. Prague, 1793

Hemmeligheden. Copenhagen, 1796
Dragedickken; Jokeyn. Copenhagen, 1797
Eric Ejegod. 1798
Naturen Roest; La Harpe d'Ossian. 1799
Le Rétour dans les Foyers. Copenhagen, 1802

NICOLO ISOUARD.

Avviso ai Maritati. Florence, 1794
Artaserse. Livorna, 1795
Il Tonneliere; Rinaldo d'Asti; Il Barbiere di Seviglia; L'Improvvisata in Campagna; Il Barone d'Alba Chiara, Malta
La Statue; ou, la Femme Avare. Paris, 1800
Le Petit Page; ou, la Prison d'Etat. 1800
Flaminius à Corinthe. 1801
L'Impromptu de Campagna; Michel Ange; Le Baiser et la Quittance. 1802
Les Confidences; Le Médecin Turc. 1803
Léonce, ou le Fils adoptif; La Ruse inutile; L'Intrigue aux Fenêtres. 1805
Idala; La Prise de Passau; Le Déjeûner de Garçons. 1806
Les Créanciers, ou Remède à la Goutte; Les Rendez-vous Burgeois. 1807
Un Jour à Paris; Cimarosa. 1808
L'Intrigue au Serail. 1809
Cendrillon. 1810
Le Magicien sans Magie; La Victime des Arts; Le Billet de Loterie; Le Fête au Village. 1811
Lulli et Quinault. 1812
Le Prince de Catane; Le François à Venise. 1813
Joconde; Jeannot et Colin; Le Siège de Mezières. 1814
Les Deux Maris; L'Une pour l'Autre. 1816

NASOLINI.

Nitteti, Trieste; L'Isola incantata, Parma. 1789
Adriano in Siria, Milan; Andromacca, London; Tesco, Vienna. 1790
La Morte di Cleopatra. 1791
Semiramide. Rome, 1792
Ercole al Termodonte, Trieste; Eugenia; Il Trionfo di Clelia; L'Incantesimo senza Magia; La Merope; Gli Opposti Caratteri; Gli Sposi Infatuati; La Morte di Mitridate; La Festa d'Iside; I due Fratelli Rivali; Gli Annamorati; L'Adimira; Merope; Il Torto Immaginario
Ferdinande in Mexico.

PORTOGALLO.

L'Eroe Cinese, Turin; La Bachetta Portentosa. 1788
L'Astutto. Florence, 1789
Il Molinaro. Venice, 1790
La Donna di Genio volubile. Parma, 1791
La Vedova raggiratrice, Rome; Il Principe di Spazzacamino, Venice; Il Filosofo sedicente; Alceste; Oro non compra Amore
Demofoonte. Milan, 1794
I Due Gobbi ossia le Confusioni nate dalla Somiglianza. Venice, 1795
Il Ritorno di Serse, Bologna; Il Diavolo a quattro, ossia le Donne Cambiate

Fernando in Messico. Rome, 1797
La Maschera fortunata
Non irritar le Donne. 1799
Idonte. Milan, 1800
Il Muto per astuzzia; Omar, Rè di Temagene; Argenide
Semiramide. Lisbon, 1802
Il Cia bottino; Zulema e Selimo
Adriano in Siria. Milan, 1815
La Morte di Mitridate.

TRAETTA.

Farnace. Naples, 1750
I Pastori Felici. 1753
Ezio. Rome, 1754
Il Buova d'Antona. Florence, 1756
Ippolito ed Aricia. Parma, 1759
Ifigenia in Aulide. Vienna, 1759
Stordilano, Principe di Granata, Parma; Armida, Vienna. 1760
Sofonisba. Parma, 1761
La Francese à Malaghera. 1762
Didone Abbandonata. 1764
Semiramide Riconosciuta. 1765
La Serva Rivale. Venice, 1767
Amore in Trappola. 1768
L'Isola Disabitata. St. Petersburg, 1769
L'Olimpiade. 1770
Antigone. 1772
Germondo. London, 1776
Il Cavalier Errante. Naples, 1777
La Disfatta di Dario; Artenice. Venice, 1778
Apele e Campaspe. Milan, 1796.

NICCOLINI.

La Famiglia Stravagante. Rome, 1793
Il Principe Spazzacamino; I Molinari. 1794
Le Nozze campestri, Milan; Artaserse, Venice. 1795
La Donna Innamorata. Alzira, 1797
La Clemenza di Tito. Livorna, 1797
I Due Fratelli ridicoli, Rome; Il Bruto; Gli Scitti, Milan. 1798
Il Trionfo del bel sesso. Indativo, 1800
I Baccanali di Roma. Milan, 1801
I Manli. Milan, 1802
La Selvaggia. Rome, 1803
Fedra ossia il Ritorno di Tesco. Rome, 1804
Il Geloso sincerato. Naples, 1805
Geribea e Falamone. Naples, 1805
Gli Inconstanti Nemici delle Donne. 1805
Abenhamet e Zoraide. Milan, 1806
Trajano in Dacia. Rome, 1807
Le Due Gemelle. Rome, 1808
Coriolano. Milan, 1810
Dario Istaspe. Turin, 1811
Angelica e Medoro. Turin, 1811
Abradate e Dircea, Milan; Quinto Fabio, Vienna; Le Nozze dei Morlacchi; La Feudataria. 1812
La Casa del Astrologo; Mitridate; L'Ira d'Achille, Milan; Balduino, Venice; Carlo Magno; Il Conte de Lennose, Parma; Annibale in Bitinia; Cesare nelle Gallie; Adolphe; La Presa di Granata; L'Ero di Lancastro; Aspasia ed Agide; Il Teuzzone; Ilda d'Avenel; La Conquista di Malacca; Wittikind; Il Trionfo di Cesare.

SPONTINI.

I Puntigli delle Donne. 1795
Gl' Amanti in Cimento. Rome, 1796
L'Amor Secreto. Venice, 1796
L'Isola Disabitata. Parma, 1797
L'Eroismo Ridicolo. Naples, 1797
Le Teseo Riconosciuto. Florence, 1798

La Finta Filosofa. Naples, 1799
La Fuga in Maschera. 1800
I Quadri Parlanti. Parma, 1800
Il Finto Pittore. Parma, 1800
Gl' Elisi Delusi. Parma, 1801
Il Gelosa e l'Audace. Rome
Le Metamorfosi di Pasquale. Venice, 1802
Chi più guarda meno vede. Venice, 1802
La Principessa d'Amalfi. Venice, 1802
Le Pôt de Fleurs. Paris, 1803
La Petite Maison. Paris, 1804
Milton. Paris, December, 1804
L'Eccelsa Gara. 1806
La Vestale. December 15, 1807
Fernand Cortez. 1809
Pélage; ou, le Roi et la Paix. 1814
La Colère d'Achille. 1816
Les Dieux Rivaux. 1816
Berenice.
Les Danaides.
Louis IX. en Egypte. 1817
Artaxerxes. 1819
Olympie. 1819
Les Athéniennes. 1822
Alcidor. 1823
Nourmahal
Agnès de Hohenstaufen. Berlin, 1827.

BOÏELDIEU.

La Dot de Suzette. 1795
La Famille Suisse. 1796
Mombreuil et Merville. 1797
L'Heureuse Nouvelle. 1797
Zoraime et Zulnare. 1798
Beniowsky. 1800
Calife de Bagdad. 1800
Ma Tante Aurore
La Prisonnière
Amour et Mystère
Calypso
Abderkan
Aline, Reine de Golconde
Joconde
Jeannot et Colin
Jean de Paris. Paris, 1812
Le Nouveau Seigneur de Village. 1813
Les Bearnais
Angela; ou, l'Atelier de Jean Cousin. 1815
La Fête du Village voisin
Charles de France
Blanche de Provence; ou, la Cour des Fées. 1821
La Dame Blanche. Paris, December, 1825.

MAYER.

Lodoiska. Venice, 1796
Telemacco. Venice, 1797
Lauso e Lidia. Venice, 1798
Adriano in Siria. Naples, 1798
L'Equivoco. Milan, 1800
Ginevra di Scozia. Trieste, 1801
Il Nuovo Fanatico per la Musica
Le Due Giornate. Milan, 1801
Argene. Venice, 1801
Il Raoul di Créqui. Milan, 1801
Amore non soffre Opposizione. Venice, 1801
I Misteri Eleusini. Milan, 1802
Ercole in Lidia. Vienna, 1803
Le Finti Rivali. Milan, 1803
Alfonso e Cora. Milan, 1803
Amor non ha ritegno. Milan, 1804
Elisa. Venice, 1804
Ernaldo ed Emma. Milan, 1805
L'Amor Conjugale. Padua, 1805
La Rocia di Fahenstein. Venice, 1805
Gl' Americani. Venice, 1806
Ifigenia in Aulide. Parma, 1806
Adalasia ed Alaramo. Milan, 1807

Nè l'un nè l'altro. Milan, 1807
Belle Ciarle e tristi Fatti. Venice, 1807
I Cherasci. Rome, 1808
Il Vero Originale. Rome, 1808
Il Ritorno d'Ulisse. Venice, 1809
Il Desertore ossia Amore Filiale. Venice, 1811
Medea in Corinto. Venice, 1812
Tamerlano. Milan, 1812
Le Due Duchesse. Milan, 1814
La Rosa bianca ed la Rosa rossa. Rome, 1814
Atar. Milan, 1815
Elena e Constantino. Milan, 1816.

CATEL.

Semiramis. 1802
L'Auberge de Bagnères. 1807
Les Artistes par Occasion. 1807
Les Bayadères. 1808
Les Aubergistes de Qualité. 1810
Le Siége de Mezières. 1814
Wallace, ou le Minstrel Ecossais; Zirphile et Fleur de Myrte. 1818
L'Officier Enlevé. 1819.

GENERALI.

Gli Amanti Ridicoli. Rome, 1800
Il Duca Nottolone. Rome, 1801
La Pamela nubile. Venice, 1802
La Calzolaja
L'Adelina
Misantropia e Pentimento, Venice; Gli Effeti della Somiglianza, Venice; Don Chisciotti, Milan. 1805
Orgoglio et Umiliazione, Venice; L'Idolo Cinese, Naples. 1807
Lo Sposo in Bersaglio. Florence, 1807
Le Lagrime d'una Vedova. Venice, 1808
Il Ritratto del Duca. Venice, 1808
Lo Sposo in Contrasto. Vienna, 1808
La Moglie Giudice dello Sposo. Venice, 1809
Amore vince lo Sdegno. Rome, 1809
Chi non risica non rosica, Milan; La Vedova delirante, Rome; La Sciocca per gli altri e l'Astuta per se, Venice. 1811
Gaulo ed Ojitono. Naples, 1812
La Vedova stravagante, Milan; L'Ordo che ci vede, Bologna
Eginardo e Lisbetta. Naples, 1813
Bajazette; La Contessa di Colle Erboso; Il Servo Padrone, Turin. 1814
L'Impostore ossia il Marcotondo. Milan, 1815
I Baccanali di Romo. Venice, 1815
La Vestale. Trieste, 1816
Il Trionfo d' Alessandro. Bologna, 1816
Elato. Bologna, 1817
Rodrigo di Valenza. 1817
Il Gabba Mondo; Elena ed Alfredo; Adelaide di Borgogna; Chiara di Rosemberg; La Testa maravigliosa; Il Divorzio Persiano o il gran Bazzaro di Bassora
Francesca di Rimini. Milan, 1829.

HUMMEL.

Le Vicende d'Amore
Mathilde de Guise
Das Haus ist zu Verkaufen
Die Ruckfahrt des Kaisers.

WINTER.

Armida; Cora e Alonzo; Leonardo e Blandine; Hélène et Paris. 1780

Bellérophon. 1782
Circé. Munich, 1788
Catone in Utica; Antigone. 1791
Il Sacrifizio di Creta, Venice; I Fratelli Rivali. Venice, 1792
Psyché, Munich; Der Sturm. 1793
Le Labyrinthe
Das Unterbrochene Opferfest; Ogus, ou le Triomphe du beau Sexe, Prague; Die Thomasnacht. 1795
I Due Vedove, Vienna, 1796
Ariana; Elisa. 1797
Marie de Montalban. Munich, 1798
Tamerlan. Paris, 1802
Castor et Pollux. London, 1803
Il Ratto di Proserpine. London, 1804
Zaira, London; Calypso; L'Amore Fraterno, London; Fraenbund, Munich. 1805
Colman. Munich, 1809
Die Blinden. Munich, 1810
Il Maometto, Milan; I Due Valdomiri. Milan, 1817
Etelinda. 1818
La Bouffe et le Tailleur. 1819.

BEETHOVEN.

Fidelio. Vienna, November, 1805.

BISHOP.

The Circassian Bride; The Vintagers. 1809
The Maniac. 1810
The Virgin of the Sun; The Æthiop; The Renegade. 1812
Haroun al Raschid; The Brazen Bust; Harry le Roi; The Miller and his Men; For England, Ho! 1813
The Farmer's Wife; The Wandering Boys; The Grand Alliance; The Forest of Bondy; The Maid of the Mill; John of Paris. 1814
The Brother and Sister; The Noble Outlaw; Telemachus. 1815
A Midsummer Night's Dream; The Slave. 1816
The Heir of Verona; The Humorous Lieutenant; The Duke of Savoy.
Zuma. 1818
The Heart of Mid Lothian; A Roland for an Oliver; The Comedy of Errors. 1819
The Antiquary; The Battle of Bothwell Bridge; Henry IV. 1820
Twelfth Night; The Two Gentlemen of Verona; Montrose. 1821
The Law of Java; Maid Marian. 1822
Clari; The Beacon of Liberty; Cortez. 1823
Our Native Land; The Fall of Algiers. 1824
William Tell. 1825
Aladdin. 1826
The Englishman in India; The Rencontre. 1827.

COCCIA.

Il Matrimonio per Cambiale. Rome, 1808
Il Poeta Fortunato, Florence; La Verità nella Bugia, Venice. 1810
Voglia di Dote e non di Moglie. Ferrara, 1810
La Matilde. 1811
I Solitari. Venice, 1812
Il Sogno verificato. 1812
Arrighetto. Venice, 1814
La Selvagia. 1814
Il Crescendo; Euristea; Evelina. Milan, 1815

I Begli Usi di Citta, Milan; Clotilde, Venice; Rinaldo d'Asti, Rome; Carlotta e Werter. 1816
Claudine, Turin; Etelinde, Venice; Simile, Ferrara. 1817
Donna Caritea. Turin, 1818
Fayel. Florence, 1819
Atar. Lisbon, 1820
Mandane, Regina di Persia. 1821
Elena a Costantino. 1821
La Festa della Rosa. 1822
Maria Stuarda. London, 1827
L'Orfano delle Selve. Venice, 1829
Rosamunda. Naples, 1831
Edoardo Stuart. Milan, 1832
Enrico di Montfort. 1832
Caterina di Guisa. 1833.

MORLACCHI.

Il Ritratto, Bologna; Il Poeta in Campagna. 1807
Corradino; Enone e Paride, Livorna; Oreste, Parma. 1808
Rinaldo d'Asti, Parma; La Principessa per Rimpiego, Rome; Le Avventure d'una Giornata, Milan. 1809
Le Danaïde. 1810
Raoul de Créqui. Dresden, 1811
La Capricciosa Pentita. Dresden, 1812
Il Nuovo Barbiere di Siviglia. Dresden, 1815
La Badicea. Venice, 1818
Da Semplicetta di Pirna
Donna Aurora. Dresden, 1819
Tebaldo ed Isolina. Dresden, 1820
La Gioventù di Enrico V. Dresden, 1823
Laodicea. 1825
I Saraceni in Sicilia. Venice, 1827
Il Colombo. 1828
Gioanni di Parigi. 1829
Francesca da Rimini. Venice, 1836

SPOHR.

Der Zweikampf der Geliebten; Der Berggeist; Faust; Jessonda; Zemire et Azor; Pietro d'Abano; Der Alchymist, Berlin.

WEIGL.

La Précaution Inutile; La Sposa Collerica; Il Pazzo per Forza; La Caffetiera; La Principessa d'Amalfi; Giulietta e Pierotto; L'Amor Marinaro; L'Accademia del Maestro Cisolfat; I Solitari; L'Uniforme; Le Prince Invisible; Cleopatra; Il Rivale di se stesso; L'Imboscata; L'Orfana d'Inghilterra; Le Petit Homme Pierre; Le Village dans les Montagnes; La Maison des Orphelins; La Famille Suisse; Françoise de Foix; Le Feu de Vesta; La Chute de la Montagne; L'Empereur Adrien; La Jeunesse de Pierre le Grand; La Chute de Baal; La Porte de Fer; Ostade; L'Ermite; Le Rossignol et le Corbeau; Waldemar; Edouard et Caroline; Il Ratto di Proserpine.

ROSSINI.

La Cambiale di Matrimonio. Venice, 1810
L'Equivoco Stravagante. Bologna, 1811
L'Inganno Felice (Ven.); Ciro in Babilonia (Ferrara); La Scala di Seta (Ven.); L'Occasione fa il Ladro (Ven.). 1812
La Pietra del Paragone. Milan, 1812
Demetrio e Polibio. Rome, 1812
L'Italiana in Algieri. Naples, 1813
Tancredi. Venice, 1813

Il Bruschino; o, il Figlio per Azzarde. Venice, 1813
L'Aureliano in Palmira. 1814
Il Turco in Italia. Milan, 1814
Sigismondo. Venice, 1815
La Gazetta. Naples, 1816
Otello. Naples, 1816
Il Barbiere di Siviglia. Rome, 1816
La Cenerentola. Rome, 1816
Armida. Naples, 1817
La Gazza Ladra. Milan, 1817
Mosè in Egitto. Naples, 1818
Elisabetta. Naples, 1817
Ricciardo e Zoraide. Naples, 1818
Torwaldo e Dorliska. Rome, 1818
Adelaide di Borgogna. Rome, 1818
Adina; o, il Califfo di Bagdad. 1818
Ermione. Naples, 1819
Eduardo e Christina. Venice, 1819
La Donna del Lago. Naples, 1819
Bianca e Faliero. Milan, 1819
Maometto. Naples, 1820
Matilda di Shabran. Rome, 1821
Zelmira. Naples, August 13, 1822
Mosè in Egitto. Paris, 1822
Semiramide. Venice, 1823
Il Viaggio a Rheims. Paris, 1825
Le Siége de Corinthe. Paris, 1826
Le Comte Ory. Paris, 1827
Guglielmo Tell. Paris, 1829
Robert Bruce. Paris, 1846.

CARAFA.

Il Vascello; L'Occidente. 1814
La Gelosia Corretta. 1815
Gabrielle di Vergi. 1816
Ifigenia in Tauride. Naples, 1817
Adele di Lusignano. Milan, 1817
Berenice Siria. Naples, 1818
Elizabeth in Derbyshire. Venice, 1818
Il Sacrifizio d' Epito. 1819
Gli Due Figaro. Milan, 1820
Jeanne d' Arc. Paris, 1821
La Capriciosa ed il Soldato, Rome; Le Solitaire, Paris; Tamerlano, Paris; Eufemio di Messina Abufar, Vienna; Le Valet de Chambre, Paris; L'Auberge Supposée. 1823
La Belle au Bois Dormant; Il Sonnambulo, Milan, 1825
Sangarido. Paris, 1827
Le Nozze di Lammermoor. Paris, December, 1829
La Violette; Masaniello; Jenny; La Prison d'Edimbourg. 1833
La Grande Duchesse.

PACINI.

Anetta e Lucindo. Venice, 1814
Rosina. Florence, 1815
L'Ingenua. Venice, 1818
Adelaide e Comingio. Milan
Il Barone di Dolsheim. Milan, 1818
L'Ambizione Delusa; Gli Sponsali di Silfi; Il Falegname di Livonia; Ser Marcantonio; La Sposo Fedele; La Schiava di Bagdad; La Gioventù d'Enrico V.; La Vestale; L'Eroe Scozzesse; La Sacerdotessa d'Irminsul; Atala; Isabella ed Enrico
Temistocle. Lucca, November, 1823
Alessandro nell' Indie. Naples, 1824
Amazilia. Naples, 1825
L'Ultimo Giorno di Pompei. Naples, November 19, 1825
Niobe. Naples, November 19, 1826
Il Crociato in Tolomaïde. Trieste, 1828
Gl' Arabi nelle Gallie. Turin, December 25, 1828
Margherita d'Anjou
Cesare in Egitto
Gianni di Calais
Giovanna d'Arco, Milan, March 12, 1830; Berta; Muletiere di Toledo

Malvina di Scozia (Naples); Cinq Mars (Palermo). 1852
Il Cid (Milan); La Cantatrice di Madrid. 1853
Allan Cameron; La Punizione (Venice); Romilda di Provenza; Elisa Valasco (Rome). 1854
Luisetta. Naples, 1855
Margarita Pusterla. Naples, 1856
Gianni di Nisilda. Rome, 1860
Belphegor. Florence, 1861
Giovanni di Marana. 1862.

VACCAJ.

I Solitari di Scozia. 1814
Il Lupo d'Ostenda. 1818
Pietro il Grande. Parma, 1824
La Pastorella Feudataria; Zadig ed Astartea. Naples, 1825
Giulietta e Romeo, Milan; Fuccine di Norvegia; Giovanna d'Arco, Venice; Bianca di Messina, Turin; Saladino, Florence; Saulle, Milan; Il Marco Visconti; Giovanna Gray; La Sposa di Messina.

DONIZETTI.

Enrico, Conte di Borgogne. Venice, 1818
Il Falegname di Livornia. Venice, 1819
Le Nozze in Villa. Mantua, 1820
Zoraïde di Granata. Rome, 1822
La Zingara. Naples, 1822
Chiara e Serafina. Milan, 1822
Il Fortunato Inganno. Naples, 1823
Aristea. Naples, 1823
Una Follia. Naples, 1823
Alfredo il Grande. Naples, 1823
L'Ajo in Imbarazzo. Rome, 1824
Emilia; o, l'Ermitagio di Liverpool. Naples, 1824
Alahor in Granata. Palermo, 1826
Il Castello degli Invalidi. Palermo, 1826
Elvira. Naples, 1826
Olive e Pasquale. Rome, 1827
Il Borgomastro di Saardam; Le Convenienze Teatrali; Otto Mesi in due Ere. Naples, 1827
Giove di Grano; L'Usule di Roma; Gianni di Calais. Naples, 1828
La Regina di Golconda. Genoa, 1828
Il Paria; I Pazzi per Progretto; Francesca di Foix; La Romanziera; Il Castello di Kenilworth; Zaida; Il Diluvio Universale; Imelda di Lambertuzzi. Naples, 1829
Anna Bolena. Milan, 1830
Fausta. Naples, 1831
Ugo Conte di Parigi. Milan, 1832
L'Elisir d'Amore. Milan, 1832
Sancia di Castiglia. Naples, 1832
Il Furioso, Rome; Parisina, Florence; Torquato Tasso, Rome. 1833
Lucrezia Borgia, Milan; Rosmonda d'Inghilterra, Florence; Maria Stuarda, Naples; Buondelmonte. 1834
Gemma di Vergy. Milan, 1835
Lucia di Lammermoor. Naples, 1835
Marino Faliero, Paris; Betly, Naples; L'Assedio di Calais, Naples; Il Campanella di Notte, Naples; Belisario, Venice. 1836
Pia di Tolomei; Roberto Devereux. Naples, 1837
Maria di Rudenz. Venice, 1838
Gianni di Parigi. Milan, 1839
La Figlia del Reggimento; La Favorita; Les Martyres. Paris, 1840
Adelia. Rome, 1841
Linda di Chamouni, Vienna; Maria di Rohan, Vienna; Maria Padilla, Milan. 1842

Don Pasquale; Dom Sebastien. Paris, 1843
Catarina Cornaro; Gabrielle de Vergi; Le Duc d'Albe. Naples, 1844
Rita. Paris, 1860.

MERCADANTE.

L'Apoteosi d'Ercole. Naples, 1818
Violenza e Costanza. Naples, 1819
Anacreonte in Samo. Naples, 1820
Il Geloso Ravveduto. Rome, 1820
Scipione in Cartagine. Rome, 1820
Maria Stuarda. Bologna, 1821
Elisa e Claudio. Milan, 1821
Andronico. Milan, 1822
Adele ed Emerico. Milan, 1822
Amleto. 1822
Alfonso ed Elisa. Mantua, 1823
Didone. Turin, 1823
Gli Sciti. Naples, 1823
Gli Amici di Siracuse. Rome, 1824
Doralice. Vienna, 1824
Le Nozze di Telemacco ed Antiope. Vienna, 1824
Il Podesta di Burgos. Vienna, 1824
L'Erode. Venice, 1825
Nitocri. Turin, 1825
La Donna Caritea. Venice, 1826
Ezio. Milan, 1827
Il Montanaro. Milan, 1827
La Rappressaglia. Cadiz, 1829
La Testa di Bronzo. Madrid, 1830
Zaïra. Naples, 1831
I Normanni a Parigi. Turin, 1831
Ismala ossia Morte ed Amore. Milan, 1832
Il Conte d'Essex. Milan, 1833
Emma d'Antiochia. Venice, 1834
I Briganti. Paris, March 22, 1836
La Gioventù di Enrico V.
Il Giuramento. Milan, 1837
Le Due Illustri Rivali. Venice, 1839
Leonora
La Schiava Saracene. 1850
Statira; Violetta. Naples, 1853
Pelagio. Naples, 1857.

NOTE.—Signor Mercadante has written fifty-two operas in all.

MEYERBEER.

Romilda e Costanzo. Padua, 1818
Marguerite d'Anjou. Milan, 1822
L'Esule di Granata. 1823
Il Crociato. Venice, April, 1824
Emma di Resburgo. 1825
Robert le Diable. Paris, 1831
Les Huguenots. Paris, 1836
Nabuco
Attila. Venice
Giovanno d'Arco
Camp de Silesie. Berlin, 1844
Le Prophète. Paris, 1849
L'Etoile du Nord. Paris, 1854
Le Pardon de Ploërmel (*Dinorah*). Paris, 1859.

WEBER.

Die Macht der Liebe und des Wiens. Salzburg, 1798
Silvana. Munich, 1800
Peter Schmoll und seine Nachbarn. Salzburg, 1801
Rubezahl. Breslau, 1805
Abon Hassan. Darmstadt, 1810
Der Freischütz. Berlin, 1821
Euryanthe. Vienna, 1823
Preciosa. 1825
Oberon. London, April 12, 1826
Der Berherrscher der Geister. 1826.

HALÉVY.

L'Artisan. Paris, January 30, 1822
Pygmalion
Phidias. 1827

Les Deux Pavillons. 1827
Le Roi et le Batelier. 1828
Le Dilettante. Paris, 1829
Clari. Paris, 1829
La Langue Musicale. 1831
Ludovic. 1832
La Tentation. 1833
Les Souvenirs de Lafleur. 1834
La Juive. Paris, 1835
L'Eclair. Paris, December, 1835
Guido e Ginevra. Paris, 1838
Cosme de Medicis. 1839
Les Treize. 1839
Le Drapier. Paris, 1840
Il Guitarero. Paris, 1841
La Reine de Chypre. Paris, 1842
Charles VI. Paris, 1843
Il Lazzarone. Paris, 1844
Les Mousquetaires de la Reine. Paris, 1846
Le Val d'Andorre. Paris, 1848
La Fée aux Roses. Paris, 1849
La Tempestà. London, 1850
La Dame de Pique. 1850
Le Juif Errant. 1852
Le Nabob. 1853
Jaguarita. 1855
Valentine d'Aubigny. 1856
La Magicienne. Paris, 1857.

AUBER.

Le Séjour Militaire. 1813
Le Testament et les Billets-doux. 1819
La Bergère Châtelaine. 1821
Emma. 1821
Leicester. 1822
Le Neige; ou, le Nouvel Eginard. Paris, October 8, 1823
Le Concert à la Cour. Paris, 1824
Léocadie. Paris, November, 1824
Le Maçon. Paris, May, 1825
Le Timide. 1826
Fiorella. 1826
La Muette di Portici. Paris, 1829
La Fiancée. Paris, January, 1829
Fra Diavolo. Paris, January, 1830
Le Dieu et la Bayadère. Paris, October, 1830
Le Philtre. Paris, June, 1831
Le Serment. Paris, 1832
Gustave III. Paris, 1833
Lestocq. 1834
Les Chaperons Blancs. 1836
Actéon. Paris, January 25, 1836
L'Ambassadrice. Paris, 1836
Le Domino Noir. Paris, 1837
Le Lac des Fées. Paris, 1839
Zanetta. Paris, May, 1840
Les Diamans de la Couronne. Paris, March 6, 1841
Le Duc d'Olonne. Paris, 1842
Le Part du Diable. Paris, 1843
La Sirène. Paris, 1844
La Barcarolle. Paris, 1845
Haidée; ou, Le Sécret. Paris, 1847
L'Enfant Prodigue. Paris, 1850
La Corbeille d'Oranges. Paris, 1851
Marco Spada. Paris, 1852
Le Cheval de Bronze. 1853
Manon Lescaut. 1855
Jenny Bell. 1855
La Circassienne. 1861.

GNECCO.

Gli Bramini; Argete; Le Nozze de Sanniti; La Prova d'un Opera Seria; Le Nozze di Lauretta; Carolina e Filandro; Il Pignattaro; La Scena senza Scena; Gli ultimi due Giorni di Carnovale; La Prova degli Orazzi e Curiazi; Arsace e Semira; Amanti filarmonici.

HÉROLD.

La Gioventù di Enrico Quinto. Naples, 1812

Charles de France; Les Rosières; La Clochette. Paris, 1816
Le Premier Venu. Paris, 1818
Les Trocqueurs; L'Amour Platonique. Paris, 1819.
L'Auteur mort et vivant
Le Muletier; Lasthénie; Vendome en Espagne. Paris, 1823
Le Roi René. Paris, 1824
Le Lapin Blanc. 1825
Marie. Paris, November, 1826
L'Illusion. Paris, July 19, 1829
L'Auberge d'Auray. Paris, 1830
Emmeline; La Marquise de Brinvilliers. 1830
Zampa. Paris, May, 1831
La Médecine sans Médecin. Paris, October 19, 1832
Le Pré aux Clercs. Paris, 1832.

BELLINI.

Andelson e Salvina. Naples, 1825
Bianca e Gernando. Naples, 1826
La Straniera. Milan, 1829
Il Pirata. Milan, 1829
Zaira. Parma, 1829
I Capuletti e Montecchi. Venice, March 12, 1830
La Sonnambula. Milan, 1831
Norma. Milan, January 1, 1832
Beatrice di Tenda. Venice, 1833
I Puritani. Paris, 1835.

PERSIANI.

Piglia il Mondo come viene. Florence, 1826
L'Inimico Generoso, Florence; Attila, Parma. 1827
Danao Rè d'Argo. Florence, 1827
Gaston de Foix; Inès de Castro.

BENEDICT.

Giacinta ed Ernesto. Naples, 1827
I Portoghesi in Goa. Naples, 1830
Un Anno ed un Giorno. Naples, 1836
The Gipsy's Warning. London, 1838
The Brides of Venice. London, April 22, 1844
The Crusaders. London, 1846
The Lily of Killarney. London, February, 1862

NIEDERMEYER.

Il Reo per Amore, Naples; Une Nuit dans la Forêt, Paris; Marie Stuart, Paris
Stradella. Paris, 1836
La Fronde. 1853,

COSTA.

Il Carcera d' Ildegonda. Naples, 1828
Malvina. Naples, 1829
Malek Adel. Paris, 1837
Don Carlos. London, 1844.

FLOTOW.

L'Ame en Peine; Stradella
Die Matrosen. Hamburg, 1845
Marta. 1848.
La Grande Duchesse. Berlin, 1850
Rubezahl; Sophia Catharina; Indra, Vienna. 1853
Albin. Vienna, 1855.

ADOLPHE ADAM.

Pierre et Catherine. Paris, 1829
Danilowa. Paris, April, 1830
Le Morceau d'Ensemble. Paris, March, 1831
Le Grand Prix. Paris, 1831
Le Proscit. Paris, 1833
Une Bonne Fortune. 1834
Le Châlet. 1834

Le Postillon de Longjumeau. Paris, October 15, 1836
Le Brasseur de Preston. 1839
La Reine d'un Jour. 1840
La Rose de Peronne. Paris, 1840
Le Roi d' Yvetot. 1843
Richard de Palestine. Paris, 1844
Le Toréador. 1849
Giralda; ou, la Nouvelle Psyché. 1850
La Poupée de Nuremberg. 1852
Le Bijou Perdu. 1853
Le Roi des Halles. 1853
Le Muletier de Tolède. 1854
Le Fidèle Berger. 1855
Falstaff. 1855
Le Houssard de Berchini. 1855
Mamz'elle Genévieve. 1856.

BALFE.

I Rivali di Se Stessi. Palermo, 1829
Un' Avvertimento in Gelosi. Pavia, 1830
Enrico IV. al Passo della Marna. Milan, 1831
The Siege of Rochelle. London, October 29, 1835
The Maid of Artois. London, 1836
Catherine Grey. London, 1837
Joan of Arc. London, 1837
Diadeste; or, the Veiled Lady. London, 1838
Falstaff. London, 1838
Keolante. London, March 3, 1841
Le Puits d'Amour. Paris, 1843
Geraldine; or, the Lover's Well. London, August, 1843. (Translation of Le Puits d'Amour.)
The Bohemian Girl. London, November 27, 1843
Les Quatre Fils Aymon. Paris, July, 1843
The Daughter of St. Mark. London, November 27, 1844
The Enchantress. London, 1845
L'Etoile de Seville. Paris, 1845
The Bondman. London, 1846
The Devil's in it. London, 1847
The Maid of Honour. London, December 20, 1847
The Sicilian Bride. London, 1852
Pittore e Duca. Trieste, 1856
The Rose of Castile. London, 1857
Satanella. London, 1858
Bianca; or, the Bravo's Bride. London, December 5, 1860
The Puritan's Daughter. London, November 30, 1861
The Armourer of Nantes. London, February 12, 1863.

BARNETT.

The Mountain Sylph. London, August 25, 1834
Fair Rosamond. London, 1837
Farinelli. London, 1839

LODER.

Nourjahad. 1834
Francis the First. 1839
The Night Dancers. London, 1847
Robin Goodfellow. 1849
Raymond and Agnes. 1859

VERDI.

Oberto, Conte di St. Bonifacio. Milan, 1839
Un Giorno di Regno. Milan, 1840
Nabuco. Milan, 1843
I Lombardi. Milan, 1843
Il Tancredi
Ernani. Milan, 1844
I Duo Foscari. Rome, 1844
Giovanna d'Arco. 1845
Alzira. Naples, 1845
Attila. Venice, 1846
Macbeth. Florence, 1847

Jerusalem. Paris, 1847
I Masnadieri. London, 1847
La Battaglia di Legnano. 1849
Il Corsaro. Trieste, 1849
Luisa Miller. Naples, 1849
Stiffelio. Trieste, 1850
Il Finto Stanislas. 1850
Rigoletto. Venice, 1851
Il Trovatore. Rome, 1853
La Traviata. Venice, 1853
Les Vêpres Siciliennes. Paris, June 13, 1855
Simon Boccanegra. 1857
Un Ballo in Maschera. Paris, 1861
La Forza del Destino. 1862.

MACFARREN.

Devil's Opera. London, 1838
Don Quixote. London, 1846
Charles the Second. London, 1849
Sleeper Awakened. London, 1850
Robin Hood. London, 1860.

AMBROISE THOMAS.

Le Panier Fleuri. 1839
Mina.
Le Caïd; Songe d'une Nuit d'Eté. 1850
Raymond. 1851
La Tonelli. 1853
La Cour de Celimène. 1855
Le Carnaval de Venise; Psyché. 1857
Le Roman d'Elvire. 1860.

WALLACE.

Maritana. London, 1845
Matilda of Hungary
Lurline. London, February 23, 1860
The Amber Witch. London, 1861
Love's Triumph. London, 1862.

SCHIRA.

Mina. London, 1849
Nicolo di Lapi. London, 1863.

GOUNOD.

Sappho. Paris, 1851
La Nonne Sanglante. Paris, 1854
Le Médecin malgré Lui. Paris, 1858
Faust. Paris (Théâtre Lyrique), March 19, 1859
Philemon et Baucis. Paris, 1860
Colombe. Baden-Baden, 1860
Le Faucon. Baden-Baden, 1861
La Reine de Saba. Paris, 1861.

GLOVER.

Aminta. London, 1852
Ruy Blas. London, Oct. 24, 1861.

MELLON.

Victorine. Covent Garden, 1859.

NOTE.—This List of Operas does *not*, with very few exceptions, include Operettas, Musical Pieces, Musical Farces, Entertainments, or Interludes.

ALPHABETICAL LIST OF DRAMATIC COMPOSERS,

NOT PRE-EMINENT AS OPERATIC WRITERS.

Abadia
Abert
Acciajuoli
Aimon
Alary
Albinoni
Aldrovrandini
Alessandri
Andreozzi
Apell
Ardita
Arienzo (d')
Arion
Ariosti
Arrietta
Astaritta
Attwood

Barata (Dalla)
Barbate
Bassani
Batistin
Battista
Beck
Beer (Jules)
Beffroy de Reigny
Bellermann
Benda (G. & F. L.)
Beninconi
Benvenuti
Berendt
Bergson
Berlioz
Bernabei
Bernardini
Bernasconi
Bertin (Mdlle. Louise)
Berton (P. M. & F.)
Bertoni
Berwald
Bianchi (F.)
Bierey
Bigaglia
Biletta
Bioni
Blaise
Blamont
Blangini
Blavet
Blum
Blumenthal
Boïeldieu (Adrien)
Boisselot
Bondineri
Boniventi
Bononcini
Borde (De la)
Boretti
Borghi
Boroni
Boscha
Bottesini
Bousquet
Bouteiller
Boyce
Braeunich
Braga
Brandl
Brassac
Bristow
Bronner
Broschi (R.)
Brown
Brunetti (A. B.)
Bruni
Buini

Cacciati
Cadaux
Cagnoni
Caldara
Campra
Candeille
Capecelatro
Capelli
Carrer
Caruso
Cary
Cavalli
Champein
Chancourtois
Chapelle (P. D. A.)
Charpentier (M. A.)
Chelard
Chelleri
Chiaramonte
Chiochetti
Ciampi
Ciebra (José de)
Clapisson
Clayton
Cocchi
Conradi
Consolini
Conti
Cooke
Coppola
Cordans
Cortesi
Cousser (or Kusser)
Cramer (F.)

David (F.)
Davies
Davy
Defferrari
Della Maria

Deluse
Desmarets
Dessaue
Dezede (or Dezaides)
Ditters de Dittersdorf
Doerstling
Dominicetti
Doppler
Dorn
Dourlen
Draghi
Dugazon
Duggan
Dumoulin
Duprato
Duprez
Durette
Dutillieu

Ebell
Eccles
Eckert
Ehrlich
Elsner
Erkel

Fabrizi
Farinelli (J.)
Federici
Feo
Ferrari (J. G.)
Fétis
Finger
Fioravanti
Fischer (A.)
Fischietti
Floquet
Foertsch
Foignet
Fraenzl
Franck (J. W.)
Francoeur

Gail (Mdme.)
Gambini
Garcia
Gasparini (F.)
Gasse
Gassmann
Gaveaux
Gavinies
Gazzaniga
Gentili
Gerl (or Goerl)
Gevaert
Giacometti
Giardini
Giordani (J.)
Giosa (Di)
Glinka
Godefroi
Gollmick
Grand
Graun
Gresnick
Grisar
Guglielmi
Guhr
Gürrlich
Gyrowetz

Haeffner
Haeser (A. F.)
Hanssens
Hart (J.)
Haydn (J. M.)
Heinricken
Hellwig
Helmesberger
Hermann
Hiller
Himmel
Holzbauer
Horn (Chas. Edw.)
Huber
Hullah (J.)

Inenga

Jadin (L. E.)
Jones
Jozzi
Jullien

Kaffka (J. C.)
Keiser
Kelly
King
Kinki
Kirchhof
Kittel
Kozeluch (J. A. & L.)
Kreubé
Krieger

Labarre
Lampe (J. F
Lampugnani
Langert
Langlé
Lannoy
Laruette
Lasser
Leblanc
Leborne
Lebrun (L. S
Légat de Furcy
Lescot
Leveridge
Lillo
Limnander
Lindpaintner
Linley (T.)
Litolff
Liverati
Lobe
Locke (M.)
Lotti
Louis
Louis (Mme.)
Lucchesi
Lutz (Meyer)

Mabellini
Maillard
Maillart
Mangold
Mansfield
Marais
Marschner
Massé
Mattheson
Mazzinghi
Membrée
Micelli
Michl
Mijore
Milototti

Minoja
Mononyi
Monteverde
Montfort
Monti
Morel
Moroni
Mortellari
Mosca
Moscenza
Moscuzzi
Mouret
Muhle
Muzio

Nargiller
Naumann
Nicosia
Nini

Offenbach
Orgitano
Orlandi
Orlandini
Ottani

Paganini (E.)
Paini
Pallavicino
Pappalardo
Parenti
Pavesi
Pedrotti
Pellaert
Penso
Pentenrieder
Perez
Peri
Perillo
Perti
Pescetti
Petrella
Petrocini
Philidor (F. A. D.)
Piccinni (Louis)
Pignatta
Pistilli
Pixis

Poise
Polarolo (or Pollarolo)
Ponchielli
Porta (Jean)
Potier
Predieri (L. A.)
Propriac
Pucitta
Pugnani
Puzone
Puzzi

Raff
Raimondi
Rampini
Raphael
Rastrelli
Rauzzini
Rebel
Reeve
Reicha
Reissiger
Ressell
Reyer
Ricci (F. & L.)
Righi
Righini
Ritter
Roesler
Roeth
Romani
Ronzi
Rooke
Rosi
Rota
Rubinstein
Rust

Sabadini
Saint Amans
Salvator
Sanelli
Sarmiento
Schauensée
Schëfer
Schindelmeisser
Schmidt (J. P. S.)
Schuster

Schwab
Schwanberg
Schweitzer
Sciroli
Scolari
Secchi
Sellenik
Semet
Simons Candeille (Mme.)
Sinico
Smith (Robt.)
Sola
Solié
Soliva
Spaeth
Steibelt
Stolz
Stöpler
Strungk
Stukersky
Sussmayer

Taddei
Tadolini
Tarchi
Taubert
Taylor
Tell
Thalberg
Tommasi
Tori (or Torri)
Tozzi
Traversari
Trento
Tritto
Tuczek
Tully

Umlauff

Valente
Vancorbeil
Van der Does
Vannacci
Vento
Vera
Villebois
Villebranch

Vivaldi
Vivier

Wagner
Webbe (E.)
Weber (C. G. & B. A.)
Wély

Werstowski
Westmeyer
Williams
Witt
Woelfl
Wolf (E. G.)
Wolfram (J.)

Wollanck
Wraniczky (or Wranitzky)
Würst

Ziani
Zoppi
Zumsteeg.

NOTE.—An enumeration of the works of these Dramatic Composers will, for the greater part, be found in the *Dictionnaire des Musiciens* of M. Fétis.

INDEX.

THE END.

CPSIA information can be obtained
at www.ICGtesting.com
Printed in the USA
LVHW110803120522
718525LV00003B/29

9 783375 004897